A Singular Hostage

A Singular Hostage

Thalassa Ali

BANTAM BOOKS

A SINGULAR HOSTAGE

A Bantam Book / December 2002

Excerpt on page 83, translation from an unknown poet by Mir Ijaz Mahmood.
Excerpt on page 123, translation of a poem by Mir Taqi Mir by Ahmed Ali from *The Golden Tradition, An Anthology of Urdu Poetry,* Columbia University Press, New York and London, 1973.
Excerpt on page 237, translation of a Punjabi fable by R. C. Temple.
Excerpt on page 346, translation of two fragments of Hafiz by: Rifaat Ghani.

MAP ILLUSTRATION BY LAURA HARTMAN MAESTRO

BOOK DESIGN BY GLEN EDELSTEIN

Library of Congress Cataloging-in-Publication Data
Ali, Thalassa.
A singular hostage / Thalassa Ali
    p. cm.
ISBN 0-553-38176-8
1. Auckland, George Eden, Earl of, 1784–1849—Fiction. 2. Ranjit Singh, Maharaja of the Punjab, 1780–1839—Fiction. 3. India—History—19th century—Fiction. 4. Eden, Frances, 1801–1849—Fiction. 5. Eden, Emily, 1797–1869—Fiction. 6. British—India—Fiction. 7. Afghan Wars—Fiction. I. Title.

PS3601.L39 S56 2002
813'.6—dc21   2001056591

Published simultaneously in the United States and Canada

Bantam Books are published by Bantam Books, a division of Random House, Inc. Its trademark, consisting of the words "Bantam Books" and the portrayal of a rooster, is Registered in U.S. Patent and Trademark Office and in other countries. Marca Registrada. Bantam Books, 1540 Broadway, New York, New York 10036.

PRINTED IN THE UNITED STATES OF AMERICA

BVG   10 9 8 7 6 5 4 3 2 1

To the memory of
Sayed Akhlaque Husain Tauhidi,
who showed me the Path to Peace through scattered pearls

ACKNOWLEDGMENTS

Among those who helped me with this book were Arthur Edelstein, who taught me to write fiction and my writing group, who made wonderful suggestions and bore with me every step of the way. My friend and agent Jill Kneerim, editor Danelle McCafferty, Peter Scholl, Lois Ames, and Bill Bell were the first to take the book seriously. Gillo Afridi, Tony Mahmood, Samina Quraeshi, and many other friends in the U.S., India, and Pakistan also offered me advice and encouragement. Kate Miciak, my meticulous editor at Bantam Dell, held my feet to the fire. I cannot praise or thank her enough. I also thank Sophie and Toby, my closest allies of all.

HISTORICAL NOTE

This story takes place in the north of India, now Pakistan, in 1838–1839, the first year of Queen Victoria's reign. By that year, Britain, through its proxy, the Honorable East India Company, controlled most of the Indian subcontinent. To the north, the Great Game—the nineteenth-century struggle between Britain and Russia for control of Central Asia—was gathering speed.

By 1838, the British feared a Russian threat to their Indian territories. Determined to outwit the Russians by gaining political control of Afghanistan, Lord Auckland sent his armies to Kabul on a military adventure later known as the First Afghan War.

Before launching his Afghan Campaign, Auckland took the extraordinary step of traveling twelve hundred miles across India to enlist the aid of the dying one-eyed Maharajah Ranjit Singh of the Punjab, whose independent military state lay between the British territories and Afghanistan. That year-long journey—on which Lord Auckland was accompanied by his two spinster sisters, his entire government, and a ten-thousand-man army—culminated in the great *durbar,* or state meeting, at Firozpur, on the border between British-controlled India and the Punjab.

A treaty between the two was essential to the British campaign. Maharajah Ranjit Singh knew this and delayed signing the treaty for a month, forcing Auckland to send his troops across the mountain passes into Afghanistan in deep winter.

This story takes place during that month.

. . .

LORD Auckland, his sisters, his political secretary, and his chief of protocol are real historical figures, as are Maharajah Ranjit Singh and his Chief Minister. The durbar took place much as I have described it, and the subsequent movements of the British camp are generally accurate.

Mariana Givens, Harry Fitzgerald, the baby Saboor and his family, and Saat Kaur, the Maharajah's youngest wife, are products of my imagination.

A Singular Hostage

CHI

Transport
camels

Kabul
Khyber Pass
Peshawar
AFGHANISTAN
Qandahar

KASHMIR

Indus R.
Jhelum R.
Chenab R.
Lahore Amritsar
Ravi R.
Kasur Simla
Firozpur

Indus R.
Sutlej R.

Delhi

HIMALAYA
Mt. Everest

NEPAL

Brahm

RAJASTHAN

Jodhpur Jaipur Agra
Ajmer Chambal R.
Chitor Kotah
Udaipur MALWA

Ganges R.
Jumna R. Allahabad
BIHAR
BENGAL
Calcutta

Ganges R.

Cambay
Narmada
Surat

Mahanadi R.

INDIA

Bombay
Ahmadnagar Godavari R.

Bay of
Bengal

Golconda
Bijapur Hyderabad
GOA

Kistna R.

Penner R.

Madras

ARABIAN SEA

Kaveri R.

CEYLON

INDIAN OCEAN

Mariana
Givens

Tame
Spotted
Deer

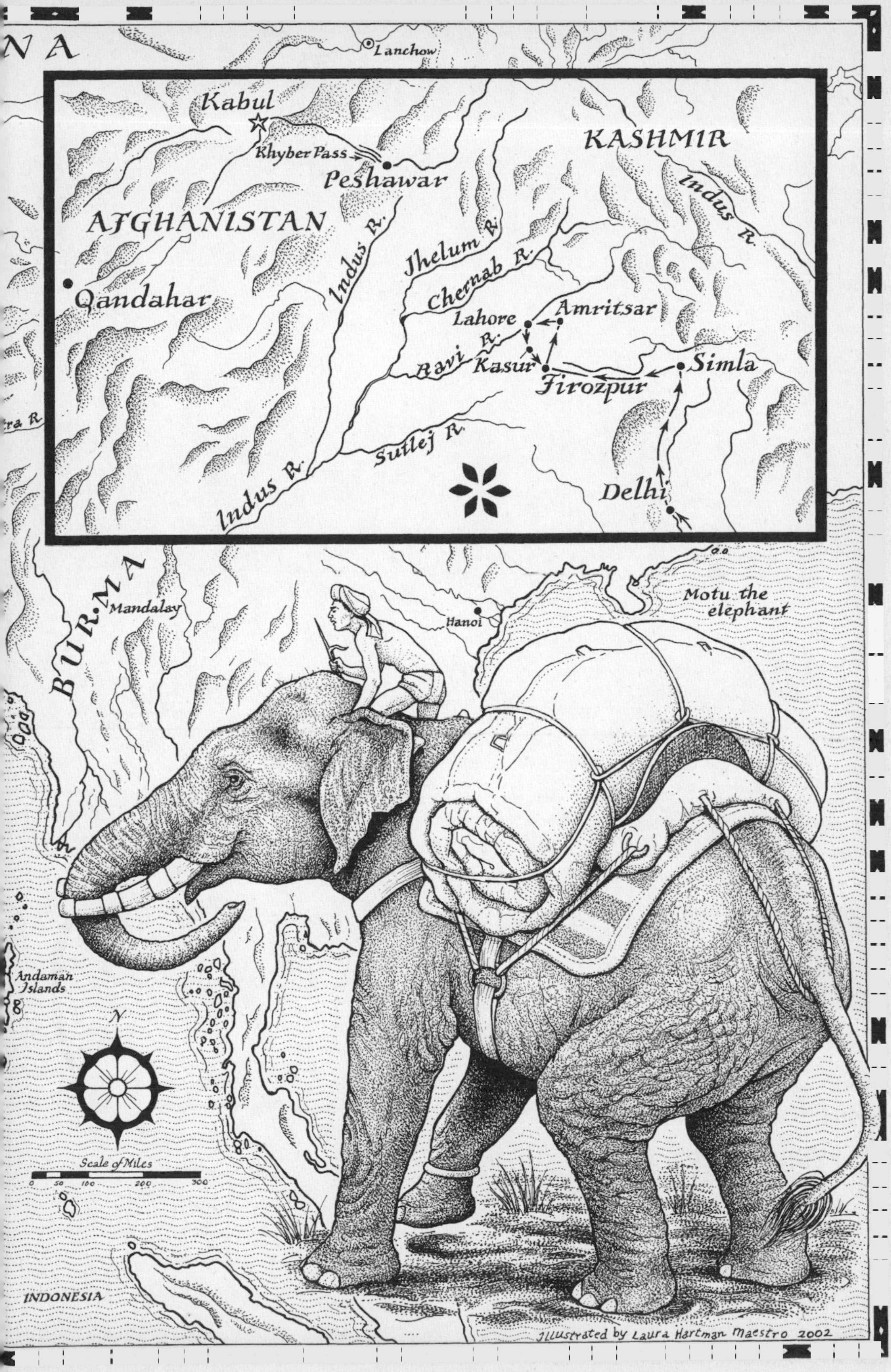

CHINA

Lanchow

Kabul

Khyber Pass → Peshawar

KASHMIR

AFGHANISTAN

Indus R.

Qandahar

Jhelum R.

Chenab R.

Lahore → Amritsar

Ravi R.

Kasur

Firozpur

Simla

Indus R.

Sutlej R.

Indus R.

Delhi

BURMA

Mandalay

Hanoi

Motu the elephant

Andaman Islands

N

Scale of Miles
0   50   100   200   300

INDONESIA

Illustrated by Laura Hartman Maestro 2002

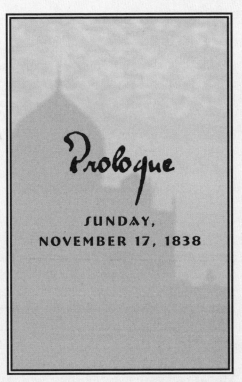

At 2:00 A.M., Shaikh Wali-ullah Karakoyia opened his eyes. Years of offering his prayers at the appointed hours had given him a delicate sense of the passage of time. Sometimes he allowed himself to imagine that, should he be sent to the windowless dungeons of the Lahore Citadel, whose walls shut out the call to prayer, he would still know when to wash himself and stand before his God.

He shivered and reached for his shawl. Moonlight filtered its way through the latticework balcony outside and fell like coins on the prayer rug that lay ready, pointing west to Mecca, its corner turned back to avert evil. Wooden curtain rings clicked softly as he padded through a doorway to the little table that held his water vessel and brass basin. The water was cold as he washed for the postmidnight prayer, a prayer optional to all save those schooled in the mystical traditions of Islam.

"God is great," he murmured, as he dried his face.

Facing the wall so that no creature might come between him and God, the Shaikh stood straight, his hands folded, his eyes half-closed.

*"In the name of Allah Most Gracious, Most Merciful:
Praise be to Allah, Cherisher and Sustainer of the Worlds;
Most Gracious, Most Merciful,
Master of the Day of Judgment.
Thee alone we worship, Thee alone we ask for help.
Guide us to the straight path: the path of those whom Thou
hast favored;
Not of those who have earned Thy wrath, nor of those who
have gone astray."*

As he recited, he abandoned himself to his dreams: mind pictures so dazzling that he found them difficult to describe, even to the most advanced members of the mystic brotherhood he had led for more than twenty-five years.

Eyes on the mat before him, the Shaikh moved through the slow dance of his prayer. He bent, straightened, and bowed, his forehead to the tiles beneath the threads of his prayer mat, as his fellow Muslims had done for thirteen hundred years, the venerable Arabic coming in whispered cadences in the moonlight.

BY sunrise, the rain that had poured in torrents before dawn had nearly ceased, leaving only a faint light to shine on the Shaikh's house and on the cobbled square upon which it stood.

The light strengthened and found its way into the narrow lanes and bazaars of Lahore City. It spread over the wet pavilions and court-yards of Maharajah Ranjit Singh's Citadel, the great marble fort that shared with the city the protection of its ancient fortified wall.

In an octagonal tower set into the Citadel's northwest corner, the Maharajah's youngest hostage was refusing a cup of milk.

Saboor would not drink from the cup the servant girl held out invitingly. Compressing his lips, he turned his head away.

"Oh, Saboor Baba," the girl crooned, looking about her cautiously as she held out the cup, "drink this, it is sweet."

"No," said the child firmly, and trotted away, his little shoulders bouncing. Reaching the safety of the bed where his mother sat loosening her hair, he crouched beside her and followed the servant with round, anxious eyes.

"What is the matter, my darling?" His mother pursed her lips and made a kissing sound. "Why don't you want your milk? You love your milk." Cocking her head, Mumtaz Bano studied Saboor and smiled. Auburn hair cascaded over her shoulder and lay in a shining coil in her lap.

"Oh, Reshma, is Saboor not the sweetest baby in all of Lahore?" she asked in her child's voice.

"Yes, Bibi," murmured the servant girl, her head swaying in agreement. The cup she held trembled, making little waves in the milk.

But Saboor would not have his milk. He crawled beneath the bed, his bare feet disappearing from view. There he sat, obstinately refusing his breakfast.

"Well, then, your *ammi* will have to drink it instead," his mother said. "Ammi loves warm sweet milk."

Mumtaz Bano reached for the cup, heavy embroidered silk falling back from a delicate wrist. The servant, her eyes widening, tried to take it back. "No, Bibi. This milk is for Saboor," she protested, but Mumtaz Bano would have it. She made a polite but commanding gesture.

As his mother took the cup from Reshma's fingers, Saboor crawled hurriedly from his hiding place, his mouth open, his breathing rapid. At the edge of the bed he dragged himself upright at his mother's knee, his face flushed, in time to see her lift the cup to her mouth and swallow.

For a moment there was silence. Then Saboor began to scream.

"What is the matter, my darling?" Mumtaz Bano asked, reaching out and stroking Saboor's face with her free hand, but he could not answer. He could only scream and shake his head back and forth, his mouth stretched open as far as it would go, his eyes screwed shut.

The servant girl stood immobile, her hands pressed over her ears to shut out the child's voice. Then, mumbling an excuse, she snatched him up and fled.

Without stopping outside the door for her slippers, Reshma flew, the child shrieking on her hip, past other rooms whose languid occupants scarcely looked up. Breathing hard, she climbed a flight of stone stairs to the outer door and ran out across a damp courtyard to the ladies' garden.

They were alone. A nearby fountain burbled. Reshma set Saboor down on its cold marble edge, then wiped tears and mucus from his face. The grinding, desperate sound of his screams told her that his heart was breaking.

"Why do you cry?" she asked him, her voice trembling. "Nothing has happened. Nothing."

Guards shared a water pipe near the tower door. Shielded from their eyes by a cypress tree, Reshma tugged her unclean veil over her head and crouched beside the child, willing him to fall silent. Now, her terrible work gone all wrong, she could only wait until Saboor's mother fell, unknowing, into deadly sleep. Later, when the body was discovered and Reshma questioned, she would swear that she and the child had been outdoors all along.

Saboor's mouth was still stretched wide, although he gave only a single, drawn-out cry. Reshma reached toward him, then drew her hand away.

Today's evil had begun a year ago, with jealousy and whispers, after the old Maharajah ordered Saboor and his mother to the Citadel from their home in Shaikh Waliullah's house half a mile away. Only Saboor's presence, the Maharajah had insisted, would protect him from illness and death. Saboor was, after all, the grandson of Shaikh Waliullah, a man whose mysterious abilities were known to all.

A myna bird shrieked in the cypress tree overhead. Reshma wrapped her fingers around her knees. Saboor's mother, whom Reshma had once envied for her beauty and her station, now lay mortally poisoned in her bedchamber. If Saboor had been helpless to save her, what use was he to the Maharajah?

Reshma looked down at the child. If he did possess special powers as people claimed, they had done him no good: they had only brought him to his present exile among the Maharajah's many queens, and the loss of his pretty mother.

He was quiet now. Reshma lifted him to her lap where he lay hiccuping and listless, refusing to meet her gaze. She bit her lip. What would the Maharajah do when he learned of Mumtaz Bano's death? Aware of the jealousies swirling within his household, would he guess the truth: that the poisoned cup had been meant not for the mother but for her child, his favorite, his tiny magician, his pearl of pearls?

Reshma looked past the tree at the guards who now dozed beneath a portico, their forearms shading their eyes. The Maharajah, at least, was far away, encamped on his border with his bejeweled court, awaiting his meeting with the English people. It was his youngest queen whom Reshma feared more, Saat Kaur, whose own infant son had failed to attract the Maharajah's love. The queen waited in a downstairs room for the screams that would herald Saboor's death. How was Reshma to explain her failure?

She wiped Saboor's wet face with a corner of her veil. How different he looked now, his brightness gone, his soft, questioning look replaced by blank exhaustion. Before today, save for the old Maharajah with his constant demands, Saboor's sole companion had been his lonely young mother. Alone and friendless now, how would he survive?

Reshma closed her eyes against her tears, but they seeped from beneath her lids and trickled down her cheeks. Why had she, who had never deliberately caused harm, consented to be the bearer of the poisoned cup? Was it her terror of the young Queen's rages? Had her own deprivation, her bondage, made her hard?

"Forgive me, Saboor," she whispered. "Forgive me."

A new fear clutched at her. Saboor had refused his milk. He had crawled as fast as he could from beneath the bed when his mother had taken the cup. Had he been trying to stop Mumtaz Bano from drinking the poison? *Had he known?*

She glanced at the silent child. It could not be possible. Saboor Baba, after all, was only one and a half years old.

Chapter 1

As a watery light filtered into her tent, Mariana Givens awoke with a start. Overhead, rain whispered against canvas.

She sat up and pushed her hair from her face. Why had she awakened so suddenly? Had an unusual sound, a voice, come from outside?

As she reached for her boots, a familiar scuffling at her doorway signaled the arrival of Dittoo with her coffee. She dropped the boots, flung herself down impatiently, and dragged the covers to her chin. Feigning sleep was the only way she could prevent Dittoo from talking to her. Even among Indian servants, Dittoo could win a prize for talking.

She breathed evenly, watching through her lashes as he pushed his way inside, past the heavy blind that served as a door, bringing with him a wave of damp chill and the scent of cooking fires. His bare feet on the striped rug made wet sounds that grew louder as he advanced toward her bed, wheezing a little, the tray rattling in his hands.

She forced herself not to wince as the tray clanked noisily onto her bedside table. Above her, Dittoo cleared his throat. Mariana had thought of asking the advice of the Governor-General's two sisters regarding Dittoo's habit of standing over her while she was in bed, but had refrained, knowing they would only insist that he be sent immediately away. Whatever the sisters might think, Mariana was certain Dittoo's behavior had nothing to do with her being twenty and unmarried.

When he turned, she opened her eyes and watched him shuffle toward the door, his shoulders stooped under their usual invisible burden, then remembered what had awakened her. It had been the silence outside her tent. Where were the coolies who daily dismantled the red canvas boundary wall in her corner of the state residence compound? Where were the shouts of the men, the grunts of their pack animals?

Her tent floor was wet, the air damp and cool. She remembered the sound of rain pounding on the roof in the night. That was it, the rain!

"Dittoo," she called after him, making a mental note never to do it again, "are we traveling today?"

He swung back, beaming. "That is what I wanted to tell you, Memsahib. They do not know as yet. Everything depends upon the big elephant. I heard them saying—"

"Thank you, Dittoo," she said, and waved him away.

The blind closed behind him. Mariana sat up. She scooped up her boots and banged them upside down against the side of her bed, then looked down, as she always did, to see if some interesting creature had tumbled out of one of them.

The red wall outside her tent would be taken down only if the camp's biggest baggage elephant proved able to carry his load. If she hurried, she might see the elephant for herself.

Hopping first on one foot and then the other, she fought her way into her boots, shrieking at the cold water that squirted up through the holes in the striped cotton rug under her feet. After flinging off her nightdress and grappling with her stays, she buttoned herself into her favorite tartan gown, pushed a handful of brown curls inside her matching tartan bonnet, and tied its ribbons carelessly under her chin. She ignored the ewer and basin waiting on their stand. There was no time to wash her face: she had an elephant to visit.

Leaving her coffee steaming untasted, she hurried across the soaking rug, Miss Emily's voice sounding in her ears. "How many times must I warn you, my dear," Miss Emily had said only yesterday afternoon while regarding Mariana severely over her reading spectacles, "that you must *not* forget your position. *Never* allow a native to see you confused, upset, or less than *perfectly dressed*."

Mariana took an impatient breath and stepped out into a misty early morning.

Her tent was well located. Tucked sideways into a front corner of the Governor-General's own residence compound, it had a clear view of the residence tents and a good, if distant, view of the principal gate, a folded entrance in the red canvas wall that enclosed the entire compound. Intriguing sounds often drifted into her tent from the other side of the wall, causing Mariana to spend much time imagining the various origins of the people and animals passing by on the avenue outside.

Smooth, shiny mud marred only by Dittoo's footprints covered the distance from her modest doorway to the compound's center. There, arranged in a square, the three riotously patterned tents of Lord Auckland and his two unmarried sisters, and a dining tent large enough to seat twenty, billowed wetly in the dawn breeze.

Beside Mariana's tent, the red canvas wall stretched away toward the guarded gate. Holding her skirts away from the mud, she hurried along the wall.

She should have waited in her tent until the march. That was the rule for ladies traveling in camps. If there was no march, a lady waited until nine o'clock before going across to the dining tent for breakfast. She then returned to her tent to read or write letters until lunch. After lunch, she paid calls, in this case upon Miss Emily or Miss Emily's younger sister, Fanny, in *their* tents. Before dinner, she went out for a ride. Mariana knew these rules because Miss Emily had repeated them to her countless times.

But Mariana would not shut herself away behind canvas. Ladylike idleness would certainly drive her mad. Besides, she would miss everything, and it was her duty to learn all about the camp, and about India. If she did not, her twice-weekly letters to Papa would never be good enough.

She risked a glance toward the residence tents. There was no sign of activity: no tattletale ladies' maid carried things across the compound, no English-speaking native manservant stood watching her. If she could get past the gate, then across the avenue and back again without being seen, she would be safe from Miss Emily's glares at breakfast.

She followed the wall, avoiding the stout guy ropes pegged to the ground every eight feet. The wet ropes and the gusting wind reminded her of the dream from which she had awakened. In her dream she had shivered in the prow of an unfamiliar ship as it sailed headlong through a dense fog toward a destination she could not guess.

It seemed odd to dream of a ship as she lay in a tent on the flat plain of northwestern India, a thousand miles from the sea, but odd as it seemed, the dream had come twice, perhaps three times, before.

Beside her, the ruddy canvas was stained with rain. High, grimly heavy, designed to keep out thieves, to Mariana's eye the red wall blocked out too much of the excitement of living in a traveling camp. Even the Eden sisters felt the same. "It would be almost worth the horror of discovering a knife-wielding savage under one's bed to be able to see more of the avenue from our tents," Miss Emily had remarked only last week as she, Miss Fanny, and Mariana negotiated the entrance.

By 6:00 A.M., the folded entrance, like the wall, should have been collapsed on the ground, tended by coolies coiling guy ropes and rolling up sections of canvas. Like the wall, the entrance was still standing.

Ignoring the salutes of the sentries, Mariana passed through and emerged onto the avenue. A hand to her eyes, she peered up and down the avenue's length toward the flat open plain at one distant end and the orderly horse and elephant lines at the other.

The wide avenue looked much as it had last evening, lined with office tents and the tents of senior government officials. Only the great durbar tent, missing from its place opposite the guarded entrance, had been replaced by an empty rectangle of churned mud where several hundred coolies stood watching something she could not see.

She hurried toward them.

The big elephant, Dittoo had informed her, was nearly twelve feet tall. The largest of the hundred twenty-seven baggage elephants attached to the British camp, he was the only animal strong enough to carry the durbar tent, the great reception tent essential to Lord Auckland for the entertainment of native princes. The elephant's name, Dittoo had said, was Motu. Such an elephant as Motu, Dittoo had added, was born only once in a hundred years.

Rain was Motu's sole enemy. The tent, an enormous weight when dry, became an intolerable burden after a soaking rain. As it was unthinkable for the Governor-General to be without his durbar tent, and as Motu was unable to carry it more than one day's march at a time, the elephant was never left behind. If after a rain Motu could not carry his burden, Lord Auckland and his spinster sisters, the British government of India, ten thousand soldiers, thirty-odd thousand government officials, shopkeepers, servants and coolies, and countless pack animals waited, squatting in the mud, until he could.

Mariana reached the muddy space and swept to a stop, craning to see over the pushing, half-naked coolies. A few turned to watch her. Oh, please let the big elephant be able to carry his load! How could she bear any more delays in the journey, when she was on pins and needles to meet Ranjit Singh, the legendary Sikh ruler of the Punjab?

From where she stood, she could see nothing. Hesitating only a moment, she plunged into the crowd.

"*Hattho, hattho,* move out," she commanded, and the coolies obliged, pushing against each other to open a narrow pathway through their ranks.

She was nearly there. Ahead of her, someone called out orders. An animal grunted. Staccato shouting erupted nearby. An elephant's trunk waved in the air. She had never looked closely at this elephant. How high would twelve feet be? Would he be strong enough to lift the wet tent even after—

"Miss Givens! *Miss Givens!*"

Mariana froze in midstep. A fair-haired Englishman had appeared, standing on a bale of baggage a little distance away. He waved a blue-uniformed arm.

She could not avoid him. Collecting herself, she waved in return. The mist had now become a soft rain that soaked through the shoulders of her gown. *Why,* if she must be caught alone outdoors, mingling with half-naked coolies at six in the morning, must she be caught by Lieutenant Fitzgerald of the Bengal Horse Artillery, the first man she had liked in the *whole camp*?

She braced herself and started toward him, tucking a damp strand of hair into her bonnet as she walked. Should she avert her unwashed face from his when she reached him? No, it was too late for that.

Fitzgerald and a dozen young officers, all suitable marriage prospects, had been invited three evenings before to the Governor-General's dining tent.

Fitzgerald had sat across from her at dinner. Mariana had seen immediately that he was a possibility, with his square, handsome face and high Roman nose, his hair smoothed unfashionably with pomade. After the soup he had put back his head to laugh at someone's remark, and that gesture, the angle of his head, the shape of his mouth, had caught her eye. Later, risking a glance, she had found him looking at her speculatively over the chicken fricassee.

His expression gave nothing away, but his look had excited and disturbed her. For the rest of dinner she had labored to converse with the man beside her, rationing her glances across the table, but Fitzgerald had not met her eyes again.

"Miss Givens," Fitzgerald called again, over the crowd's noise, frowning as he climbed down from his bale, smart in his uniform, "surely you should not be here. If you will wait a moment, I shall escort you to your tent."

"Thank you, Lieutenant," Mariana shouted back, "but I have come to see the elephant."

As she approached him, he looked at the front of her gown, then glanced hastily away. She glanced down and saw a telltale bubble of cloth poking up where she had missed a button.

Her whole gown must be buttoned wrong. Her hair was coming loose from her bonnet. She bit her lip and raised her eyes to find the lieutenant smiling.

He offered his hand. "Since you have come to see the elephant," he said, "you had better climb up here with me. This promises to be interesting."

She scrambled to the top of the bale, breathing in the rain-soaked mustiness of his wool uniform, feeling the warm pressure of his fingers.

Steadying her by her elbow, Fitzgerald pointed. "There he is."

Mariana looked out over the crowd and drew in her breath.

In front of them, ringed by coolies, a massive bull elephant struggled to rise to his feet, the Governor-General's rolled-up durbar tent creaking and swaying on his back.

A *mahout* straddled the elephant's neck, beating at the huge head with an iron prod, shouting at him in Bengali, while the crowd, already liberally splashed with mud, argued and speculated and laid wagers. Ignoring them all, the big elephant steadied himself while he searched for purchase in the glassy mud, and then, with a fearful, trembling effort, heaved his tottering burden upward.

At the last instant, a great hind leg gave way. Mariana felt Fitzgerald stiffen beside her. The coolies groaned. Overbalanced by the sodden canvas, the elephant rolled, squealing, onto his side, scattering the coolies like so many chickens and sending his mahout scrambling for balance.

What a perfect scene for today's letter to her father. Mariana turned to Fitzgerald, her face alight. "This is what I like about India: real Indian things, not imitation English things. We try so hard to be English, with our tents and food and furniture, but it doesn't—"

"I am sorry, Miss Givens," Fitzgerald interrupted, letting go of her elbow, his gaze traveling past her as if he were looking for someone, "but I must inform General Cotton at once of the elephant's failure." He swung himself to the ground and held up a hand, looking both military and apologetic. "Allow me to help you down."

She looked at the elephant a moment longer, impressing his picture into her memory, then took the hand Fitzgerald offered.

When she reached the ground, he raised an elbow to take her arm. "I must see you to your tent, Miss Givens. It's too far for you to walk alone."

His hair gleamed as he bent to her. He had missed a spot on his cheek while shaving. His eyes, like hers, were green. He smiled crookedly.

Tempted to accept, Mariana hesitated. In the ten minutes it would take to reach her tent, they would converse. She could learn much about him in ten minutes; but what of the toppled elephant that breathed harshly behind her in the mud, the tent still roped to the wooden frame on his back? Could he get up again? Was he hurt? Dear Papa, waiting at home in Sussex for her letters, must be told.

"That is kind of you, Lieutenant," she replied, "but I shall stay here a moment longer. I wish to have a word with this elephant's driver."

Fitzgerald took his arm away. "A word with his mahout?" he repeated, frowning. "But how can you—ah, of course, you speak their languages." He hesitated. "But surely I should not leave you alone here." He looked over his shoulder, as if seeking help.

Mariana planted her feet in the mud. "I came here alone, Lieutenant Fitzgerald," she replied. "But I am sure," she added, looking him full in the face, "that we shall see one another again soon." She glanced away, certain she had held his gaze too long.

He hesitated again, then bowed. "I am flattered that you remember my name, Miss Givens. And you will be all right here?"

Mariana nodded, her lips pressed together, then offered him her wide, impulsive smile.

He smiled in return. "Then I shall tell no one I have seen you."

When she looked back, he had gone.

The elephant still lay on his side, weighed down by the sodden tent, a gray mountain with one visible, bloodshot eye. The mahout moved around him, crooning as he went, a large, wicked-looking knife in his hand, slicing a rope here and a strap there, expertly loosening the animal's load.

He started when Mariana cleared her throat.

He was smaller than she was, and wiry. His shoulders moved awkwardly when he greeted her, as if he were unused to foreigners.

"What is your elephant's name?" she asked, in her careful Urdu. Being English, she was entitled to be imperious. She chose to be civil.

"It is Motu, Memsahib," he replied over his elephant's whistling breath, departing from his own language to answer her. His face was deeply seamed. The whites of his eyes were the color of old ivory.

She nodded. "Motu. And yours?"

"Hira Lal."

Behind Hira, the elephant twitched and raised his trunk. Without an apology, the mahout turned from Mariana and went back to his work.

Well, then, she would speak to his back. She raised her voice. "Why are you cutting all the ropes? Won't they be angry with you?"

"What do I care for their ropes?" Hira's fingers shook as he cut through a thick leather strap. "I told them we should not try to move the tent today." His own voice rose. "I told them Motu would fall. I warned them of the danger to Motu."

"Danger?" Mariana took a step closer. "What danger?"

Hira made one last cut and the load fell away like a huge, cold sausage. Motu lay still for a moment, then rolled onto his knees, the empty frame still tied to his back.

The little man turned to face Mariana. She could not imagine how he could bear the chill, wearing only a loincloth and a strip of worn cotton. He was covered from his carelessly tied turban to his bare feet in the pungent smell of elephant. "An elephant's spine is delicate," he told her. "If something causes the load to shift, the frame may shift, and press upon the spine. Such accidents cripple or kill elephants. An elephant must never fall when loaded."

When his face relaxed, Mariana saw how frightened he had been.

At Hira's command, Motu lumbered to his feet and towered above them both. It was the unusual length of his legs, like four great tree trunks, that made him so tall. While Mariana watched, he bent his front legs and lowered his face to his mahout. Hira Lal spread his arms and took hold of the two great ears, then set one foot high on the elephant's trunk, mounted in one nimble motion, and seated himself twelve feet above the ground.

"How long have you been his mahout?" Mariana tilted her head upward, a hand on her bonnet, not wanting them to leave.

"Since he was small," Hira replied. The heavy elephant prod appeared in his hand. "I hope," he said, "that we die at the same time. We are used to one another."

Shivering at the thought, she turned back toward the avenue.

So Dittoo had been right about the elephant's name, Fatty. Perhaps Motu had been a little tub when he was small, like her baby nephew, Freddie. Whatever the elephant had been then, he was now an immense gray animal, wrinkled and covered with coarse black hairs. Mariana sighed. She would never have enough of elephants.

Freddie must have changed in the year since she had left England. He had been an energetic, sticky-faced little creature then, with pudgy legs and feet and a halo of golden hair. By now he would be nearing his third birthday.

A large puddle of shiny mud blocked her way. Mariana stopped and contemplated it, as the breeze sent a little shower of rain onto its surface. Freddie would be five in two years, the same age her brother had been when he died.

Poor little Ambrose. He had been playful one day, hot and agonized the next, and gone forever soon after that.

For a long time after he died, she had thought she would never recover.

From the moment of his birth, Ambrose had been in her charge. At eight, her sashes untied and dangling at her sides, she had walked the gravel paths in the garden with him cradled in her arms. When he had begun to speak, it had been she who translated his first words. "He wants another potato, Mama," she had said. "He wants to pat the dog."

Later, Ambrose had been her constant curly-haired companion. He had followed her everywhere, never telling her, as others did, that she was untidy, or too noisy, or that she talked too much. She had shown him her private hiding places in the garden, and they had crouched together beneath the bushes, their clothes speckled with burrs, while she spun tales for him of talking frogs and fairies who dwelt at the bottom of the garden.

Holding her skirts aside, she circled the mud puddle, ignoring the stiffening breeze. She had been twelve, her sister Charlotte fourteen, when Ambrose died. Whenever she thought of that time, she remembered her mother and her aunt Rachel standing grim faced and exhausted at the door to the bedroom where Ambrose lay, quiet now, in the sleep that precedes death.

"Come inside," Mama had said to Mariana and her sister, "and bid your brother good-bye."

Together, the two girls had tiptoed to his bedside and found him snoring, his mouth open, his little face wasted, his head, shaven against the typhoid fever, ugly upon the pillow. Certain that he would open his eyes for her, Mariana had taken his hand, but he had not awakened, and his small fingers had felt devoid of life. Realizing the truth, sick with pain and fear, she had dropped to her knees and thrown her arms about his small body.

"Do not die, Ambrose, *please,*" she wailed, while Charlotte sobbed quietly beside her.

Mariana pushed chilled hands into her sleeves as she made her way to the avenue. Ambrose had not been the first to die. Two other Givens children had been lost to measles when Mariana was four: Colin at two, Janet, at six months. She did not remember them well, although she did remember her panic when, after her own slow recovery, she had noticed the silence in the nursery.

The lost children were never mentioned, and Mariana had never seen her mother weep for them. White-faced and trembling, her mother had not wept for Ambrose either. Her silence terrified Mariana, who thought it meant she was to blame. And why not? Talkative and clumsy, she had gone on living while the precious babies had all died.

"But why must we be brave?" Crumpled on a chair before the sitting room fire, Mariana had searched her mother's still face for consolation and forgiveness. "Why may I not cry for Ambrose when my heart is broken?"

"Because, Mariana," her mother had said before turning away, "what we need at times like these are resignation and fortitude. Weeping will only make us ill."

Her hollow-eyed father had smiled wanly. "We must sustain ourselves," he had added, "with the knowledge that God is good."

From that day, they had rarely spoken of Ambrose. While Charlotte tried to behave normally, Mariana had trailed about the garden alone, weeping painfully in the hiding places where she and Ambrose had played, Ambrose who had thought her perfect, who had smacked his lips as he watched her spread fresh strawberry jam on his scones.

She kept his favorite wooden soldier, concealing it by day and sleeping with it by night. The sight of strawberry jam sent her sobbing from the dining table.

She found herself noticing other people's pain. She burst into the kitchen and flung herself into the arms of a scullery maid whose sister had died. She often said awkward, truthful things.

Mama and Aunt Rachel had fumed at her odd behavior. Only Papa never said a cross word to her, dear Papa to whom her heart went out even now, as she stood beside the avenue in the rain, miles away from him. Absorbed in his work, he had not foreseen the deadly swiftness of Ambrose's illness. He had not expected his little son to die.

But now there was little Freddie. Perhaps Charlotte's son would take Ambrose's place in Papa's heart. One day, perhaps, Mariana's own babies would do the same for her.

That, of course, would be soon, if her mother in England, her aunt Claire in Calcutta, and the matchmaking Miss Emily had their wish.

"It is my plan, Fanny," Miss Emily had confided to her younger sister a week ago as they waited to be handed into the dining tent, unaware that Mariana had moved up behind them, "to have Mariana meet *every* unmarried officer in camp. They shall sit beside her by turns. If I have my way, we shall have a wedding before the end of December."

Miss Emily's enthusiasm, maddening to Mariana, must be gratifying to Mama, who waited patiently at home in Sussex for news.

"One year," Mama had told her as she packed a newly stitched gown into the largest of Mariana's three trunks, "is all you shall have until the next lot of unmarried girls arrives in Calcutta. I hope and pray that, in that time, you find a suitable match. If not, people will think you shopworn. It will be *too late*."

A string of camels blocked Mariana's way, padding along the avenue, their brass ankle bells chinking. She tapped a fretful foot, eager to get across the avenue and inside the guarded entrance before she was seen again.

Since her arrival from England, India, not marriage, had absorbed Mariana's attention. Now that her year was nearly over, she must find a husband. Lest she forget, letters warning of approaching doom arrived every third day in the mail pouch from her aunt Claire in Calcutta.

Mariana was only too aware of the progress of the other potential brides who had arrived last winter with her. Aunt Claire's most recent letter had described the engagement of the plainest of them, a Miss Finchley, who had made a surprisingly good match, while one of the prettiest girls had become ill with smallpox, and was expected to be disfigured for life by the scars.

"They are sending her home." Miss Emily had shaken her head as Mariana folded Aunt Claire's letter away. "What a pity. I understand Miss Ranier was a lovely girl, with every chance of success. Now, if she is fortunate, she will live her life out of a trunk, a kind maiden aunt to one family member after another. If not, she will be forced to hire herself out as a governess."

Miss Emily had sighed. "How suddenly things change."

The camels were still passing. Mariana fidgeted on the avenue's edge. Her year was very nearly over and she was not yet engaged, but her position was most enviable, nonetheless. The great moving camp, her home for the past three weeks, was also temporary home to more than half the British government and all but a handful of Calcutta's British-born army officers, most of whom were young and unmarried. It was a rare opportunity, as both Miss Emily *and* Aunt Claire had pointed out. Had Mariana been one of a hundred girls with only one available man, she would have had no chance, with her inquisitiveness, her untidinesses, and her unconventional behavior. Yes, Mama had echoed in her letters from Sussex, what chance could Mariana have, with her unmanageable curls, her too-wide smile, her square shoulders?

But there were disadvantages to being the only young lady among so many eager men. Mariana had long ago tired of anxious strangers. Jaded by too much choice, she noticed only their missing teeth, their protruding ears, their desire to please her. Her dinner partner last night had looked so exactly like a white rabbit that she had scarcely been able to make conversation.

Miss Emily and her sister, of course, had their own opinions. They seemed more interested in the men's qualities than in Mariana's affections. Miss Emily's candidate was a lively man with an odd-shaped head, whose family was reported to be very generous. "We must remember, Mariana," Miss Emily had pointed out, "that most of these men are second or third sons." Miss Fanny's favorite was a tall, lugubrious person who had a habit of bursting into tears. "Nothing," Miss Fanny had observed, "is more important in a husband than a kind heart."

They both liked the White Rabbit.

The camels had gone by. Mariana lifted her skirts and began to dash across the avenue just as a European on horseback appeared suddenly from between two tents.

She stopped hurriedly. Major Byrne, commanding officer of the camp, pulled abreast of her, a stout figure, upright in the saddle. His black boot shone at the level of her chest. Spiked brass spurs caught the sun.

He gazed meaningfully down a ruddy nose, first at the departing elephant, then at Mariana. "Good morning, Miss Givens," he drawled. "Out for a stroll this morning, are you?" His eyes drifted to the front of her gown.

"Yes, indeed, Major Byrne," she replied. She forced a smile as heat rose to her face. Water dripped from the rim of her bonnet.

He returned her nod with a sharp little one of his own, then spurred his horse and rode away down the avenue, his horse's tail flicking.

She kicked up an arc of mud with the toe of her boot. Why should it matter to Byrne that her gown was buttoned all wrong? Her chin high, she hurried across the avenue. She *would* cross the avenue when she wanted to. She *would* look at elephants or speak to mahouts when she chose to. *They* might expect her to sit all morning in her damp little tent staring at the walls, but she would not. She could make no new discoveries for herself and Papa by looking at the openings in those walls, to Dittoo's corridor, to her cramped bathing space, to the space where, terrified of the sudden appearance of Dittoo or the sweeper, she gripped the inner and outer curtains closed while using her chamber pot.

Who was fat Major Byrne to be superior? Mariana did not make honking noises the way he did when he thought no one was listening. She had *not* missed the honk he gave just now as he rode away. And what of his friend William Macnaghten, who had given her the post of lady translator, with his great bushy eyebrows and his habit of studying his tongue in a pocket mirror? What was wrong with them all? Could they not see what an adventure this was?

Lieutenant Fitzgerald, at least, had understood. She marched past the sentries at the gate, her own nose at a severe angle. "Dittoo," she snapped as she swept into her tent, "bring my riding habit, and tell the grooms to saddle one of the mares."

Chapter 2

Miss Emily had instructed Mariana to take at least two grooms with her whenever she went out riding. Although she hated being followed on foot over miles of ground, Mariana did not send her trio of underfed youths away at once, but out of deference to Miss Emily, allowed them to trot behind her past the large tents of senior government officials, past office tents and veterinary tents, until she had reached the horse lines at the avenue's end. There she reined in her mare and sent her attendants off.

At the lines, hundreds of animals stood tethered in long, orderly rows, tended by a host of natives. Between the horses, guinea hens, natural enemies of snakes, picked at the muddy earth.

Mariana watched the dark-skinned grooms going about their work, wrapped against the chill in lengths of cloth. Her favorite, a tall, bony-faced senior groom, saluted her as he strode by, leading a mare with a cut on her glossy neck. Mariana always looked for the tall groom when she came to the lines. He never hurried and he rarely spoke, but there was something about him that drew her attention.

Whatever that was, it was not lost on the other grooms. All treated him with great respect, although he did not seem to notice.

She sighed. What could be more different from home than this place! Try as she might, she could never capture in her letters one-tenth of what she had seen and smelled of India. Everything was exotic here, the sudden dawns and dusks, the taste of everything, even the feel of the air.

Modeled after the legendary camps of the Moghul emperors who traveled with their governments, armies, wives, and slaves, the British camp was at once grand, complicated, and squalid. Mariana never tired of its myriad lanes and tents, its colorful, noisy bazaars. With a population of only forty-odd thousand, it scarcely counted compared to the Moghul emperors' camps, which, she had learned, would have been three times as large. Nevertheless, the British tents stretched for several miles over what was now an ocean of mud broken only by an occasional ruin or cluster of thorn trees.

The camp's departure for the Sikh kingdom had taken place at Calcutta the previous October. Mariana, newly added to the Governor-General's party, had missed that exciting event as well as the first six months of the camp's travels. What information she had about the journey had been gleaned from dinner table conversation and from Lord Auckland's sisters, both of whom had pointed out that having suffered the journey once already, they had no need to suffer it a second time in recollection.

The camp traveled, as the Moghul camps had, at the rate of ten miles a day. Each morning at six o'clock sharp, as the last trunks were being loaded onto wagons and pack animals, Lord Auckland and his sisters left for the next campsite, traveling in a carriage in fine weather, in closed palanquins carried by bearers if there was a threat of rain. After some three hours of hard cross-country travel, they would arrive at the next campsite where, barring disaster, their breakfast, sent ahead in the night, waited for them in the spare dining tent.

Blue smoke from cooking fires hung in the air. Suddenly hungry, Mariana sniffed, enjoying the scent of charcoal and unfamiliar spices. But, hungry or not, she should not expect a lovely breakfast at nine o'clock. By now the breakfast wagons, their drivers alerted by runners, would be on their creaking way back with the brioches and the smoked duck, too late to do Mariana any good.

On the march, traveling as she did with the Governor-General's own party, Mariana had no need to fend for herself in the great procession that followed after them, prodded by professional camp drummers. Ill or well, in whatever conveyance they could find, everyone else in camp, from the senior-most official to the lowliest sweeper, rushed to stay ahead of the dust or the mud thrown up by ten regiments of marching soldiers and by the baggage train with its straining bullock teams, laden camels, quick-moving donkeys, and the slower elephants hauling artillery and wagons full of grape-shot and cannonballs.

Thanks to the efforts of thousands of coolies, the camp was reborn at each new site within hours of arriving, with every shop and servant's quarter in its appointed place, and the grand avenue, as if by some miracle, precisely as long and as wide as it had been the day before.

It had taken from October 1837 until the end of March 1838 for the camp to make the journey from Calcutta to the northwest corner of British India. There, when the raging heat of summer overtook the tents, Lord Auckland, his sisters, and his senior officers had abandoned the army and the baggage train to their own devices and traveled up to the hill station at Simla to rest from their journey in rose-covered cottages and to entertain themselves with dinners, fêtes, and theatricals. It was there that Mariana had made their acquaintance and had been invited to join the Governor-General's party.

Now November had arrived, with its cooler days and balmy evenings, and the camp was traveling once again. Its final destination—Firozpur on the British side of the Sutlej River—was now only fifty miles away. Across the Sutlej, which marked the northwestern border of British India, stood the independent Kingdom of the Punjab, home to the old Lion of the Punjab, Maharajah Ranjit Singh, who even now waited on the border at his own lavish camp for the British to arrive.

In less than a week now, the camp's long journey would end, and the great durbar would begin: the state meeting for which Lord Auckland, his government, and his army had traveled so far. At the end of the durbar, after its many military reviews, its dinners and entertainments, the moment would arrive when Lord Auckland and the Maharajah signed the important treaty sealing their joint promise to combine the British and Sikh armies, and together, or "hand in hand" as the Maharajah had put it, conquer Afghanistan.

Conquer Afghanistan . . . Mariana clucked to her little mare. Leaving the horse lines behind her, she began to cross the two miles of open plain separating the government and army camps. For the next weeks, news of the durbar and the Afghan campaign would fill the letters she wrote to Papa, while her letters to her mother and her sister Charlotte would be full of the doings of Lord Auckland and his sisters, and of her own prospects for marriage.

She yawned. Her family. The warming air felt moist. She reached up and opened the top button of her riding habit. It was Sundays she thought of when she thought of home, Sunday lunch in the vicarage dining room with its tall windows and everyone at table.

"*THIN* slices, please, Wilfrid," her mother would say in her penetrating voice, as Papa carved the mutton, while at the end of the table Mariana's sister Charlotte exchanged glances with her husband, and Baby Freddie squeaked in his little chair beside them.

Perhaps it had been the sight of Charlotte and Spencer, happily married with a son, that had prompted Mariana's mother to send her to India.

"She is nearly nineteen, Lydia," Aunt Rachel had said a year and a half ago, her taffetas rustling as she and Mama spoke privately in the small sitting room. "This corner of Sussex has no one to offer but poor Mr. Bertram with his four little girls and young what's-his-name who has that dreadful stammer. We have no connections elsewhere, like other families. We all know Mariana's looks are far from fashionable, and much as I love him, her father can give her no fortune. India is full of ambitious young men. Send Mariana to Calcutta, to Claire and Adrian. Her bad habits will matter less there."

"I suppose you're right, Rachel." Mama's voice had dropped. From her listening post in the passage, Mariana held her breath.

A new rustling sound meant Aunt Rachel had drawn herself upright on her favorite straight-backed chair. "Of course I am right. The girl's tactlessness is legendary by now. Who can ignore her remark at church, in front of their grandmother, about your cousin's twin babies, 'two misshapen peas in a single pod.' And what of the frights she has given us? What of the time she disappeared when she was sixteen, and came home hours later covered in mud, saying she had fallen into the river?"

"Please, Rachel," Mama said quietly. "I believe we had agreed never to mention that awful time again."

"Of course, Lydia." Mariana imagined her aunt waving an impatient hand. "But what of her curiosity? Do you know that Mariana *listens behind doors*?"

"Yes, Rachel, I do." Her mother's sigh washed over Mariana's hiding place.

Mariana did, indeed, listen behind doors. She had done so ever since the summer after they had buried Ambrose, when she had gone to her father's study to tell him dinner was ready.

It had grown late, and he had not appeared at the table. Sent to call him, Mariana rushed across the passage in her usual headlong way, then stopped abruptly, horrified at the sounds coming from behind his closed study door. She had always believed that her father never cried: now, his surreptitious, muffled sobbing cut her to the bone. "My boy, my poor little Ambrose," she heard him moan over and over.

Mariana crept away to tell her mother that Papa was busy and would be coming presently, but the echo of his sobs never left her. From that day, she had never entered a room without first listening outside.

The week after her conversation with Aunt Rachel, Mama broached the subject of India, looking hard at Mariana between rapid jerks of her knife as they cut delphiniums for the front hall.

"I do not know what I shall do without you, my child, in spite of all the trouble you give me," she announced in her usual ringing tone, causing two men in the kitchen garden to look up from their hoes, "but your aunt Rachel is correct. Young ladies do go out to India these days, properly chaperoned, of course. It really is the best thing for you, considering your prospects here." She shook her head. "If you had blue eyes and a neat rosebud mouth like your sister, things might have been different. I know your father finds that great, broad smile of yours enchanting, but subtlety is now the order of the day. As for your hair— If you stay here, Mariana, you will spend your life changing the flowers and the library books. Claire and Adrian have not seen you since you were Freddie's age. Having you there will give them pleasure. After all, they have no children of their own. Go to India, darling."

India. The East. Until that moment, for all Aunt Rachel's advice, Mariana had never pictured herself actually sailing to India to marry someone there, perhaps never to return. But now that it was to happen, India beckoned her. There she would start her life anew, her slate wiped clean, free of the troubles of her past, and of the restrictions of English village life.

During the following six months, while they awaited Aunt Claire and Uncle Adrian's response to her father's letter, Mariana, already missing her family, showered sudden kisses on Mama, Charlotte, and little Freddie.

"For goodness' sake, girl," Mama said, "stop flinging yourself at everyone. You haven't gone yet."

But as much as she loved them all, it was her dear, soft-hearted papa whom Mariana would truly mourn.

"I shall miss you dreadfully, my darling," he had said on her last day in Sussex, taking her hands into his own, and looking sadly at the three trunks standing ready to be loaded onto the carriage. "You must remember that we are here, and that we will always love you."

How would Papa manage without her? Since Ambrose's death, who besides Mariana had undertaken to make him happy? Not

Mama, bearing her loss in tight-lipped silence. Not Charlotte, trying her best to be brave, and too preoccupied to notice his misery. It had been Mariana who had taken it upon herself to cheer her father.

She had found a path to his heart in his passion for military strategy: all that now remained of a thwarted military ambition, quashed by his clergyman father twenty-five years earlier.

She had read the books in his study and pored over battle plans. When she found him pale and distracted, she chattered of the great battles: Marathon, Hastings, Waterloo. Later, as their bond and her own interest grew, she mastered the histories of other battles. At the age of fifteen she horrified Aunt Rachel by discussing the Battle of Agincourt in the garden with her father and a gentleman neighbor.

It was Mariana who appreciated her father's sermons.

"How do you expect, Wilfrid," Aunt Rachel had said after church on Mariana's last Sunday at home, "to inspire people like Miss Pringle and Mrs. Brownley to Christian works by citing Alexander the Great? What do you mean by instructing them always to 'attack the enemy's strongest sector'?"

As Aunt Rachel shook her head, Mariana and Papa had exchanged their special look for the last time.

And when she was sixteen, Papa had kept her secret after Jeremy Harfield had nearly drowned in the river.

Jeremy, a tall boy in laborer's homespun, had been picking apart a rope with his fingers when she chanced upon him on one of her solitary rambles along the riverbank.

"Caulking my boat," he had replied, when she asked what he was doing. He pointed to a little dinghy that bobbed beside him in the weeds. "I'm stuffing fiber into the cracks to keep the water out."

Jeremy was only a raw village lad, but she was glad to see him occasionally, glad of the smile he gave her when she appeared, hatless, on the path.

He said he did not mind her questions. He seemed to enjoy her company.

One day, however, he had looked up when she came, but he did not smile. "My sister died last evening," he said baldly, after a moment's silence.

Mariana put a fist to her mouth. "Oh," was all she could say before her own remembered pain swept over her, and she began to cry, certain Jeremy would think her weak, but unable to stop herself.

He dropped his eyes. "Three days ago she was took badly," he added. "Emma had delicate lungs, you see. The doctor came, but it was no use. She died in my mum's lap. She was a tiny little thing. I used to wrap her in my muffler when she felt cold."

Mariana snuffled wetly. "I'm sorry to weep like this, especially when you're being so brave, but I can't help thinking of my brother Ambrose. He died when he was five. I loved him so much."

"I'm sorry about your brother." He smiled crookedly. "I don't mind if you weep. Perhaps you are doing my weeping for me."

They met daily after that. A week later, the dinghy was ready. Mariana helped Jeremy push it into the current, then climbed in and sat watching him pull on the oars.

The world looked different from the middle of the river. As he rowed, they talked of heaven, imagining it full of fat babies and happy children, and stocked with every possible treat and pleasure. "I hope to see Emma there one day," Jeremy said softly.

"And I my brother Ambrose," she replied.

Forgetting the time, they stayed too long. The sun was setting when Jeremy rowed to an overhanging willow tree, then stood to hand Mariana to the bank. In her haste to scramble out, she overbalanced the little dinghy, causing it to rock wildly. Jeremy cried out, then, arms flailing, was over the side.

Where there had been warmth and enjoyment, now there was only chaos. Why had she jumped so dangerously from the boat? Why had she not guessed that he, a poor laborer, could not swim?

A willow branch stretched over the water, out of his reach. "Wait," she called. Her heart hammering, she climbed onto the branch and crawled unsteadily toward him as he struggled, his eyes bulging, six feet from the bank. Almost too frightened to breathe, Mariana scrambled out along the branch, fighting her hindering skirts, gasping as she slipped sideways.

The branch dipped treacherously as she neared Jeremy, threatening to tip her into the river beside him. "Here," she gasped, reaching out to him while her skirts fell into the water, nearly dragging her down. "Catch hold of my hand!"

Somehow, he did. One hand gripping the branch, she towed him toward her, then crawled backward while he followed her, pulling herself hand over hand toward the safety of the bank.

They sat, panting, among the willow roots and rushes. Their clothes were sodden and filthy, but Mariana felt giddy with accomplishment. She had saved his life. How proud Papa would be, when she told him.

After her mother had astonished Mariana by bursting into great gulping sobs of relief when she arrived home, bedraggled and chilled, her father called her into his study.

"Early this evening," he said gravely, shutting the door, "while walking along the river, one of my parishioners thought he heard someone drowning. He rushed to help, but found that the rescue had already taken place. The victim, a laborer in dripping clothes, was on his knees, being sick into the river. You were sitting beside him."

"Mariana," her father said, when she had poured out her story, "you are sixteen, and coming out into society. It is most unsuitable for you to be seen with young laborers. We shall not tell your mother of this," he added. "We shall say only that you fell in while retrieving your bonnet. But you must promise me that you will never see Harfield again."

Never see him again? "But Papa," she begged, "Jeremy is my *friend*. *Please* don't make me give him up."

He sighed. "You have a natural curiosity, Mariana, and a quick sympathy for others, but you act too rashly. You should have known that a friendship like this one would only end in loss.

"From what you have told me," her father went on, "it was your own heedlessness in getting out of the boat that nearly killed the lad. But I must say that you showed quick thinking in a crisis." He smiled wistfully. "I should not mind having you beside me in battle."

Mariana made her promise, and did not return to the riverbank. A few months later she came upon Jeremy on his knees, rebuilding a stone wall in the village. She nodded carefully; he returned her nod.

It had not occurred to her, then, to break her word, but by the time she reached home, Mariana was so angry with herself that she barely spoke to anyone for the rest of the day.

In bed that night she had vowed she would never again turn her back on someone she cared for.

SHE spanked dust from her riding skirt as her mare plodded past an empty well hole. Three years after the incident with Jeremy, she had leaned on the rail of the *Marchioness of Ely,* watching the English coast glide past, wondering how she would survive the dreary invalid lady who was to chaperon her on the voyage out. After more than three months of listening to Mrs. Sumter describe her migraines, she had been hugely relieved to get off the ship and throw herself into Aunt Claire's arms. . . .

After Sussex, Calcutta had seemed tantalizing, worldly, and exciting. In spite of the increasingly hot weather and the absence of Lord Auckland and his camp, there had been no slowing of the city's customary social round. As one of a dozen newly arrived English girls, Mariana found herself invited to everything.

"It is your skin, my dear," Aunt Claire explained as she inspected

Mariana's appearance before a ball. "Fresh, rosy skin is admired here more than anything else. Our skin turns yellow in this climate, you see. A few good agues and pouf, you are primrose! Mrs. Warrenton next door has survived here for fifty years. That is why the poor woman is orange." She pursed her lips. "We must get you one or two new gowns. People will talk if you repeat too often."

Determined to supply her father with interesting letters, Mariana had thrown herself into investigating India. Her imagination afire, she had questioned everyone she met about the natives and their customs, but had found to her astonishment that no one wanted to tell her anything.

Calcutta, she quickly discovered, was as rigid as Weddington village. Her new life was to be exactly the same as before, only it was to take place in the heat and humidity of the East.

"It's no use, Aunt Claire," she said crossly a month later, before the third dinner in four days. "I *hate* Calcutta parties. I have met every eligible man for miles. Not one of them knows a thing about India. All they talk of is their horses and their promotions. The thought of marrying any one of them gives me a headache."

"Don't be silly, Mariana. The other young ladies like them well enough." Aunt Claire frowned. "Do you think you should wear the blue tonight? You've worn the rose already this week."

"—And the ladies do nothing but gossip."

Aunt Claire raised her eyebrows. "And why not? What else is there to do? Of course you must go to parties. There will be other men. How are you to meet them if you stay at home? And stop fidgeting, Mariana, or I shall stab you with this brooch."

Two days later, when Mariana asked to be taken to the native part of the city, Aunt Claire's hand flew to her breast. "You are not to go there, my child!" she cried. "Mrs. Warrenton's niece insisted on seeing the native city. She was next seen being carried on board a ship for home, swathed in bandages!"

Kind, balding Uncle Adrian took out a map of Bangalore and showed Mariana the route he had traveled as a young district officer in the South, journeying from village to village with a tent and a writing table, settling disputes, but he would not upset his wife by taking Mariana to see the natives.

Her diligent efforts to learn about the Black Hole of Calcutta also failed. When she asked an elderly general to describe the tactical errors leading to the disaster, he reacted with horror. "He treated me," she complained to her uncle Adrian, "as if I had committed murder."

"A hundred and twenty-three people suffocated that night in that awful little room," her uncle replied. "It happened a long time ago, and we should have recovered by now, but we have not. If I were you, I should not mention it again."

"But," Mariana had almost shouted, "if we insist upon forgetting them, how can we learn from our mistakes?"

AT the outskirts of the army camp, she stopped near a row of nine-pound cannon and shaded her eyes, studying the heavy guns. For all she knew they might be Fitzgerald's.

A troop of native cavalry had stopped to rest in the shade of the gun carriages, their mounts tied to the spoked wheels. Their hairy, bucktoothed officer stared at Mariana as if she were a mirage.

The officer's hungry gaze made her more uncomfortable than the curious stares of the native cavalrymen. She tugged on the reins and turned back toward the horse lines of her own camp.

She reached up under her wisp of veil and wiped her forehead. What an adventure this was, and all because of what had happened twelve hundred miles away in Calcutta, one summer afternoon.

SITTING idly in her window at her uncle's house one stifling morning, Mariana had noticed a piece of cloth lying on the ground near the front gate. Being the exact color of the earth on which it lay, the cloth had been nearly invisible, but when it moved slightly, the motion caught her eye. She instantly went out to investigate.

When she reached it, she saw that the cloth was about the size of a bath towel. Lifting one corner, she found underneath it a creature that must once have been human. She could not determine if the thing was male or female. All she could see in that horrifying moment were contorted black limbs and a death's-head face, the lips drawn back in a toothless grimace.

Disturbed, the creature looked up at her through runny eyes and made one gesture, an unmistakable request for water.

She turned and raced into the house in search of a servant to send outside with something for it to drink, but no one was in the kitchen. Banging about in the pantry, she found a glass tumbler, filled it with water, and dashed back to the gate.

Mariana had not taken in the condition of the creature's hands. She saw as she offered the water that they were useless, bent double, the fingers twisted inward. Still, it sat up weakly and tried to grip the heavy glass between its wrists. The effort proved too great: with a little moan it fell helplessly back to the earth.

Having come this far, Mariana refused to give up. She held the glass out at arm's length and gestured for the creature to drink.

For what seemed an eternity, the creature gulped at the water, its neck extended. Then, water dribbling from its chin, it lay back on the dun-colored dirt and began to speak. It spoke for some time, incomprehensibly, in some native language, its voice a thin whine. Finally, satisfied, it stopped speaking and closed its eyes.

Mariana felt immobilized by the sound of its voice. Bent over as if still offering the creature its drink, she was overcome by a sudden desperate desire to know what it had said. She tore herself away and hurried, the glass still in her hand, to the servants' quarters behind her uncle's house, where she stood in the dust shouting for Shivji, the servant who spoke English, to come at once and help her.

By the time Shivji emerged from his quarters and followed her to the gate, there was no longer any sign of the cloth or the wretched thing that had lain under it. At her insistence Shivji made a half-hearted effort to find it on the road, but returned to report that there was no sign of the creature she had described.

Aunt Claire ordered the tumbler to be smashed. "It terrifies me to think," she quavered from her pillow, after collapsing in the drawing room and being helped to bed, "that native lips—and most especially those of a native in the condition you describe—have touched one of my own English tumblers. The thought of that particular one becoming confused with the others and my actually drinking from it has made me quite ill. How *could* you, Mariana?"

Even Uncle Adrian tried to sound cross. "I know you only did it to be kind," he told Mariana uncomfortably, "but you must understand the danger of getting too close to the natives. There are those whom one may allow to come near, such as our own servants, but a half-dead wretch like that one might easily have given you unmentionable diseases. Promise me you will never do such a heedless thing again."

That evening, Mariana stood on the stairs listening to Aunt Claire and Uncle Adrian in the drawing room discussing taking her away from the "bad air" of Calcutta.

"*Yes, to Simla,*" Aunt Claire repeated, her voice so like Mama's carrying easily to all corners of the house. "You can always do your work in the hills, Adrian. You know how I loathe travel, especially such a great distance, but we cannot remain one more day in Calcutta in this heat. It does not suit the girl. You know what she is like at the best of times, and now she has begun to behave even more oddly. I will never forgive myself if she does something mad and ruins her chances."

Even more oddly? Ruin her chances? Mariana climbed the stairs and shut her door with a bang.

• • •

FOUR little girls walked in file beside the rough path, heavy-looking bundles balanced on their heads. Mariana watched them from her mare, envying their grace.

How could she have guessed, when she and her uncle and aunt set out seven months ago for Simla, that their summer in the hills would bear such interesting fruit?

One afternoon a few days after their arrival, as Mariana and Aunt Claire sat drinking tea in their pleasant little garden overlooking a deep valley, Uncle Adrian had stepped from the veranda, pink-faced with pleasure, rubbing his hands together.

"The most extraordinary thing has happened," he announced, pulling up a folding chair. "I have rediscovered the old man who taught me my native languages when I was a young man in Bangalore. He was passing in front of the church. I recognized him at once. He looks exactly the same, although it is nearly twenty years since I saw him last. He is a good man. I should never have mastered my languages without him." He blinked and cleared his throat. "Mariana," he said, a little frown between his eyes, "would you like to study Indian languages with my old teacher while we are here?"

The creature from Uncle Adrian's garden appeared before Mariana's eyes, water dribbling from its mouth, telling her something she could not comprehend. She caught her breath.

"But, my dear Adrian," Aunt Claire protested, turning from her husband to Mariana and back again, her upright lace parasol clutched in one hand, "the girl is not interested in studying any subject at all, far less native languages, are you, my darling?"

Mariana dared not look at Aunt Claire. "Yes, oh, yes, *please,*" she breathed.

Uncle Adrian smiled at his wife. "Here is an opportunity, my dear," he said, "for the girl to gain real knowledge instead of the silly nonsense one hears everywhere." He leaned forward and put a hand on Mariana's sleeve. "The old man will teach you more than languages," he said earnestly. "He will teach you poetry. He will give you some understanding of how the best natives think. I know that no one believes it any longer, but one can, and should, learn a great deal from the best of the natives."

Mariana nodded, unable to speak. Her uncle stared at the view. "Things have changed since I first came out," he added. "I don't like this new, snobbish attitude toward the natives. They should not automatically be treated as inferiors, regardless of their station or their learning."

He pushed himself out of his chair. "I must tell you one thing more. The Urdu word for *teacher* is '*munshi*'. You must always call your teacher Munshi Sahib. He is not, and must not be treated as, a servant."

He marched off, leaving Aunt Claire quivering and indignant in one basket chair, and Mariana beaming in the other.

The following morning as she sat in the drawing room, Mariana heard her uncle greet someone, and realized that her new teacher had entered by the front, not the kitchen, door.

A moment later, her uncle entered the room smiling delightedly, followed by a wispy old man.

"Mariana, my dear, this is your munshi, Sahib," Uncle Adrian said grandly, then stepped aside.

The munshi, who had removed his shoes outside the door, came forward and stood in his stocking feet. His eyes, fixed on hers, seemed benign. A worn woolen shawl thrown about his narrow shoulders covered the top half of a snowy shirt that fell below his knees over a pair of carefully ironed pajamas. The white stubble of his beard might have looked seedy on another face, but she thought it gave him a bookish air. His face, an even shade of brown, exactly matched his hands.

"Peace be upon you, Bibi," he said in English. "I understand that you wish to learn some languages of India."

Mariana let out a great sigh of gratitude.

FROM that day, Munshi Sahib called on Mariana twice daily, once after breakfast, and once in the afternoon. Driven by a passionate desire to learn, she studied day and night, practicing the sounds of Urdu whenever she was alone. As helpless as an infant at first, she gained a measure of fluency within three months, astonishing her uncle.

"We must," he decreed one day at lunch, "find a way to make use of this talent of yours."

And they did. In early November, the need had arisen suddenly for a lady translator for Lord Auckland's two sisters. The next day, after being handed over to the care of Miss Emily and Miss Fanny Eden by a proud uncle and a tearful aunt, Mariana left the Simla hills, accompanied by Munshi Sahib and her servant Dittoo, for the great British camp on the plains below.

HER mount shied abruptly on the muddy path. Keeping her seat on the trembling mare, Mariana looked for danger but saw none. Was it a snake? Jackals? She leaned forward to stroke the animal's neck, then started with a cry as a scarecrow of a man erupted from a large thorn tree, barring her way.

His hair was matted, his stare hot and otherworldly. He clutched a heavy wooden staff in one hand, and with the other he stabbed a knotted finger in her direction. "You, Memsahib," he quavered, his body swaying, "listen to what I am telling you!"

Mariana glanced desperately about her. Was there no one to help? Why had she left her grooms behind? Where were bucktoothed officers when they were wanted?

Very well, then, she would have to escape on her own. Her heart pounding, she bent forward in the sidesaddle, preparing to dig her spurred heel into the mare's side.

With a howl, the man dropped his staff. He raked the air above him with his hands, causing the frightened mare to jerk sideways. "The path you will take requires courage," he shouted hoarsely, "but it will bring you peace. Be careful, careful! That is all."

Before Mariana could move or speak, he scooped up his staff, and without another word, strode swiftly away and vanished into the tangle of thorns.

Light-headed with fright, she stared into the silent trees, then breathing hard, spurred her mare.

"*India is full of soothsayers and magicians,*" Uncle Adrian had warned her once. "*Everyone who comes out here is exposed to them at one time or another.*"

Afraid to look behind her, she cantered past dusty trees and ruins, past an abandoned well, hearing only the pounding of the mare's hooves which matched the quick beat of her heart.

After reaching the safety of the horse lines, she signaled to her waiting groom to follow her to her tent.

"*The natives are a superstitious race,*" Uncle Adrian had added. "*Most of them believe that nonsense. But you, Mariana, must always remember who you are. Do not listen to native fortune-tellers. If you do, you will never be the same again.*"

The White Rabbit from last evening bowed eagerly as she passed him on the avenue. Deep in thought, she scarcely nodded in reply. What *path* had the madman meant? Why should she take such a path if all she would find there was peace? And why should a path to peace require courage? She dismounted in front of her tent and handed the reins to the groom. She wanted all sorts of things: her father's happiness, excitement and adventure, knowledge of India, and an English husband. But she most definitely did not want peace.

. . .

"MEMSAHIB, your munshi sahib approaches."

Dittoo's voice broke into Mariana's thoughts twenty minutes later as she sat at her table in the light of the open doorway. Now that she was safely in her tent, her encounter with the madman seemed more dreamlike than real. How mysterious the natives were, appearing and disappearing without warning, offering bewildering advice in strange languages! Had the misshapen creature under the towel been a sooth-sayer too?

Miss Emily would insist that she pin up her loosening hair before her munshi arrived. Still feeling the madman's hot stare, Mariana reached up, then exhaled crossly at the sound of her favorite tartan gown giving way under her arm.

A discreet commotion outside her doorway told her it was too late to change her gown. If she kept her arms down, the old man would never notice. "Come in," she called.

A brown hand appeared, grasping a handful of canvas, and her teacher stepped with his usual care into the tent on stocking feet. The rug made a small, wet sound.

"Oh, Munshi Sahib," Mariana said quickly, "please be careful. The rug is very wet."

Her teacher seemed not to have heard. He came and stood beside her, long feet planted firmly. "*As-Salaam-o-alaikum*, Bibi, peace be upon you," he intoned, as if she had not spoken.

"And upon you," she replied, returning his greeting. "I am so sorry, Munshi Sahib," she added in her best Urdu, or high Hindustani, as Uncle Adrian called it. How stupid to have begun her lesson with a mistake. No matter how severe the emergency, greetings always came first. "It was just that I—"

Her munshi raised a hand. "It does not matter," he said mildly. Water had seeped through the striped rug. The English hose that covered his feet were already turning dark. "It does not matter."

She was not to mention his socks again.

He raised his chin and clasped his hands behind his back, signaling that the lesson had begun. "Today, Bibi, we will talk of Lahore. As you may visit there, you should know something of the city."

Mariana brightened. "Oh, yes, Munshi Sahib. I am very anxious to see Lahore!"

"Lahore, of course, is the capital of the Punjab." The munshi leaned back, his hands still clasped behind him, and fixed his eyes on the curved ceiling of the tent. "What, Bibi, do you know of Lahore?"

Mariana arranged her skirts. "The city of Lahore is so old that no one knows when it was founded. It is surrounded by a thick wall, pierced by twelve gates. The Citadel, which is the Maharajah's palace and fort, and the Badshahi Mosque take up the northwest quarter of the walled area. The rest is occupied by the city itself."

The munshi rocked on his heels. "That is correct. Do you know that Lahore once stretched far beyond its present boundaries? Two centuries ago, before invaders came through the northwestern passes, Lahore reached far beyond its fortified walls, with gardens, bazaars, and countless houses." He spread his hands. "The city which now has nine *guzars,* or quarters, once had thirty-six. There was a great jewel bazaar outside its walls called the Palace of Pearls. Even today, small pieces of jewelry and gold can be picked up there in the mud after a heavy rain."

Rain. Water. Mariana looked again at her munshi's feet. His socks were now stained with water, all the way to his ankles.

This was unbearable. "Munshi Sahib, please forgive me," she wailed, clutching at her forehead, "but I have a sudden headache. I beg your leave to rest."

The old man's expression did not alter. "Bibi," he said, "I am sorry you are unwell. I will return when you are able to receive me. In the meanwhile," he added, his eyes on hers, "please remember that there is little time to waste. Your Governor-General's great meeting with the Maharajah will begin quite soon. You must be ready." He smiled.

He knew she had told an untruth about her aching head.

He reached into his clothes and produced a paper folded in four. "Here is a poem for you to translate. Please prepare it for our next meeting."

Maintaining his usual distance, he laid the paper on the corner of her table, then took a step backward. She unfolded it and saw that it contained four lines of verse in his flowing, right-to-left Urdu script.

Mariana practiced the *salaam,* right hand to her forehead, as the munshi, his back to her, grasped the reed curtain and stepped from her tent into his shoes. She watched pensively as he strode away, without looking back, toward the guarded entrance.

Munshi Sahib knew Uncle Adrian well, although no two people could have been less alike. Not one of her teacher's gestures, no turn of his head, no hunching of his shoulders, was like that of an Englishman.

Who was he, really? The old man never allowed idle conversation during their meetings. When she asked where in India he had been born, he replied that she would be able to answer that question for herself when she became familiar with the various people of India. When she asked about his family, he had said that his family was of no consequence to her study of languages. When she inquired how he had come, genielike, to be in Simla where Uncle Adrian encountered him, he had said nothing at all.

She turned back to her desk and picked up the paper again. She, Mariana Givens, was about to translate a poem that looked like this, *into English*.

She yawned, stretching her arms over her head, then brought them sharply down, too late to prevent the tartan gown from tearing past repair.

Bother! She had meant to ask Munshi Sahib about the madman's message—"*The path you will take,*" he had told her, "*requires courage—*"

After the poisoned milk had done its work in the Maharajah's Citadel, word of Mumtaz Bano's death spread swiftly into the old city that pressed against the Citadel's walls, speeding from mouth to mouth through cobbled lanes until it reached Qamar Haveli, home to three generations of Shaikh Waliullah's immediate family and a score of his more distant relations.

Wailing arose at once in the upstairs ladies' quarters of the house, while downstairs the high carved doors swung open to admit the first somber-faced male visitors into the inner courtyards. As the day progressed, servants from neighboring houses crisscrossed the narrow streets, carrying vessels of food to the *haveli*'s back entrance, observing the tradition that no food is cooked in a house of mourning. Incense, painful to all, heavy in its associations, made its way on the breeze over the roofs of nearby houses.

"Shaikh Waliullah's daughter-in-law has died," the incense proclaimed, with more finality than any human voice. "Mumtaz Bano, mother of the Maharajah's hostage child, is dead."

As the tall haveli doors opened, a horseman rode out, his weapons rattling at his sides, his horse's hooves echoing in the brick entrance-way. Head down, he rode along curving lanes until he reached one of the twelve gates leading out of Lahore City. Seeing him pass under the Kashmiri Gate, an ironmonger called out, "Godspeed, O messenger of the Shaikh!" From his saddle Yusuf Bhatti saluted, but gave no reply.

He rode north, taking the ancient road leading to Peshawar, then to the Khyber Pass, then to Afghanistan, three hundred miles beyond. He rode wearily, coughing at the dust that rose from underfoot, his shoulders hunched beneath the burden of the news he carried. In three hours he stopped only twice, to ask for water at the villages he passed. As he traveled, he scanned the crowded highway for a familiar figure riding south.

Near Gujranwala, Yusuf Bhatti found the man he sought. Passing through a roadside village, he caught sight of Mumtaz Bano's husband mounting his horse near a fruit vendor's stall, an orange in his hand, his neat beard and long embroidered coat tarnished with the dust of hard travel.

His jaw tightening, Yusuf spurred his horse.

Hassan Ali Khan's clever, good-natured face lit with pleasure as he leaned from his saddle to embrace his closest friend. "Yusuf, may you have a long life!" he cried. "I was thinking of you just now. What a journey this has—"

When Yusuf pulled mutely back, Hassan's smile faded. He drew himself up and sat warily, his horse moving restlessly beneath him, his eyes locked on his friend's face.

Yusuf dropped his eyes.

After a moment Hassan Ali Khan's shoulders sagged. He took a ragged breath. "Is it my father?" he asked.

"No, it is not Lala-Ji." Yusuf raised his head and looked into Hassan's face. "It is not your father," he said, his eyes filling. "It is your wife."

"What? When?" Hassan's voice sounded like dry leaves.

Yusuf looked away and wiped his eyes on his sleeve. "This morning."

A pair of donkeys pulling a cart loaded with bricks minced past, sidestepping the two riders. Seeing one man's gray face and the other man's tears, their driver spoke aloud to no one in particular. "So," he said, "in this world, ill news comes to both great and small."

A passing merchant grunted his agreement.

"How?" Hassan had squeezed his eyes shut.

Yusuf hesitated, then told him the truth. "They are saying she choked on some food. We do not like the story."

"We do not like the story?" The reins shook in Hassan's fingers. "Do they think someone has *killed* her? *Killed* my Mumtaz Bano?"

"We have no proof," he said, "but we think there was jealousy in the Jasmine Tower. One of the wives—"

"What of Saboor?" Hassan interrupted. "Where is my son?"

"Saboor is still at the Citadel." Yusuf spoke gruffly to cover the additional pain he knew this news would cause. "The people there have refused to release him without the Maharajah's permission, and the Maharajah has already gone south to meet the British. Those at the Citadel say they have sent a message to his camp."

"I know the court people. They will never dare give this news to the Maharajah, for fear of being blamed." Hassan brushed his fingers across his face. "My baby is alone there. Oh, Allah!"

Yusuf's sword clanked as he leaned toward his friend. "I will ride to the Maharajah's camp myself. I will leave now. I will ask for Saboor to be sent home."

Hassan raised his head and looked into the distance. "Home," he repeated. "Oh, Yusuf, why did I take Saboor to see the Maharajah last year? Why was I so proud of my son that I ignored the risk?"

"Why blame yourself?" Yusuf asked. "None of this tragedy is your doing. How could you have foreseen the Maharajah's passion for Saboor, or that he would order him to live at the Citadel?"

"That moment has never left me. I see it daily: Saboor on the Maharajah's lap, turning his head to look at the bright colors and the jewelry, the old Maharajah peering at him out of his one good eye, stroking him and crooning to him. 'This baby has a light in his heart,' the Maharajah said to everyone, 'a bright, sweet light. This child will stay with me and bring me health and good fortune.' My Saboor was only six months old."

He sighed. "My poor Mumtaz Bano—forced to leave us and live with the Maharajah's wives. They terrified her, with their falseness and their cruel ways. Now they have killed her. I failed her, Yusuf, I failed them both." He dropped his head into his hands.

Yusuf sat silently. Poor Hassan. Over the past year he had tried many times, with increasing desperation, to retrieve his wife and son from the Jasmine Tower. Hassan was a skilled courtier and well connected, but the Maharajah, as his health weakened, had refused to give up Saboor. Instead, he had clung to the child as if to life itself.

"Saboor and the Koh-i-noor diamond are my most treasured belongings," the Maharajah had said countless times.

Yusuf reached for his friend's shoulder, but Hassan straightened with an impatient jerk, and reached for his horse's reins.

"We must hurry home to Lahore," he said. "We must not miss Mumtaz's burial."

THEY had been riding in silence for nearly an hour. Yusuf shifted in the saddle. What was Hassan feeling? What did he see at this terrible time? Did the villages in the distance shimmer before his eyes? Did the road rise and fall like a live thing before him? Aching to embrace his grieving friend, Yusuf glanced sideways, but saw only Hassan's shuttered face.

Saboor must be miserable at the Citadel, although that particular misery would most likely end soon, when the order came for him to join the royal camp sixty miles south of Lahore. But who knew what would happen to the child there, alone and unprotected?

Yusuf slapped at a fly. If Hassan's father, with all his spiritual abilities, had been powerless to protect his own daughter-in-law, it was doubtful that he could help his grandson. People were saying that Shaikh Waliullah should have saved Hassan's wife with magic. People talked all kinds of nonsense. Like the Maharajah, they too claimed Hassan's baby son had powers, that five minutes of Saboor's infant company could lift a man's darkest mood.

Hassan's grim voice broke the long silence between them. "I hate the Maharajah," he said quietly. His eyes were half-closed, his face wan above his beard.

Yusuf stared at his hands. A great soldier and statesman, Maharajah Ranjit Singh was loved by most, if not all, of his subjects. A soldier himself, Yusuf had admired the old one-eyed Maharajah all his life.

"I have told no one, not even you, Yusuf, what I have suffered over this past year," Hassan went on, keeping his voice low, even though the road was nearly deserted. "I have worked for the Maharajah, traveled to distant cities for him, collected his taxes, argued with his enemies; and all this time I, myself, have hated him more than all his enemies together." His fist tightened on his knee. "All this time I have thought that if I said it aloud, if I let myself speak my hatred, I would go mad. He has torn my very soul from me, but I cannot fight him for fear of causing my family more harm. Today that harm has come, in spite of all my inner struggle." He looked hollow-eyed at his friend. "Allah help me, Yusuf, I never thought I could feel such hatred toward anyone."

Yusuf tugged on one of his ears, then the other. "In that case, Hassan," he said, "God help us both."

Two hours later they reached Lahore.

It is sympathy that breaks reserve. At the first sorrowful greeting from a gentle-eyed Hindu blacksmith near the Masti Gate, Hassan's face crumpled. Yusuf urged his own horse ahead, allowing Hassan to follow him, however blindly, to his father's house.

At the periphery of the city, they passed rope makers and coppersmiths. Nearer to the center, they made their way past cloth sellers, acknowledging as they passed the grave salutes of all who knew their story. They maneuvered their horses through the congested streets, past spice sellers and goldsmiths, diamond merchants and weavers of the softest silk. At length they reached Wazir Khan's Mosque, home to the most precious of goods: incense, perfumes, and illuminated books.

Opposite the mosque stood the Waliullah family's ancestral home.

The tall doors of the haveli stood open. Male members of the Shaikh's family stood outside greeting visitors. All were ushered inside, each visitor directed, either to the Shaikh's presence or to the main courtyard, depending upon his degree of intimacy with the family. Palanquins with tightly closed side doors passed through on their way to the ladies' quarters. A crowd of onlookers craned to see each new arrival.

"Stand back," cried a voice from the crowd, as the two horsemen approached the gate. "Hassan Sahib has come!"

The crowd moved aside, staring, to let them pass.

"May Allah Most Merciful grant you patience," shouted someone. The crowd lent its voice in agreement.

"May the lady's soul rest in peace," said another voice.

"Yes, yes, may she rest in peace," answered the people at the door.

Their horses' hooves echoed hollowly as Hassan and Yusuf rode into the haveli's high, vaulted entrance. They dismounted and made their way past clusters of men, then through a gate with a carved wooden lintel. There, in his small courtyard in front of a decorated portico, Shaikh Waliullah had already risen from the padded platform where he sat daily among his close companions. He opened his arms to receive his son.

Yusuf stood at the back of the crowd. He had his instructions. Immediately after Mumtaz Bano's burial he was to ride out of the city again, and head south to the Maharajah's camp. Once there, he must find a way to persuade the Maharajah to return the infant Saboor to his grieving family.

He grimaced at the prospect. A soldier, quick with a *tulwar* but clumsy with words, Yusuf had no golden, persuasive tongue like the courtier Hassan, but the work must be done, and there was no one else to do it.

He must not fail.

• • •

AT the Maharajah's camp two days later, Yusuf made poor headway as he rode along a crowded avenue. "Move out, move out," he bellowed, fighting impatience as he forced a path for his horse through the throng of merchants and hangers-on. He pushed by a cluster of silk-clad riders who scowled and whispered as he passed. Dandified fools, let them talk.

He skirted a line of carts piled high with blood oranges. He should find food, but he was too angry and disappointed to eat. In his haste to cover the distance between Lahore and the Maharajah's camp he had bypassed the small, walled city of Kasur. Now his inquiries had yielded bad news: the Maharajah's Chief Minister, Faqeer Azizuddin, childhood friend of Shaikh Waliullah and Hassan's patron at court, had been at Kasur when Yusuf passed by. No one but Faqeer Azizuddin would be able to gain Yusuf an interview with the Maharajah. No one knew when the minister was to return.

Faqeer Azizuddin had been their best hope.

Yusuf turned toward the Maharajah's horse lines. His mount, at least, should eat and rest. If only he and Hassan could rescue the child themselves after Hassan's duties at the funeral were done . . . Yusuf had thought of it, without hope, all the way from Lahore. No one entered the Citadel's gates unnoticed. Even if they could, by stealth, reach the inner gardens, how would they gain entry to the women's quarters? The Jasmine Tower, home to the Maharajah's Queens, was walled off from the rest of the palace grounds. Armed sentries guarded its single, low door. Only Allah knew how many eunuchs were within, protecting the inhabitants of the Maharajah's harem.

No, Hassan's baby would be rescued with cleverness, not force.

A naked Hindu mendicant strode along the margin of the camp's main avenue, a begging bowl in one hand, his body covered with ashes. Yusuf glanced at the man, then away.

He had never seen Hassan's wife. Hassan, her distant cousin, had not seen Mumtaz Bano himself until after the marriage papers had been signed, the blessing given. Only then would the figured mirror have been produced and held at an angle, to show the groom, indirectly, the face of the bride who sat beside him, her head bowed modestly under her scarlet wedding veil. Whatever Hassan had seen that day, it did not matter now.

Yusuf rubbed his eyes. He would make himself eat, and then, putting his trust in Allah, he would go on to his next task.

Leaving the Maharajah's camp behind him, he would continue

south across the Sutlej River and travel deep into British territory, searching out the British camp as it made its way north toward the border. There, among the British tents, he was to find a man who, like Faqeer Azizuddin, had been a childhood friend of the Shaikh. This man, like the Faqeer, must be told in person of the tragedy at the Jasmine Tower.

With luck, on his return journey, Yusuf would not miss the Faqeer a second time.

Dense clouds obscured a quarter moon as Yusuf rode south on a borrowed mount, ignoring the discomfort of traveling without rest. As darkness descended, he followed a pitted track past ragged trees and empty fields to where a fortified mud village stood on its mound of earth, presenting eyeless walls to the outside world. Directed by a boy driving a bony cow, he presented himself, dusty and famished, at the headman's house.

After dining on *chapatties* and boiled lentils cooked over a dung fire, he lay down to sleep on a string bed in the headman's courtyard. Looking into the blackness, he listened to the grunting of the animals.

How was Hassan bearing this loss? He, like Yusuf, must be lying awake tonight.

Within hours of her death, Mumtaz Bano had been buried beside Hassan's mother, who had died when Hassan was only nineteen. Nine years ago, Yusuf had been among the men carrying the body of Shaikh Waliullah's wife out through the carved haveli door, wrapped in its winding sheet and decked with flowers, while behind him, the family women wailed. Two days ago, the same friends and Waliullah family members had borne Mumtaz Bano on their shoulders as the sound of the final prayers rose and fell behind them.

What would happen to Hassan's poor baby? How long could Saboor survive alone at the Citadel?

"*Allah-hu-Akbar,*" he said aloud, consoling himself. "*Allah-hu-Akbar.*" God is Great. If God were willing, help for the child would arrive in time.

THE only real garden in the Lahore Citadel was the Queens' Garden.

Twenty years before, at the desire of the Maharajah's second wife, the garden, a square space adjacent to the ladies' tower, had been returned to the graceful formality of its Moghul days. It had been a symmetrical Persian garden then, divided into four squares, with a marble fountain at its heart. In each cypress-shaded square, paths led to a smaller fountain between plantings of jasmine, gardenias, oranges, and roses, whose perfume was carried by the breeze from one end of the garden to the other.

The central fountain had been set into a marble platform, where on pleasant days the Maharajah's ladies enjoyed themselves, screened from idle onlookers by a row of cypresses that cast their shade along the gravel walks. In warm weather the younger ladies played by the fountain, giggling and trying to push one another into the water, while their serving women waited on their pleasure in the shade of nearby trees.

It seemed that this morning was too cool for such games. The Maharajah's thirty-seven wives seemed satisfied to recline on carpets in the garden, leaning against bright-colored bolsters like resting butterflies, their loose garments falling into silken folds against their bodies.

The senior-most wife rested near the fountain, her hooded eyes expressionless, her two legs spread apart, each one kneaded rhythmically by a serving woman, while the other Queens positioned themselves close by, nudging one another discreetly out of the way, vying to be close to the center of influence.

The old Maharani grimaced. "Not so hard," she said sharply to one of her servants. The woman nodded and went on with her work. The Maharani closed her eyes, ignoring the competition that boiled silently around her.

Crouching under a tree a little distance from the other serving women, a young servant girl glanced down at the disheveled baby who squatted at her side, his eyes passing from queen to queen, as if he were searching for someone.

Was he looking for his mother? Reshma did not believe so. She was certain he had known the milk was poisoned. She was sure that when Mumtaz Bano took the cup, Saboor had understood that she was about to die. His screams in the garden, she now knew, had been screams of loss.

What then, or whom, did he seek? If only his color were not so poor. If only his cheeks were still plump.

"Look at Saat Kaur," said one queen, a tight-faced woman, jerking her chin without sympathy toward Reshma's own mistress, a gray-eyed sixteen-year-old who sat apart from the others, a frail baby on her lap. "That boy of hers is certain to die soon. No child so weak and unhealthy can live for long."

The Maharani opened her eyes briefly and gave the sick baby an incurious glance, but did not favor the speaker with a reply. Biting her lip, the woman subsided into silence. Near her in the crowd, a second, harsh-faced woman smiled bitterly.

Reshma shivered. How these queens hated one another! How they feared for their future!

Saat Kaur did not look up, although color stained the dewy cheeks that had first caught the Maharajah's eye. Yawning deliberately, the little queen lifted her baby, whose skin was as yellow as turmeric, put him down beside her, and turned her head toward the row of cypress trees. Reshma shrank into her loose clothes and tried to tuck Saboor behind her. Oh, please let Saat Kaur not see him. . . .

The little queen narrowed her eyes, then started, her body stiffening. Reaching for a silver tray, she took a sugary sweetmeat. "Send the boy here, Reshma," she commanded.

Saboor ceased his searching from face to face and looked at the young Maharani. Trembling, Reshma pushed him forward.

Saat smiled and called softly to the child, the orange sweet glistening in her fingers. "Come here, take this."

Saboor hesitated, then trotted shyly to the young queen's side. As he stretched out his hand for the treat, she snatched it away and slapped his fingers sharply.

"There," she said, her mouth curling downward at his tears. "That is what you get for making yourself a favorite of the Maharajah. *Nothing* is what you get." With a disdainful gesture, she dropped the sweet into the fountain where it sank and rested, still tempting, under the water.

Her voice had a knife's edge. "Who gave you permission to spend hour after hour in the company of the Maharajah while his own son waits here, unnoticed?"

His cheeks wet with tears, Saboor gazed uncomprehendingly up into her face.

"And what is this 'light' you are said to have? I see no light," Saat Kaur added as he stumbled away. "Pah! I see only a dirty, foul-smelling boy whom no one loves." She gestured after the child with a finely painted hand. "Reshma, why do you keep bringing him here? He does not belong among royalty. Take him from my sight, and do not give him food. Why should we feed him?"

She had raised her voice. The other Queens nudged one another. "He is no child of ours," Saat Kaur added.

Reshma scrambled to her feet, tugging her veil forward to hide the pain on her face. She caught Saboor up and lifted him onto her hip. "Of course not, Bibi," she mumbled. "Of course we need not feed him."

She carried him away, out of sight of her mistress, away from the uncaring faces around the fountain. Once out of their sight, she buried her face in his small shoulder. A damp spot appeared on his shirt.

"Oh, Saboor," she whispered. "How can I leave you alone and attend only to Saat Kaur? How can I then atone for my crime? Who will care for you?" She looked anxiously over her shoulder. "Come, do not weep so. I will find you some dry chappatti while the queens amuse themselves in the garden."

Chapter 4

WEDNEJDAY,
NOVEMBER 20

The best horses in the British camp were to be found at the Governor-General's own horse lines. Separated by a hundred yards from the mounts of lesser camp members, the animals stood tethered in glossy rows, resting from the day's march, served only by the most experienced of the camp grooms. At the far end of the second row, Yar Mohammad, senior groom, straightened from inspecting a bruised leg on one of the mares and strode toward a nearby cooking fire to have his food.

As he squatted, warming his hands before the flames, he had an acute sensation that something important was about to happen. He closed his eyes and found himself looking at a strange and vivid scene.

He saw a fire before him, much like the one whose warmth he could feel on his face, but the blaze in his vision gave off a great cloud of dust and smoke. For an instant he could see nothing more. Then, padding toward him out of the haze, came a lioness. She moved carefully, for she was carrying something heavy in her jaws. Once clear of the fire, she paused and looked about her as if to satisfy herself that she was safe, then deposited her burden on the ground.

Yar Mohammad now saw that the big cat had been carrying a baby, a boy the same age as his own youngest daughter. The boy's face was fair, broad, and sweet of expression.

He sat on the ground with the lioness, watchful, above him. After a moment her long body stiffened. In one swift motion, she picked up the child again and moved off, her tail twitching, his small body dangling from her careful jaws. An instant after she had carried him away, a dense new cloud of smoke and dust enveloped the place where they had been sitting.

Yar Mohammad opened his eyes. The campfire with its suspended cooking pots crackled before him. Men chatted idly, their hands outstretched to the fire's warmth, their bodies neatly folded like his, their feet flat on the ground, their arms resting on their knees. Yet, when he closed his eyes again, the cloud of dust and smoke appeared once more, and once more the tawny cat appeared, carrying the soft-eyed child.

Yar Mohammad lowered his head, allowing his turban to shield his face from the eyes of the other grooms. The length of unstitched homespun that served him as a shawl trailed on the ground beside him as he moved closer to the fire.

Remembered words came to him as clearly as if they had been spoken moments before. *"If you see or hear something out of the ordinary, you must tell your murshid, your spiritual guide. These events often contain in them instructions, or important information. To reveal these things indiscriminately is wrong, but to conceal them from your spiritual teacher is also a grave mistake."*

For all that he remembered those instructions, Yar Mohammad could not obey them. The only spiritual teacher he knew, the very man who had once said those words to him, was out of reach, eighty miles away.

Yar Mohammad looked up and gazed into the distance. His lips tightened. By Allah, there was something he could do. He could tell the great man.

He did not know the great man's name; but three days earlier the mere sight of him, a Muslim stranger passing on the avenue, had caused Yar Mohammad to stop so abruptly that the ladder-carrying carpenter walking behind him had very nearly knocked him down. The stranger's eyes had reminded Yar Mohammad so forcibly of that faraway spiritual teacher that his breath had caught in his throat.

He had met his teacher only once, but the meeting remained vivid in his memory. The man's eyes had been deep, filled with profound knowledge. He had radiated goodness and strength. He was Shaikh Waliullah, leader of the Karakoyia Brotherhood, one of the five hidden brotherhoods of India, whose members taught and practiced the mystical traditions of Islam. Something about this elderly stranger so closely resembled the Shaikh that Yar Mohammad had forgotten the oats he had come for, and had followed the stranger from place to place in the camp, watching him as he went about his business, marveling at the man's calming effect upon others, at the kindness with which he addressed a fruit seller, a scribe, children begging on the avenue. When the old man returned to his tent, Yar Mohammad had gone back to the horse lines, satisfied that this stranger, like Shaikh Waliullah, was well versed in the mysteries of the heart.

Yar Mohammad gathered his shawl around him and rose silently from the fire. Although he did not change his long, unhurried stride, he took the shortest route, down alleyways, between ramshackle tents, past small bazaars where men stood arguing over mounds of fruit, until he reached a neat tent whose door was at that moment being propped open by a small boy.

"Is the most respected sahib available?" he inquired.

Gesturing for him to wait, the boy vanished inside, but before Yar Mohammad could sit, the boy put his head out again, beckoning with a raised hand.

Standing shoeless and uncertain inside the doorway, Yar Mohammad saw that the tent was bare except for a single tin box that stood in one corner, and a string bed on which the great man sat writing on a paper with pen and ink. Looking up from his task, the old man pointed to the ground beside him.

Yar Mohammad felt once again that he was in the presence of no ordinary person. Although the man's face and dress were unremarkable, he exuded a calm that poured over Yar Mohammad like honey.

Yar Mohammad squatted down beside the bed and began to speak, describing without preamble his vision of the lioness and the child.

The old gentleman listened without comment, nodding from time to time. When Yar Mohammad finished speaking, the old man sat silently for some moments, his eyes closed. When at last he opened his eyes and spoke, his tone carried no trace of superiority. "You have done well to come to me at once with this information."

Yar Mohammad's heart swelled. The great man had spoken, not to his station as a groom but to his soul. It had been years since anyone had addressed him like that.

"This vision of yours contains a cloud of dust and smoke, signifying an emergency of some kind." The old man's face puckered in thought as he picked up a *tasbih* of black onyx beads from a square of cotton cloth beside him. "Although it concerns an emergency," he went on, his eyes traveling around the tent as he fingered the beads, "it does not appear to be a vision that gives instruction, but rather one that only conveys information. Now tell me why you have come to me with your story."

Yar Mohammad, his eyes on the ground, considered his answer. "Seeing you walking on the avenue," he began carefully, "caused me to remember someone in Lahore, whom I hold in great respect. I had hoped—"

"And what is the name of this gentleman?"

"His name, Sahib, is Shaikh Waliullah Karakoyia."

The old man nodded several times. After a moment he called the little servant boy. "Bring this man tea, Khalid," he instructed, then turned back to Yar Mohammad and regarded him seriously. "I know Shaikh Waliullah," he said, "very well." Yar Mohammad's heart quickened. "There is no question that this vision of yours is intended as a message to the Shaikh," the old man continued, nodding again. "Otherwise, why would you have been sent to recount it to me? You must, therefore," he added, his eyes returning to Yar Mohammad's face, "borrow from the lines a strong horse that will not be missed, depart at once, and ride north until you reach Firozpur on the banks of the Sutlej River. That will be a twenty-mile journey.

"See if the Maharajah's new bridge of boats is ready. Should you find the bridge unfinished, a barber named Kareem who lives near the great mosque will arrange for you to cross the river by ferry." He paused briefly, his lips moving as he thumbed his beads one by one, then continued, nodding to himself. "Once you reach the far bank, you must ride without stopping the sixty miles to Lahore City. There you must deliver the full story of your vision, with no omissions, to Shaikh Waliullah Karakoyia. Is that understood?"

Yar Mohammad nodded.

"Tell him," added the old man, "that I have sent you. My name is Shafiuddin."

He picked up his paper and pen. "And now," he said with a little nod, "Khalid will bring your tea outside. Drink it before you start."

Yar Mohammad found himself dismissed by a single, tidy motion of the old man's hand.

AS Yar Mohammad finished the last of the tea the boy brought him, scenes rose before him of the triumph and shame of his other, long-ago meeting with the Shaikh Waliullah. Of course he and his first teacher, the good-natured Abdul Rashid, had both been young then. If he had known better, Abdul Rashid might have kept his imperfect knowledge to himself, and not tried to show his village cousin the profound mysteries of the Path, but he had tried to teach Yar Mohammad, and the knowledge he so generously shared had made Yar Mohammad the clumsy practitioner he was in that faraway time. Without Abdul Rashid, he would not have had the vision that sent the two men on the long journey to Lahore from their mountain home six months after Yar Mohammad received his first lesson.

Yar Mohammad put down the teacup and stood, shaking out his clothes. He must start for Lahore.

After passing rows of tents, each with its group of string beds standing in the sun, Yar Mohammad caught the welcome smell of the horse lines. He walked by the pits where blacksmiths heated iron bars in trenches of fiery charcoal. Two sweating blacksmiths greeted him. He returned their greeting without looking up.

When that vision came so many years ago, he had been young. He had not yet understood the need for discretion in spiritual matters. Overcome with confusion and a sense of his own unworthiness, he had told his wife what he had seen. A Personage whose name he dared not utter, he told her, had appeared before him and handed him a ceramic vial that, it seemed, fitted warmly and perfectly into the palm of his hand. In her simplicity, his wife had run to her family with the news that her young husband had seen a vision of the Prophet Mohammad. Scandal and misery had followed. Some villagers, believing Yar Mohammad had developed great powers, had come to him expecting miracles and been disappointed. Others had called him a liar. In the end, he and Abdul Rashid had set out for Lahore to discover the truth.

Seated on his padded platform, the Shaikh had heard their story. The Shaikh had then explained to them both, kindly but with great firmness, the importance of disclosing spiritual events only to the proper people. Finally, he had turned his powerful gaze onto Yar Mohammad's face.

"I believe," he had said, "that the meaning of your vision is that you have been given a gift. It is no small gift, Yar Mohammad. You may not yet know what it is, but when the time comes, you will know. Coming from such an august source, it is a tremendous gift indeed. You are a fortunate man."

Yar Mohammad had not tried to conceal the tears that ran down his face and dripped onto his clothes. From that instant on, although he had never failed to treat Abdul Rashid with affection and respect, tending him faithfully in his last illness, he had always regarded Shaikh Waliullah as his true murshid.

As he scanned the horse lines choosing his own mount, a horseman approached. Yar Mohammad noted with annoyance the animal's drooping head and uneven gait. The rider was a strong-looking man with burly shoulders, perhaps a well-to-do Kashmiri. Such a man should know better than to ride a horse to exhaustion. Approaching him, Yar Mohammad opened his mouth to point out the necessity of caring properly for one's mount, but the traveler addressed him first.

"I am looking for one Shafiuddin who is also known as Shafi Sahib," he said in a dry voice. His hair and his jutting beard were gray with dust. "I have important news," he added, dismounting stiffly and rubbing his face absently with a thick hand.

Yar Mohammad studied the weary stranger who had asked for the great man. Should he point the way, and then, without further delay, follow his own instructions and mount quickly for the ride to Lahore? Should he wait and take the man back the way he had come?

"I have ridden, with little rest, directly from Lahore City." The stranger looked as if he might fall asleep where he stood.

No longer hesitating, Yar Mohammad reached for the man's reins. "Take this horse," he told another groom, nodding toward the rows of well-muscled animals. "Care for him as if he belonged to the Governor-General himself." He inclined his head toward the stranger. "Come with me, Huzoor. I will take you to Shafi Sahib."

Shortening his stride to accommodate the other man's tired legs, he walked back the way he had come.

When they reached the tent, the stranger nodded to Shafi Sahib's little servant boy. "My name is Yusuf Bhatti. Please tell your sahib that I have come from Lahore, from the house of Shaikh Waliullah."

The Shaikh's house. As the man shouldered his way inside, Yar Mohammad followed, glancing cautiously toward the string bed as he lowered himself, uninvited, to the floor near the tent's open entrance. He waited without moving, containing his excitement.

The visitor saluted the old man. The handle of a large dagger peered from his cummerbund. "Peace be upon you, sir," he offered.

Shafi Sahib replied serenely, his eyes on the newcomer's face.

"I have come with unfortunate news." The visitor glanced at his hands, then put them behind his back. "The daughter-in-law of Shaikh Waliullah Karakoyia of Lahore has died."

The news fell on Yar Mohammad's chest like a heavy blow. The chill that followed told him there was more to this tragedy than he yet knew.

"Poor Waliullah, poor young Hassan," Shafi Sahib said mildly, shaking his head. "May God rest her soul in peace, and grant them all patience."

The visitor lowered his gaze to the floor. The old gentleman looked at him expectantly. "There is more," he said gently.

The man called Yusuf was perspiring. He sighed. "Unfortunately she did not die at home, but at the Citadel, where she and her son were being held hostage by the Maharajah. The child, who is only a baby, has not been returned from the court."

"Ah." The old gentleman stared thoughtfully in Yar Mohammad's direction, then his eyes returned to his visitor's face. "Is the Maharajah still at Lahore?" he inquired.

"He has left Lahore, sir. He is at his camp, preparing to meet the British officials."

"Then he may not yet know of this sad event. And you have come straight from Lahore?"

Yusuf shook his head. "No, sir," he replied. "I stopped at the Maharajah's camp to ask for help in freeing the child."

"Ah." The old man tapped his fingers together. "Whom did you see there?"

"No one, sir. I was to meet Faqeer Azizuddin, but he was not there. He had gone away to Kasur."

"So you did not meet the Chief Minister. Did you ask anyone else for help regarding the child?"

"No, sir, those were not my instructions. I have not yet been able to help the family at all."

In the ensuing silence, Shafi Sahib closed his eyes. His lips moved silently. At length he spoke, but not to his visitor. "Go, Khalid," he said decisively to the servant boy who materialized out of the shadows, "and bring this man water and food. Bring him plenty of both. And then show him where to bathe. Yar Mohammad!"

He had not been wrong to intrude. Praise be to Allah!

"Arrange for provisions and for three horses. We will begin our journey as soon as this gentleman has rested and eaten."

Turning to his visitor, Shafi Sahib spoke with gentle authority. "I will leave you now. After a few hours, when you are ready, we will start for Lahore."

Before his guest could offer polite protest, the old gentleman got up from the bed, and was out the door.

THE servant boy reappeared, carrying a brass basin and a water vessel. Yusuf grunted his thanks while the boy poured a stream of water over his outstretched hands.

A little later, the boy backed through the door with a loaded tray.

Yusuf glanced at the food in front of him. This was princely fare, not the simple meal of boiled lentils he had expected. A thick buttery round of bread hung over the edges of a straw plate, its center laden with chunks of spiced meat. Oranges, guavas, and pomegranates rolled on the tray beside the bread. There was even an earthen dish of yogurt. Sighing with anticipatory pleasure, Yusuf tore off a piece of bread and used it to pick up a bit of meat. He ate rapidly, using only his right hand to serve himself, picking dexterously at the food with his fingers. For all the simple poverty of Shafi Sahib's tent, the old man had resources.

When Yusuf could eat no more, he washed his hands again. Leaving his weapons with the boy, he carried the string bed outside. There he lay down gratefully, one arm shading his eyes.

The sounds of the camp flowed around him. He would now forget the privations of his journey south, his failure to find Faqeer Azizuddin on the way, his long night of traveling toward the British camp, partly on foot, leading his horse by instinct in the near blackness.

All that remained now was to ride north with Shafi Sahib to the Maharajah's camp. *Inshallah,* God willing, the Chief Minister would be there. If anyone could help them free the baby, it would be Shaikh Waliullah's childhood friend who was also, by all accounts, the Maharajah's closest advisor. This duty done, Yusuf and Shafi Sahib would then travel with all speed for Lahore.

He yawned. If this effort failed, he would do whatever was needed to restore Saboor to his father. If killing would bring Saboor back, Yusuf would kill. Why not? Yusuf, unlike Hassan, was a fighter and a hunter. Hassan had never fought as Yusuf had with the Maharajah's irregular cavalry, or traveled to the hills to hunt white leopard. He had never shot pigs in the forests near Chhangamanga.

Yusuf gave a curt, barking laugh. Hassan, his clever, city-dwelling, silk-wearing friend, at a pig shoot? He would pay good money to see that.

He grunted. Would Hassan kill for him? What did it matter? Hassan was no soldier, but he was Yusuf's friend. Hassan would certainly die for him.

Die for him—die for him. Yusuf floated, weaponless, over the Citadel, the hostage child in his arms. Eunuchs on horses leaped into the air beneath him. Hassan appeared, a great sword in his hand, and spurred his horse through the air to guard his son.

TWO hours later, his hair still wet from a bath, Yusuf sat watching from a fresh horse as Yar Mohammad helped Shafi Sahib into his saddle. There could be no mistaking the groom's solicitous manner, or his choice of an ancient mare for the old gentleman. If the old man had ever ridden a horse, it had not been for years. What had possessed him to come on this journey where haste meant everything?

Good manners did not allow Yusuf to show his feelings. Keeping his face still, he watched Shafi Sahib climb creakily into the saddle, then sit gripping its pommel while Yar Mohammad gathered up the reins, mounted his own horse, and led the mare with her elderly passenger away toward the avenue.

When the two men had passed out of earshot, Yusuf allowed himself a snort of annoyance, then joined them, spurring his own gelding unkindly. The journey to the Maharajah's camp would now require frequent rests. Those twenty miles alone, accomplished by him in one night, would take them two days. The remainder of the distance to Lahore might require as much as four infuriating days more.

The track they followed was deeply rutted from past rains. The clay under their horses' hooves had cracked into a crazy pattern as it dried. Dust hung in the stillness, coloring distant villages with soft hues. There was little vegetation, only an occasional spreading thorn tree. Here was a land good only for lizard hunters and cattle thieves.

Yar Mohammad rode beside him, leading Shafi Sahib's mare. A small ax was tied to his saddle. A heavy Gurkha knife hung from his waist. At least the man would prove useful if they were attacked. Moving so slowly, they made a perfect target.

"How," Shafi Sahib asked from behind them, "did Saboor come to be the Maharajah's hostage? Is there some dispute between the Waliullah family and the court?"

"No, sir." Yusuf slowed his horse, allowing Yar Mohammad to pull ahead. "It has to do with the child himself."

"Ah." The old man nodded, swaying in his saddle.

Yusuf slapped at a fly. "You may already know that Hassan is assistant to Faqeer Azizuddin, the Chief Minister. He was appointed to the post because of the friendship between the Faqeer and Shaikh Waliullah."

"Yes," replied Shafi Sahib. "I knew of that."

"After Saboor was born," Yusuf continued, "Hassan went, as a courtesy, to show his son to the Maharajah. Unfortunately, the Maharajah fell in love with Saboor at first glance." He sighed. "Since that day, he has not been allowed to leave the Maharajah's side."

TWO hours later, Yusuf scanned the horizon, his shoulders hunched. After all this time, they were less than halfway to the Sutlej. Shafi

Sahib had not spoken since they had passed the last outlying sentry at the British camp. The time had come to decide on a plan of action.

"When we have crossed the river, shall we go straight to the Maharajah's camp?" Yusuf asked, turning politely in his saddle.

Shafi Sahib did not reply. Yusuf tried again. "Once we cross the river," he repeated more loudly, "we can inform Faqeer Azizuddin of the tragedy, and ask him to help us to free Waliullah Sahib's grandson."

Again there was silence. Had the old gentleman gone deaf? He had not, but when he spoke it was in a tone that put an end to any further conversation. "We shall see," Shafi Sahib replied, without inflection, as if to himself. He sat, bent forward on his mare, his knuckles pale on the pommel of his saddle, his eyes closed, his lips moving.

So be it. The old gentleman was dear to Shaikh Waliullah. That and his age made him the senior member of the party, the person whose wishes must be respected. But what had he meant by "we shall see"? Was it possible that he would refuse to let them stop at the Maharajah's camp? No, that was out of the question. The poor old man must be desperate to reach a tent and a cooking fire; he could scarcely sit straight on his horse.

Yusuf squinted into the northern distance, hoping for some sign of the green belt of trees that followed the riverbank, but saw only an empty plain dotted with mud villages. They should travel for another hour before resting and offering their prayers. He glanced backward again at a sudden noisy fit of coughing from Yar Mohammad to see the groom gesture with his eyes at Shafi Sahib. The old gentleman was swaying, gray faced, in his saddle.

Horrified, Yusuf pulled up. When had they last had water? What a careless fool he was!

They stopped in the shade of a tangle of thorn bushes whose branches swept the ground. It was not the old man's fault that he could hardly ride. He was poor. Poor men did not own horses, or even ride horses. Poor men *walked*. Yusuf tugged savagely at the water skin while Yar Mohammad helped Shafi Sahib to the ground.

LATER, lying on Yar Mohammad's coarse shawl, his head propped on one of the saddles, Shafi Sahib had begun to revive.

"Do not apologize," he said in a faint voice, flicking long fingers in Yusuf's direction. "I should have said something." Drops of water clung to the stubble of his beard and spotted his snowy shirt.

Before Yusuf could reply, a noisy thrashing erupted from inside the bush nearest to Shafi Sahib's makeshift bed. The dusty branches parted as if by themselves, and a ragged figure of a man lurched into the sunlight. Brandishing a wooden staff, the man turned his head rapidly from side to side as if looking for someone, then, his staff high, moved jerkily to where Shafi Sahib lay full-length on the earth.

With a hasty prayer that Yar Mohammad knew how to handle his knife, Yusuf reached for his tulwar, his eyes moving rapidly from the attacker to the bushes. Where was the rest of the gang? How many were there?

"You are the one," the intruder cried, his voice a dark, rasping sound, "who can tell the foreign lady, who can tell her—"

"Stop!" Yusuf shouted to the man's back as he struggled to free the heavy, curved sword from its scabbard. "Do not move!"

Ignoring his warnings, the stranger took another step toward Shafi Sahib.

Yusuf's blade slid free. As he swung back, preparing to slice the intruder in half, fingers gripped his forearm.

"Wait," said Yar Mohammad into his ear. "Look at Shafi Sahib."

The old gentleman had made no move to shield himself. Instead, he peered interestedly at the tattered figure standing over him. "Speak," he commanded.

The stranger's staff fell to the ground as he raised his arms over his head. "You must tell the foreign lady," he said, "whose horse bears the five lucky signs, that the path she takes will bring her peace."

"Which foreign lady?" Shafi Sahib raised himself on one elbow.

The madman ignored him. "Tell her to be careful." His voice sounded like stones rolling down a hill. "Tell her, *khabardar, khabardar*—"

Without finishing what he had begun to say, he reached for his rod and strode to the bush. Ignoring the long, cruel thorns, he parted its branches with his bare hands, turned, and stepped backward into the thicket. The branches shuddered, then closed upon him.

Baffled, Yusuf peered into the silent bush. Seeing nothing, he turned away, shaking his head, to find Shafi Sahib on his feet.

"We must go now," he said. His face, ashen when they had stopped, was now fresh and animated.

Yusuf and Yar Mohammad stared.

"We must start for Lahore at once," Shafi Sahib insisted, in the voice of one accustomed to command.

"But," Yusuf protested, "we are going to the Maharajah's camp, are we not? We must find the Faqeer and—"

"No," the old gentleman said firmly. "We have no need of the Chief Minister. Come, there is no time to be lost."

Once again he had to be helped onto his ancient mare. Once mounted, he waved an arm toward the north. "Lahore," he cried, "we must ride for Lahore!"

TWO days later as they traveled the busy road, Yusuf kept his face averted from his two companions. There was nothing to be gained from letting them see his rage. Why, oh why, had Shafi Sahib insisted on bypassing the Maharajah's camp?

Yusuf let a lungful of air out through tight lips. He had done his best to explain their urgent need to contact Faqeer Azizuddin, but his efforts had come to nothing. Ah, if Allah in His wisdom had given Yusuf a golden tongue, he could have made the old gentleman see reason. But Yusuf's gift, useless in this case, had been the steady hand and tight-clinging knee of a cavalryman.

He leaned and spat into the dust. Surely this change in their plans was not because of a stick-waving madman? Surely Shafi Sahib did not believe in that nonsense? Yusuf steered his horse impatiently around a bullock cart piled high with firewood that crawled, groaning, toward the Maharajah's camp, the same camp that they were to leave, unvisited, behind them.

If it were safe to do so, he would gladly have turned back and galloped alone toward the line of tents still visible behind them in the distance. Once there, he would have begged the Maharajah's Chief Minister for his assistance in freeing little Saboor, then hastened back to join his companions. But Yar Mohammad was not a professional man-at-arms, and Allah knew the road was not safe. Among the crowds of merchants and travelers between Lahore and the Maharajah's camp, there were certain to be cutthroats and thieves. Left to themselves, Shafi Sahib and the groom could be robbed and killed ten times over before he returned.

No, the facts could not be changed. There was now no hope of Yusuf's carrying out the instructions he had been given. If he survived, Hassan's poor little son would have to be rescued by someone else.

Yusuf skirted a deep rut in the road. All this had happened because, by some ill fortune, Shafi Sahib, the Shaikh's trusted friend, had gone quite mad. Tears stung Yusuf's eyes. How could he face Hassan, his most loved friend, with this news?

Shafi Sahib had begun to speak. Was it to him? Yusuf turned to look behind him.

"Yusuf Sahib." The old gentleman's tired voice held a teasing note. "Why do you try to do all the work yourself? Do you not remember

Allah, the All-Powerful? If it is His will that the child is to be rescued, then no one can keep him at the Citadel. If it is not His will to spare the child, then no power on earth can save him. Is that not so?"

Yusuf nodded numbly. The old man cleared his throat. "In any case, O kind and honest soldier," he added, smiling serenely, "there is no need to worry. Your prayers have already been answered."

Chapter 5

**MONDAY,
NOVEMBER 25**

A troop of Bengal Lancers trotted past Mariana on the avenue, their black mustaches bristling. Artillery shots boomed in the distance. She slowed her mare, her eyes following the lancers. Her father would enjoy as much as she did all the preparations for this campaign into Afghanistan. She imagined him bent over a map at her writing table, working out the various roles of the British and Sikh forces in the campaign, his gentle face alight as he spoke of the difficulty of moving the heavy British guns over the mountain passes into Afghanistan, and of the likelihood of Afghan resistance to the British-leaning monarch who would replace their present king.

The Governor-General, together with everyone else, was looking forward to the moment when Shah Shuja, their handpicked Afghan prince, would enter Kabul at the head of the triumphant Sikh and British armies, to be installed upon the throne of the most strategically valuable country in Central Asia.

What would be the result, Mariana wondered, of this exciting invasion whose preparations had taken two years? British supremacy in

Afghanistan would of course quash forever the Tsar of Russia's ambition to control Central Asia, but surely there would be other changes. Surely there would emerge a new, almost British Afghanistan, with English officers in the streets, and English horse races being held in its faraway cities with wonderful names: Kandahar, Jalalabad, Kabul . . .

One day, she would see Afghanistan for herself, eat its fabled fruits, breathe its air, and read its poetry.

Ahead of her, a British officer rode toward the red gate. Mariana watched the sentries stiffen to attention as he passed through. If Papa were here, he would understand her passion for languages, as she understood his passion for war. He would appreciate Munshi Sahib.

She nodded to the sentries as she rode through the entrance. It had been days since her last lesson. Was Munshi ill? He had not looked well since the day he had come to her in the rain. She must talk Major Byrne into giving her a second chair. The poor old man should not be made to stand all the way through their lessons.

People had begun to gather in the doorway of the dining tent. She was late once again. It was lunchtime already, and she was still wearing her riding clothes.

A man in a blue uniform stood talking to the White Rabbit. Was it Harry Fitzgerald? Mariana strained to look, leaning awkwardly in the sidesaddle, and saw that it was, just as her mare stumbled, wrenching her from her seat, and knocking her foot from the stirrup. Unable to stop herself, she plunged, headfirst, to the ground.

Someone approached. She sat up, gasping at a sharp pain in her shoulder. Her skirts had now settled modestly about her, but her legs had flown into the air in front of everyone. She must get away at once. Where was her riding hat?

"It's lucky her foot came out of the stirrup," said a man's voice. "She might have been dragged. Look at these sharp stones. She may be hurt. Call the doctor."

"No," Mariana tried to say over the sound of someone running off.

She forced herself dizzily to her feet, crying out when a hand gripped her injured arm. It was the White Rabbit. He peered at her, his chinless face full of concern. "We must get you to the shade, Miss Givens. Allow me to help you into the dining tent."

To be gaped at by everyone in camp? Absolutely not. She pulled away, shaking her head. "No, thank you, Lieutenant Sotheby," she said hastily. "Please help me to remount my horse."

"But your horse has been taken away, Miss Givens."

"*What?*" Mariana looked behind her. It was true. Her mare was gone. "Well then, Lieutenant Sotheby," she said, holding out her good arm, her teeth clenched in a smile against a sudden desire to weep, "you must walk me to my tent."

"Of course, Miss Givens," said the Rabbit, who then pretended, all the way to her tent, not to have seen the tears of mortification she could not hide.

"MEMSAHIB, Memsahib!"

Dittoo's voice pierced Mariana's sleep. She sat up. She was still wearing her riding habit. Her mouth tasted sour. Her head ached from her fall. What time was it?

"The ladies are calling you, Memsahib! They want you to join them outside their tents before dinner."

Injured or not, she could not refuse. She stood and began to undo her buttons. The last thing she wanted to do was face them all now. Wincing, she pulled her injured arm from its tight sleeve. She could not bear to think what had come into view when her legs had gone over her head.

She pulled her second-best gown from her trunk, and wriggled into it. She had thought of asking Miss Emily to seat her with Fitzgerald at dinner tomorrow or the next day, but would the lieutenant wish to sit beside someone who could not stay on a horse or button her clothes properly?

She paused, her mouth full of hairpins. Of course he *had* disappeared after her accident. Surely he had not rushed away after seeing her fall. That could not be a good sign in a prospective husband.

"I did not mean to hurt his feelings, poor little Rajah." Miss Fanny adjusted her shawls as Mariana raced into the square of ground between the residence tents in a flurry of skirts. "But as none of us can endure the smell—"

"Ah, there you are, Miss Givens." His jowls wobbling, Lord Auckland rose from a basket chair and towered above Mariana.

"I am sure Mariana will agree with me, Fanny," Miss Emily said from her own folding chair. "You should not have sent them back." A corner of her thin mouth turned up. "You do not have a sufficient number of animals in your tent. Two camels would do nicely if your spotted deer should die, although of course, we should need a larger sofa if they wanted to lie down."

It was nearly sunset. Mariana lowered herself into a chair and accepted a glass of sherry as a pair of Miss Fanny's peacocks picked their way past her tent, their iridescent tails dragging behind them.

Miss Fanny bent forward. "Mariana, we heard of your accident this afternoon. Are you hurt? Ah, here is Dr. Drummond, the very person we need." She nodded as the doctor bowed formally to the little group, his heels together.

The doctor sat down with a groan and put his cane on the ground beside him. "Are you all right now, Miss Givens?" He removed his spectacles and frowned at Mariana. "I tried to see you earlier, but your servant told me you were sleeping."

"I am quite well, thank you, Doctor." She refused to think of her sore shoulder.

"That is a great relief." He nodded several times, then turned. "Well, Miss Emily," he declared heartily, "no rain today!"

The conversation drifted from the weather to lepidoptera collecting. As soon as the doctor had gone, Mariana decided, she would ask Miss Emily about Fitzgerald. If only the doctor would go away—

"Is that not true, Miss Givens?" The doctor was looking expectantly at her across the dusty space between their chairs. He raised his eyebrows.

What had he said? Was it about butterflies? "Yes, of course, Doctor," she agreed, smiling.

"I do not find this a smiling matter." Miss Fanny's golden eardrops shook gently. "I, for one, am disgusted by the natives. I cannot abide their peculiar habits and their grinning idols. One even hears of human sacrifices. . . ." Her voice trailed off.

What had she agreed to? Mariana sat up. "But I do not believe," she heard herself say, "that one ought to feel disgust at the natives, unless they are mad or diseased. Of course," she added, thinking back, "if they are, one might be able to help them."

Miss Fanny gasped. Dr. Drummond laughed aloud. "My dear young woman, what a preposterous remark!"

As heat rose to Mariana's face, Lord Auckland, who had not appeared to be listening, sat forward in his chair. "Let me give you some advice, Miss Givens." He spoke slowly and distinctly, as if addressing a half-wit. "As long as you are in this country, you must make every effort to avoid the natives. Do *not* speak to them unless absolutely necessary. They are an uneducated, heathen people, and must be treated as such."

"But, my lord, I myself am being educated by a native. Munshi Sahib comes every—"

"Munshi *Sahib*?" Dr. Drummond made a snorting sound. "Munshi

Sahib? You address a native in a manner reserved for Europeans?" He turned to Miss Emily. "Miss Givens, I must say, is a most *extraordinary* young person."

Mariana reached out and dropped her sherry glass noisily onto the tray.

"MY dear girl," Miss Emily said after the doctor had departed, turning a sharp blue eye on Mariana, "I have rarely seen anything as transparent as your temper just now. What did you mean by banging down your sherry glass?"

Mariana's head had begun to throb. She did not answer.

Her sister sniffed. "I cannot imagine what the poor doctor could have done to offend you. He has made a point of studying the natives, and he knows much more about them than we do. You made a silly remark, and he had every right to correct you."

"I certainly hope you will behave properly at dinner," said Miss Emily, changing the subject before Mariana could reply. "I have had a request from someone who wishes to be seated beside you tonight."

Richard Sotheby, of course. Mariana should be grateful. One could do worse than to sit beside a kindly rabbit.

"I am sure you will remember him. He came to dinner ten days ago. He is the younger of two brothers who came out here within a few years of each other. Major Byrne describes him as 'a promising young horse gunner,' which I take to mean he is in the Horse Artillery. His name is Fitzgerald."

Miss Emily picked up her parasol and got out of her chair with a rustling of skirts. "Let us go in. They are all waiting."

It was only by chance that Mariana had made a real effort to arrange her hair, although, possessing only a small hand glass, she could never tell how she really looked. A few loose curls had already fallen to her shoulders. Oh, please, let her hair, for once, not come out of its pins. . . .

Lieutenant Fitzgerald stepped forward, even handsomer by candlelight than he had been in the rain. His braid and buttons shone; his white doeskin breeches fitted him to perfection. Mariana took the arm he offered her and steadied herself, willing away her increasing dizziness.

Beside her at the table, a spidery stranger bowed elaborately. She inclined her head to him, aware that on her other side, Fitzgerald had pulled his chair so near to hers that their knees touched. She turned from the stranger and opened her mouth to speak, but found herself about to address a blue-clad shoulder.

"Ah, Peter," Fitzgerald was saying to someone across the table, his animated baritone carrying so far that Miss Fanny caught Miss Emily's eye, "I have been looking for you all day. I shall not let you get away until we have settled our argument."

The man named Peter, a round-faced man with black curls, smiled broadly. "You are wrong, my boy. The French artillery would never have won the day. The whole battle was decided by our infantry squares against their cavalry. We exhausted them into defeat."

"Nonsense." Lieutenant Fitzgerald waved a hand over his soup. "The French had us outgunned nearly three to two. If they had defended their forward guns properly—"

The Battle of Waterloo!

"We should have lost," Mariana put in, more loudly than she had planned.

Four seats away, his spoon in midair, Dr. Drummond gazed at her as if she were a talking parrot. Miss Emily froze.

Someone nearby clicked his spoon against his teeth. In the silence, Fitzgerald turned to Mariana. "I beg your pardon?"

"I agree with you." She nodded seriously. "If the French had resisted the charge of Ponsonby's Union Brigade and saved the seventy-four guns we took early in the battle, we should have lost."

Fitzgerald lowered his soup spoon.

"Of course Marshall Grouchy's failure to join the battle was also important. . . ." Her voice faded under his stare. Could he tell how much she liked him? What should she do now?

Around them, conversations started up again. Mariana clearly heard her name pass up and down the table. She looked at her plate, feeling her stays bite uncomfortably into her ribs.

Fitzgerald's napkin was at his mouth. He seemed to be choking, but he was not.

She cleared her throat. "My father," she said, answering a question he had not asked, "is interested in military history. I've read all his books."

Why was Fitzgerald laughing?

He lowered his napkin. "Forgive me," he said. "I am glad to have you *and* your father on my side when it comes to Waterloo. I hope you will forgive my rudeness just now. It's just that we shall all be leaving for Afghanistan soon. I am not myself. I can't seem to think of anything but the army."

"Oh." Mariana looked away.

"What an insensitive brute I am!" He leaned toward her. "I should have asked if you are recovered from your fall. I went to fetch the doctor, but when we returned, you had gone to your tent. We came there, but your servant turned us away. Were you injured?"

"Not at all, thank you." She dropped her eyes. Those running feet had been his, but what had he seen as she fell?

"I also want to say," he added, "that I was very sorry to abandon you with the elephant the other day. I missed a great opportunity. You could have translated my questions."

"You like elephants?"

"I like everything in this country, but I have not learned much, except about the army. But I've wanted to ask you, how have you come to be on this journey with us?"

Mariana watched as he buttered a piece of bread. Fitzgerald's hands were square and competent looking. Her other prospects never asked questions. They tried only to impress or please her. "It was my uncle Adrian's idea," she replied. "We were at Simla, and I had begun learning Urdu and Persian from his old munshi. Lord Auckland and all of you were about to come down from the hills and begin traveling again when the real lady translator fell ill. When we got the news, my uncle dragged me to the political secretary's cottage in the middle of dinner to offer my services. He thought the post would give me a chance to see more of India."

"The *real* lady translator?" Fitzgerald gave her a crooked smile. "But whatever did Macnaghten say when you appeared at his door with your dinner napkin still under your chin?"

"He stared as if we were mad, but my uncle Adrian is such a darling, no one can refuse him, so Mr. Macnaghten let us in, then, very stiffly, as if he were doing my uncle the most *enormous* favor, he asked me to describe, in Urdu, the scene outside his window, which wasn't exactly fair because it was pitch-dark outside. I said something about the scent of roses under the window and distant mountains, and Mr. Macnaghten gave me the post." She smiled. "He had no choice, really. There was no lady for a thousand miles who spoke Urdu or Persian or anything."

Fitzgerald nodded seriously. "You are new to translating, and this is my first campaign. Everything is new, isn't it?" He sighed. "I do not know when I shall be getting my next leave. It might be a long time."

The table was turning. With an apologetic smile to the bewhiskered general on her left, Miss Emily turned brightly to the sharp-faced general on her right. At the other end of the table, Lord Auckland nodded to Macnaghten, then turned, smiling wearily, to a small, energetic-looking foreigner on his other side. Up and down the table bodies turned in unison. Fresh conversations began.

Harry Fitzgerald's face reddened suddenly as he nodded to Mariana before turning away from her. Suddenly wanting to touch him, she tried to brush against his shoulder, but he was too far away.

"Well, Miss Givens, how great a pleasure it is to sit beside you on this lovely evening." The Spider's smile revealed several missing teeth.

LATER, as she undressed for bed, the stiffness in Mariana's shoulder made every movement painful, but she did not mind. After dinner Lieutenant Fitzgerald had somehow intercepted the Spider and seen her to her tent. When they reached her door he had bowed politely, then looked hard, not at her face but at her mouth. His eyes had swept the front of her gown, not as they had before when her buttons were crooked, but as if he were looking at what lay beneath the silk of her bodice.

She reached to undo her gown, remembering the delicious feeling that had swept over her at that moment. She would not mind having that feeling again. No, she would not mind at all.

She tugged her gown over her head. *"Do not marry the first man who asks you,"* Mama had instructed, as the gardener carried Mariana's trunks to the carriage. No one *had* asked her except seventy-year-old Colonel Davenport in Calcutta, who asked everyone. Until now, Mariana had not cared. Since her arrival, she had been too captivated by India and too concerned about her letters to her father to think seriously of marriage. In spite of a hundred warnings, she had given no thought to her own future happiness.

Time was getting very short. As soon as Lord Auckland and the Maharajah signed the treaty, Fitzgerald would march for Afghanistan, and she would begin the long return journey to Calcutta. When would that be? Had Macnaghten really said three weeks? *Three weeks?*

Why had she not met Fitzgerald *earlier*? She dropped onto her bed and reached to unbutton her boots, remembering that only days ago she had bristled with impatience to reach Firozpur. How wrong she had been. The journey must last as long as possible. Let there be a disaster of some kind, a month-long downpour or, if necessary, a plague among the camels or the bullocks. Yes, a plague would be acceptable, as long as there was no danger to the elephants.

Would there be time enough for courtship, even marriage, before it was too late? Her brain whirling with possibilities, Mariana dropped her second boot, lay down, and pulled the covers to her chin.

Chapter 6

MONDAY,
NOVEMBER 25

A blacksmith's son recognized Yusuf Bhatti and raced off, a small barefoot figure in filthy clothes, to bring the news of their arrival to the Shaikh's house. As he ran, his treble shouts pierced the din of the crowded streets so successfully that by the time the three men reached the haveli, the carved doors had already been thrown open.

Handed down from his mare, Shafi Sahib shuffled toward the inner courtyard, waving away solicitous strangers. "Yar Mohammad will help me," he told them, his impatient voice echoing around him in the vaulted entranceway. "Someone else can look after the horses."

Yar Mohammad's heart filled. He glanced upward at the carved balconies overlooking the main courtyard, and the arabesques painted high on the courtyard walls. He had come here only once, years ago, but he had never forgotten this house. Now, as he led Shafi Sahib through the seated crowd, Yar Mohammad could see that like his house, Shaikh Waliullah was unchanged. He still wore his tall, starched headdress, and his expression was still as deceptively calm as a banked fire.

The seated men fell silent as the Shaikh and Shafi Sahib embraced. Weak-kneed from excitement, Yar Mohammad took his place against a wall. The Shaikh had not seemed to notice him.

A young man, too, embraced Shafi Sahib. Yar Mohammad nudged his neighbor. "Who is that?" he asked.

"That is Hassan Ali Khan," the man replied, "husband of the dead lady, and father of the baby Saboor."

Hassan was as tall and lean as his father but his face told a different story. While the Shaikh was as dark and wrinkled as a raisin, his face all liveliness and sharp points, Hassan was fair and smooth-faced above his beard. As they sat together, the son on a straw stool beside his father's platform, the Shaikh's gaze moved slowly through the crowd, fixing on one man at a time, while Hassan's eyes darted from face to face, gathering nods of recognition and half smiles of greeting.

Yusuf Bhatti pushed his way to Hassan's side. Yar Mohammad watched the Shaikh's son stand and wrap his arms about his friend. For all his grace, Hassan looked ill. His lips were cracked; his hair looked dull and dry. He seemed like a man with more than one tragedy to bear.

"*Your prayers have already been answered,*" Shafi Sahib had assured Yusuf as they rode for Lahore. If prayers for the child's safety had been answered, Yar Mohammad thought, the child's father had not yet been told. Catching Hassan's traveling red-eyed gaze, Yar Mohammad thought he felt something leap from Hassan's heart into his own. Before he could guess what it was, the Shaikh put his feet over the side of his platform and felt for his slippers.

"If I am not mistaken," he said, addressing the crowd as he stood up, "the Call to Prayer is about to come. So come, my friend," he added, holding out a hand to Shafi Sahib. "You and I will offer our prayers in my room."

As he strode off, with Shafi Sahib wobbling slightly beside him, Shaikh Waliullah's voice carried across the courtyard. "Speak, Shafi," Yar Mohammad heard him say. "Tell me what knowledge has come to you. Teach me that which I do not know."

Shafi Sahib's reply floated behind them as the two old men began to climb a flight of stairs. "Wali, I have no knowledge. I am as ignorant as the buffalo that turns the water wheel on the roof of this house. But I have brought with me a groom whose name is Yar Mohammad—"

"*Allah-hu-Akbar, Allah-hu-Akbar,* God is Great, God is Great," cried the *muezzin,* leaning from a high minaret of Wazir Khan's Mosque, cupping his hands over his mouth to be heard in the streets below. "Come to prayer, come to prayer!"

Yar Mohammad closed his eyes and was immediately transported to an empty plain far from the busy courtyard. Shaikh Waliullah stood in front of him, his gaze a silent question. In the palm of his hand, Yar Mohammad could feel the smooth weight of a small ceramic vial, the same vial that he had received years before, in his first vision. He opened his eyes and looked out at the scene before him. There were the high, frescoed walls of the Shaikh's house, the carved balconies, the eddying crowd. He opened his hand and found it empty. That was the reality. But what was the dream? He closed his eyes again and once more found himself standing in the same barren site of his vision. The Shaikh's eyes did not leave his face as Yar Mohammad began to open the small, flat bottle.

What had he been given? Was it a gift he could offer to others, even those as elevated as Shaikh Waliullah? The thought of actually helping the great man caused sweat to form on Yar Mohammad's forehead. He reached behind him for the tail of his turban and wiped his face. But perhaps the Shaikh *did* need help. For all his strength, how could he not weep for his murdered daughter-in-law? How could he not fear for his tiny grandson?

The crowd in the courtyard had begun to funnel slowly through the gate toward the mosque. Near Yar Mohammad, Yusuf Bhatti raised his voice over the muezzin's cry. "Surely they will have found someone to look after Saboor."

Hassan smiled wanly at his friend. "Those courtiers care nothing for my son," he replied. "And now, God help us, news has come that the Maharajah fell ill yesterday at his camp. All this must be causing trouble among the women here at the Citadel."

"Trouble?" Yusuf raised his eyebrows.

"Who knows which queens will die on the Maharajah's pyre? The choice of *suttees* is the province of the senior queen. Some will want to die. Others will not. All will be trying to please her. No one will think of my son." Hassan shook his head. "The pushing, the lying, the cruelty between people at court is beyond our imagining. We may be sure," he added as he and Yusuf turned to follow the crowd, "that the Maharajah will now send for Saboor to cure him of his latest illness."

Yusuf snorted. "What madness this is! How can the poor child cure anyone?" He rested a thick hand on Hassan's embroidered sleeve. "Do not worry, my friend. We will find a way to get Saboor away from the Maharajah. We will do it during the confusion of the durbar. If you and I and others are there, and we work together—"

"But, Yusuf," Hassan interrupted, his eyes alight, pushing away Yusuf's protecting arm, "how could I have forgotten your journey?

Tell me of your visit to Faqeer Azizuddin at the Maharajah's camp. Surely you have some good news for me?"

Yar Mohammad had enough time to see the other man's face tighten grimly before his attention was caught by one of the Shaikh's servants who edged up beside him, a man whose henna-dyed hair was a flaming red.

"You are to go to Shaikh Sahib's rooms as soon as you have offered your prayers," the red-haired man told him. "When you are ready I will show you the way."

A short while later, Yar Mohammad followed the man up the same stairs the Shaikh had climbed with Shafi Sahib, and found himself outside a curtained doorway. As he scuffed off his sandals, he heard a light voice coming from inside.

"Well, my dear Shafi," the voice was saying, "I must confess that what you suggest seems unlikely. After all, the Maharajah and his people, too, style themselves as lions. Why should the rescuer be English and not one of their Sikh women? But it is you, not I, who are the interpreter of dreams."

The red-headed servant gestured impatiently toward the threshold. Yar Mohammad stepped nervously into the room.

As the room's two occupants looked up, Yar Mohammad noticed that the Shaikh had exchanged his tall, embroidered headdress for a fitted cap. Without the headdress he seemed sharper and more forceful than ever. Although they were the same height, he seemed to tower over Shafi Sahib.

How should Yar Mohammad greet his true murshid, his spiritual teacher? Should he touch the great man's knees, his feet? He started forward, but something in the narrow face caused him to stop and salute in the usual way, his head bowed, his cupped hand to the center of his forehead.

"*As-Salaam-o-alaikum,* Shaikh Sahib," he said to the floor.

"*Wa'alaikum Salaam,* and upon you, peace." The Shaikh pointed downward. His heart pounding, Yar Mohammad sat a little distance from the Persian carpet where the other two men sat, their backs to the wall.

"Tell us," ordered the Shaikh, "the five lucky signs of a horse."

The question was so unexpected that Yar Mohammad did not grasp it at first.

The Shaikh frowned at him. "You do not know the signs?"

So, Shaikh Waliullah and Shafi Sahib wanted only to understand the ravings of the madman who had jumped from the thorn bush. Why was Yar Mohammad disappointed? Had he really expected to be remembered after so many years?

"I do, Huzoor," he said, recovering his voice. He would not have these great men believe him ignorant. "The five lucky signs are these: that a horse should be marked with four white stockings to the knee and a white muzzle rising to a blaze on the forehead."

The two men on the carpet exchanged a glance. "And is there such an animal at the horse lines of the British camp?" the Shaikh asked.

Yar Mohammad nodded. "There are two such horses."

"And are either of these horses ridden by the ladies?"

"No, Huzoor." Forgetting his nerves, Yar Mohammad grew fluent. "The first of these is a stallion, very wild, unsuitable for women. Even his owner, a captain in the British army, is afraid of him. Each day he comes with a new reason why he cannot ride the horse."

"And the other?"

"The other is an old mare, weak in her legs. She was included in a lot of animals we bought when the hot weather killed some of our riding mares. The ladies ride the better animals. I expect that this mare will be killed soon. She is not worth her feed."

"Ah." The Shaikh turned to his companion. "And there are three ladies attached to the British camp?"

"Yes, there are three." Shafi Sahib helped himself to a handful of pomegranate seeds offered by a servant who had appeared silently through a curtained doorway. "The youngest I have already described. The other two are sisters of the Governor-General."

The Shaikh nodded, waiting.

Shafi Sahib poked through the seeds in his hand, ruby-red juice staining his fingers. "What can one say about these foreigners? They have strange habits, to be sure, and an odd manner of dressing. They wear tight clothes, even in hot weather. But I believe both ladies are kindhearted. One of them," he added, looking up from his seeds, "keeps a pair of spotted deer and several other animals in her tent."

Yar Mohammad looked from the startled Shaikh to Shafi Sahib. Where had Shafi Sahib learned this? Surely the old man did not frequent the camp's cooking fires?

Shaikh Waliullah turned and stared at the wall, his face softening. For a moment, hunger and sadness seemed to pour out of him. Yar Mohammad dropped his eyes. Yes, the Shaikh did, indeed, fear for his grandson and grieve for his daughter-in-law.

"I have told Shaikh Sahib of your vision of a lioness," Shafi Sahib said gently. "Tell us, are you a practitioner like us, a follower of the Path?"

At last they were to talk of spiritual matters. Yar Mohammad took a long breath. "I am, Huzoor."

"And you perform the necessary spiritual exercises?"

"Yes, Sahib." Yar Mohammad could not keep his voice from shaking with excitement. "To the best of my ability, I try to be honest and charitable. I offer my five daily prayers, and also one optional prayer. I perform *Zikr,* the repetition of the name of God. I invoke Allah's blessings on the Prophet Mohammad both night and day."

"And what is the name of your Brotherhood? And your murshid—who gives you spiritual guidance?"

How could he meet his teacher's eyes? "I belong to this Brotherhood, to the Karakoyia, Huzoor." Yar Mohammad stared down at his hands. Rough and callused, they were not the hands of a mystic. "It is you who are my true murshid. I came to that knowledge many years ago after meeting you for the first time."

Shaikh Waliullah, spiritual leader of the vast Karakoyia Brotherhood, pushed a long finger under his embroidered cap. His eyes narrowed. "Tell us of your first visit to me."

Yar Mohammad cleared his throat. If he did not say it now, he might never have another chance. "I came to you once, in the company of my cousin. We had traveled from our village to tell you of an event concerning me that had recently occurred."

Shafi Sahib sat straighter. Shaikh Waliullah leaned forward on the Persian carpet.

"I had seen a vision of our Prophet," Yar Mohammad went on, "upon whom be Allah's blessings and peace. In that vision, he had given into my hand a small ceramic vial which I took to be a container of perfume or of scented oil. Perhaps you do not remember."

For a long moment, the Shaikh and Shafi Sahib stared wordlessly at each other. Disappointed, imagining his interview finished, Yar Mohammad moved to stand. The Shaikh's voice struck him like a blow.

"*You* are the man who received the vial? *You?* You fool!" The Shaikh's voice rose. "If you are the same man who was given the vial, why did you not tell this to Shafi Sahib when you first went to him at the British camp?"

Yar Mohammad felt each word as if it were a dagger. The Shaikh pointed at him. "What was wrong with you that you withheld this information?"

His bowels churning, Yar Mohammad stared at the tiled floor in front of him, unable to reply.

"Shafi and I had assumed that the lioness dream was your first important vision. Now you tell me that it was you who received the ceramic vial. You should have told Shafi Sahib of this." The Shaikh tugged a bolster toward him and leaned against it with an impatient sigh.

Yar Mohammad sat under the Shaikh's accusing gaze, tears of

shame leaking from his eyes. There must have been a mistake. The vial must have been meant for another man, one who would know what to do, who would not make error after error in the telling of the story.

A small, comforting noise came from Shafi Sahib. A sigh. Yar Mohammad looked up to find Shaikh Waliullah peering at him in surprise.

"Did I frighten you?" The Shaikh's voice had returned to normal. "I should not have spoken so harshly, but you do not know how long we have searched for you."

Searched? Yar Mohammad's brain emptied. Searched?

"You had received an important vision. I wanted to know who you were and where you lived. It never occurred to me on that day that your cousin was not still attached to this household. When I discovered that he had returned with you to an unknown village in the north, I sent people to look for you, but they failed to find you. Since then, we have waited for your return, hoping another vision would bring you back to seek my advice." He sighed again. "Eleven years have passed since that time.

"In any case, do not worry," he added, speaking directly to Yar Mohammad's fear, "there has been no mistake. It is Allah Most Gracious who sends visions. Unlike us, He is perfect." The Shaikh's gaze seemed far away. "I have often thought of your vision," he said absently. "I have wondered if my interpretation was correct." His eyes shifting abruptly to the present, he waved an impatient hand. "And stop worrying about everything, Yar Mohammad. You still have much to learn. Remember that too much humility is a bad thing."

Yar Mohammad, who had known only the simple tutelage of his cousin, buried his face in his sleeve. Air escaped him, hissing into his clothes.

"Shafi Sahib, here," the Shaikh said, laying a hand on Shafi Sahib's knee, "is the foremost interpreter of dreams and visions among the five Brotherhoods." His voice was almost tender. "Teach us, Shafi. Tell us the meaning of Yar Mohammad's dream of the vial."

Us. Yar Mohammad's heart rose.

Shafi Sahib coughed delicately. "The vision of the vial," he began, "means only one thing: that the recipient has been chosen to do a particular task, and that he has received all that he needs in order to accomplish it. This task most assuredly is of great importance and concerns the lives of many people."

Yar Mohammad blinked. *His* work was to be of great importance? Was he dreaming?

"That is not my exact interpretation, but it is near enough." The Shaikh sounded pleased. "Go on, Shafi."

Shafi Sahib took another handful of pomegranate seeds and studied them, his mild face drawn in thought, as if there was wisdom to be found in the palm of his hand. "The second lioness vision shows an important rescue in which you, Yar Mohammad, will play a major part."

"And the baby?" the Shaikh asked softly.

Shafi Sahib's eyes closed. "In a vision," he said, "a baby signifies the future of the Brotherhood. I believe that Yar Mohammad's vision tells us two things: first, that Saboor is to be rescued, and second, that he is to be the next Shaikh of the Karakoyia Brotherhood."

He looked up and turned his fingers over to indicate that he was finished.

The Shaikh let out a long breath.

Yar Mohammad could not move. His heart seemed to have stopped beating.

After a moment the Shaikh turned to Yar Mohammad. "Now do you understand the importance of your visions? You are an uneducated man and the goal is still very far distant, but you have traveled much farther than you realize on your journey toward God."

He raised an admonitory finger. "Remember, each vision, no matter how small or how insignificant it may seem, must be reported immediately to me, your murshid."

Your murshid. Yar Mohammad wanted to weep with relief, but there was more to be said. "Shaikh Sahib," he said, fidgeting where he sat, "I have seen something else."

He forced the words out quickly, afraid of another mistake. "Just now I saw myself standing in a barren place, the ceramic vial from my first vision in my hand. You, Shaikh Sahib, stood before me, watching as I reached to pull the cork from the vial."

"Is that all?" The Shaikh's voice seemed to tremble.

"Huzoor, that was all."

"So," Shafi Sahib put in quietly, "your work is about to begin."

Yar Mohammad's head suddenly felt as heavy as a cannonball. He clenched his teeth against a yawn he could not stop.

The Shaikh shifted on the carpet. "Although I am your murshid, you must understand that the gift you have received and the task you will perform are yours alone. It is you, and no one else, who will know when the time has come to act. We can only offer you our advice."

Our advice. So he was to have Shafi Sahib as well. Yar Mohammad could scarcely contain his joy. Shaikh Waliullah sat in silence, then turned toward the door. "Tariq," he called.

A servant boy pushed back the curtain.

"Call Allahyar."

"You will have your food downstairs," the Shaikh told Yar Mohammad briskly, as the same fiery-headed servant who had shown him upstairs reappeared in the doorway. "Allahyar here will show you where to sleep. Tomorrow, after your observances, you will take your horse and Shafi Sahib's, and return to the British camp. It is fortunate that the camp is now closer than it was when you set out on your journey to this house."

But what of—

The Shaikh held up his hand, reading the question before it was formed. "Shafi Sahib has done enough horse riding. He will travel to your British camp in one of our palanquins.

"You have done good work already," he added, nodding to Yar Mohammad. "I expect that very soon you will find that there is more to do. In the meantime, follow the instructions of the madman on the road. Two horses at the British camp bear the five lucky signs you have described. One of these will, Inshallah, be given to a memsahib to ride. When that happens, relay the message to her. And stay in touch with Shafi Sahib. Godspeed."

As he reached the door, Yar Mohammad looked back at the two men. Shaikh Waliullah and Shafi Sahib, their hands moving in arcs and arabesques, were already deep in a discussion of the Essence of Love.

The red-haired servant stole a curious glance at him as they descended the stone stairs toward the kitchens. "Shaikh Sahib gives no more than a few moments to any of his followers," he commented, as they reached the kitchen door where thick rounds of bread had been stacked high, fresh from the baker.

Yar Mohammad blinked. How long had he been in that room? "You see," he said politely, "due to unusual circumstances, I have not seen Shaikh Sahib for more than ten years. It took some time for me to tell him all that has happened."

The servant nodded dubiously. "I see."

At her writing table, pen in hand, Mariana stared out through her doorway, watching camp servants as they hurried back and forth between the tents. A flock of sheep passed by on its way to the back of the compound, each animal decorated with vivid splotches of orange dye.

On the table lay a half-written letter to her father. *"We have reached Firozpur at last,"* it said.

As only two days remain before the great procession that will begin the durbar, the camp is in a frenzy of activity, practicing intricate drills on the parade ground, beating the carpets, building places to sit. All the preparations seem to require shouting, and as many of them are carried out at night by torchlight, no one has slept properly for days. To think we used to complain about the servants' nightly coughing!

The state visit will last about seventeen days, with marches past, trick riding, dancing girls, and hundreds of wonderful elephants, all taking place in a spirit of vigorous competition to see whether it is we or the Sikhs who are richer and grander.

A lizard clung to her tent pole, watching her. Where was Fitzgerald? Why had he let two precious days go by without coming to see her?

Apparently even the handsomest of our men will be no competition for the Sikhs. They are said to be extraordinarily good-looking and marvelously well dressed in exquisite shawls and Moghul jewelry. The only one of them who is neither handsome nor elaborately dressed is the Maharajah himself, a tiny little man who has only one eye, having lost the missing one in battle. He, apparently, wears only the simplest of clothes and very little jewelry, unless you count his enormous diamond, the Koh-i-noor, or Mountain of Light. He is said to be a magnificent horseman who commands the absolute loyalty of his people. His army, after ours, is the best fighting force in India.

Speaking of someone who is no competition for the Sikhs, fat Major Byrne has become frantic about the Maharajah's tents. We hear they are made of silk and cashmere, while our camp, after all its travels, is a sea of dilapidated, mud-covered canvas. Major Byrne was so nervous at lunch yesterday that he honked in front of everyone! But he says our gifts, at least, will be more dazzling than Ranjit Singh's.

Since Ranjit has a passion for horses, the Major has ordered all our best ones to be kept aside to be preened and polished for the durbar. We are to ride only the ones that remain. As I am very far down the list, I am sure mine will be a thousand years old.

She put down her pen. It was no use. She was too distracted to write, even to Papa. The letter must wait. Since Fitzgerald had not come to her, she must go to Fitzgerald.

"Dittoo," she called. "I wish to ride."

Yesterday's ride had been an ordeal of nerves. Remembering the lunatic's bewildering appearance in front of her the day before, she had brought her grooms with her and had taken a different path, this one away from the army camp. Certain that she was being observed, she had hurried through her ride, starting at every sound, peering into each thorn bush. Then, returning to the safety of the compound, she had been so unwilling to fall again that she had walked her horse all the way to her tent. Worst of all, Harry Fitzgerald had appeared at neither lunch nor dinner.

She put away her half-written letter and closed her writing box. Everyone who rode a horse fell occasionally, even Lord Auckland, who had broken several ribs only two months ago. *"The path you will take requires courage,"* the mad soothsayer had said. As for native fortune-tellers, what could *they* know of her future, of her feelings?

"Remember who you are," Uncle Adrian had told her.

Of course, if the adventure with the lunatic had happened to someone else, she would have been panting to know every detail of the encounter, down to the ragged clothes he had been wearing when he lurched out of the thorn bush. It would seem exciting rather than unnerving, exotic rather than unsavory. It had, after all, been a very *Indian* experience. But the effect was sometimes quite different, she decided, when the adventure happened to oneself.

Hearing a clopping sound outside, Mariana quickly tied on her riding hat and stepped into the sunlight, then stared in surprise. Instead of the usual half-grown boy, her favorite senior groom waited at her doorway, his bony face intent beneath a roughly tied turban, the reins of a little mare in his hand.

She had only ever seen him in the distance. She smiled, pleased that he had come.

He bent to greet her, a hand over his heart. "Peace," he said in a resonant voice.

The mare he had brought was old and her ribs jutted from her sides, but she had spirit. She pawed the ground with a frail white-stockinged foot when the groom handed Mariana the reins, and nudged his shoulder with a muzzle from which a white blaze rose and flared between her eyes.

"Patience, my friend," the groom murmured.

As she arranged herself in the sidesaddle, Mariana felt the tall groom fix his attention on her. "There is a message for you, Memsahib," he said, glancing at her, then away. He shifted his weight as if reluctant to speak, his hands moving aimlessly in and out of invisible pockets in his clothes.

"The path you will take," he continued, "leads to peace. You must be careful, very careful."

Startled, she gaped at him. "My name is Yar Mohammad," he added. "I will send two men to accompany you on your ride."

Without seeming to hurry, he moved away before she had found her voice.

Mariana willed her hands to stop their trembling as she clucked to the mare and started for the gate, her thoughts whirling. What did these natives want from her?

Later, as she crossed the open stretch of ground between the government and army camps, she glanced over her shoulder. Who was sending her these messages? Were they watching her now?

At the army camp she avoided the stares of the British soldiers who sat outside their tents, waiting to be called for afternoon drill, and rode with determination toward the newly cleared parade ground, her pair of grooms trotting behind her.

WITH no idea how to find Fitzgerald in the huge, busy army camp, she followed the margin of the ground, uncertain of what to do next.

Fifty yards from her, native infantrymen marched up and down to shouted orders, their shabby red coats buttoned tightly over their chests, their faces sweating in the sun. A pair of elephants crossed the ground, each carrying half a dozen men.

In a veterinary tent at the far end, an Englishman in high boots swabbed the back of a handsome bay horse. As she rode past him, Mariana began to perspire. Perhaps Fitzgerald had not liked her as much as she had thought. Perhaps she had said something tactless at dinner that had driven him away, something she could not remember. Perhaps he was even now avoiding her, laughing with his friends, waiting until she had gone. She patted the little mare's neck with an absent hand. Mama and Aunt Rachel had warned her endlessly against tactlessness.

A British army captain passed her, riding the other way. She returned his greeting with a stiff little nod. If anyone asked, she would say she had come simply to see the preparations for the campaign.

Someone was about to overtake her on the path. She turned in her saddle and saw Fitzgerald thundering toward her on a gray horse. Barely avoiding her grooms, he pulled up beside her, red-faced. "Forgive me, Miss Givens," he said, breathing hard, "I've only just learned that you are here."

He seemed genuinely upset. In her lap, Mariana's gloved hands loosened on the reins.

They rode side by side, his gray dwarfing her little mare. "I have hoped since our dinner that your ride would bring you here," he said. "I've been too desperately busy with my men to call on you. I cannot even come to meals."

They turned from the path and started across open country. One of his hands held the reins, the other rested on his thigh. His legs were long and muscular. "It's the drilling that takes so much time," he added, then turned to meet her eyes. "I hope you will come again."

Mariana pushed a curl under her riding hat. "Only if you promise to describe all your preparations for the campaign."

"I promise to shower you with every tedious detail." He gave her his protective smile.

Her dreams fulfilled, Mariana beamed beneath her veil.

"War lasts longer than we think," he said suddenly. "Look." He pointed to the horizon. "This country was reduced to emptiness by pillage a hundred years before Ranjit Singh came to power. It has never recovered. I believe that violence can soak into the soil and become a part of a place. I feel it here."

"You feel violence *here*?" Mariana looked toward the placid scene where he pointed, with its distant mud villages and a single ragged man leading a black buffalo. The soothsayers had not mentioned violence, but they had mentioned courage. Of what future calamity had they tried to warn her?

They had reached a stand of feathery trees. Fitzgerald reined in his horse. "Shall we stop for a moment in the shade? I do not believe," he added, seeing her hesitate, "that anyone knows we are here. Besides, it's only for a little while."

Before she could make up her mind, he called to her grooms, "Leave us. Return to the horse lines."

"I am not sure you should ride alone with native menservants," Fitzgerald added seriously as they watched her escort trot away toward the government camp. "Men like those may not be safe."

She dismounted. "Men like my grooms?" she asked, as Fitzgerald tethered their horses. "Are *those* poor underfed creatures your idea of a pillaging horde?" She sat on a stone under the trees and swept a spider from her skirts. "It would be worse to ride out with no escort at all," she added, thinking of the mad fortune-teller. "Besides, a senior groom has chosen them for me."

"Still," Fitzgerald said softly, as he came and sat beside her, "they *are* native men. You should be careful." His voice sounded hoarse, as if he needed something to drink.

His face neared hers. "I wished to speak to you alone," he said, dropping his eyes, "because I must know . . ."

Her hands were clasped together in her lap. Reaching out swiftly, he took them in his, his square fingers brushing her thighs through the wool of her riding habit. "I should not say this, Miss Givens," he murmured, turning her fingers over in his, "but since dinner, I have thought of nothing but you."

As he spoke his eyes roamed over her face and the front of her body as they had two days ago. Unable to stop herself, she bent toward him, her eyelids drooping.

In an instant, he dropped her hands and raised the veil from her face. Gripping her shoulders, he pressed his mouth over hers.

He smelled of horses. The bite of his fingers into her shoulders and the moist pressure of his mouth swept her away from everything she knew. As she pressed toward him, one of his hands, then the other, slid behind her back. Heat rose from the center of her body and spread to her face.

"Oh, Mariana." His cheek to hers, he rocked from side to side, breathing rapidly, as if he had run up a flight of stairs.

He had called her by her name. She wanted to reach up and touch his lips with her fingers.

An artillery shot crashed in the distance. Shouts closer by signaled that someone was approaching.

She started backward. What had she done? They would be seen coming out from the trees alone, without even her grooms for propriety! Pushing him away, she jumped to her feet.

He, too, rose. "It's all right," he assured her as he untied the horses. "We can ride around the far side of these trees. No one will see us."

Afterward, they hardly spoke, but as they parted, he studied her again, his eyes luminous in his square face.

"Mariana," was all he said before he left her.

LATER, still rosy and breathless, she stood over her basin, splashing water on her cheeks, remembering the exact moment when Fitzgerald's lips had met hers. Her riding habit lay in a black heap where she had dropped it when she changed into a fresh gown.

"Memsahib!" Dittoo cried, rushing inside, shattering her reverie, "your clothes! If they lie on the floor, a snake or a scorpion might get inside!"

What did she care for snakes and scorpions? Mariana groped blindly for her towel as Dittoo snatched up her riding coat and shook it vigorously, thickening the air with dust.

"A snake, even a small one, can kill you with one bite, Memsahib," he prattled on, now shaking her skirt. "It can come into this tent through the tiniest hole. As for a scorpion, its sting can make the strongest man scream. That is why the other memsahib did not come with us to translate for the Governor Sahib's ladies. She was bitten by a scorpion that got inside her clothes."

Was she not to be allowed a moment's peace? Mariana flung her towel onto the chair and pointed to the doorway. "Take those clothes outside, Dittoo!" she snapped.

Unperturbed, Dittoo gathered up her habit, then waved a careless hand. "You should be getting ready, Memsahib," he told her. "Your munshi sahib is coming this way."

If Munshi Sahib had been ill, he was now recovered. Her lesson! How could she have forgotten the poem he had given her, so full of feelings that mirrored her own? Mariana turned a softer eye on Dittoo.

"Ask him to wait a moment, until I am ready to receive him," she ordered.

She returned to her table, opened her writing box and took out the paper on which he had written the poem in Persian ten days ago, and the larger piece on which she had copied her translation. She smoothed them carefully out on the table.

"Are you quite well now, Munshi Sahib?" she inquired moments later, searching her teacher's face, noticing that he looked a little wan. Careful of the formality between them, she did not mention his new lamb's wool hat.

"I am quite well, Bibi," he replied, nodding gravely. "And now, let us see how you have translated our poem."

Mariana had worked on the poem until late the previous night, her lamp flickering beside her, dreaming of Harry Fitzgerald as she chose her words. Now he had kissed her. Her voice trembling a little, she began to read.

"I, the candle, burn myself away
For thee, the blazing morn, my heart's desire.
Consumed by heat of longing for thy face,
At thy first glance I perish in thy fire.
Far distant yet close by, I die for thee,
Whose radiant being lights my funeral pyre."

She looked up, delighted with her accomplishment.

For a time her munshi rocked silently on his heels, his eyes moving over the walls of her tent.

"Bibi," he said at last, poking a long finger at the paper in her hand, "you have taken words from the page I gave you and written your own poem. You have not translated *that* poem," he added, gesturing toward the paper on the table.

Mariana picked up the page decorated with his delicate Persian writing. "But Munshi Sahib, I *have* translated it. There it is—'*Main shama jan gudazan—*' "

"No, Bibi." He shook his head firmly. "The poem I gave you is about a candle and about the morning light, that is true, but it does not contain the sentiments you have expressed."

"Sentiments? But Munshi Sahib—"

"Moreover, fire does not appear in the original poem, and there is most assuredly no mention of a funeral or a funeral pyre. I regret, Bibi, having given you this poem when you were not in a frame of mind to do a proper translation. It is my mistake. Do not concern yourself. We will not mention your poem again."

Her poem. *Her* frame of mind. Suddenly hot, she looked away. What had she revealed? What had he guessed?

"I will now give you a better translation," he went on in a businesslike tone. "This one is not in poetic form, but it is, nonetheless, better."

His hands clasped behind him, he recited in his curiously accented English:

"I am the self-consuming candle.
Thou art the brilliant morn that draws the heart.
I burn with desire to see thee,
Yet I perish before thy glory.
I am both close to thee and immeasurably far away.
Separation from thee is like dying,
Yet in thy presence I cannot survive."

Scarcely hearing him, Mariana stared at her hands. He knew. He read her so easily. He was worse than Miss Emily. "Oh, Munshi Sahib," she said, "I do not think I—"

"This," her teacher interrupted solemnly, "is not a simple poem. It does not concern itself with fires and burning. It concerns itself with the pain of separation. Its subject is the striving of the soul to reach God."

"Oh," she murmured uncomfortably.

"Yes," the munshi continued, "this poem describes the pain of longing. It says that the soul is a candle burning in the darkness, longing for the morning. But when the sun appears, the candle's light diminishes to nothing. Like a candle in sunlight, the soul becomes nothing in the presence of God. That is why the candle and the soul both fear that which they long for most.

"And that," he said, his old eyes on Mariana's face, "is what you are to learn from translating this poem."

Her munshi had a curious ability to focus Mariana's attention. Against her will, his words reached her and dominated her thoughts, temporarily driving away even Fitzgerald's kiss.

She nodded. "The candle and the soul," she repeated, "both fear what they long for. That is sad but lovely, Munshi Sahib. But," she asked, needing suddenly to know, "to what religion do you belong, Munshi Sahib? Are you Hindu?"

"No, Bibi, I am not Hindu, although there are many noble and God-fearing Hindus in India. In fact, there are noble men of all religions in India. But I, myself, am Muslim." Her teacher smiled. "That much you may know of me."

When he had gone, Mariana read her own poem once more, then crossed out its original title, *Love's Candle,* and replaced it with *To H.F.* After folding it carefully, she slipped it beneath the papers at the very bottom of her writing box.

She shivered. So much had happened today, but for all the beauty of Munshi's poem, for all the excitement of Fitzgerald's kiss, she could not forget the groom's eerie message. A groom, a madman, even Fitzgerald, had now warned her to be careful. But of what?

Chapter 8

WEDNESDAY, NOVEMBER 27

Quiet had settled over the Lahore Citadel. The usual jostling throng of nobles, traders, soldiers, and servants was missing from the outer courts, having gone to wait upon the Maharajah at his distant camp, leaving the fountains to play to an audience of sweepers who stood knee-deep in the water, their garments tied high, scrubbing slime from the waterways.

Only the Jasmine Tower, home to the Maharajah's thirty-seven queens, was as busy as usual. Throughout the afternoon, maidservants had covered and re-covered the distance from the kitchens to the tower, carrying the ladies' meal—twenty-one dishes of goat, fish from the Ravi River, quail, venison, duck, wild mushrooms, rice dishes cooked with saffron and scattered with almonds, rounds of bread, mountains of fruit. The eunuch guards lazed, waiting in the marble court, while servant children, their clothes the color of dust, watched from the shade of nearby porticos.

In the long room with the delicately fretted window at its end, the meal had finished. The silk squares still lay in a line on the carpet, but the dishes and platters that had covered them were now gone. Still sitting, the queens waited, greasy fingers held away from their clothes, for slave women to come and pour a stream of rose water over each pair of royal hands.

For the remainder of the afternoon, the ladies would rest. They dried their fingers, then moved, still chatting, to the cool walls to arrange themselves on bolsters and let the servants cover them with satin quilts. The ladies stretched, curled, and sighed, their bangles clashing musically in the perfumed air.

While the queens dozed, those servants who had not stayed to fan away the flies snatched their own sleep on reed mats thrown onto the bare tiles of the women's servant quarters. There they would lie until the sonorous voice of the court caller summoned them back to serve their queens.

They, too, had eaten. The eunuch guards, as always, had pounced on the leftover delicacies from the tower, leaving only morsels for the senior-most women servants, and nothing for the others but rice and boiled lentil mush.

After swallowing the last of her dry bread, Reshma had found a mat in the larger of the two women's quarters. She liked to sleep in a corner but, being young and unimportant, she rarely had her wish. Today, she was crowded into the middle of the room with a pair of feet inches from her face.

The afternoon was bright and not too hot for rest, and the morning's work had been easy. Preoccupied, Saat Kaur had not pestered Reshma to bring her this, no, bring her that, no, take it all away.

But Reshma had worries more serious than cracked looking glasses and misplaced lengths of brocade. She reached out with cautious fingers and felt for the small body that shared her mat. Yes, Saboor was still there. When she dared a hasty glance, she saw that his eyes were open, fixed on the cobwebs that clung to the rafters overhead.

He, who used to chatter to his mother every waking moment, had not spoken since excited voices from the ladies' tower had called them from their hiding place in the garden. The running servants had been too breathless to explain, but Reshma had not needed to be told of the horror that had occurred. Surrounded by panting women, she had carried Saboor down the stairway to the crowded room where his mother lay dead, and from that moment he had lapsed into a heavy, unbroken silence. His slight body in its starched cotton pajamas had also changed, its bright energy replaced by leaden sadness. Her arms had ached as she dragged him away from the sight of his mother.

Dead, the lady had seemed asleep. Only the liquid that had trickled from the corner of her mouth to stain the scarlet bedcovering hinted that something was amiss, that she would not at any moment sit up and reach for her tortoiseshell comb with the pearls set into its frame. The silver cup, fallen from her fingers, had rolled away across the floor. It was the cup that had betrayed the source of the poison.

Reshma raised her head and looked cautiously about before she rolled onto her back and turned her own eyes to the rafters. There never seemed to be a moment when she was not watched.

Without the Maharajah's protection, Saboor had suffered since his mother's death. His starched clothes were now limp and unclean; his head, shaven to thicken his curls, was scabby. He ate only the mouthfuls that Reshma saved from her own poor meals and fed him hastily, looking over her shoulder, afraid to be seen. He had endured blows.

Worst, in all that time, no one had embraced him. Before his mother's death, Saboor had never been more than an arm's length from someone who loved him, and now he had only Reshma to carry him here and there, and she did not dare to embrace him with kindness, or show her grief at what she had done. How could she, when all eyes were upon her, when Saat Kaur, frightening murderess that she was, had now offered a pair of ruby earrings to the first servant to see him dead?

All this was because the Maharajah was old and ailing. Some of the queens wanted to burn alive on his pyre after he died, but not Saat Kaur. Terrified for her life, she had tried to gain importance through her sickly little princeling, but it had been Saboor, not her own baby, who had won the Maharajah's love. For this, she had ordered Reshma to poison Saboor.

Saboor sighed. Reshma heard him, but did not move. Children were said to forget quickly. He should have forgotten his mother by now, but she knew with certainty that he had not. She knew that, since his mother's death, there had been no moment when he did not long to hear her voice, to feel her arms about him. Reshma squeezed her eyes shut against the panic that threatened her every waking moment.

She wished he would look at her. It would lighten her burden to feel he understood her efforts to help him, but even when she fed him, he looked into the distance, as if dreaming of some far-off place. When he swallowed the water she brought, he stared away from her, refusing to meet her sorrowful gaze. Was he thinking of the sweet sherbets his mother used to stir into his drinks?

Only one thing seemed to interest him: the queens of the Jasmine Tower. Whenever he came near them, he looked eagerly from face to face, lapsing after each search into a dark, disappointed sadness.

Now he sat day after day, alone in the shadow of a portico, watching the ladies in the garden. Every day he grew weaker.

Reshma sat up on her mat. "Come," she said loudly, keeping her voice careless. "You must come to the latrine before you soil yourself or me."

She stood and dragged the little boy to her hip. Her hands shook. She should call the sweeperess to do this, but the woman's hands stank, and she, the poorest of all the servants, who craved the earrings most, was the cruelest of all.

Avoiding the gaze of the other servants, Reshma carried Saboor away to the noisome cupboard behind a rotting wall.

As they returned, a eunuch appeared in the doorway.

He was no ordinary eunuch, but a functionary of the court. His tall, pear-shaped form was clothed in silk, not cotton. His turban was elaborately wrapped, and he wore a gold bangle on one wrist.

"The Maharajah," he announced languidly, "has called for the child Saboor to be sent to him at once. His best clothes are to be sent as well, the ones he wears at state functions."

The women servants stared. The eunuch scowled.

"Do not gape like a herd of camels. Go and fetch the child. He is to leave without delay. The Maharajah's own palanquin is waiting by the door. You," he added, pointing to one of the senior servants, "are to tell the senior queen of these instructions. And tell her that since there is no accommodation for ladies at the Maharajah's camp, the child's mother is to remain here until Saboor returns."

No one had told the Maharajah of Mumtaz Bano's death. A murmur ran through the group of women. Again, their eyes fixed on Reshma as a hollow voice echoed from the courtyard outside. "Reshma, Reshma, go to Rani Saat Kaur."

God help her, it was the caller. The little queen was awake.

Reshma seized Saboor, pushed through the crowd, and ran for the ladies' tower.

She carried him up the stone stairs to the dusty storeroom at the top of the tower, high above the room where the queens lay sleeping. There, breathing hard, she put him down and began to throw aside boxes of all sizes as she searched for the little basket where his mother had stored his embroidered court clothes.

"We must hurry, Saboor," she panted. "We must get you away before Saat Kaur learns you are going to the Maharajah." Her hands trembled as she worked. She imagined the young Queen, her face twisted with rage, appearing at the head of the stairs, snatching up the little boy, and hurling him from a tower window. "Poor Saboor. Your light, if you have it, has brought you no luck."

Too weak to stand for long, Saboor had sat down, silent and dirt smeared, at the top of the stairs, his hands open at his sides.

"How little our lives matter, Saboor," Reshma said as she turned over tin trunks and leather boxes. "We are nothing to these important people. The queens have not even told the Maharajah that your mother is dead, although their silence may be due to fear. But if we hurry, we can at least save you from Rani Saat Kaur. Now you will go to the Maharajah, who will give you the best food. He will protect you from harm. This will be better, you will see. This will be better."

As Reshma found his basket and snatched it up, the caller's distant voice found its way up the stone stairs.

"Reshma, oh, Reshma."

Saboor on her hip, Reshma clutched the basket with one thin arm and took the stairs two at a time down to the doorway where the palanquin waited.

Before she carried him out into the sunlight, the child turned his head and looked solemnly into her face for the first time since his mother's death. Reshma's eyes filled with tears.

IN the marble courtyard by the ladies' garden, there stood a magnificent carved palanquin with its curtains closed, the long carrying poles protruding front and back from a curved roof. Twelve bearers in the scarlet uniform of the Maharajah's service stood ready, while mounted guards waited on impatient horses, the blades of their ceremonial spears flashing in the sunlight. The eunuch leaned against a second, plainer palanquin, picking his teeth with his thumbnail. A little distance away, another group of bearers sat, watching silently.

Reshma bundled Saboor into the grand palanquin and pushed the basket of clothes in after him.

"Wait, stupid woman, daughter of an owl." The eunuch was beside her. "What is this nonsense? What filthy brat are you passing off for the child Saboor? You will be punished for this."

"Reshma!" The caller's hollow voice had grown impatient. "You must go at once to Rani Saat."

Reshma's eyes jerked from the eunuch to the doorway. She stepped back from the palanquin. "That *is* the child Saboor," she said.

"What?" he asked, his dusky voice high and startled.

"Please. His mother died ten days ago. Please take him away quickly."

The eunuch's eyes widened. "The mother is dead?" Recovering himself, he flapped his fingers at the palanquins. "Never mind. This is no time to be concerning ourselves with details. We must hurry." He glanced at Reshma. "Women," he said, and spat upon the marble paving.

With a ceremonial groan, four bearers hoisted the Maharajah's palanquin to their shoulders. The head bearer gave a command, and all twelve men began to trot. In seconds, the palanquin with its relief bearers and mounted guards rounded the corner of the courtyard leading to the elephant stairs. Following closely, the eunuch's palanquin with its own complement of bearers and guards passed out of Reshma's sight.

"May God forgive me for my crime," she whispered, when they had gone, "and give my Saboor a safe journey."

Turning away, she ran as fast as she could to Rani Saat Kaur's room.

S A A T Kaur's child was coughing when Reshma entered, a weak, unpleasant sound.

"Where have you been?" Saat Kaur snapped irritably from her bed. "Where is the brat Saboor?"

"He has gone, Bibi." Reshma's throat was dry. When she closed her mouth, grit from the storeroom cracked between her teeth. "The Maharajah has sent for him. He has gone in the Maharajah's own *palki* to the royal camp."

Saat Kaur sat up, her eyes stretched wide. "In the Maharajah's *own palki*?"

When Saat Kaur rose from the bed, Reshma stood motionless, although her heart beat thunderously and she longed to run. But where was there to run in this enclosed tower? An instant later, her head snapped sideways as Saat's open hand struck her, leaving a fiery imprint on her cheek.

This time one slap would not suffice. Panting with fury, Saat Kaur reached for her shoe.

Reshma sought to save herself from the next blow, but she was not quick enough. It fell sickeningly on her ear. She covered her head with her arms and hunched her shoulders against the blows that followed.

"For this," Saat Kaur gasped, out of breath from the work of beating her servant, "my father brought me at the age of eleven to run beside the Maharajah's palanquin so he would notice me? For this, I enticed the Maharajah to take me as his youngest wife?"

Reshma waited, whimpering, for Saat Kaur's arms to tire. Her own arms ached and burned. The blows to her body echoed in the small room. When at last they weakened, she ran for the doorway, but fingers grasped her braid and yanked her back.

The red of Saat Kaur's embroidered clothes signified joy. The Rani's eyes were swollen. The little queen had been weeping even before she heard the news of Saboor's departure. Now she reached out, her fingers bent into claws, her voice a coarse whisper, while on the bed, her son began to wail fretfully.

"People will tell the Maharajah what I have done! What will become of me now?"

"No, Saat Bibi," Reshma protested, "he will not know, he—"

"Liar!" A sour smell rose from Saat Kaur's pretty body. She shook Reshma by her battered shoulders. "He will see the brat's condition. The others will tell him of the poison. They have guessed. I can feel it. *Why did you not wash the cup?*"

She let go of Reshma and clutched her own face. "What will save me from the pyre now? They would not burn the mother of a beloved son, but the Maharajah cares only for the brat Saboor. It should be my son, *my son* in that palki! This is your doing. I will kill you for this. I will kill you—"

She flung herself onto the bed beside her wailing son. Reshma crawled to a corner and huddled there, her arms wrapped around her body. Helpless tears ran close upon one another along her nose and dripped onto the front of her long, worn shirt.

From the bed, Saat Kaur sighed. "Come here, Reshma," she commanded, rolling onto her stomach. "I want you to press my back."

Her body still trembled with shock and fright, but Reshma did as she was ordered. She bent over the bed, and pressed her hands rhythmically up and down the length of the little queen's back until Saat Kaur fell asleep.

Chapter 9

The two palanquins had made good time along the road to the Maharajah's camp. In three hours, they had covered a little over twelve miles. The Maharajah's personal head bearer called a halt, and the running men and their escort left the road.

They set the palanquins down and squatted beside them while the armed guards tethered their mounts. The relief team would come soon. With luck, they would do eleven more miles before dark.

The bearers stretched. Since they had started their journey, there had been no sound from within the royal palanquin.

"We might as well be carrying an empty palki," remarked one man. He yawned. "I wish we had such small passengers every time."

"His condition is bad," remarked another. "I will be surprised if he lives to finish the journey."

"The child's condition is no concern of yours." The eunuch pushed his way past the men who now sat grouped around the silent box. "Your only concern should be getting him to his destination the day after tomorrow morning. Show him to me."

A bearer held a tasseled curtain aside. The eunuch put his head inside and withdrew it instantly. "He stinks," he cried, his face puckering. "He cannot have been bathed for days."

The bearers and the guardsmen peered into the palanquin. Saboor's stained shirt had lifted as he slept, exposing protruding ribs. His body and clothes smelled. He looked at the men with lightless eyes.

"This evil is the work of women," said one of the guards, shaking his head. "Who but a jealous woman would harm a lovely child such as this?"

"HAH, hah, hah." Two days later, breathing in harsh rhythm in the way of bearers, the final team was only five miles from the Maharajah's camp. They would arrive with time to spare.

The palanquins skirted a dead jackal on the road, scattering a flock of carrion crows. Neeloo, the head bearer, turned to the man trotting beside him. "The child is too quiet. I am worried about his condition. He came with no food or drink for his journey. The previous bearers have fed him from their own meals, but he has not eaten since this morning."

"Where is his food?" asked Neeloo's companion. "Why is he traveling in the royal palanquin with nothing to eat or drink?"

"Perhaps he is dying," suggested another man.

Neeloo did not reply.

Small muffled sounds now came from behind the closed curtains. Neeloo signaled for a stop, then squatted beside the royal palanquin and pulled apart the curtains. Saboor lay whimpering on the satin sheets, his hands opening and closing at his sides.

"What is this? Why have we stopped?" The eunuch climbed from his palki.

A hand on his tiny passenger, Neeloo looked up. "The child needs food."

"Food? Now? Do not be stupid. Move on."

Neeloo looked from the eunuch's retreating back to the baby, then pointed to a village near the road. "Gupta," he told a young bearer, "fetch some dung from there. We must make a fire and cook for the child."

The other bearers stared. They were Kahars from Farrukhabad. Hereditary palanquin bearers did not fetch dung from villages, and they never cooked or ate food during the day.

"What? Cook for the child?" The eunuch swung around. "Are you mad?"

Neeloo spread his hands. "The child is valuable to the Maharajah. He must be delivered to the camp alive."

The eunuch paced, muttering to himself, while they made a small fire and stirred a pot of lentils. He fumed aloud, glaring as the child opened his mouth like a baby bird's to receive his food.

"He is very hungry," said a bearer.

"These cruelties happen over deaths and marriages," agreed a guard, shaking his head as Neeloo tore off a child-sized morsel of flat bread and scooped up a little of the yellow mush.

But it seemed that food and drink alone would not satisfy Saboor. As soon as they started off again, wailing arose from inside the curtained box. On and on it went, wavering a little with the bouncing of the palki, pausing as the child breathed, only to begin again.

The running bearers shouted encouragement. When the cries did not stop, Neeloo and the unburdened bearers opened the palanquin's curtains and trotted alongside, arguing with the little boy's tears.

"Come, child, do not weep," they called, putting their hands inside to pat his dirty little body. "Look, there are so many things to see. We will open the curtain on the other side, also. There is not far to go. You will have so many things to eat at the Maharajah's camp!"

But Saboor went on wailing, his eyes squeezed shut, his mouth stretched wide.

"You are making us late!" shouted the eunuch as Neeloo stopped again and lifted the child once more from the Maharajah's satin sheets. "I order you to move!"

Neeloo did not look up. He folded Saboor onto his lap as he had done for his own children when they, too, had wept from want and misery. "We will wait until he has ceased crying," he declared, as he wiped Saboor's wet face with a callused hand. "No child should be left to weep alone."

The other men nodded their agreement.

The eunuch raged, but for all his authority, he was only one, and there were twenty-four bearers and twelve armed guards. Their backs to the eunuch, all waited by the beautiful carved palanquin until, cradled in Neeloo's arms, Saboor had sobbed himself to sleep.

Chapter 10

THURSDAY, NOVEMBER 28

Miss Fanny rocked a little on the narrow seat as she, Miss Emily, and Mariana returned on an elephant from the parade ground. "I must say, our troops made a stirring show this morning," she remarked.

Miss Emily, who sat hunched over with fever beside her sister, pulled her shawls closer about her in the morning heat. "Did you enjoy our practice review, my dear?" She peered out at Mariana from the shade of a large purple silk bonnet.

"Oh, yes," Mariana cried, "it was marvelous! How do you suppose they persuaded the baggage elephants to behave so well on parade?"

For her, the best part of the show had been the horse artillery, especially Lieutenant Fitzgerald on his tall gray gelding, his brass dragoon helmet flashing as he led a team pulling a twenty-pound gun.

"I hope they do as well at the real review." Miss Fanny sighed. "I always think I have become used to seeing our British soldiers in India; but when the Queen's Buffs marched past this morning . . ." Her voice quavered.

"Yes, indeed, Fanny," put in Miss Emily, speaking through gently chattering teeth, "you always weep at the sight of the Buffs. For my part, a bagpipe always fills me with excitement. At the first hint of a drone I long to snatch up a weapon and attack someone."

Miss Fanny tugged her bonnet lower over her eyes. "And whom would you attack? I can only imagine myself attacking rampaging natives."

The two ladies subsided into silence, their eyes on the horizon. Opposite them, Mariana fidgeted on her seat.

"Miss Fanny," she asked after a moment, "do you really dislike the natives?"

"In a way I do, Mariana," replied Miss Fanny, as she took out her handkerchief. "There is something far *too* foreign about them: something mysterious and upsetting." She pointed down at a group of dark-skinned men walking beside the elephants, wearing only dirty-looking loincloths, their hair tangled and uncombed. "Look at those men. How can one not feel distaste?"

She sniffed, her handkerchief to her nose.

"But not all of them are like that, surely." The elephant shifted her weight, causing the open box where the ladies sat to lurch sideways, pushing Mariana against the railing. "Surely some of the natives are worthy of respect. My munshi says there are noble and God-fearing men of all religions in India, and—"

"Their worthiness, or lack of it, is not the point, Mariana," Miss Emily interrupted from her corner. "The point is that you show far too much interest in their affairs. You have been seen poking about with elephants and mahouts. You speak of helping diseased natives. I worry about that munshi of yours. I fear he has filled your head with unsuitable ideas.

"The only way to behave with natives," she added, tightening her shawls, "is to ignore them. Do not like them, do not hate them, do not fear them. Those who do pay a heavy price. Our previous lady translator, silly woman, developed a horror of natives. I am told she barricades her bedroom door at night for fear one of them will get in while she is sleeping."

Miss Fanny put a hand to her bonnet. "Something happened to her, you see. People are saying she will never be the same again."

"The lady," said Miss Emily, "was awakening from sleep one morning when her serving man came in with her coffee. As he put down the tray, he noticed a scorpion on the bedclothes. It was, if I am correct, crawling up the lady's person, on its way to her face."

She turned to Mariana. "Hill scorpions, as you know, are large, black, and very fierce."

Mariana remembered Dittoo shaking out her riding habit. "The sting of a scorpion," she repeated, "can make the strongest man scream."

Miss Emily did not seem impressed with Mariana's knowledge. She pointed into the air with a gloved hand. "The servant tore open the mosquito curtains, reached out with his bare hand, and swept the scorpion to the floor, where he killed it. The lady began to shriek at the top of her voice. People rushed to her room to find her fainting with terror, but not," she added, closing her eyes as the howdah rolled, creaking, to one side, "from fear of scorpions."

"From what, then?" Mariana looked eagerly from one sister to the other. This was perfect for her next letter to Papa. "What was the lady so afraid of? Why did she faint?"

Miss Emily pressed her lips together. "She fainted because a native man had touched her. The servant was dismissed. And the lady, since then, has been unable to be left alone for five minutes."

"What a fool the woman must be!" Mariana exclaimed.

"Yes, she is a fool, because she gave in to fear." Miss Emily frowned. "Now, Mariana, you *must* do as we say. Natives are very different from us, although most of the time I would not go so far as to call them 'savages' as some of our Englishmen do."

Savages? Her dear old Munshi Sahib? Her irritating, clumsy, harmless Dittoo? Mariana opened her mouth to protest, then closed it.

"And now, my dear," Miss Emily continued, fixing her gaze on Mariana's face, "I understand you have taken an interest in Lieutenant Fitzgerald."

By now, everyone must know. Mariana felt herself blush.

Yesterday, returning to their grove of trees, she and Fitzgerald had talked animatedly of the intricacies of artillery drills, of the Afghan campaign, and of his uncle's estate in Sussex, not ten miles from her own village. Alone together, they had kissed again. This time he had laid a hand on her breast. She flushed, remembering the heat of it, and the longing it had aroused in her.

"I am sorry to say that we have had a bad report of him." Miss Emily pronounced her words with care.

A bad report? Mariana smiled uncomprehendingly. "Miss Emily?"

"It seems Lieutenant Fitzgerald jilted a young lady in Calcutta a year ago. He and the girl had been engaged for months when he broke it off with no explanation, leaving her to return, unmarried, to England." Miss Emily sighed. "He has very much blackened his name in Calcutta." She folded her gloved hands. "I am sorry, Mariana. I wish we had known this earlier."

On the elephant ahead of them, Mr. Macnaghten laughed loudly at something Major Byrne had said. Mariana clutched at the howdah railing. "Blackened his name? But Miss Emily, there must be some explanation. I cannot believe he would do such a cruel thing."

"It seems," Miss Emily continued, "that he did it after meeting a *second* young lady with a greater fortune. *She* had the sense to refuse him. Since then, he has not been received in proper society. It was his good fortune that his regiment, where he was still popular, left Calcutta soon afterward to join this camp."

Miss Fanny nodded from her corner. "Of course it will not be long before the entire camp learns of this."

"But Miss Emily, Miss Fanny, we *must* hear his side of the story!"

"No, Mariana." Miss Emily peered from the depths of her bonnet into Mariana's face. "It is too late for explanations." She sighed again. "Your connection to Fitzgerald must be severed. I am sure this is painful for you now, but, in time, you will be grateful."

In her mind's eye Mariana saw her father's grave face as he told her she was not to see her friend Jeremy again. How could this happen a second time? How could she be forbidden the only person she wanted, the only one in India whose presence gave her joy?

Miss Emily leaned forward. "You will not need to break off the friendship yourself," she added briskly. "I shall have a word with General Cotton. Fitzgerald's commanding officer will speak to him tomorrow morning. After that, he will not approach you again, you may be sure." She smiled kindly. "Do not worry, my dear. There are several suitable men in this camp with spotless reputations. I am sure one of them will make you *very* happy."

Miss Fanny patted Mariana's knee. "My sister is right. Good looks are all very well, but they do not last. A kind heart and a sufficient income are what make a good husband."

"Miss Emily," Mariana declared as firmly as she was able, "I cannot sever my connection with the lieutenant until I have spoken to him myself."

"You may *not* speak to him." Miss Emily drew herself up on her seat. "Believe me, my dear, men like Fitzgerald are great charmers, capable of getting young women like you into all sorts of trouble."

Mariana's thoughts flew to the grove of feathery trees, and Fitzgerald's hand on her breast. She could not bear the unfairness of this. She had come all the way from Weddington village to find everything exactly the same here as it was there.

Miss Emily pursed her lips. "And now, let us cease this unpleasant conversation. We have no need to speak of the young man again."

•   •   •

THE sky through Mariana's doorway seemed drained of color. In Sussex, it would be cool and rainy. If she were wearing her blue striped gown there, she would need a hood for her cape when she and Fitzgerald drove to his uncle's house to be received as husband and wife.

She dipped her pen into her inkpot with a little stabbing gesture.

"*As for me,*" she wrote to her mother, "*I look constantly into my boxes to make sure nothing awful has happened to my gowns. Several of them are borrowed from ladies in Simla whom I hardly know, and I am terrified of losing or ruining one of them.*"

She wiped her pen. She could write no more of this drivel. Having saved her news about Fitzgerald until she was certain of him, she now had only her hurt and fury to report, and they were too painful to put on paper.

She thrust herself from her chair and paced to her bed, then flung herself around and paced back to her desk. Then, she jerked open her trunk and pulled out her riding habit. "Dittoo," she called out, "get me a mare and two grooms."

THE little mare had been brought to her by a silent stranger, which meant she had been spared any further messages from the groom Yar Mohammad. That was a good thing. She did not think she could tolerate any more advice from soothsayers.

At the army camp, she rode toward the parade ground, aware that people were watching, that someone might report her to General Cotton. She did not care. Who was General Cotton anyhow but a fussy old man with a scarlet face and bushy sideburns, who sat beside Miss Emily at dinner?

Activity surrounded Mariana as she rode past rows of tents. Soldiers, both native and European, were polishing weapons and repairing uniforms. A team of bullocks hauled a gun carriage out of the way. English officers inclined their heads as she rode by.

She had circled the parade ground only twice before Fitzgerald rode toward her, waving, from between two tents.

At the sight of him, she began to perspire.

When he reached her side, smiling happily, she tried to smile in return, but could not.

"Is something wrong?" He studied her.

"Yes," she forced out, knowing she was about to ruin everything forever. "Miss Emily spoke to me this morning. There has been a bad report of you from Calcutta."

"What did she say?" His voice was level, but his knee jogged up and down on his saddle. "Did she say I had jilted someone, that I had ruined the girl's chance at marriage?"

Someone had lit a campfire nearby. The smell of burning wood reached them. Under her veil, Mariana's hair was sticking to her forehead. "Did you do it?" she asked.

"Yes. No." Fitzgerald looked away, then into her face. "I did not jilt her. I refused to marry her when I learned what she was. That is all."

That could not be all. Mariana bit her lip. "Please tell me what she did. You know I will believe you, Harry." She longed to touch him. Birds chattered in a nearby tree.

He shook his head. "What good would it do? The girl is ruined, and so am I." He stared past Mariana, into the distance. "I never thought her lies would reach all the way to the Punjab. Has Miss Emily told you not to see me again?"

Mariana took a shaky breath. "Your commanding officer will speak to you tomorrow morning."

Horses were approaching. Collecting herself, she nodded to two officers as they rode past, then turned back to Fitzgerald.

He looked so forlorn, his face averted, his shoulders sagging, that she stretched out a hand not caring about the consequences. "I am sure there was a reason for what you did. You don't need to tell me now," she added, when he did not respond. "I mean, we can meet tomorrow when nobody is—"

"I am an officer in the Bengal Native Artillery," he cut in harshly. "If I am ordered not to see you, I cannot disobey orders." He dropped his head into his hands. "Oh, God, why did they bring the *army* into it?"

She must return to camp before they guessed where she had gone. "But," she asked, needing to know, her body steeled against his answer, "were you—would you have married me?" She twisted the reins in her fingers.

"Of course, Mariana." He kicked his horse. "Whatever did you think?" he added over his shoulder as he rode away.

SHE would not break her connection to Fitzgerald. She did not care what anyone said. As she dismounted angrily by her tent, a forceful, irritated voice came from beyond the red wall.

"I do not care in the slightest what the carpenters think," the loud voice declared. "The stairs will be erected *there,* and they will be erected *now.*"

It sounded like Major Byrne.

"And," the voice continued, as flat as a file, "you *will* find the stair carpeting and you *will* have it nailed onto the stairs."

It *was* Major Byrne. Mariana took off her riding hat and shook out her hair. Must he shout so, when her emotions were in such turmoil?

"And, Sotheby," the major added, "you are to make absolutely certain that the gifts are presented in their proper order. Repeat your instructions to me."

Stairs? Gifts? The durbar. Unable to resist eavesdropping, Mariana crossed to the red wall and looked through her hole in the canvas.

Major Byrne stood planted on the avenue, his back to her, addressing the White Rabbit, who stood at rigid attention. Across the avenue, a group of native workmen gestured at a stack of wooden boards.

"Yes, Major." The Rabbit's scarlet coat was stained with perspiration. When nervous, he tended to shout. He had talked so loudly when he sat beside Mariana at dinner that Miss Fanny had kept her napkin in front of her mouth for most of the soup course.

Her eye to the hole, Mariana shook her head. How could the Eden sisters *ever* have imagined her marrying the White Rabbit?

"The portrait of Her Majesty," Sotheby yelled, "is to be given first, arrayed upon a velvet cushion—"

"Has the goldsmith returned the frame yet?" the major interrupted, tapping an impatient boot.

"The gold—"

"I certainly hope you told Johnston not to take his eyes off the jeweler while he set the diamonds into the picture frame." In order to interrupt Sotheby a second time, Major Byrne was obliged to raise his voice to a bellow. The carpenters stared. "They *all* steal, you know. They must be watched every moment."

"Sir, the frame is ready," Sotheby yelled, his eyes bulging out of his chinless face.

"Yes, yes. Go on, man, repeat your instructions." The major took out his watch. "I do not have all day."

At the sound of Dittoo's voice behind her, Mariana flapped a hand for silence.

"Following the presentation of the smaller gifts, the two guns will be brought forward, and—"

"By God, Sotheby," the major bellowed from the avenue, "I most particularly told you that those howitzers are to be *in place* for presentation by the time the two elephant processions have met at the midpoint of the avenue, there."

Howitzers! Here was something Papa would enjoy: short-barreled cannon made especially for firing shells at a high angle of elevation. He had never seen one close by. . . .

Papa. If he were here, he would see that she was right about Fitzgerald, who loved her, who loved India as much as she did. This time he would not close the door and make her promise to give up her only friend, the only person she wanted. He would see that Fitzgerald must have left his bride-to-be for a reason.

Major Byrne was still talking. "—I have told you at least twice that you are to have them moved by coolies, and not by animals. The ground near the tent will have been swept, and I will *not* allow pack animals to tear it up. And you must not forget that the ammunition is to be arranged *close by* for the Maharajah's inspection. I want two hundred shells over there, and they *must* be stacked properly. If I find they have been thrown carelessly onto the ground, you shall be called to account. Do you understand me?" The major pointed at Sotheby's chest. "And make sure the groom Yar Mohammad comes himself. He is not to send that fool Gulab Din with the horses. And mind that the grooms leading the animals for presentation are in *clean clothes*. We made a poor showing last time. I should not have to remind you that it is *not* the business of the British East India Company to be outdone on these occasions by native princes, whatever their pretensions may be. Remember that, my boy."

Smiling suddenly, he clapped Sotheby on the shoulder. "Cheer up, lad, we'll show Ranjit Singh a thing or two. You'll see!"

He turned on his heel and strode across the dusty avenue, a barely discernible honk hanging in the air behind him. A moment later the sentries at the entrance came to clanking, stamping attention.

FIVE miles away, two horsemen rode across the broad parade ground at the Maharajah's camp.

"Since I do not have a quarter of your eloquence," Yusuf Bhatti was saying, "I am glad we are doing this together."

"Eloquence?" Hassan made an exasperated gesture. "In this case, eloquence has no value. There it is." He pointed to a tent made of yellow woolen shawls that had been set up near a spreading tree at the very edge of the ground.

"No one is here but the guards." Yusuf frowned as they approached the silent tent.

Hassan shook his head. "A saddled horse is tethered outside. That means the Maharajah is here. Even when he is ill, his horse is kept ready for him. He is very weak, I am told. We need only wait there." He pointed to a group of reed stools outside the tent. "If Uncle

Azizuddin is not with him now, he will be here soon. He rarely leaves the Maharajah's side."

A short while later a stooping, bearded figure emerged from the tent's doorway. Yusuf and Hassan got to their feet.

"Ah, my dear boy," cried Faqeer Azizuddin, the Chief Minister, as he reached for Hassan. "I am so sorry to have missed you at Lahore. You had just left when I arrived there. I am heartbroken at the terrible news of your wife."

Hassan accepted his patron's embrace, but did not reply.

"Please, let us sit." An arm around Hassan's shoulders, Faqeer Azizuddin guided him toward the stools. "We do not wish to disturb the Maharajah."

Yusuf studied the Chief Minister as he lowered himself onto a stool. His long woolen coat was creased, his beard untrimmed. The man looked as if he had not slept for days. The Maharajah must indeed be ill, perhaps more than ill.

The Faqeer signaled to a servant to bring water. He turned to Hassan. "You have come," he said, "to ask for Saboor's return."

Hassan nodded. Beneath his elegant turban, his face was as still as stone.

"I cannot lie to you, my boy." Faqeer Azizuddin took a crumpled handkerchief from the folds of his coat and wiped his face. "The Maharajah needs your son. I know it does not seem reasonable, especially at this sad time, but he does." He glanced toward the yellow tent. "When Saboor is beside him, the Maharajah feels hope. He comes alive. He is able to rule. Without Saboor, he is weak. He falls victim to illness, to fits of paralysis and despair. Who can explain such things?"

He returned his handkerchief to its hiding place in his clothes. "As to your son's whereabouts, I can tell you this much—he left the Citadel yesterday. He will, God willing, arrive here tomorrow morning, in time for the beginning of the durbar. After he arrives, he will remain with the Maharajah until the close of the durbar."

Hassan stiffened. Beside him, Yusuf flexed his shoulders, his weapons clashing against one another.

The Faqeer looked briefly at Yusuf. "Do not worry," he continued, turning back to Hassan. "I have arranged for a reliable servant to look after Saboor. I promise you that after the state visit is concluded, you may take your son home to Qamar Haveli."

"Faqeer Sahib, I *must* see Saboor before then."

"Of course you will, son." Faqeer waved an airy hand. "Of course you will. And now, Hassan," he continued briskly, "we all know that the business of the Maharajah does not stop for durbars. The leaders of Kasur have again refused to pay the Maharajah's tribute money. You must go there and get it from them. It will take no more than a few days. After that, you will see Saboor." He nodded toward Yusuf. "And take your friend with you. At this painful time, you should have your friends."

The Faqeer's voice softened to velvet as his eyes moved from Yusuf's weapons to his face. "I am sure," he added, "that there will be no attempt to take Saboor away before the close of the durbar in fifteen days' time. You should know that anyone who tries to do so will be risking his life."

Yusuf did not look in Hassan's direction. Both men got to their feet as the Chief Minister stood and took his leave.

As they walked back to their horses, Yusuf spat onto the ground. "So even now you must wait fifteen days to embrace your son while the Faqeer caters to the Maharajah's whims!"

He tugged angrily at his horse's reins. "How can the Faqeer not take your side? Is it for the sake of the villages the Maharajah gives him? How can your father bear to be his friend? I myself would willingly kill him for his greed."

Hassan sighed wearily. "As cruel as he seems, the Faqeer is not to be hated. My father and I know what you do not. The Maharajah is dying, and has not yet chosen his heir. Faqeer Azizuddin is only trying to keep him alive until he names his successor, for if he dies without choosing, who knows what evil will befall us all? The Faqeer humors the Maharajah for the sake of the Punjab, not for himself. How can I refuse him, when so many lives are at stake?"

He shook his head. "No, it is the Maharajah whom I cannot love. And now we must do his work, but we will be back soon. Here, at least, my son will be safe from the queens."

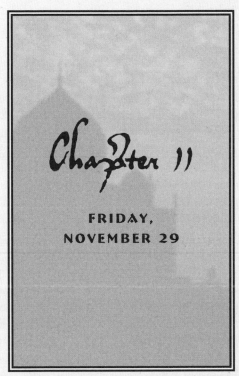

Chapter 11

**FRIDAY,
NOVEMBER 29**

At all times of day," Mariana's munshi told her one afternoon as they stood outside her tent, "there are vultures overhead. They look like black spots circling in the sky." He waved a wiry arm. "Can you see them?"

Her hand over her eyes, Mariana peered upward.

"They are searching," the munshi explained, "for dead and dying creatures on the ground below. Some people believe that they have not always been here. They say that when the Moghul king Babur first entered India, he was shocked to find the carcasses of animals lying where they had fallen, with only ants and crows to carry away their rotting flesh. 'Has India no vultures?' King Babur asked. When he was told that it did not, he sent for several pairs to be snared and brought back to him from his homeland in Central Asia. According to the story, they have remained here ever since. Whenever you look up, you will see them, making their slow circles in the sky."

Vultures soaring on their appointed rounds high above the Sutlej

River looked down on two camp cities that had arisen there in the space of only a few days.

South of the river's east-west course stood a large, orderly camp divided into two parts. In one, soldiers in red coats and white cross-belts marched to shouted orders on a newly cleared parade ground, while rows of heavy wheeled guns waited, their barrels pointing to the north.

The other part boasted a grand avenue with a red-walled compound and spacious tents. From the avenue, smaller streets spread in all directions. Thousands of tents clustered around fires whose smoke joined together to form a horizontal cloud over the camp. Men and boys tended long lines of horses, elephants, camels, and bullocks. At three separate bazaars, each a small city, men, women, and children busied themselves at various tasks—cooking, stitching, throwing pottery, hammering brass, cleaning ears, shaving hair.

At the midpoint of the camp's avenue, between the red wall and a grand tent with dancing pennants, a dozen decorated elephants knelt on the ground, their velvet housings trailing in the dust. At the avenue's far end, several troops of cavalry in dress uniforms waited on gleaming horses.

Across the river stood another camp city. This was similar to the first, but more fanciful in style, with an expanse of garden blooming at its center and a sea of silk, Kashmir shawl, and striped canvas tents stretching in gay profusion into the distance.

Here, a different body of infantry in native costume practiced intricate drills on their own new parade ground. Howitzers boomed practice shots into stands of distant trees. Brightly dressed cavalry charged imaginary enemies.

Making their way south from this camp toward a newly constructed bridge of boats across the Sutlej River, painted elephants marched behind a detachment of troops in yellow silk and chain mail along a newly cut road toward the river's bank. Beside and behind them, horses danced impatiently in the morning light, their riders aglitter. Bare-chested men in loincloths and loose, waist-length hair followed on foot. Drummers beat a steady tattoo as the procession prepared to cross the bridge on its way to the great camp on the other side.

As the first elephant stepped onto the bridge, running men carrying two palanquins approached the Maharajah's camp from the north. A dozen armed horsemen rode in their wake.

Groaning with fatigue, they made their way toward the camp's center, passing at last under a carved wooden archway into a great crowded square where broad pathways led between masses of potted chrysanthemums. The mounted guard shouted, pushing aside excited children and men carrying cloth-covered trays.

They deposited the palanquins by a silk tent, the largest of those fronting the square. The scents of musk and amber spilled from the tent, joining other smells—jasmine, orange blossoms, cooking spices, horse and elephant.

But there was only one elephant to be seen. It knelt twenty yards away, its gold-tipped tusks catching the light while courtiers climbed, one by one, up a ladder to its howdah. More men on elegantly caparisoned horses rode off toward an archway in the distance. Of a royal procession there was no sign.

With an echoing groan, the eunuch stretched his legs from the smaller palanquin and held out a hand until one of the guards pulled him to his feet. He peered about him. "Where is the Maharajah's procession? Where is it?"

Perspiration ran down his dismayed face. "We are too late!" His silks flapping, he rushed toward the squatting bearers. "This is your doing, Neeloo. You insisted on feeding the child! It is you who are to blame!"

As he swung, openhanded, at the head bearer's face, a white-haired man with a full silver beard appeared in the entrance of the silk tent.

"Stop," he said.

Arrested in midair, the eunuch's hand fell to his side as Faqeer Nuruddin, manager of the Maharajah's vast household, strode toward the palanquins. "The Maharajah waited half the morning for you to bring the child," he snapped. "Did I not tell you to have Saboor here before noon?"

The eunuch gave a high squeak, but the silver-bearded man waved an unforgiving hand. "I have no time for your lies, Gurbashan. Where is the child?"

Neeloo pointed to the carved palanquin, where a small foot protruded from beneath a curtain.

Gurbashan the eunuch bent himself nearly double. "Most Respected—"

"The boy's servant is there," Nuruddin interrupted, pointing to a small man with a sparse beard who squatted in the shade of a nearby tent. "His name is Ahmad. He is to dress the child and take him to the Maharajah."

He smiled grimly. "You are fortunate that one of the elephants was kept back."

His attention snagged by another problem, Nuruddin moved off, leaving the eunuch to dart away toward the waiting servant.

"—very important to the Maharajah." Gurbashan gestured grandly as he hurried back, followed by Ahmad, who walked with a long, rolling stride. "He is the son of Hassan Ali Khan of the Maharajah's court, and the grandson of Shaikh Waliullah of Lahore City."

At the sound of those names, the little servant's eyes widened briefly.

They had reached the palanquin. Gurbashan flung back the curtains, covered his nose, and bent down.

He pulled back, his face puckering in disgust as the sweetish smell of unwashed human skin rushed out of the palki. "I do not care what you do with him," he told Ahmad, "only do it quickly. I have had enough of this brat."

"He is hungry," the head bearer offered, as the servant squatted down and looked inside. "We last fed him—"

"Quiet! What have you to do with this?" the eunuch snarled at Neeloo. "You will be punished for making us late. Do not think you will evade my wrath. And you, Ahmad," he said, turning to the servant, "dress him in his court clothes and be quick about it. And do not forget his necklace of emeralds and pearls, his gift from the Maharajah."

He glanced down briefly as Ahmad the servant lifted the baby from the palki. "We are fortunate. He is most likely too ill to cry. Let us hope," he added briskly, "that he does not die before the end of the day. But if he does," he raised his hands, palms outward, "it will not be my work."

Neeloo and the other bearers did not speak as they trotted away to find water, food, and a place to rest.

"Do you think, as I do," asked the oldest bearer finally, "that the child in the palki is different from other children?"

Neeloo nodded. "Yes," he replied firmly, "he is different."

SABOOR sat unmoving on the ground while the bearded servant studied him carefully, examining bruised skin and frail limbs.

"Look at this small one, grandson of Shaikh Waliullah," Ahmad said aloud. "What does he need?" He poked through Saboor's things. "He needs his clothes and he needs his necklace. But as to his state, it is very bad."

He shook his head worriedly, looking about him at the people eddying to and fro on the paths of the Maharajah's potted garden. Among them, a water carrier swung his goatskin, spraying the path with droplets of water to keep down the dust. The little servant stood up and beckoned. "Oh, Bhisti, come this way!"

"What do you need?" the man asked with the good nature of all water carriers. The full goatskin on his back dragged one of his shoulders downward. The bhisti was small and wiry, but he walked with the characteristically wide, heavy gait of the water carrier. He looked down at the child. "Ah," he said, comprehending, "the boy needs a bath."

He readied his skin as Ahmad pulled off Saboor's unclean shirt and pajamas, then poured water over the child's head until his hair ceased to be matted and his skin no longer stank of neglect. Ahmad wiped the crust from Saboor's nose and the tear stains from his cheeks, then dried and dressed him in a pair of fine satin pajamas and an embroidered satin tunic with gold buttons. While the bhisti looked on with interest, his now empty goatskin slung over his shoulder, Ahmad set Saboor's round embroidered cap on his wet curls and hung the rope of emeralds and pearls about his neck.

"What bruises he has," remarked the water carrier as they admired their work. "May whoever has hurt this beautiful child endure ten times his pain in retribution."

"God is Great," replied Ahmad sadly as he drew Saboor to him and got to his feet.

A man passed carrying a heavy tray of sweetmeats. "Stop," Ahmad called, and ran after him, the child bouncing in his arms.

Moments later, holding Saboor against his shoulder with one hand and a milky sweet in the other, Ahmad the servant climbed up the elephant ladder and into the crowded howdah. There he broke the sugary square into small pieces and put them, one by one, into the baby's mouth.

Chapter 12

"Memsahib, Memsahib, you must hurry!" Dittoo cried, hoarse from excitement. "Maharajah Ranjit Singh has come. He is at the end of the avenue with all his nobles, readying himself for the procession!"

Mariana stabbed a last pin into her hair, snatched up her bonnet, and rushed toward the main entrance.

Miss Emily and Miss Fanny sat in front of the great tent, in the first of a double row of occupied chairs. As Mariana crossed the avenue past Major Byrne's new staircase, Miss Fanny beckoned her to hurry, pointing to the lone empty seat beside her.

Behind the chairs, an expanse of white cloth covered the reception tent floor. Someone had lined the walls with chests of drawers, tables, and chairs, in an effort to imitate an English drawing room. Beyond, in another, smaller tent, Miss Emily's sofa and the least travel damaged of the dining-room chairs had been arranged in a half circle.

Miss Emily turned and surveyed the arrangements. "I am sorry for poor George," she sighed. "I can see his bedside table by the doorway. They might at least have left him somewhere to put his book."

"I am pleased they have not taken my bed," returned Miss Fanny in a stage whisper.

A large crowd had gathered along the avenue. Mariana stirred in her seat. Where was *he*? The red coats across the avenue belonged to the infantry. The blue-coated artillery, Fitzgerald among them, must be somewhere else.

Miss Fanny leaned confidentially toward her. "Poor Emily has had dreadful stomach spasms all morning. I do not know whether she will be able to last out the durbar."

On Miss Fanny's other side, Miss Emily sniffed. "I most assuredly *will* last out this durbar. If necessary, I shall have my bed carried to every review and every dinner. I have not come all this way to—"

The crowd's voices rose with excitement. Children ran out of sight around the side of the tent, then reappeared, dancing excitedly, as Lord Auckland rounded the corner on a large elephant, alone save for his mahout.

"Ah," breathed Miss Fanny, "have you ever seen the like of George's elephant? What artists these natives are!"

The elephant's state housings of ruby red velvet, heavily worked in gold, fell below its knees. Its massive face, above gold-painted tusks, was a mask of indigo and carnelian. A fringed canopy of gold brocade on four gold posts shaded the curved, golden howdah.

Miss Emily pursed her lips. "A charming effect, like that of a fairy tale. I have never seen George dressed entirely in gold tissue and brocade. What a pity," she added as her brother looked down and offered her a private, lopsided smile. "I don't think he *likes* being a fairy prince."

European and native soldiers now lined the avenue, craning their heads expectantly in both directions. Children of shopkeepers and camp servants ran, shouting with excitement, among the crowd. Behind the troops, servants stood on boxes, grinning and pushing one another.

Where *was* Fitzgerald? Mariana peered up and down for several breathless minutes, until a British officer galloped past at full tilt, waving his hat over his head, signaling that the Maharajah's party had begun its advance. Orders echoed up and down the avenue. The rows of troops jerked to attention and presented arms.

THE Maharajah rode alone in his gem-encrusted howdah, his tall elephant dwarfing the horses of his mounted guard. Behind him, among a group of dignitaries, the king's only legitimate adult son, Kharrak Singh, gnawed his fingernails and stared vacantly down at the pageantry while, in one corner of the howdah, a little servant gripped a frail baby with one hand and the railing with the other.

The Maharajah's most senior ministers and advisors followed on other elephants, also surrounded by a swirling throng of men and horses. Riders danced their horses in the Maharajah's train, while behind each horse, grasping its tail as he ran, flew a half-naked man, his long hair streaming out behind him. Village children darted in and out of the line of elephants, risking death for the sake of the coins the Maharajah showered onto the crowd from a basket at his feet.

At a command, the Maharajah's wiry little mahout leaned over and spoke to his charge. As the elephant, responding, began to trot, the Maharajah tossed the last of his coins over the side of the howdah and reached, smiling, for a handhold. Little boys broke from the fighting crowd and raced beside the lumbering procession, coughing at the clouds of dust that rose from under the elephants' feet.

On the second speeding elephant, the servant Ahmad began to pray soundlessly, his eyes closed, while the baby drooped in his arms.

AS the Maharajah's train came swaying into view, Lord Auckland's mahout urged his own elephant to a lumbering trot. Behind him, the decorated elephants of the other officials followed suit. Peacock feather fans, tasseled standards, and crook-shaped silver sticks bobbed beside the lead animal, their bearers sprinting now to stay abreast of the elephants.

Alone in front, Lord Auckland jounced on his flimsy golden seat, his face pale with nerves. "Slow *down,* slow *down,* I say!" he shouted, one hand holding down his golden tricorn.

The mahout, who understood no English, took Lord Auckland's shouts for cries of encouragement, and urged his elephant to run faster.

BAGPIPES began to wail. Mariana searched the avenue with her eyes. Miss Fanny reached for Miss Emily with one hand, and for her handkerchief with the other.

"Oh, Emily," she quavered, "I am so very proud of George, and of England!"

The music grew louder. Cheers erupted from the troops along the avenue as the two parties advanced toward each other, each one heralded by a great storm of dust.

"Something is wrong," declared Miss Fanny, as two British cavalry officers rode, shouting, into the avenue, waving their swords. "I think they are coming too fast."

"Look!" Miss Emily pointed to their right as the first of the Maharajah's elephants appeared, as if from a dusty dream, two hundred yards away.

It came at surprising speed, its single passenger shielded from the sun by a great tasseled parasol. More elephants and a swirling throng of outriders and standard bearers followed. Chain mail flashed in the sun.

A moment later, Lord Auckland burst out of the swirling dust cloud to their left, leading his own running elephants and four companies of Bengal Lancers straight at the Maharajah's procession.

"They can never stop now," breathed Miss Fanny.

Miss Fanny and Miss Emily sat rigidly upright in their pale silks, neither moving nor speaking. Mariana held her breath and looked from side to side at the two processions. How were they to escape crashing into each other? She looked behind her and found Dr. Drummond, the vicar, and an elderly visiting scholar wedged together behind her in the second row of chairs. All seemed mesmerized by the impending collision.

As the two trains closed rapidly on one another, the lead mahouts stood on their elephants' necks, iron prods waving, their shouted commands lost in the martial din of the bands. Deserting both processions, runners and outriders dropped their tasseled standards and peacock feathers and raced for the margins of the avenue. Soldiers and onlookers scattered as they ran.

"Get up, man, run for your life!" cried the doctor from behind Miss Fanny's chair. As one, the three men behind Mariana bolted up and began to climb over their chairs. Mariana half stood, then realized that she could not get over her own high-backed chair while wearing six yards of blue-striped skirts. She had waited too long to run onto the avenue. She bent double on her seat, making herself as small as possible.

Abandoning language at last, the mahouts signaled wildly with their arms. The Maharajah's elephant veered left. With a great tearing sound, it crashed past Lord Auckland's elephant, carrying away with it a dozen yards of velvet housings and a corner of the British state howdah.

"Ahhhhh!" Abandoned by the doctor and the vicar, the poor old scholar let out a terrified scream.

Dust filled Mariana's nose and mouth. Waves of chaos washed over her as the remaining animals, still advancing at speed, sought a way out of certain disaster, their frightened trumpeting accompanied by the bellows of excited natives and the clamor of competing bands.

Some were able to turn aside, but others could not help but collide while their mahouts clutched the harnesses for balance and the occupants of the howdahs were flung about like rag dolls.

Had anyone been thrown out of the howdahs? If so, they had certainly been killed. Mariana gripped Miss Fanny's hand as Lord Auckland's elephant, trembling with fright, its damaged howdah apparently now empty, stumbled toward their row of chairs.

"*Shabash,* well done!" its mahout shouted happily, slapping away at his elephant's head as Lord Auckland reappeared suddenly, miraculously upright on his seat, knocking dents from his tricorn hat. "Well done!"

Beside Mariana, Miss Fanny remained immobile, her eyes straight ahead, a statue in dusty silk and ribbons.

The mahouts maneuvered the two lead elephants until the animals were side by side. Many hands dragged the Maharajah's small, red-clad figure headfirst into the Governor-General's howdah. A swarm of grooms led Lord Auckland's nervous elephant to the specially constructed stairway where Lord Auckland and Ranjit Singh, one tall and pale, the other tiny and dark skinned, offered one another their embraces—the Maharajah with enthusiasm, Lord Auckland with solemnity.

Only then did Miss Fanny turn, her face alight, to Mariana. "Is this not marvelous, my dear?" she cried. "Is this not a wonderful spectacle?" She pressed her hands together. "One can only wonder what will happen next!"

Chapter 13

The child Saboor still in his arms, Ahmad the servant looked down from the kneeling elephant. The clash at the meeting had thrown them to the howdah's floor injuring Ahmad's wrist, but the child seemed unhurt.

They were alone on the elephant. When the confusion waned, their fellow passengers had all scrambled down the elephant ladder to the ground and followed the Maharajah into the durbar tent. Even the elephant's mahout had now vanished.

Men surged along the avenue, soldiers and onlookers swirling around the row of kneeling elephants. Ahmad rubbed his swelling wrist while the baby lay silent on his shoulder. "Baba is not well," he said aloud, his eyes on the durbar tent. "He should not be taken into that crowd."

He wiped his forehead with his uninjured hand. "Baba must have his food. Who knows when this meeting will finish?"

Holding Saboor, he climbed gingerly down the elephant ladder, then stood still, searching the torrent of soldiers and onlookers for someone useful.

"Oh, cook," he called to a man whose clothes smelled of wood smoke and spices, "will you make me food for this child?"

The cook, a round-faced man, came near. He peered at the baby who lay unmoving against Ahmad's shoulder. "I am a poor man," he replied seriously, "and this child is of rich birth. Surely you can pay for what I give him?"

When Ahmad did not answer, the man poked a thick finger at Saboor's fine clothes.

"Give me a gold button from this baba's suit and I will make you both a dinner fit for the Maharajah himself."

MARIANA let herself be swept with everyone else toward the durbar tent. Dark-skinned men with silk turbans, earrings and necklaces, men with luxuriant beards and mustaches, seemed to be everywhere. Behind her, a horde of British officers pushed aside sentries and aides-de-camp in their own rush to gain admittance to the tent.

Inside, the crowd surged forward, carrying Mariana through the main tent and toward the inner tent with its sofa and dining chairs. Someone barked an order and, with a rush of canvas, the main door flap unrolled to the ground, drenching the packed tents in near-perfect darkness.

The small tent's outer doorway had also been closed, cutting off air circulation. Murmuring arose around Mariana as she groped her way to the half circle of dining chairs and seated herself. She waited for her eyes to adjust to the darkness, then blinked with relief when she made out Miss Fanny beside her, struggling to get out of her shawls in the sudden stifling heat, and Miss Emily, fanning herself on one end of the sofa.

Her chair rocked as someone pressed against it from behind. Where was the Maharajah? As Mariana strained to see, Lord Auckland appeared, one hand gripping the red silk elbow of a tiny, one-eyed, silver-bearded native, the other arm straight out before him as he battled their way toward the sofa. Arriving, he pushed the old Maharajah down without ceremony next to Miss Emily, then sat on his other side.

The hot air thickened. An English voice shouted an order and the crowd edged back as the blackness of the inner tent turned to gray. "Someone has opened the main entrance again, thank goodness," murmured Miss Fanny, "but whatever is wrong with George?"

Turning to look, Mariana saw Lord Auckland sitting perfectly still at the Maharajah's side, his eyes starting from his head as he stared at someone behind her.

No—something was wrong with the little Maharajah. His red-turbaned head had fallen forward onto his chest; his long silver beard rested against the row of fat pearls at his waist. He seemed unconscious of the handsome youth draped in emeralds who had appeared at his feet and now sat kneading his legs and gazing up anxiously into his face.

The perspiring throng shifted. A group of Sikhs forced their way toward the sofa, their eyes on their stricken king, their hands on the dagger handles protruding from their sashes.

Near Mariana, a pair of unarmed British officials watched nervously. Major Byrne caught hold of a young officer of the Thirteenth Foot, whispered to him, then pushed him toward the doorway.

A trickle of perspiration began at the crease behind Mariana's knee and ran down the back of her calf. Behind Mariana, the Sikhs muttered to each other. Every one of them carried at least two weapons. Lord Auckland edged away from the Maharajah and perched, his jowls quivering, on the edge of the sofa.

At last the air began to move. The outside door of the small tent was open.

The old Maharajah raised his head and looked straight at Mariana. Ignoring her sudden lightheadedness, she gazed back at him, avidly memorizing his appearance: his long, pointed silver beard, his closed blind eye, his luminous, intelligent seeing eye, the humor on his face.

As a wave of collective relief blew through the tent, a shrewd-looking man with a thick black beard and a coarse woolen robe sat down at the Maharajah's knee, greeted Lord Auckland, and began, without irony, to deliver, in Urdu, a series of elaborate compliments involving perfumed gardens and the song of nightingales, while Mr. Macnaghten the political secretary translated rapidly from his chair beside the sofa.

The man on the floor speaking with such ease, turning his hands for emphasis, must be Faqeer Azizuddin, the Maharajah's Chief Minister. His title of Faqeer, Munshi Sahib had told her, denoted humility, although seed pearls gleamed on the loose shirt he wore under his cheap-looking robe. Mariana surreptitiously mopped her face. It was astonishing that anyone could talk of gardens in this stifling, noisy place.

As the crowd parted again to allow an officer to carry in Queen Victoria's portrait upon its plump velvet cushion, a new unpleasant feeling in Mariana's stomach joined the one in her head. She closed her eyes, measuring her discomfort. This was too unfair. It was Miss

Emily who had suffered all morning from spasms. And yet *she* now sat, smiling composedly, on her end of the sofa. Mariana, who had waited months for this moment, realized that if she did not immediately leave the tent, she would either fall from her chair in a dead faint, or be sick onto the carpet, or both.

As the Maharajah reached for the Queen's portrait, a deafening noise erupted outside, eclipsing the voices around Mariana. The pain sharpened in her head. She thrust herself to her feet, a hand to her mouth.

"I hope they are firing that salute away from the horses," she heard a British voice say as she clawed her way toward the doorway. Ahead of her, a tall bearded native was also leaving the tent, helping her unknowingly by opening a way for her, his long embroidered coat acting as a beacon guiding her through the half-dark. After reaching the entrance, he paused for a moment, as if searching for someone, then strode rapidly across the avenue.

YAR Mohammad's eyes roamed the avenue as he waited by the durbar tent with Major Byrne's gift horses. When Shafi Sahib had instructed him to locate the Shaikh's grandson among the members of the Maharajah's court, he had thought his task would be easy; but of a small male child there was no sign. Perhaps Saboor Baba was already inside the tent, having passed invisibly by in the crowd.

Beside Yar Mohammad, a young groom smacked dust from his new clothes. "What riches, what jewels we have seen!" he marveled.

Yar Mohammad nodded. Even Qamar Haveli, the most important house he had ever visited, did not compare in wealth to this. For all his fame, not even Shaikh Waliullah owned an animal like the draped and painted elephants that stood tethered across the avenue, or even the horses like the one whose bridle he now held.

A sudden movement caught his eye. A familiar-looking man erupted from the durbar tent, glanced about him, then hurried onto the avenue toward the elephants.

Behind him, another figure staggered into the sunlight, a hand to her head. It was the young memsahib.

Yar Mohammad turned back to the avenue in time to see Hassan reach the tethered elephants and begin speaking, his hands moving, to someone squatting in the shade.

Hassan was still breathing hard when Yar Mohammad arrived at his side. The former looked less ill than he had at his father's house, but shadows still marked his eyes. He was glowering at the squatting man, who scrambled to his feet.

"You are saying that the child came here on your elephant, but now he is gone?"

"As I have told you, Huzoor," replied the mahout, "the servant must have taken the baby with him. I did not see which direction he took. If I had known . . ." He shrugged.

Hassan glanced at Yar Mohammad without recognition, then turned back to the mahout. "Describe the servant," he ordered.

"He walks with long strides," said the man, "and he stands like this." He bent his shoulders forward to hollow his chest. "His name," he added helpfully, "is Ahmad."

Yar Mohammad shifted his feet. "Peace, Sahib," he offered.

Hassan turned. At close quarters he was nearly as tall as Yar Mohammad himself. "Speak," he ordered carelessly, his impatient gaze wandering past Yar Mohammad's shoulder to the men on the avenue.

Yar Mohammad pointed to where the gift elephant and horses stood waiting. "If what this man says is true, Saboor Baba was not carried past the horses. If he had been, I would have seen him."

Before Yar Mohammad could add anything more, Yusuf Bhatti joined them, red-faced from hurrying, and took hold of Hassan's arm.

"I have waited by the guns since the processions arrived," he said without preamble. "I have not seen Saboor. He must not have come with the procession."

"He came." Hassan waved irritably at the kneeling animal whose ladder still stood against its side. "He was on this elephant, and now he has gone, no one knows where."

Yusuf Bhatti blinked. "What is to be done now?"

"Saboor is not lost."

All four men turned toward the gentle voice beside them. Shafi Sahib, friend of Shaikh Waliullah and interpreter of dreams, gestured toward the guarded entrance in the red canvas wall. "I, too, waited," he told them. "Although he is not to be seen, I can assure you that Saboor is not lost. Have patience, my dear Hassan. God is kind."

"Shafi Sahib," Hassan said, opening his hands, "the Chief Minister has ordered me to go to Kasur this afternoon. If I do not see Saboor now, when will I see him?" He closed his eyes. "Pray, Shafi Sahib, that I will see my son alive."

Poor man. Yar Mohammad thought of Nusrat, his solemn little daughter, the light of his eyes, who waited for him in his mountain village. How would he endure her absence if she, too, were to vanish?

Shafi Sahib nodded. "Your father and everyone at Qamar Haveli are praying for you. *Inshallah,* if God wills, we will all see Saboor soon."

"Look." Yusuf pointed across the avenue.

At one side of the durbar tent, a score of coolies with ropes over their shoulders dragged a pair of howitzers toward a pyramid of gunpowder shells.

Sikh nobles and British officers began to pour from the durbar tent and move toward the guns.

"ARE you quite well, Mariana?" The dry voice startled Mariana as she slumped, pushing loose hair into her bonnet, in one of the visitors' chairs.

"I am astonished at your behavior," Miss Emily added as Mariana got, waveringly, to her feet. "Why did you rush out of the tent just when we were presenting the Queen's picture? Everyone saw you do it."

"I suddenly felt very unwell. I am sorry, Miss Emily, Miss Fanny." Mariana patted her upper lip with her crumpled handkerchief.

Miss Emily sniffed. "I do not care how you felt. You must never behave that way again." She held out an armful of shawls. "And take these. I cannot carry them a moment longer."

The air had done Mariana some good. Clutching the shawls, she followed the two sisters to the side of the tent, where they watched the presentation of the animals. But it was the guns she really needed to see, brand-new and gleaming, each barrel emblazoned with the Maharajah's crest. It was often the heavy guns that decided a battle. She could name several important—

She gasped. In front of her, at attention before the two howitzers, stood a double row of men in the dress uniform of the Bengal Horse Artillery. At one end of the first row, his saber at his side, stood Lieutenant Harry Fitzgerald, his eyes fixed on the air above her head.

"Oh, dear," murmured Miss Fanny.

"There is *no* need for us to notice the honor guard." Miss Emily gripped Mariana firmly above the elbow and marched her toward the pile of artillery shells. "The view is perfectly good from here," she declared as she stopped. "Look, here come my brother and the Maharajah!"

A sound beside Mariana caused her to turn her head. The tall bearded courtier who had preceded her from the tent now stood beside her. He raked the crowd with weary eyes, as if searching for something he had lost.

Sadness seemed to pour from him. When he moved, his beautiful coat gave off the scent of sandalwood.

Munshi Sahib had once brought her vials of scented oil: rose, amber, musk. Her favorite had been the warm, inviting, complicated scent of sandalwood.

Fitzgerald might have worn sandalwood, if she had asked him to.

The crowd shifted to let Lord Auckland and the Maharajah approach the waiting howitzers. Both men looked exhausted after so much ceremony, Lord Auckland clammy faced in his wilted finery, the little Maharajah tottering weakly beside him.

Major Byrne and Sotheby had stationed themselves behind the pyramid of shells, the major red-faced and smug, Sotheby blinking anxiously.

As the Maharajah approached to inspect the guns, the crowd pushed forward. A voice shouted a warning as someone knocked into the carefully arranged shell pyramid. As Mariana watched, still holding Miss Emily's shawls, the top shell slowly disengaged itself from the others and rolled down one side of the pyramid into the Maharajah's path.

He saw it too late. Gaining speed, it caught him at his ankles, knocking him off balance. Before anyone could catch him, Ranjit Singh, Maharajah of the Punjab, lay flat in the dust before the British guns.

Miss Emily's hand closed on Mariana's wrist as, aroused, the Sikh bodyguards reached once again for their weapons. The sad man beside Mariana launched himself forward, his fine coat flapping, but before he could reach the Maharajah, Major Byrne and the White Rabbit had dragged the old man to his feet, while Lord Auckland stared into the distance, pretending not to have seen.

"A bad omen, very bad," someone muttered in Punjabi. "These British will bring nothing but evil to this country."

Mariana looked to see who had spoken, but could only make out the back of the clever-looking Chief Minister's coarse robe as he led his Maharajah away.

Chapter 14

SUNDAY,
DECEMBER 1

"We need not have worried so about the Maharajah's camp," Miss Fanny remarked two evenings later, over the drumming of the Maharajah's musicians, as her eyes studied the embroidered canopy above their heads. "His tents are very fine, to be sure, but they are quite as dusty as ours. And have you noticed the plants? No one could have watered them for days."

Hundreds of small oil lamps flickered in the outdoor enclosure where they sat wrapped against the evening chill, the Maharajah with his feet under him on his golden, bowl-shaped throne, his egg-sized Koh-i-noor diamond refracting the flames of the lamps from a heavy bracelet upon his upper arm.

Behind Lord Auckland's silver chair, Harry Fitzgerald looked over Mariana's head, unbearably handsome in gold braid. Moments ago, he had caught her eye and given her the faintest of nods.

The Maharajah was now talking to Lord Auckland through his black-bearded Chief Minister, his hands rising and falling. Earlier in the evening he, too, had caught Mariana's eye, but the old ruler's look had held no warmth, only appraisal, as he leaned from his throne to speak to his minister. Now she felt his single eye on her again, and saw to her discomfort that it had fastened upon her bare chest and shoulders, both exposed by the pretty neckline of her borrowed gown. Before she could look away, he had treated her to an open-faced leer.

"If consulted," said Miss Emily in an undertone as the seated musicians began to play faster, "I should say we have had a sufficient number of dancing girls for one evening. I believe I have seen all the undulating and stamping I can endure. Look, here is a fresh one, just when I had hoped it was all over. And Mariana," she added, raising her eyebrows, "why have you wrapped yourself like a mummy in that shawl? I thought you looked quite nice in your blue-and-white."

A girl with a dozen gold bangles on each arm stepped forward to stand before Lord Auckland. While he gazed over her head, she began a delicate, soaring song, accompanied by the twanging of the instruments. Her voice was fine and supple and so filled with longing that Mariana shivered.

"In pursuit of your image
My distracted thought
Has wandered everywhere,
Like a pauper's lamp."

"What is that fat girl shrieking about?" Miss Emily asked. "She seems to have fallen in love with George at first sight."

Mariana sighed. Did this song, too, describe the soul's longing for God, or was she allowed to give it her own meaning?

"She says her thoughts have wandered everywhere in pursuit of her beloved. It is a poem."

Miss Emily sniffed. "How they do exaggerate. It would have been quite enough to say she was pleased to see George."

How well Mariana understood those plaintive words! For all his nearness, Fitzgerald might have been a thousand miles from her.

"I am both close to Thee," her own poem had read, *"and immeasurably far away—"*

"Ah," Miss Emily said later, nodding with satisfaction toward the dancing girls and their musicians, "that must have been the final song. See, they are all going away. We shall leave soon, thank heaven."

As the last of the entertainers drifted away, a small servant appeared at the Maharajah's side, carrying a baby boy. The child in his arms, he followed the Maharajah toward the waiting elephants. Mariana stared after them. How curious these people were, letting such a tiny child stay up until midnight! Why would the Maharajah want to have a baby with him now? The child's eyes drooped with exhaustion, but, strangely, he turned his head, searching the crowd as if he were looking for something important.

"I have invited Lieutenant Marks to dinner, Mariana," Miss Emily announced the following evening, smoothing her blond satin skirts with her palm, "in hopes that he will see the need to show his hand. There is not much time left before we sign the treaty and the army leaves for Afghanistan."

Mariana felt her toes curling inside her boots. "Show his hand, Miss Emily?"

Miss Emily opened her fan with a little snap. "If he is interested, he should say so. And since a little competition might be encouraging, you are to have Peter Edwardes on your other side. Edwardes has been pestering me about it for days."

The breeze from Miss Emily's fan carried a hint of violet water. Mariana bit her lip. Colin Marks, Peter Edwardes, the White Rabbit—they were all the same to her. Let Miss Emily marry them herself.

"The girl needs to be pushed," Miss Emily whispered loudly, as she and Miss Fanny walked toward the dining tent with Mariana close behind. "Marks is the most suitable of them. I know his uncle. There is no point in her waiting, now that Fitzgerald has been disqualified. She should choose *someone* before they all leave for Afghanistan. A number of them are quite eager. . . ."

As they entered the tent several young officers stopped talking and bowed in their direction.

"There you are, my dear." Her skirts rustling, Miss Emily turned. "You remember Lieutenant Colin Marks of the Queen's Buffs." She nodded toward the little man who bowed elaborately beside her. "I have put him on your left this evening."

Marks's ears were not only large, they were hairy. Behind him, also bowing, was Harry Fitzgerald's curly-haired friend from the Waterloo dinner.

Fifteen minutes later, as conversations rose and fell around the table, Marks bent toward her, his soup spoon in his hand. "I fear, Miss Givens," he said, favoring her with a patronizing smile, "that I sit here under false pretenses."

"False pretenses, Lieutenant Marks?" This was agony. Mariana stole a glance toward Peter Edwardes on her right. He was Fitzgerald's friend. How much did he know of the past?

"Yes." Marks lowered his voice confidentially. "My name is not Colin, it is actually *Bartholomew* Colin. I wish you to know *everything* about me."

The hair sprouting from his ears appeared thicker than ever. His shin was within reach of Mariana's booted foot. She crossed her ankles decisively under the table.

It was another full hour before the table turned. At last, her face stiff from trying to smile, she turned to her right in time to see Lieutenant Edwardes tip back his head and swallow half a glass of wine in one gulp.

"Good evening." He inclined his head. "Glad to sit beside a woman who knows military strategy. Heard you talking about Waterloo some time back. You agreed with Fitzgerald. Good man, Fitzgerald." He nodded several times.

Mariana pushed bits of vegetable around her plate. Her appetite had long since vanished. "Have you and Lieutenant Fitzgerald known each other long?" she asked cautiously.

"Since I came out here. Must be three years now. We are the best of friends," Edwardes added, nodding significantly.

Three years! Mariana put down her knife. "And were you in Calcutta a year ago?"

"I was."

"Then you must know what happened with the young lady, his fiancée?" She held her breath.

He swayed toward her, red-eyed in the candlelight. "You have heard ill of him," he said in a stage whisper, "and you want the truth." His head bobbed up and down. "Thought you would ask."

This was madness. The man had clearly had too much to drink.

"I'll tell you, then, but you, Miss Givens, must keep it to yourself." Edwardes wagged a finger in her direction. "People know you are fond of Fitzgerald. If you repeat this story, they will, if you will excuse me, think you are stupid with love."

Stupid with love! Mariana snatched up her knife and fork and attacked her roast venison.

"Two years ago," Edwardes began, ignoring her scowl, "a young lady came out from England. Exceptionally pretty she was. Miss Owen was her name. Several men took a liking to her, Fitzgerald among them. I was not in Calcutta at the time, so I missed his marriage proposal."

Edwardes glanced at her. "Are you all right, Miss Givens?"

"Yes," she snapped, so loudly that the White Rabbit glanced up from across the table.

"Harry and Miss Owen became engaged," Edwardes went on,

"not officially, of course, as they had not yet had permission from his commanding officer or her guardian. Only one or two of us knew."

He took another gulp of burgundy, then wiped his mouth, trailing his napkin in the gravy on his plate as he did so. "By the time I returned to Calcutta and met Harry and Miss Owen at the usual dinners and balls, she had begun paying attention to another man. This man, you see, was to inherit a little money, while Harry has no prospects of that sort. When Harry found them together, he understood her game, and broke the engagement."

"Game?" Mariana repeated.

"Miss Owen had been using Harry for safety while she pursued the other man, who naturally dropped her when he learned what she was doing. She returned, husbandless, to England." He snorted. "Served her right."

A pair of finely wrought silver peacocks stood opposite Mariana in the center of the table. She stared past them at the tent's open doorway. The woman had been an adventuress! How could Fitzgerald have been taken in?

The White Rabbit giggled at someone's joke. Edwardes yawned behind his stained napkin. "Later, to save face, Miss Owen told people that Harry had jilted her for someone with a better income."

Mariana picked up her wineglass, then put it down again.

"Harry took it well, good man, and never revealed the truth, but life in Calcutta was difficult for him afterwards. The Afghan Campaign was a godsend for him. Got him out of there. But now, of course, everyone here knows, so it's all the same." Edwardes shrugged.

"Does *everyone* in Calcutta know?"

"Oh, yes. *Her* version." He sighed. "Poor Harry."

Mariana pushed away her uneaten food. In her mind's eye, Fitzgerald rode his gray horse, stood guard at the howitzers, kissed her. "Why doesn't he tell the real story now?"

"Who would believe him? It is too late."

THE fruit had been taken away. The men stood as the Eden sisters and Mariana rose from the table and made their way out of the dining tent's back entrance, leaving the gentlemen to their brandy.

"Well, Mariana," began Miss Emily as she subsided into a basket chair positioned between the tents, "I observed you deep in conversation with Lieutenant Marks over the fish."

Over the fish, Marks had given Mariana a scrupulously detailed account of trout fishing in Galway with his rich uncle.

"Colin Marks is well suited to you, my dear," said Miss Fanny warmly. "According to everyone, he is an able young officer, and he stands to inherit property. It is thought he will go far in the army."

Miss Emily shook out her skirts. "Now we shall see whether he offers to see you to your tent."

Unable to contain herself, Mariana let out a great, noisy sigh. Both sisters frowned.

An hour later, sounds faded inside the dining tent as the dinner guests began to leave by the main doorway. Servants shouted to each other across the compound. Jimmund, the servant of Miss Emily's dog, came out of Miss Emily's tent with Chance under his arm. The Eden ladies rustled quietly.

"Ah, here comes someone," said Miss Emily with satisfaction.

A figure emerged from the dining tent's back door.

"May I have the honor of seeing Miss Givens to her tent?" inquired a swaying Peter Edwardes.

She was to be spared Colin Marks. Mariana made no effort to contain her broad, delighted smile.

As she and Edwardes started away, she looked over her shoulder to see the Eden sisters gazing after them in the semidarkness.

"Sorry I took so long," Edwardes muttered, when they had rounded a corner of the tent. "Had to outflank that fool Marks. I have a surprise for you, Miss Givens."

Waiting in the shadow of the dining tent, a finger to his lips, stood Harry Fitzgerald.

"Are you surprised?" he asked quietly as they watched Edwardes weave his way toward the main entrance.

"Yes," she whispered. She looked over her shoulder, her heart thumping. "You have taken such a risk!"

"It doesn't matter," he said. He looked strained, but his hand felt warm and strong when he squeezed her fingers. "I could bear it no longer. Yesterday evening you were not seven feet from me, and I could scarcely look at you for fear Miss Emily would see. And Marks has been puffed up for days."

"I *hate* Colin Marks," she whispered.

Fitzgerald's uniform was unbuttoned at the neck. Mariana drank in his profile as he walked beside her. "What has Peter told you?" he asked, after a moment.

"Everything," she replied.

Her heart was still racing as they reached her tent. She stopped, anticipating Fitzgerald's embrace, but before she could close her eyes he grasped her by the shoulders and kissed her awkwardly, his teeth banging hers.

"Oh, Mariana . . ." His breath thickened as he fumbled at the front of her gown.

"Stop! What are you doing?" She took a step backward and glared at him. "I do not like that at *all*."

Still breathing hard, Fitzgerald peered at her in the shadows. He dropped his hands. "I'm a clumsy fool," he muttered. "Forgive me, Mariana. I've been miserable without you."

His brass buttons gleamed in the starlight. He *was* clumsy, and he *had* been duped by Miss Owen in Calcutta, but he had not jilted her, and Peter Edwardes had called him a good man. Best of all, he had been miserable without her.

"Well," she offered, "other people can be clumsy, too. Last Monday I fell off my horse in front of everyone."

He returned her smile, then wrapped his arms about her and gave her the kiss she wanted.

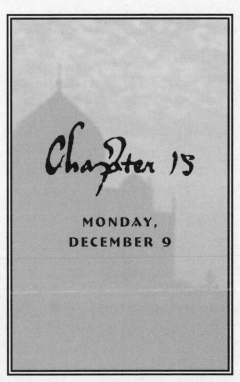

Chapter 15

**MONDAY,
DECEMBER 9**

"Nine days, Macnaghten." Lord Auckland stopped partway up his elephant ladder to look balefully down at his political secretary. "Nine days and nights of drinking, dancing girls, bawdy jokes, fireworks, lavish costumes, and potted plants. Nine days of gifts given and received, and not one hour of real facts. Not *one moment's* discussion of the Afghan Campaign. We *must* get Ranjit Singh to come to terms over the campaign and sign this treaty."

He climbed into the howdah, sat down on the narrow satin-covered seat, and rested a hand gingerly on his waistcoat. "I did not sleep at all last night after his dinner party. Never mind the poisonous food—whoever drew up the regulations on durbars and native princes should have been warned about the man's *wine*. Englishmen should be expressly forbidden to drink the stuff." He sighed. "I had at least three glasses of it. I was forced to keep one foot on the floor all night to stop my bed from turning somersaults. I suppose, Macnaghten," he added, as his political secretary climbed up, puffing, and took his seat, "as you were sitting on the Maharajah's blind side, *you* were able to pour *your* wine onto the ground."

"I was, my lord, yes," replied Macnaghten apologetically. "I poured it away all evening."

Lord Auckland stared glumly down at the honor guard below. "The old goat did not take his eyes from my cup. Someone told me his wine is made from raisins and ground pearls. Tell me, Macnaghten, when you poured it away, did it actually burn a hole in the carpet?"

The political secretary would have preferred to ride, as he usually did, with his dear friend Major Byrne, but this time there had been no escaping the Governor-General. "My lord," he said, gripping the howdah's railing with unnecessary tightness, "I have attempted every possible stratagem to get the Maharajah to come to terms. I have exhausted my store of compliments. At today's meeting I had just started off with some nonsense about the sun shining down a hundred years from now on the glories of both England and the Punjab, when the old man actually *interrupted* me to say in that irritating way of his that the two nations, hand in hand, would conquer Afghanistan, that it would be a 'great show.' "

Lord Auckland gave a wan smile. "A 'great show'! What a waste of time this is!"

THE next day's meeting had already consumed two hours. Outside the Maharajah's grand reception tent, the sun had shifted. It gleamed down nearly vertically on the rows of potted crotons and chrysanthemums along the pathways, shrinking the shadows of passing men and horses.

From his seat beside Lord Auckland, the little Maharajah spoke animatedly in a combination of Urdu and Punjabi, his good eye on Lord Auckland's expressionless face. Behind his throne, Sikh grandees, three deep, murmured their approval.

"I see," William Macnaghten translated without inflection. "The colors of the silks are meant to show the identities of the owners. *Wah, wah,* how clever!"

Lord Auckland smiled politely at the Maharajah, then turned to his political secretary. "Macnaghten, this must stop. I will *not* discuss horse racing."

The baby on the Maharajah's knee watched them listlessly. On the carpet before the Maharajah's feet, Chief Minister Azizuddin smiled knowingly.

Catching the man's expression, Lord Auckland blinked and straightened. "Ask the Maharajah how long it will be before his army starts for Afghanistan."

The Maharajah replied to Macnaghten's question in his soft, rapid-fire voice, his hands waving.

The political secretary folded his own fingers over his dove-colored waistcoat. "He says that it will be soon, but that when they go, they will cross rivers. He, of course, will have bridges of boats built for the crossings. He wishes to know how many stone bridges England has, and how they are constructed."

"I do not know!" Lord Auckland's jowls shook. "Tell him anything. I cannot bear any more of this. I have never been so suffocatingly bored in all my life. What is the old fool saying now?"

"He wants to know," Macnaghten replied, "the difference between a Sikh temple and a Christian church."

"Macnaghten, you must ask him how many of his troops he intends to commit to the campaign," Lord Auckland said later, taking advantage of a conversation between the Maharajah and his Chief Minister. "And ask when he intends to send them." He shifted irritably in his seat. "It *must* be soon. He cannot mean to send an army to Kabul in deep winter, when the mountain passes are full of snow. None of our troops except the Gurkhas are accustomed to the cold.

"And tomorrow," he added with determination, "we will discuss laying our supply lines and moving our troops across his territories."

The frail baby had fallen asleep facedown on the Maharajah's lap. "That child looks even feebler than the Maharajah," murmured Macnaghten.

"Why are they all in such bad health?" asked Lord Auckland querulously. "The Maharajah pretends to be in the peak of condition, but anyone can see the man's as weak as a cat. As for that child—" he made a face while pretending to cough. "How unpleasant it is to deal with such poor-looking people. And the Chief Minister," he added, his eyes on Faqeer Azizuddin, "now, *there* is a man *not* to be trusted."

Outside the tent, people moved to and fro. On the Maharajah's lap the child lay motionless. Resting one hand on the tiny back, the Maharajah beckoned with the other to one of his courtiers.

"Please," murmured Lord Auckland, as the Maharajah spoke animatedly to the thin, dark-skinned man who stood before him, a hand over his heart, "let the old man not be sending for wine!"

After the dark-skinned man had gone, the Maharajah poked a small brown finger into Lord Auckland's uniformed side. "Governor Sahib," he announced, jerking Lord Auckland to startled attention, "I have great news!"

Sitting back in his throne he threw out an expansive arm. "Tomorrow," he declared, as Macnaghten translated, "we will all go to Amritsar. I wish to show you and your party the Golden Temple, the seat of our Sikh religion, before we travel on to Lahore to enjoy further entertainments."

Amritsar, Lahore. Lord Auckland sat up. "Is this a good sign?" he whispered to Macnaghten.

"Yes, my lord," replied Macnaghten, "I believe it is!"

Lord Auckland's fingers tightened on the arms of his chair.

"Yes, yes, we will have a great show." The Maharajah beamed, his good eye alight. "After we have seen the Golden Temple, we will go to my treasury and armory at Gobindgarh."

A silken rustle ran through the crowd of Sikhs. Two tall men nudged each other.

The Maharajah leaned forward to peer into Lord Auckland's face. "The English are our dear brothers from whom we must never be parted. It is therefore our duty to share with them the innermost secrets of our kingdom. They must see Gobindgarh, and look with their own eyes upon my fort, my riches, and my weaponry." He laughed aloud, suddenly, clapping his hands, waking the baby on his lap.

"My lord, he keeps all his artillery at Gobindgarh," Macnaghten explained animatedly. "We will see not only Maharajah Ranjit Singh's treasure but also his guns. He must have brought only a small part of his artillery to the durbar. What a grand opportunity for the generals! This must mean something, my lord, it must!"

Lord Auckland smiled crookedly. "Now, then, Macnaghten," he murmured, "you must flail your imagination back to life and compose a suitably splashy answer. Perhaps all this wasted time here at the Sutlej has been some mysterious native preliminary to the *real* talks. Perhaps the real negotiations were never meant to take place until after we reached Amritsar."

"You will of course leave your army at Firozpur," the Maharajah was saying, "and bring the ladies, and an escort of your soldiers." He waved a hand in the direction of Lahore. "When you cross my bridge of boats with your party and enter my territories, it will be a great show, a great show!"

The rustling among the *sirdars* had been replaced by murmuring. A hundred dark eyes moved from Maharajah Ranjit Singh to Macnaghten and Lord Auckland.

Macnaghten cleared his throat. "There is," he pronounced, gesturing at the bright sky outside, "a canopy of stars covering our two nations, now bound together forevermore in loving brotherhood."

"*Wah, wah,*" returned the Maharajah, clapping his hands. "Excellent! And they are never to be parted."

"There is a saying," Macnaghten remarked later to Lord Auckland as the Maharajah and his Chief Minister escorted them to their elephant, "that if no heir is chosen, whoever holds Gobindgarh after Ranjit Singh's death will rule the Punjab. His treasure and his guns are the cornerstone of his power."

"Indeed, Macnaghten," Lord Auckland replied, smiling with satisfaction as he began to mount the elephant ladder. "Indeed."

THE little servant stood inside the entrance of the elaborate reception tent, his bare toes pushed into the thick carpet. "Maharaj," he said, interrupting the Maharajah's conversation with Faqeer Azizuddin, "Baba must have his food." He pointed to the child.

Ranjit Singh looked up from the child on his lap, his expression blank. "Now?" He stroked the baby's face. "My little Saboor," he crooned, "my Pearl of Pearls! How dear he is to me!"

Ahmad did not budge from his post. "Maharaj, it is time for his food. I must take him now."

"Yes, yes, all right." The Maharajah lifted his hands. "You may take him to the kitchens," he said as Ahmad crossed the tent and took hold of the child, "but I must have him back the moment he has eaten."

From his place at the Maharajah's feet, Faqeer Azizuddin spoke softly. "Maharaj, do you remember that we decided to send Saboor back to his family after fifteen days?"

"Of course I remember." The Maharajah waved dismissive fingers. "But we are not going to Lahore now; we are going to Amritsar. He can go to his family later."

"Why," the servant muttered as he carried Saboor toward the kitchen tents, "does Maharaj not see how unhealthy Baba has become?" He patted Saboor's back, his face creasing with worry.

At the royal kitchens, he stood outside the door of the first tent, watching a row of cooks slicing onions and crushing garlic, ginger, and spices on a great stone surface.

A shaven-headed cook looked up and saw Ahmad and the child. "Ah, there you are," he said. He wiped his forehead with his sleeve and bent to smile into Saboor's solemn face. "We are ready for you, Baba. We have baked a quail for you today. Come, see what you will eat!" His eyes met Ahmad's. "Has he smiled yet?"

"No, not yet." Ahmad sighed. "He only stares, as if he is waiting for something. Perhaps he is waiting to die. Every day he grows weaker. He cares for nothing."

"He is missing his family." A second cook with a jutting belly had joined them. "He grieves for his own people."

"When will Baba see his father, his grandfather?" asked Ahmad as he squatted down in the shade, Saboor on his lap. "When will he see the ladies of the Shaikh's family? The Maharajah wants Baba beside him every moment. He has promised to return him soon, but I do not think he will keep his promise."

The shaven-headed cook strode off, then returned, balancing a round of bread and a tiny baked bird on a leaf plate. "Do not give him the quail yet," he cautioned, "it is still too hot."

"Can we not take him away ourselves and send him to his family?" As Ahmad tore off a piece of bread for the child, the second cook eased himself down with them by the sheltering wall of the kitchen tent. He pushed greased hair from his eyes. "So many merchants are going back and forth from here to Lahore. Surely there is one good-hearted man among them."

The bald cook shrugged. "Who can tell a good heart from a bad one, Rana? Besides, who would take the chance of being caught with one of the Maharajah's hostages?"

The fat cook nodded. "But what of the foreigners who have come to meet the Maharajah? He wouldn't kill his guests, even if they were found with the child. I am told there is a woman among them who speaks Urdu. If we ask her, she might take Saboor Baba to his family."

"She might treat him badly." Ahmad put a sliver of the quail's breast into Saboor's mouth. "She might sell him."

"She will not sell Baba," put in the shaven-headed cook. "These English do not traffic in children. But as for kindness, who knows?" He shrugged again.

"She is a woman." The fat cook yawned. "A woman will know what to do with a child. Any life is better than the life he has now. The Maharajah loves Baba, but does not see his misery. If Baba remains here much longer, he will die."

Saboor refused to have yogurt, but he drank water from the battered tin cup they offered him. The cook shook his head. "Poor little thing. You should watch for an opportunity to give him to the Englishwoman. When you have done it, we will find a way to send a message to his family, telling them where Baba can be found. He won't have to stay with her for long."

After a moment, Ahmad nodded.

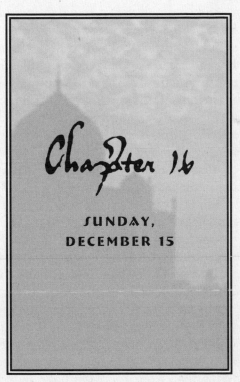

Chapter 16

Leaving the army with all its guns and its animals behind at Firozpur, a much reduced British camp containing Lord Auckland and his party, senior government officials, a cavalry escort, and a military honor guard set off for Amritsar. The sixty-mile journey took six days. Ranjit Singh's own bright and noisy camp had gone first. At each halt, the British reviewed the Maharajah's troops and watched trick riding and artillery displays. In the evenings, they sat under his embroidered canopy and watched his entertainments.

On the sixth day, they were five miles from Amritsar, the city most holy to the Sikhs. At just after ten o'clock, breakfast was nearly over at the British camp.

William Macnaghten sat at one end of the dining table, stirring a rapidly cooling cup of coffee. He looked mournfully at his companion.

"Did you achieve anything last night?" asked Major Byrne.

"Nothing." Macnaghten drew a pattern on the tablecloth with one finger. "Everything is exactly as it has been. The Maharajah talks of infantry maneuvers, or God, or steeplechasing, any subject but the Afghan Campaign."

Major Byrne's nose looked even redder than usual. He sniffed and fumbled for a handkerchief. "It is odd to have the preliminary courtesies extend this long, but cheer up, William. His offer to show us his arms and treasure must mean something."

"God knows how much he is spending to feed us, never mind the bags of rupees for our escort and all those greasy sweetmeats. Why would he do all this if he didn't intend to sign the treaty? Why would he show us his treasure and his guns?" Macnaghten glanced over his shoulder and bent closer to Major Byrne. "I fear something is wrong, Byrne. I fear we may have blundered, that for all the Maharajah's courtesies, he is making fools of us. We have brought a ten-thousand-man army all the way from Calcutta, believing that within days of our arrival, our army and Ranjit's would be on their way to Afghanistan together, but Ranjit Singh shows no interest in the campaign. He laughs when we try to discuss the treaty. Lord Auckland is beginning to blame *me* for the Maharajah's behavior." His fingers trembled a little on the handle of his cup.

Major Byrne blew his nose vigorously. "True enough, but we have the upper hand. The old boy knows a real army when he sees one. His troops look smart enough on parade, but I'll wager they'd run away in a real fight. We have Europeans, the cream of our native infantry, and the best horse and foot artillery in India. Maharajah Ranjit Singh will never cross the Army of the Indus."

Macnaghten sighed as a servant took away his coffee cup. "Have you considered the possibility of a trap?"

Major Byrne frowned. "What are you saying, man?"

"Our party, including three ladies, is now sixty miles inside the Maharajah's territory. We have only an honor guard and a cavalry escort. We are surrounded by the Maharajah's huge army, as he reminds us daily with his endless reviews and artillery displays. The rest of our army and all our heavy guns are out of reach at Firozpur," Macnaghten said miserably. "If it came to a fight, Major, what chance would we have?"

THE postbreakfast elephant procession to the Golden Temple was to be informal, allowing the Governor-General to travel with his political secretary.

His eyes half closed against the sun, Lord Auckland winced as their elephant shifted his weight, rocking the howdah. Beside him, Macnaghten tugged at his collar. "My lord," he said, his eyes moving from Lord Auckland's hollow gaze to the mahout riding on the elephant's neck, "I have one or two suggestions regarding our afternoon conversation with the Maharajah. If, at this afternoon's meeting, the Maharajah still refuses to discuss committing his troops to the campaign, I think we must assume that he does not intend to do so. In that case, sir, I suggest we proceed into Afghanistan without him."

Lord Auckland looked silently down on his cavalry escort as they waited for the Maharajah's elephants to join the march. "I agree. We mustn't wait any longer for the old man." A sigh shook his large frame. "All this is most disappointing. I shall be very sorry to lose the Maharajah's army, although our own force is certainly strong enough to take Kabul without him. But we *must* get written assurance of a right-of-way up to the Khyber Pass. We *must* have a signed treaty before another week goes by."

Macnaghten wiped his face. "I believe we will, my lord."

"Then get it for us." Lord Auckland tugged his brocade coat over his midriff. "The Honorable East India Company cannot be held hostage by a petty Maharajah."

Macnaghten swallowed. "No, my lord, of course not."

THREE elephants behind Lord Auckland, the two Eden ladies perched on their seats like a pair of bonneted birds. Across from them, Mariana looked ahead for a sight of Fitzgerald riding with the honor guard. She had not seen much of him in the evenings recently, as the ladies had been excluded from Ranjit Singh's nightly drinking parties, orgies by all accounts, most unsuitable for gentlewomen.

That exclusion had been a relief. The old Maharajah's leering glances at Mariana had been unnerving enough in the daytime when he was sober. Heaven only knew how he would behave when tipsy.

As if he had read her thoughts, Ranjit Singh and his elephants materialized like a mirage on the plain, heralded by a great cloud of dust.

"Miss Emily," Mariana ventured, "I am sure there is an explanation for Lieutenant Fitzgerald's broken engagement. Can we not ask *him* what happened? Perhaps the story has been exaggerated by gossip."

If only they would speak to Peter Edwardes. . . .

Miss Emily turned a stern blue eye on Mariana. "My dear child, we would all like to think well of the young man, but I do not believe in smoke without fire. While I agree that some details of the tale may have been exaggerated, I cannot allow you to risk your future on someone with his reputation. Deserving or not, Lieutenant Fitzgerald has been *disqualified*."

The Maharajah's procession had drawn closer. The discordant

sounds of his music, the bellowing of his men, the circling of his nobles' horses all came into focus through the dust. Mariana bit her lip.
This should be one of the great moments of her life. She would never
see a durbar like this one again. She turned her bonneted head away
from the advancing native train and wiped away her tears of frustra-
tion with the back of her hand.

India was ruined for her.

VILLAGERS squabbled over the Maharajah's shower of coins.
Petitioners ran, shouting and gesturing, beside his elephant. His band
played "God Save the Queen," leaving out several parts of the
melody. Slowly, noisily, the Sikh and British elephants merged into
one procession.

"Poor George," sighed Miss Emily as they watched Lord Auckland
climb into the royal howdah and embrace Ranjit Singh. "I do believe
he could almost bear this durbar if he did not have to keep hugging
the Maharajah."

Peacock feather fans, yak tails, and silk standards were raised. At a
signal, the official drummers began their steady pulse and the band
took up the marching song. One by one, the elephants shifted their
weight. The ponderous, gaudy, noisy procession began to move. The
march to the Golden Temple began at last.

As they set off toward the city and the temple whose dome gleamed
in the distance, Mariana caught sight of one of the honor guard riding
ahead of the elephants. He wore the blue dress uniform of the Bengal
Native Artillery and a shiny dragoon helmet whose red horsehair
plume rippled in the sun. He looked back briefly, a hand shading his
eyes, then turned and rode on toward Amritsar.

TEN miles behind the marching elephants, a small caravan of horsemen and loaded camels followed the same road.

Yusuf Bhatti turned to Hassan, his saddle creaking. "If we do not
stop for food, we should reach Amritsar by early evening. In that
case, we may see the Maharajah tonight."

"No, Yusuf, we must eat," said Hassan beside him. "God willing,
my Saboor will be waiting for me whenever we arrive."

Yusuf nodded silently. He did not have Hassan's patience. Even in
his agony, the man had done his duty. Days and nights spent arguing
with the leaders of Kasur had gained him half the tribute money he
had been ordered to collect. Now, with a line of laden camels roped
together behind them, he and Yusuf had hope. Saboor's fifteen days

had now passed. Surely the Maharajah would keep his word and return the child, especially when he saw the camel-loads of treasure they had brought him. But, Yusuf asked himself, if all were well, why had Hassan's father sent that mysterious letter, delivered three days ago by an exhausted courier from Lahore to their camp at Kasur?

"My son," the Shaikh had written, *"I have not told you this before, but according to Shafi Sahib, Saboor is to be rescued by an outsider whose identity is yet to be determined. As Shafi Sahib is rarely wrong, I believe you may comfort yourself with this news."*

Yusuf had seen the letter himself. He knew that it now lay in the pocket over Hassan's heart.

Rescue. The Shaikh used no word lightly. He must mean that the Maharajah would refuse to return Saboor. He might also mean, although Yusuf had not said this aloud, that Saboor's condition was worse than they had imagined. Who, then, would intervene, and return the child, alive, to his family?

"Hassan," Yusuf said carefully, "if, God forbid, all does not go as planned, there is the letter."

The air had grown cold. "Yes," Hassan said, as he drew his shawl about his shoulders. "There is the letter."

Chapter 11

The interior of the Golden Temple, spiritual center of the Sikh religion, was airy and cool, but it lacked chairs. The three Englishwomen lowered themselves as decorously as they could to the expanse of carpet covering the floor.

Mariana crossed her legs under her skirts and looked over the men who sat facing each other at the center of the vast space. Lord Auckland looked most uncomfortable on his backless cushion. Fitzgerald must be there, too, but she could not see him.

"I do not know how much longer I can bear sitting like this," Miss Fanny murmured, wincing as she shifted her limbs beneath rose-figured skirts. "My knees are aching horribly."

Miss Emily, her face set into grim lines, said nothing.

"I see a lovely, comfortable-looking wall," added Miss Fanny mournfully, "but it's miles from here."

Above their heads, perfumed smoke from hundreds of incense sticks hung in the air, catching the light from the temple's high windows.

From the direction of the altar, stringed instruments took up a minor melody, joined by nasal voices. Along the walls, the Maharajah's turbaned chiefs stood in elegant, whispering groups.

Mariana absorbed the scene avidly. The Eden ladies had ruined her happiness with Fitzgerald, but, she realized, they had not spoiled India for her. India, with all its peculiarities, would always belong to her, and she must always share it with her father. That much, at least, they could not take from her.

On his own cushion, the old Maharajah talked steadily, weaving pictures with his hands. Facing him, Lord Auckland, his face a mask of strained politeness, nodded at intervals while Mr. Macnaghten translated, his brow knit in concentration. From time to time, Lord Auckland detached his attention from the Maharajah and gazed toward the entrance.

"He looks," whispered Miss Fanny, "as if he hopes someone will come through the door and rescue him."

"Shhh," replied Miss Emily without moving her lips.

The Maharajah looked across, noticing the Eden ladies' expressions. "Your ladies are becoming bored," he announced, and caught the eye of a white-bearded priest, who nodded. "Let them see the Granth Sahib," he ordered, then turned his attention back to Lord Auckland.

On the marble altar, beneath a golden canopy supported by silver poles, the holy book of the Sikhs lay under its many fine coverings. The priest motioned for the ladies to approach.

Miss Emily and Miss Fanny rose gratefully and, supporting each other, rustled unsteadily toward the altar and its row of elderly priests. Mariana trailed in their wake.

As she passed a shadowed corner, a small, bearded man stepped suddenly from the shadows. On his shoulder lay a baby in a round, stiffly embroidered cap, whose mouth hung open as he slept. She gasped.

The man addressed her softly in Urdu. "Memsahib," he said, his eyes not meeting hers, looking at the ground, at the ceiling, over her shoulder, "Memsahib, you speak our language."

The baby had drooled, leaving a stain on the man's shirt. He shook the child gently against him. "This little one is a hostage of the Maharajah. His condition is bad."

This was the exhausted child she had glimpsed with the Maharajah at Firozpur. "Hostage?" she asked, not certain she'd understood.

"Yes. To be sure of the loyalty of his courtiers, the Maharajah sometimes keeps their children in his Citadel. Baba has spent much of his life there with his mother. Now the mother has died, and poor Baba is all alone with the Maharajah. He cannot see his father or his grandfather, or any of those who love him."

The Eden sisters had reached the altar. They leaned over it, cooing in mannerly appreciation. The priest spoke beside them, his voice a deep rumble. They turned, uncomprehending, looking for Mariana to translate for them.

"There are those at the Citadel who are jealous of the favor the Maharajah bestows on Baba." The servant pushed up the child's scarlet sleeve. In the half-light of the temple, Mariana could see fading bruises on the small forearm. She felt her heart contract.

"Where is his family?" Her sharp whisper echoed back from the stone walls.

"They are in Lahore, except for his father, who has been sent away."

What a peculiar, cruel country this was, but what could she do? She spread her hands. "I am sorry."

The ladies beckoned. Mariana moved to pass, but the servant stepped sideways again, blocking her way. "The Maharajah loves Baba," he insisted, his voice trembling, "but he knows nothing of children. He does not see how sad Baba is, how much Baba longs for his dead mother, and for his father who loves him. Baba never smiles. I fear he will die of grief."

Music, tender and insistent, rose from the altar, surrounding Mariana. The first covering of the Granth Sahib, a fringe of enormous pearls and emeralds, hissed and clicked as the eldest of the priests lifted it from the book. The ladies beckoned again.

"What can I do," the man murmured, "I who am only a servant? How can I save him?" He blinked and raised his eyes to the ceiling. "The cooks make him the best food, others make him playthings, but all he wants is his family. The Maharajah gives him jewels, but what does poor Baba care for such gifts?" He met her eyes and his gaze was urgent. "Baba's grandfather, Shaikh Waliullah, is a noble man, Memsahib. He once saved my brother's life. Take the child from this place before he dies. Carry him with you when you leave here, Memsahib. Send him to Shaikh Waliullah in Lahore. It is Baba's only hope."

Noble. *"There are noble men of all religions in India,"* her munshi had said. She would like to meet this Shaikh. But how many children in India were lost, how many were beaten? Was this baby not one of a hundred thousand small victims of India's poverty and odd customs?

The baby's eyes were squeezed tightly shut. He stirred on the servant's shoulder. Mariana dragged her eyes from him. She should never have shown interest. "I am very sorry," she whispered firmly, "but I cannot help you. How can I steal a child from Maharajah Ranjit Singh?" She gathered her skirts. "Stand aside, and let me pass."

She stepped around the servant and child and started toward the altar. The priest had begun to read from the book, his voice a high, hypnotic singsong. Miss Fanny motioned for her to hurry.

The servant's voice followed her. "Allah will aid you, Memsahib. Allah Most Gracious will aid you."

She looked back to see him wipe his eyes with a brown finger. On his shoulder, the child still slept. She paused irresolutely, then moved away toward the altar.

THE visit to the temple had concluded. The ladies returned, smiling, from the altar. The gentlemen rose from their seats on the carpeted floor.

The Maharajah unfolded himself from his cushion, and, taking the Governor-General's hand, helped him to rise. "It is getting dark," he announced, still holding Lord Auckland's hand. "We will have a fireworks display." He looked about him, his single eye alight. "Where is my baba?"

Mariana shivered and looked away as the bearded servant stepped forward and gave the sleeping baby into the Maharajah's hands.

Wrapping themselves against the chill, the Maharajah and his guests filed out of the inlaid doorway. At the far end of the causeway they climbed a narrow stair to a group of balconies, where they looked back at the temple in its square lake of water.

The setting sun smudged the western sky over the city of Amritsar. From where she stood, Mariana could see torches moving below her. Lamplight glowed in the windows of adjacent houses.

The first explosion made her gasp. It rocked the air before her and rang in her ears. A great spray of sparks lit up the golden dome of the temple, its decorated outer walls, and the waters of the great tank in which it stood. As rocket after rocket went off, the temple became a fairy palace, now blindingly bright, now bathed in shadow, lit from every angle by sudden flares and showers of sparks.

"Look, my pearl," an old man's voice observed between explosions, "you can see the fish swimming in the waters of the tank."

Mariana turned. On the next balcony the Maharajah stood among his bejeweled chiefs, enjoying the show as if he had never seen fireworks before, the baby twisting in his arms. The child, his face puckered around the thumb in his mouth, looked as if he were trying to burrow his way into the Maharajah's chest. There was no sign of the servant.

The Maharajah laughed, throwing his head back. Against the old man's chest, the baby turned and looked directly into Mariana's face.

His body stilled. His eyes wide, he stared at her, unblinking, his gaze heavy, full of expectation.

Uncomfortable, she looked away. When she looked again, the baby still stared, seemingly oblivious to the deafening sounds and the cascades of light around them. He seemed to be drinking in her features, his mouth working around his thumb. Baby Freddie sucked his thumb too; but Freddie had been round and pink when she last saw him, with fair hair that stood out in a pale halo about his head, not at all like this brown baby in his strange, shiny clothes. Baby Freddie had never looked at her as this tiny stranger did now, as if she were the most important person in all the world.

His eyes locked on hers, the child rested his head on the Maharajah's shoulder.

"Are you all right, my dear?" Miss Emily inquired. "What are you looking at?"

Mariana shivered. "Nothing, Miss Emily."

The child had been asleep when his odd little servant had stepped out of the shadows and begged for her help. Why, then, did he look at her now with such keen recognition?

It was too late to save him. Rescue, difficult enough in the temple, was now impossible. She could not reach across the space between her balcony and the Maharajah's, and snatch the baby from the old man's grasp. She kept her eyes on the shimmering waters of the tank, knowing the child had not taken his eyes from her.

The child's fate was none of her concern. How many times had she been warned against entangling herself in the affairs of the natives? This time, she would heed the advice she'd been given. After all, even if the Maharajah were selfishly keeping the baby from his family, he was clearly fond of the poor thing. Surely he would see to it that someone kissed the baby tonight, that someone kept him warm in the cold night air. She wrapped her own shawl tightly about her. That expectant little face, she feared, would haunt her for the rest of her days.

With one last waterfall of light, the fireworks ended. As the crowd began to shuffle down the staircase, Mariana lost sight of the Maharajah. She turned to descend the stairs, relieved to be free of the baby's stare; but a high, despairing wail arose from the direction of the city gate, and she knew instinctively that it came from him. She followed the Eden ladies helplessly down the stairway as the child's cry lifted over the noise of the crowd and filled her ears.

They moved slowly by torchlight toward the rows of waiting palanquins. In front of her, Mr. Macnaghten spoke in a low tone to Major Byrne.

"—tomorrow morning," he was saying. "I cannot persuade him to meet the Maharajah more than once a day, but he *must* do so. We cannot be certain of the Maharajah's continued good health." His voice dropped to an indecipherable hiss.

Major Byrne patted Mr. Macnaghten's shoulder. "Of course, William," he soothed, then strode off to hail a junior officer, while Mr. Macnaghten's fingers knotted and twisted behind his back.

Alongside Mariana, two British officers helped a third, who staggered between them, his head drooping as if he were about to faint.

She quickened her steps. There was her palanquin, waiting on the ground, her bearers, anonymous in their shawls, crouched beside it.

As she sat, preparing to swing her legs into the curtained box, a small bearded man dashed toward her through the crowd, his head turning as if he were searching for someone, a tiny excited child in his arms. The servant's laboring breath was visible in the cold air, his neatly wrapped turban askew on his head. The baby in his arms rode his servant like a king on his way into battle, his fists pounding the man's shoulder, urging him on.

Child, servant, and young woman saw one another in the same moment.

Mariana's mouth fell open. The running man turned and came straight for her, his lips moving as if he were talking to himself, but before he reached her side, the baby in his arms lunged dangerously toward her. Without thinking, she reached up to prevent him from falling. She gathered him onto her lap and looked up, ready to scold the servant for his presumption. But where the little man had stood, there was only empty space.

Holding the baby, she stood up and searched about her, but there was no trace of the servant among the noisy throng of British officers and Sikh sirdars. His goal apparently accomplished, the small concave-looking man with the sparse beard had vanished into the crowd.

The child in her arms smelled faintly sour. Her nose wrinkling, she held him away from her. In his outlandish clothes, with black powder ringing his eyes, he seemed unpleasantly foreign. Moments ago she had wanted a second chance to rescue him, but now that the chance had come, she did not want it, or him. Foreign or not, he relaxed his dirty little body in her arms and raised solemn, expectant eyes to hers over the thumb in his mouth.

Her arms tightened around him. "You need a bath," she said.

He needed a bath, and he needed to get warm. Beneath his rich satins, the baby's skin felt clammy; his curled feet were icy. Why was there no woolly shawl for him? Why had his comfort been forgotten when evening closed in? What was it in those dark, tired eyes, Mariana wondered, as she tugged her shawl about them both, that promised her unlooked-for joy, that made her feel powerful and good?

Men swarmed past them. Palanquins edged through the crowd, their bearers shouting to clear the way. A spear-carrying Sikh, a precious Kashmir shawl tied carelessly about his waist, pushed by on a nervous horse, too close for safety, his gold-studded bridle gleaming in the torchlight.

Anyone she asked would say it was her duty to stop a British officer or one of the Sikh courtiers and hand the baby over, explaining that she had no right to him, that he belonged to the Maharajah. It was wrong, they would agree, to take away someone else's child.

The White Rabbit and two other aides-de-camp passed by, talking among themselves. Debating no longer, Mariana ducked her head and bundled the child into her palanquin, praying that they would not see, but they did not seem even to notice her. Without looking in her direction, they passed, still talking, out of sight.

Even Mariana's own bearers appeared not to have seen anything unusual. As she climbed into the box after the baby, they glanced at her as incuriously as ever, before getting languidly to their feet.

Everyone was leaving. Lord Auckland's elegant palki had passed by before the servant and the child appeared. A troop of horsemen trotted away into the dark, followed by a crowd of servants on foot carrying banners and fans on long sticks.

Only one palanquin, a tall one of colored glass, remained, fifty yards away, surrounded by gesticulating natives.

"Go," Mariana ordered her bearers as she wrapped the baby up to his eyes in her best blue shawl.

Who, exactly, was this little creature? She had not paid proper attention to the name his servant had given her in the temple, the name of the child's grandfather. But, even if she had bothered to listen, what was the likelihood of finding the man? The walled city must house ten thousand grandfathers with names like Wali Mohammad, or Wasif or Waheed.

"I have saved you from the Maharajah," she whispered as she tucked the child into the crook of her arm, "but I don't even know your name."

If he understood her words, he did not seem to care. He lay curled against her, his eyes locked on her face beneath the circular cap that had, by some miracle, remained on his head during the confusion.

She must decide what to do. She banged on the roof, urging the bearers to hurry.

The journey seemed to take forever. For an hour, as they covered the distance to the English camp, Mariana lay on one elbow, her hand inches from the baby's face, ready to clap over his mouth if he should cry out and betray them. Torchbearers galloped beside her, their open flames throwing an eerie, wavering light against the curtains. Harsh, rhythmic breathing of the bearers told her another palanquin was close by. She hoped that nearby palanquin did not contain Major Byrne. Only yesterday, she had heard him savage one of his subordinates over a brass uniform button. She tried not to imagine what he would say if he found her with the Maharajah's little hostage.

The child snuggled closer. *Had* anyone seen her take him?

It must be a serious crime to steal a Maharajah's hostage. What would happen if she were caught? Needles of fear pricked her unpleasantly.

She squirmed in the cramped space. Very well. If she *were* caught, humiliating as that would be, she would *not* apologize. If he did not belong to her, he did not belong to the Maharajah, either, and the Maharajah had obviously not cared for him properly. She touched the baby's cheek with one finger. How was it possible that in all that seething camp, only one servant had thought of his welfare, or noticed his misery?

At last, the familiar sounds of the avenue at night reached her through the curtains. Minutes later, her bearers slowed their pace. When they set the palanquin down, Mariana struggled awkwardly out of the box in the darkness, the swaddled child in her arms. Bent double so her bearers would not see, she dashed into her tent, letting out her breath only after the reed curtain flapped safely shut behind her.

Dittoo had left a lighted oil lamp on the bedside table. She carried the baby to the bed, tucked him carefully between two cushions, and was reaching to pick up the lamp when she thought of something.

She ran back to the door and pushed the curtain aside. "Munnoo," she called.

In the starlight, a figure detached itself from the group of retreating bearers and turned back. "Go and find Dittoo," she ordered. "I need him at once."

She returned inside, and holding the lamp aloft, bent over the child on the bed. The lamp carved great shadows on the tent walls, and gleamed on the tawny satin of her gown and on the baby's face. His skin, she decided, was the shade of her milky morning coffee, but with a touch of gold. Curving lashes shadowed cheeks that should have been plumper than they were.

She had seen native children rushing about naked in the villages the camp had passed, but she realized with a pang as she studied her tiny guest that she knew absolutely nothing about a native child's life. What did he do all day? What toys did he have? Did he wear leading strings when he was taken out into the garden?

One thing was certain. As soon as the bathwater came, she would wipe away the black powder that circled his eyes.

She tugged off her straw bonnet and shook out her hair until it fell from its pins and lay tangled on her shoulders, then sat down beside him on the bed.

"Well, you odd little thing," she said, a hand on the baby's body, "what should we do now?"

Still wrapped in her shawl he sighed, his eyelids fluttering.

When had he last eaten? "You need your supper," she said decisively. "Where is that silly Dittoo?"

There was nothing to eat in the tent, but her jug of water stood on the bedside table. She poured some into her tumbler, and, holding the baby carefully upright, put the tumbler to his mouth. Suddenly animated, he leaned eagerly forward, his eyes wide, and took it in great panting gulps. They hadn't given him anything to drink! Her hand holding the glass shook with anger.

When he would drink no more, she set the glass down and studied him. What if he were really ill? She pushed away the memory of another helpless native creature and another water glass.

She tucked his arms into the shawl and got to her feet, leaving him on the bed. At the doorway, she lifted the blind aside and looked out. All she could see in the starlight was the familiar expanse of clay stretching from her tent to the red compound wall, and the distant tents of Lord Auckland and his sisters.

Where was Dittoo?

He was an irritating servant—he talked on and on, dusting her tiny bedside table when she wanted most to be left alone, fussing over things that did not matter and forgetting those that did, but he was warmhearted. Now, alone with her stolen baby, Mariana could scarcely wait to hear his shuffling footsteps rounding the side of her tent.

The child lay still, his face framed by blue fringe. As she watched, he tried to free his arms, but could not, for the shawl was wrapped too tightly about his body. Whimpering, he fought with the entrapping fabric, his eyes filling with tears. As Mariana flew toward him, his embroidered cap came loose and rolled away, exposing his head. It was bald, save for a fine, newly sprouting crop of jet black hair.

At the sight of that round, shaven skull, Mariana felt herself instantly transported to another time and place. In his illness, his own head shaven, Ambrose, too, had whimpered helplessly: Ambrose who had adored her, whom she had loved more than anyone in the world.

She dragged the baby's small, hurt body onto her lap and tore away the shawl. "There, there," she whispered, rocking him, her face against his, as she had rocked Ambrose when he was a baby. "Don't cry, my darling, my lambkin."

She had feared he would give the same high-pitched wail that had carried to her over the crowd earlier that evening, but instead he hiccuped and put his thumb into his mouth.

"Oh," she cried, relieved, "you only wanted to suck your thumb!"

Like dew, tears clung to his lashes and lay on his cheeks. She touched his face. When he was better, would he flap his hands when he laughed, as Ambrose had done? Would he run to her, shrieking with pleasure, when she held out her arms? Would he die?

As her own past sorrows welled up and spilled from her eyes, bumbling sounds came from outside her door. Help, if only in the form of Dittoo, had come at last.

Chapter 18

In the mysterious way that news travels, word of the baby's disappearance had reached the English camp even before the young lady translator's palanquin had passed by the saluting sentry and into the Governor-General's compound. Within half an hour the news had made its appearance at cooking fires in all quarters of the camp.

When a water carrier arrived at the row of fires along the back wall of the compound, Dittoo and three friends had already finished their evening meal. The youngest of the four men was on his feet before the fire, a slim silhouette in motion, his feet stamping, his arms over his head. He sang as he danced, a light melody full of trills and catches. The bhisti watched, nodding.

"Look, Sonu," said Guggan, the eldest of the four, by way of greeting, pointing to a comfortable place by the fire, "Mohan thinks that's the way a dancing girl moves her arms." He gestured, palm up, at the swaying figure before them. "Look at him. Dittoo here says no real *nach* girl would—"

"Of course this is right." Mohan went on dancing, his fingers extended to resemble lotus buds. "Who was it that stood with his eye to a crack in the durbar tent while a whole troop of girls entertained the Governor-General and the Maharajah? You wouldn't know, Guggan," he added, "you were too lazy to leave the fire."

Sonu shook his head skeptically. "I can tell you one thing, Mohan," he offered, "you may know how to sing, but you cannot dance. But," he added, turning to his friends, "I have not come to your fire to talk of dancing girls. I have come to tell you some big news. The Maharajah's favorite hostage has disappeared."

He bent closer to the fire. "The hostage is a baby boy with magical powers."

Mohan's song stopped. All four servants fixed their eyes on the water carrier.

"The child's grandfather is Shaikh Waliullah of Lahore, a man of great powers," he continued a little grandly. "That is how the child came by his abilities. He is said to bring good fortune wherever he goes. The Maharajah keeps him because of this." He found a stick and poked the flames. "In fact, the Maharajah never lets him out of his sight. He calls the child his 'Pearl of Pearls.' "

His audience exchanged glances.

"This evening, the Maharajah made a great display of fireworks to entertain the British sahibs. Afterward, when it was time to return to camp in his palanquin of colored glass, he sent for his little hostage to accompany him. The servant came, bringing the child. The servant had almost reached the palanquin when suddenly, just like that, the baby vanished from his arms and into the air." Sonu the water carrier paused dramatically. "Everyone saw it happen.

"Now," he continued as he stirred the embers, "with the child disappeared, everyone fears some terrible calamity will befall the kingdom. That is why the Maharajah is offering a great reward for news of the baby's whereabouts."

His stick had caught fire. He brought its end to his lips and blew it out. "No one knows why the child disappeared. He was given everything, jewels, everything."

As the friends considered this point, the voice of the sirdar bearer came from the direction of the tents with an unwelcome message. "Dittoo, Memsahib is calling you."

Four faces bunched in disappointment.

"The boy has powers," Sita said thoughtfully. He picked at his teeth with a twig.

"Perhaps this disappearance is too great a feat for a child so small," Sonu offered. "In that case, it was his grandfather who caused the child to disappear."

All four servants nodded. "Yes," they agreed, "it was the grandfather."

Munnoo appeared from the shadows and stood impatiently over them. "What are you doing, Dittoo? Memsahib is calling."

"In any case, it is said that every person in the city, down to the humblest sweeper, is searching for the child," Sonu concluded, as Dittoo gathered himself and stood. "He will be known by his clothing, for it is red satin, embroidered with silver thread. He wears an embroidered cap, and a string of emeralds and pearls about his neck that reaches to his waist."

The men's speculations followed Dittoo as he stumbled away toward the cold English tents.

AS much as he liked to keep his distance from the Europeans he served, Dittoo made a point of talking to his memsahib.

He had made the decision to share his wisdom on his first meeting with her. Recruited at the last moment from his lowly post at Government House to serve a young memsahib on the journey to Lahore, he had put on his cleanest clothes and followed a lofty serving man of the Governor-General to a neat cottage on one of the better roads in Simla.

On their arrival, the serving man had left him standing in a heavy rain, not on the porch but under a tree, where he waited, shouted at by monkeys, with water soaking into his clothes, until an Englishwoman emerged from the house, a blue umbrella over her head, and approached him. The Englishwoman looked him up and down in a pointed, catlike way from beneath the rim of her umbrella, then, to his surprise, greeted him properly in his own language. At that moment, it had come to Dittoo that, unlike other foreigners, this person might be able to learn something about real life.

From the first days of his service, he talked whenever he was in Memsahib's presence, giving advice, imparting knowledge. Soon after they left Simla, he told her that there would be no orange ice at lunch, because no one had covered the shallow earthen dishes in which ice was made overnight, leaving the ice to be licked, or worse, by dogs or other animals. Another morning, he warned her that breakfast would be cold because one of the under-cooks had stabbed another with a bread knife, demonstrating the perils of borrowing money. His memsahib showed little interest in his stories. Sometimes, he suspected, she pretended sleep in order to avoid him, but he went on talking, sure of his mission.

He must do without his friends and Sonu's exciting story, but at least he would have the satisfaction of teaching Memsahib something tonight. Confident of her interest in his news, he crossed the compound and approached her tent. "Memsahib," he began, even before he had finished scuffing off his shoes outside the door, "a most strange thing has happened!"

There was no reply. The door hanging fell back into place with a slap as he entered. She was there, sitting silently on the edge of her bed, her back to him, bent over as if in pain. The lamp threw a long trembling shadow across the bed.

Was she ill?

She sniffed convulsively. Wondering if she had summoned him to help her bear some tragedy, he crossed the floor with his uneven gait, the woolen socks she had given him silent on the striped rug. Reaching the end of the bed, he leaned cautiously forward.

She sat bent over a bundle on her lap, rocking it as if it were a child. He blinked. It *was* a child, wrapped in her shawl, its small brown hand resting on her bosom. How had Memsahib come to have a native baby in her tent? Babies and talk of babies seemed to be everywhere tonight.

"*Ji*, Memsahib?" It was better to pretend he had not seen. He tore his eyes from the bundle on her lap.

She looked up at him, a protective hand on the baby's chest. "You must help me, Dittoo," she said urgently. Her eyes were red, but her face held a fierce resolution. "This little one needs food, and warm water for his bath, and plain, ordinary clothes. He cannot be seen in these."

She pulled the shawl aside. Under it was a native boy child, just old enough to be walking. His red satin costume was stiff with silver embroidery; a rope of pearls and emeralds lay heavily on his chest. The child, too, had been weeping.

Dittoo's chest rose and fell under his thin shawl as if he had run all the way from the cooking fire. He glanced uncertainly toward the doorway.

Memsahib's voice sharpened. "Bring him food, your sort of food, from one of the native fires. I doubt if he has ever eaten European food. And hurry. He is very hungry."

"*Zaroor*, most certainly." Dittoo nodded as if he were dreaming.

"And, Dittoo," she continued, startling him with her sudden ferocity, "if you speak one word of this, I shall dismiss you from my service and you will find yourself walking all the way from here to Simla. Do you understand me?"

"*Ji*, Memsahib." He backed out of the tent and set off toward the red wall, looking back at her once or twice to make sure he had not dreamed that his own memsahib stood in her doorway, shivering in the evening chill, the Maharajah's vanished hostage in her arms.

Dittoo hurried past the large tent of the Governor Sahib's chef and the greasy cooking tents, his mind in turmoil. How great was the reward? Was it enough to allow him to return to his village and build a proper house for his family?

He thought of Memsahib's sharp words. Once she discovered he had betrayed her secret, she would dismiss him from her service instantly; but how could he miss this opportunity to gain a princely reward? How, for that matter, could he keep such thrilling news from his friends? The baby, the very hostage whose story they had just heard, was *in his memsahib's tent*! He could scarcely believe it himself. Not only was this a good story, it was one in which he actually had a part!

Over the past month, these men at the fire had become like brothers. He hurried on, imagining their reaction to his story. Should he tell them yet, or should he savor his news?

He arrived out of breath. "Is the food finished?" he asked quickly. His story crouched in his throat, ready to spring out. He swallowed.

His friends regarded him with surprise.

"Yes," said Mohan, "it is finished. Why do you want more food?"

"Someone has asked for it. It does not matter. I will be back soon." There was no time to stop. He must find food for the child, and warm water. Then, his work done, he would return to the fire and, at his ease, tell them his news in each delicious detail. He hurried away, feeling his friends' eyes on his back.

The other fires in the Governor-General's compound were also cold. Clutching his arms against the chill, Dittoo tramped out onto the avenue, looking for a fire where men were still eating. He grunted with irritation as he stepped out of a misshapen shoe in the darkness. It was late. Wherever he went, men sat talking of the vanished child; but for the child himself there was no food.

Dittoo was a long distance from the red-walled compound when he found what he sought, a cluster of Muslim men still eating, talking carelessly amongst themselves. He lifted his chin. He must not give his secret away. It would not do for another man to report the child's whereabouts and gain all the credit and the reward.

He went straight to the man whom he took to be the senior person at the fire.

"I have need," he said, after exchanging greetings, "of food."

"Food?" A hill-man, whom Dittoo remembered to be a senior groom, looked up, interested, from where he squatted, chewing.

Dittoo looked away. "Yes," he replied, refusing to elaborate.

Feeling the man's eyes study him, Dittoo shifted nervously under the weight of his secret. His fingers twitched. He thrust his hands behind his back.

"Are you not the serving man of the young memsahib?" The man held a piece of bread partway to his mouth as if arrested in mid-thought.

Dittoo's hands clutched at each other behind his back. "I must hurry," he said. "If you have food, please give it to me."

The groom stretched his long body and stood. He bent and rummaged among the pots until he found a circular lid, and began without comment to scrape the leavings of the evening meal onto its flat surface. He laid a folded chapatti over the mounds of rice and lentils, then nodded and handed the lid to Dittoo.

Hurrying from the fire, Dittoo paused to look back. The groom once again squatted there, staring pensively into the fire. Dittoo walked on, relieved. The man had not suspected.

Were Dittoo a first-class serving man, his shoes would fit properly. His livery would be spotless, unlike the semiclean *dhoti* and shirt he wore, for his sahib would buy him many uniforms. A first-class man would have himself shaved every day, and his turban would be starched like those of the Governor Sahib's servants. But Dittoo had been born a second-class servant, attending to junior people like his memsahib, and he and his two surviving sons would forever remain second-class servants. He passed four soldiers on their way to their tents from their evening meal. They were Brahmins, high-caste men from Oudh or Bihar who looked down on him and his friends. He kicked a stone out of his way, careful not to spill the food.

He thought of his family. His wife had given birth to eleven children. Of the eleven, eight had died, most of them lost to want and illness in times when crop failures had wiped out the food supply in his small village. For Dittoo, it was not difficult to recognize need on a child's face.

He turned onto the avenue. The richly dressed child in his memsahib's tent had certainly been ill-cared-for. There was even more to this story than the water carrier had told.

His step quickened. That the boy had vanished from his servant's arms in front of witnesses did not surprise him. He had heard of such things before. What he found difficult to believe was that the child had been transported by magic to the tent of *his own memsahib*.

She, an ignorant foreigner, had taken part in a great supernatural feat. Her powers must be enormous to have been recognized by the child's magician grandfather who had to be miles away in the city of Lahore.

As he passed the uniformed sentry at the entrance, he forced his mind back over the previous months but could remember no event that even hinted at her being a sorceress. One never knew to whom such powers might be granted, but to one of *them*? Even odder, to one of their *women*?

The English were ugly, with their odd clothes and odder hair. They were often rude, demanding, difficult to fathom, and furious when misunderstood. They had yellowing skin and dirty habits and their music was agony to the senses. Once, when he served at Government House, hearing loud noises and rhythmic thumping coming from the main salon, he had stolen across the garden and peered inside. Through a window, he had seen Europeans, men and women, dancing together in clumsy groups, running into one another as they moved, laughing loudly, heads thrown back, when their horrible music stopped.

They controlled most of India, these foreigners; yet for all their great power, most of them knew as little about life as they did about dancing. Once when Memsahib had been ill and Dittoo had served her for hours with no time for his midday meal, she had actually offered him her uneaten supper—meat, possibly even the flesh of a cow, drenched with brown liquid, other things, vegetables, equally repulsive.

Had she not known what pollution she offered him?

Memsahib spent her day rushing from place to place, fearing to be late, her toilet incomplete, her curly hair escaping its pins. She seemed to have time only for the munshi who had taught her many languages, but who was not Hindu like himself, and was therefore as ignorant as the British.

She waited for him now in her small, pointed tent, whose walls glowed faintly with the light of her lamp. If she *were* a sorceress and he were to tell his friends, report the child's whereabouts, and collect the reward, she would know it at once. Dittoo would then lose both his position and an opportunity to observe this curious being—a foreign female magician—at close quarters.

He frowned. Her weeping over the child had been unexpected. Being a sorceress, she must have known the baby's condition before he arrived in her tent. Why then had she been so pained at his misery? Could her tears, like the offer of her uneaten food, be signs of a generous heart? It was certainly unusual to see an Englishwoman cradling a child of India as if he were her own.

Perhaps the instinct that had led Dittoo to talk instructively to her had been correct. Perhaps it had been her heart that he had recognized when he had first seen her on that rainy morning in Simla.

At her door, he shuffled out of his shoes. It was difficult to trust the

English, very difficult indeed, but who knew? Perhaps, reward or no reward, he could do worse than to serve this curious person and keep her secrets. Perhaps, Englishwoman or no, she deserved the finest gift he could offer, his loyalty.

HE sat on the floor, the baby's legs dangling across his lap, squeezing rice and boiled lentils into bite-sized balls with his fingers. The little fellow's head was dirty and scabby. When had he last been bathed?

"Good boy," he said, thinking of his youngest son as he pushed a ball of food into the baby's open mouth.

There was something powerful about this child. Even in his weak condition, he seemed to give off a light that drew Dittoo, making him think of shrines and offerings. Had not Krishna-Ji himself appeared as a baby, a powerful force for good, able to perform magic? Perhaps it was this same sweet strength that gave the child such value in the Maharajah's eyes.

"Dittoo," Memsahib said from the chair, "there is no sign of rain, and so I will not be traveling in my palanquin tomorrow. I certainly cannot take this baba in the carriage with the Governor-General Sahib and his ladies. You must bring him with you on the march. Pretend he is your nephew, or your own child."

Dittoo sat quite still. How little she knew of things! How could he suddenly produce a baby and make the absurd claim that the child was his relation? And what if his lie were discovered? At the very least, he would be sent away with no pay. He might even be subjected to some horrible torture at the hands of the Maharajah's men. Why did she not simply perform some feat of sorcery?

"It will be difficult for me to bring him with the baggage," he replied, using the begging singsong he reserved for refusal. He grinned, hunching his shoulders. "Everyone in camp is looking for him. Everyone knows his story."

The baby pushed Dittoo's hand away. His curled fingers rested on Dittoo's knee. Dittoo wiped the small mouth with a rag. Regarding him gravely, the baby reached up and patted his face, then turned away, his thumb in his mouth.

Memsahib was staring. "Story? What story?"

Dittoo avoided her gaze. "His story—that he is a lucky talisman for Maharajah Ranjit Singh, that he has vanished into the air from the arms of his servant in front of everyone." He looked at her out of the corner of his eye. "All the camp knows that his disappearance is the work of his grandfather who is a famous magician of Lahore, and that an enormous reward has been offered for his return."

Her mouth fell open, then shut smartly. "What nonsense." She pushed back her hair and pointed to the baby. "He was—" She stopped, let out a little puff of air, and raised her chin. "Well," she snapped, "it does not matter how he came here, does it? In any event, I shall travel in the morning with the other English ladies. You will please bring the child. I do not care what you say to the others in camp. Now, it is getting late. Bring me hot water for his bath."

Chapter 19

Yar Mohammad squatted silently in the shadows outside the young memsahib's doorway, his head and upper body wrapped in a length of cotton, his nose protruding sharply from its folds. Memsahib's voice came from the tent, speaking softly and kindly. No one answered, no shadow moved on the wall. Her servant must have gone out.

The man's appearance at his fire had mystified Yar Mohammad at first. Hindu dietary laws would never have allowed such a man to approach a Muslim cooking fire to feed himself. His memsahib could not have desired Yar Mohammad's *dal roti*, the plain bread and lentils of the people. Only a stranger in need would be fed from a random cooking pot. Then it had come to him—there could be only one stranger at the camp whose need was great enough to send an Englishwoman's servant searching for food like a beggar.

Yar Mohammad closed his eyes at the soothing sound of the woman's voice. Yes, Shaikh Waliullah's little grandson was within. *Al-Hamdulillah,* praise be to Allah.

An hour earlier at his fire, he had waited until the memsahib's servant had scurried away with the food before making his own way to Shafi Sahib's tent.

The old man's beads had clicked quietly as Yar Mohammad told his story. "I believe you have guessed correctly, Yar Mohammad," Shafi Sahib agreed, nodding, when the groom finished speaking. "Go now," he added, "and give Memsahib a message."

Yar Mohammad had gone directly from Shafi Sahib, entering the red compound through a narrow servants' entrance in its high back wall, greeting the uniformed Punjabi sentry in his own tongue as he passed, gaining the compound without difficulty. He had skirted sleeping servants and banked fires, then crossed the open space toward the great tents of the Governor-General and his sisters. Moving silently from shadow to shadow, he had approached the young memsahib's tent unobserved.

His instructions were to deliver this new message at once, but when he arrived, he had not called out, for fear of startling her. Instead, he pulled his shawl over his head and around his knees. He would wait.

He did not wait long. Footsteps approached, then the young lady's servant appeared at the tent, his eyes on the ground, muttering to himself, a brass pail in each hand. Steam rose from one pail. A bath for the child.

The servant had not seen Yar Mohammad. Without looking up, he set one pail down, then reached to lift the reed curtain covering the doorway. Lamplight streamed through the entrance. In one swift motion, Yar Mohammad got to his feet and stepped from the shadows.

"*Hai-ai-ai!*" Startled, the servant shouted with sudden terror. The pail of hot water jerked in his hand, swinging sideways, splashing scalding water into the dust.

While the servant, breathing hard, grasped for the reed curtain, Yar Mohammad stepped forward and looked past him into the tent.

He drew in a long breath. The young memsahib sat facing the doorway, satin skirts the color of a lion's coat spread about her, brown curls framing her pale face as she bent protectively over a fair and broad-faced baby. Behind her, shadows leaped on the tent wall. For an instant, she returned Yar Mohammad's gaze, her eyes wide and fearless.

The servant forced the hanging shut and stepped hastily in front of Yar Mohammad, his buckets before him on the ground. "Why have you come?" he croaked.

"I have a message for Memsahib."

"It's too late to be bringing messages." The man was trying to sound forceful. Through the curtain Yar Mohammad could hear a rustling sound. Perhaps Memsahib was trying to conceal the baby.

"This message is important." Yar Mohammad's own voice was tight with excitement. "It is to be delivered at once. Tell her that I, Yar Mohammad, must deliver this message in person."

He could see that the man wanted to chase him away with shouts and curses, but was afraid to raise his voice again, fearing, most likely, that interested people might come from the servants' quarters and ask questions. Yar Mohammad stood still, towering over the servant, and waited.

The servant looked as if he were about to weep. He raised a trembling hand and pushed aside the door hanging, then, clearing his throat, entered the tent. "A man named Yar Mohammad is outside," he said, his frightened voice muffled by the hanging. "He says he has a message for you."

There was more rustling. Memsahib put her head around the entrance, then emerged and stood in front of Yar Mohammad, her face ivory pale in the moonlight.

"Yes, what is it?" White fingers gripping the doorway, she shifted her weight to block his view of the interior.

"Peace be upon you, Memsahib," Yar Mohammad began. "I bring a message. It is this: You have done well. Tell no one what you have done. Wait for your instructions."

She remained motionless, her skin white and luminous, then gave a high little laugh and wiped her hand on her skirt. "Thank you, Yar Mohammad, although I have no idea what your message means."

"Wait." Yar Mohammad put up a hand as she moved to withdraw. "I have something for you."

Whimpering came from within. Memsahib glanced over her shoulder, then back to Yar Mohammad. "Go away," she commanded, her eyes darkening. "Go away."

Without answering, he squatted down and took from his clothes the muslin-wrapped packet of coarse brown sugar that he always carried for his horses. As she watched him, her slender body erect, he took out his small, crooked knife and cut off a square of muslin, wrapped two lumps of the raw sugar in it, and held it out to her.

"Children like to eat this," he said. "The horses will not miss it."

She took the sugar and turned away, her glistening skirts swishing in the darkness.

As he strode away, he pondered how afraid the young woman had been when he handed her his gift. And yet, he had seen clearly that if he had tried to force his way into the tent, it would have been she, not her servant, who would have fought him.

He looked back over his shoulder at the small tent whose walls glowed faintly from the lamplight within. What had the two old men said to him at Shaikh Waliullah's haveli?

"Your work is about to begin," Shafi Sahib had told him.

"Only you will know when the time has come to act," the Shaikh had said.

MARIANA opened the flap and turned back to the tent, the little packet of sugar dangling from her fingers. "You told Yar Mohammad," she said accusingly. "Dittoo, what have you done?"

Ditto stood still in the center of the floor, the baby in his arms. When Mariana looked at him, her face drained of color, he bent double over the child. "I swear," he burbled, tears spurting from his eyes, "I swear I did not tell. The groom is an odd man. I do not know how he could have guessed. Oh, I beg of you, Memsahib, I am telling the truth! Please, oh, please, Memsahib, do not send me away!"

"What does this mean, Dittoo? Does everyone in camp know the baby is here in my tent? Does the Maharajah know?"

The baby reached for her. She took him from Dittoo and sat down at the table. "I thought we were safe, but we are not." She untied the packet, broke off a piece of the sugar, and put it into the baby's mouth.

"And do stop weeping, Dittoo," she added sharply. "Of course you must stay." She sighed as he mopped his eyes with his rag. "I cannot be left all alone with a native baby."

"The groom brought a message, did he not?" Dittoo asked. "What was his message?"

"It was nothing, Dittoo," she replied. "His message was nothing."

It was not nothing. She feared it, this third message. No longer vague and dismissible, this warning proved that someone was indeed watching her. *"Tell no one,"* Yar Mohammad had said. *"Wait for your instructions."* She wrapped the baby in her arms and held him tightly.

She must not give in to fear. Along with his message, Yar Mohammad had brought a gift. However afraid she was of the message, he had not threatened her.

"Dittoo," she said, "if Yar Mohammad had meant to betray us, he would not have given Baba the sugar. He would have told us that he knew, and then he would have tried to snatch Baba away. I think no one knows about Baba but Yar Mohammad, and perhaps one or two others. But I do not think they mean us harm."

Relief rushed over her. "And, oh Dittoo," she added, her face alight, "did you not fear, when he came, that he would take Baba away from us?"

She patted the baby's face. "Did you not think at first that Yar Mohammad was bent upon carrying away our baby and claiming the Maharajah's reward?"

She laughed, and then Dittoo laughed, and seeing them, the baby brightened and he smiled, his eyes becoming two half moons in his broad face, and she got to her feet and spun his little body in a circle, her tawny skirts swinging about her, in the middle of the lamplit tent.

Chapter 20

The moon sent a faint silver light onto the Maharajah's yellow shawl tent and the tall palanquin of colored glass that stood empty before its entrance. Guards spoke quietly among themselves as Faqeer Azizuddin walked Maharajah Ranjit Singh up and down, an arm protectively about the old man's shoulders.

Yusuf glanced at Hassan as their camel caravan approached. Something was indeed very wrong. It must be true, the frightening news they had heard upon reaching the Maharajah's camp.

"Yes, Saboor *is* missing." Hassan's voice sounded flat, as if all his feeling had been lost, along with his son. "But why, Yusuf? Who would steal my son from the Maharajah?"

"Do not fear, Hassan." Yusuf reached out a steadying hand as they halted before the yellow tent. With news this bad, he must think for them both. "Saboor will be found. Remember your father's letter."

"Where is Saboor?" Even before they dismounted, the Maharajah pushed his Chief Minister aside and hurried toward them. "Where is my little pearl?" he cried. "What have you done with him, Hassan, you and your magician father?"

Before Hassan could reply, the Faqeer seized the old man by the elbow and guided him back toward the tent. "Come, Maharaj," he soothed, throwing Hassan and Yusuf a warning glance. "Speak to Hassan inside. You must rest now."

Once inside the tent, Yusuf watched Hassan as he approached the Maharajah's bedside. "Maharaj," Hassan began, standing beside his king, his eyes on the carpet, "I arrived from Kasur only this evening, while you were at the Golden Temple. I came to bring you the first part of—"

"What do I care for gold and riches?" The old voice trembled. "All that matters to me is my Saboor."

Yusuf sweated at his post near the door. At least the guard had not disarmed them; they were not under arrest. But all those days and nights in Kasur—the discussions, the warnings, the flattery, all Hassan's patient efforts to win the Maharajah's tax money, his prayers that the Maharajah would allow him to take Saboor home at last, his quiet anxiety on the journey here—all were for naught, or were they?

Had someone already rescued Saboor? If so, who had risked death and a king's anger to save his child? Where had this person taken Saboor?

"Maharaj," interposed the Faqeer caressingly, "Hassan cannot have had a hand in this terrible business. He has been at Kasur on your work. He has come from there only this evening, carrying news and part of the tribute money. He is not to blame."

The Maharajah signaled for his quilt. "Bring me my Saboor," he said simply, reaching for the Faqeer's hand as a servant pulled the red satin quilt to his shoulders.

A faint motion of Faqeer Azizuddin's head told Hassan and Yusuf to leave. As the two men backed from the yellow tent, Yusuf saw tears on his king's face.

IT was still dark when Mariana was startled awake by the sound of hoarse, urgent whispering.

"Memsahib, Memsahib," Dittoo was saying, "I must take Baba outside."

Baba, who was Baba? Must Dittoo talk even at night? Moaning, she turned over, then found herself jerked into wakefulness by a small stirring at her side.

The stolen baby!

"But Dittoo," she whispered into the blackness, a hand on the little body beside her, "it's still the middle of the night!"

"No, Memsahib, it is nearly morning. Baba must come outside and do *soo-soo*."

"*Soo-soo?*"

"*Pishab.*"

Pishab? What important word had her munshi neglected to teach her?

"He will wet your bed," Dittoo hissed, arriving at her side and groping for the baby. "Babies must do their soo-soo at the proper time," he decreed, his voice reproving as he pushed open the blind, the child in his arms.

Mariana touched the warm place left by the sleeping baby and listened to Dittoo's muffled wheedling through her tent wall. There was so much to do. Lahore was still four marches away. However would she conceal a baby on a four-day march?

She thrust her covers aside and, without bothering to light the lamp, groped for her boots. There was no time to find fresh clothes; she would wear the same ones she had worn the evening before.

She had dreamed again of the ship. As she fumbled with hooks and buttons she tried to recapture her dream, but was able to conjure up only a vague image of taut rigging above her head and wind-carried spray stinging her face.

The dream reminded her of yesterday's poem.

Grieve not, O heart,
For Noah shall be thy guide:
Thy pilot-master of the deluge.

She reached to light her lamp. If only Noah were guiding *her*. Believing that, she could endure anything. But perhaps she *had* been guided to steal the Maharajah's hostage. What other explanation could there be?

The baby had wanted her to steal him, of that she had no doubt. It was he who had reached out to her from his servant's arms, he who had worn that expectant look on his little face. But why?

"*You have done well,*" the groom had told her last night.

Yar Mohammad. He was no simple groom, to be bringing her these mysterious messages. He denied it, but he, too, must be a soothsayer, like the madman on the road and the creature in the garden. Soothsayers seemed to be everywhere, giving her advice about courage and about the path she was said to have chosen. . . .

At least Dittoo was no soothsayer, she decided, as he returned with the baby.

"It's far too cold," she said worriedly, a little while later, pacing the floor. "How can you take him outside without any clothes? He will take ill—and what a pity to dirty him after his nice bath."

His round eyes fixed on Mariana, the baby stood shivering in the lamplight before Dittoo's squatting figure, one small arm in a firm brown grip as Dittoo smeared cold mud onto his naked body. Miserable sounds came from around the baby's thumb.

"They are searching for a rich child," Dittoo explained as he worked. "If Baba is naked and dirty I can say I found him on the road. These things happen all the time."

"I suppose you're right, but wait—" Mariana crossed to her dress trunk and dragged out her ruined tartan gown. She found the torn place, then with a grand gesture, tore the woolen skirt from seam to seam, filling the air with dust. "Wrap him in this. Tell them I saw the baby and took pity."

Moments later, a tartan-wrapped baby struggling under his arm, Dittoo tramped away toward the red wall while Mariana watched from the doorway, her heart thudding anxiously.

IT was cold, even at the fire. From Dittoo's lap, the child looked steadily from face to face, returning the curious gazes of Dittoo's three friends, while one tiny foot, free of the torn dress, swung rhythmically back and forth.

"How could I leave him alone on the road for the jackals and hyenas?" Dittoo demanded, pushing a wad of bread into the baby's open mouth with a practiced hand.

"Of course you could have left him there. Why is he any concern of yours?" asked Sita from where he sat drawing circles in the dust with a stick of kindling wood. "And what of his caste? For all you know, you have an untouchable child on your lap and are putting your fingers into his mouth."

With an apologetic grunt, young Mohan edged away, leaving a meaningful space between himself and the baby.

Guggan chewed thoughtfully on a *neem* twig. "The children one finds here and there on the roads are nothing but trouble. Of course," he added, changing his tone, "if he were the Maharajah's hostage—"

"I know he will be trouble," Dittoo interrupted hastily, wiping the baby's mouth. "But what could I do?" His fingers shook as he wrapped the baby more securely in his tartan rag.

"You are too softhearted, Dittoo." Sita reached over his head to scratch his back with his stick. "Of course you can always sell him. You might get a good price from Sirosh the tailor or what's-his-name, the blacksmith—"

"No, do not do that." Guggan peered into the baby's attentive face. "After all, he is here now. We can look after him. A blacksmith—pah! Who can entrust a child to a blacksmith?

"He's different, you know," he added thoughtfully. "He is not like most babies." He spat a bit of bark into the fire and poked a pudgy finger at the tartan rag. "He should have clothes. A man from my village does tailoring for the army. I'll ask him."

Nodding, Dittoo held a cup to the child's lips. As he did so, the baby's body went rigid. Then, in one startling motion, he reached a small hand up and dashed the cup from Dittoo's fingers. The four men watched as it tumbled to the ground and rolled away, spilling drops of milk into the hissing fire.

"GOOD gracious, Mariana, this is the second time you've asked," Miss Emily remarked after breakfast, shading her eyes with a gloved hand. "It's never any use wondering where our things are. I, for one, expect to be reunited with my parasol precisely at sunset. But I must say, I never saw anybody so feverish for the sight of a muddy tent and an incompetent servant."

"I quite understand," put in Miss Fanny kindly. She shifted in her folding chair. "I like to know where *all* my things are after every march, especially the spotted deer. I always worry until everything is just as it should be."

"Not that in India anything is ever as it should be," added Lord Auckland. He yawned as he consulted his timepiece. "Thank goodness we need not entertain a single native until four o'clock." He leaned back in his basket chair with a sigh.

"Why not go out for a nice ride later, my dear?" said Miss Emily, studying Mariana with a shrewd blue eye. "It will do you good to exercise. You are probably a little overwrought after all the excitement of yesterday."

Excitement. Mariana felt her throat go dry.

"It *was* exciting, was it not?" Miss Fanny said animatedly. "I thought the fireworks made the temple and water tank seem like a fairy palace!"

Miss Emily's eyes had not left Mariana. "You really do look pale, my child. I shall arrange for you to ride one of the nicer horses. I have seen the poor little nag they've given you. No wonder you have not been riding."

HOT in her tawny silks, Mariana stood an hour later before her collapsed tent, watching a group of coolies lay out ropes and tent pegs. Where in the chaos of the rising camp was her small charge?

As soon as her tent was standing and its furniture arranged, she rushed inside and stood impatiently in the center of the striped floor, anticipating the familiar but now thrilling sound of Dittoo blundering into her tent.

At last he stood before her, his face creased in a smile, the child wriggling under his arm.

"Oh, thank goodness you have returned," she breathed, burying her face in the baby's neck. She laid him down on the bed and cooed delightedly at his slow, lovely smile. "He should have another bath. Were you seen?"

"No, Memsahib." Mud streaked the gray stubble on Dittoo's chin, making him look even shabbier than usual. "We were—"

"Hush!" she warned at the sound of two men talking outside accompanied by the clopping of a horse's hooves. Her grooms had arrived with one of Miss Emily's horses.

"Go," she urged Dittoo, waving a hand toward the entrance, "and send them away. Tell them I do not wish to ride today."

As Dittoo put his head out through the entrance, she let the baby down and watched as he trotted across the floor. He stopped, balancing carefully, then squatted down, reaching out with delicate fingers to pick something up from the floor.

"No, darling, not Mariana's hairpin," she whispered, snatching him up and opening his small fist.

The diminishing sound of hooves was replaced almost at once by the sound of someone clearing his throat outside. Dittoo jerked his head back inside. "Memsahib," he whispered hoarsely, "we have forgotten your munshi!"

Mariana thrust the baby at Dittoo and pulled open a canvas curtain on the inside wall of her tent, but as she motioned Dittoo to step into her tiny bathing space, a clanking of pails from outside told her that the sweeper was about to enter. Was everyone converging on her tent at once? Swiftly, she secured the curtain, shutting the sweeper out, then turned back, her finger to her lips, searching desperately for another hiding place.

Outside the entrance, a second throat-clearing held mild impatience.

"What can I say to make Munshi Sahib leave?" she whispered urgently to Dittoo.

Her servant shrugged, the baby in his arms.

It was too late to hide the baby now. Mariana held out her arms for the child. "Come in," she called, her voice cracking.

Her teacher stepped carefully inside, stooped as usual, blinking in the dusky light. At the sight of the baby in Mariana's arms, he took a step backward.

Munshi was not a man to be lied to. Before he could speak, she crossed the floor to him. "Munshi Sahib," she whispered, as the sweeper banged pails together behind the curtain, "this child is the son of a great man from the walled city of Lahore. No one must know he is here."

"Ah," replied the munshi.

One arm curled tight around Mariana's neck, the baby gazed bright-eyed at their elderly visitor.

She drew herself up. "I have stolen him from the Maharajah. People had been unkind to him. Look."

"He's been hurt." She clasped the baby's hand and held it against her cheek.

"How did you come to steal him?" asked the old man, his expression unreadable.

"His servant came to me in the Golden Temple and showed me all his poor little ribs and his bruises. I could not help him then."

She shivered, remembering. "But at the end of the evening, the same man rushed up and simply handed him to me. I put him into my palanquin and brought him here."

"Did anyone see you?" The munshi's face was grave.

"No. It was quite curious," she answered slowly. "I felt almost invisible. Everyone walked past as if I weren't there. No one, not even the Indians, looked my way."

She stroked the baby's cheek. "It was all so simple and happened so quickly—I could have stolen several children and no one would have cared."

"There you are mistaken, Bibi." Putting his hands behind him, the munshi straightened his back. "Very much mistaken. There are those who care very much about this child. To help anyone to escape the Maharajah's household, especially if that person is one of the Maharajah's hostages, is a serious crime. Had your action been discovered," he added, narrowing his eyes, "the alliance between your people and the Maharajah would have been most severely tested. The child would have been returned to the Maharajah and you would have been sent back to Calcutta in disgrace."

She tightened her grip on the baby.

Seeing her response, his face softened. "But you were *not* seen."

Approaching, he bent formally and peered into the baby's face. "What is your name, son?"

The baby took a breath, then spoke his first word in Mariana's hearing. "Thaboor," he said, wriggling in her arms.

The old man smiled. "Saboor, is it? Well, well."

"What should I do now, Munshi Sahib?" Mariana asked. Tingles of fear ran down her spine. Whatever had she done? "What should I do?"

"It is clear that to save an ill-treated child is a good and charitable act. It is also clear that what has happened thus far has been the work of Allah Most Gracious, who inspired the servant to give you the child and who protected you from discovery once you had taken him. You ask me what to do. I suggest that you pray."

"Pray?" Mariana watched Saboor totter to where Dittoo held out his arms.

"You offer your prayers to God the All-Powerful, do you not, Bibi?" the munshi asked mildly.

"Yes," she returned, "but surely there is—"

"I must have time to think," her teacher interrupted, raising an admonitory finger. "And you, Bibi, must put this whole affair into the hands of Allah Most Merciful."

At Mariana's forlorn sigh, Munshi Sahib made an indefinable gesture indicating the subject was closed.

"As to our lesson," he added, smiling at Saboor, "this is a most unusual day, not the proper day for a lesson. Today shall be a holiday. If I may have your permission, Memsahib," he said, inclining his head, "I will leave you. If you should need my help, Dittoo knows where to find me."

Without looking back, he stepped from the tent. Mariana sat down on the edge of her bed, a little giddy, a hand to her breast.

In the munshi's wake, faint wisps of fog seemed to hang in the air. In the first moments they had spent together, the baby Saboor had magically taken hold of her heart. He was hers, and she was now his. No one could tell her otherwise. Perhaps, in taking him, she had chosen a path of some kind, as the soothsayer had predicted. But whether or not she had taken a path, she would be careful, for Saboor's very life depended on her, she was certain of it. Yes, she would most certainly be very careful.

Half-awake under her covers, Mariana listened to the rain falling on the canvas above her head.

"But Memsahib, he must sleep with *me*," Dittoo had insisted the previous evening as the baby in his arms reached out to her with urgent cries. "The other servants will be expecting him. They will ask questions if he is not with me."

He had been right. How could they pretend Saboor was a lost child if he disappeared at night to someone else's bed?

Unable to argue, she had waved Dittoo and Saboor away, then slept badly, certain that Dittoo had not wrapped the child well enough against the cold.

Now she rolled onto her back and pulled her pillow over her face. In spite of Munshi Sahib's warnings, how easy it had been, first to steal, then to harbor Saboor. . . .

Only Dittoo, Munshi, and Yar Mohammad knew of the baby's whereabouts, and none of them seemed inclined to give him away.

The English were not even aware of his existence. If they were, they would never imagine that one of their own people had stolen him.

Someone else knew. Mariana pushed away the pillow and opened her eyes. How could she have forgotten Yar Mohammad's message? No, she must not think of that. She must think of how to keep darling little Saboor safe, and fatten him up and make him happy.

Footsteps approached. "Memsahib, I have brought Baba," Dittoo whispered. "Rain has begun, and so you will be traveling to the next camp by palki. I have told my friends that I have sent Baba to travel in a covered cart with a barber's family."

"*Shabash,* Dittoo, well done," she said, smiling her wide smile as she rose to greet them. "Well done indeed."

" 'MATTHEW, Mark, and Luke, and John,' " she sang softly an hour later, her voice echoing inside the closed palanquin, " 'bless the bed that I lie on—' "

A gusting wind threw spatters of rain against her palki's thin walls. Outside, the steadily panted "hah, hah, hah" of her bearers told her all was well.

"How kind of the weather to let us travel together," she whispered. "Wasn't Dittoo clever to knock over the coffee things and distract our bearers while I bundled you inside!"

The shaven-headed babe in the crook of her arm did not have her brother Ambrose's rosy skin, and his eyes were brown, not deepest blue, but his small weight against her eased her old sense of loss. His eyelids drooped, and he made little effort to sit up, but he seemed content in her company. He gazed into her face, letting her nuzzle and stroke him as much as she liked. She sat up, stuffed the pillows behind her back, and pulled him onto her lap.

"There," she said softly, as Saboor rested against her breast. She closed her eyes. If only she could show him to her family, especially to Papa—

She was glad that the baby did not fidget. The space inside the palki was long enough, extending past her feet, but it was barely wide enough for her to move, and each time she sat up, the roof grazed her head.

"Listen to the rain on the roof, my pet," she whispered. "Today we *love* the rain, do we not, my little treasure?"

She rubbed her nose against Saboor's cheek. "You see," she whispered, as he reached for the locket she wore on a gold chain around her neck, "you and I are quite safe and happy together!"

• • •

BECAUSE of the rain, the march took longer than usual. Breakfast, usually served as soon as everyone arrived at the new site, was late and crowded. Officers and staff members who would otherwise have taken their breakfast outdoors had elected to join the Governor-General and his party under cover. The dining tent was filled to capacity. Unable to sit at the table, the younger men ate standing, juggling crockery and teaspoons.

A servant pulled out a chair for Mariana beside Miss Fanny. Mariana sat and arranged her skirts, surveying the laden breakfast table. Turning Saboor over to Dittoo at the end of the march had been tricky but successful, and now she was free to enjoy her breakfast. She took a brioche and reached for a butter knife.

Harry Fitzgerald had appeared in the crowd. She glanced up, wishing she could edge over and tell him all about the baby while no one was looking.

Lieutenant Marks, who, thanks to Miss Emily, was also in the honor guard, hovered by Miss Fanny, eating a plate of eggs and attempting to catch Mariana's eye. He was invited for a glass of wine tomorrow, and Miss Emily expected her to attend *and* be civil, although she had twice been quite clear about her feelings. The second time, she had even rashly mentioned Marks's ears.

"The lieutenant's ears," Miss Emily had replied, "are of no consequence. In time, you will cease to notice them."

Mariana would *never* cease to notice them. They symbolized all her feelings about being pushed into a marriage of convenience. This morning, as Marks smirked at her over his fork, she imagined them growing longer and longer until they drooped to his shoulders.

Beyond the simpering Marks, Fitzgerald balanced his cup on a plate, his fine profile turned to Mariana. His hair looked ruffled, as though he had not slept well. She would run away with him tomorrow if there were anywhere *to* run in the Maharajah's territories, or if he were not leaving any day to march for Afghanistan.

She turned deliberately, avoiding Marks's stare, and gazed with pretended fascination at a servant balancing a tray of dirty plates. All she could do now was travel back to Calcutta with Lord Auckland and his party, praying all the way that Fitzgerald would finish his tour of duty in Afghanistan and return to her. Sooner or later his true story would reach Miss Emily. Sooner or later, everything must be all right.

"Where is Major Byrne?" Miss Fanny's voice broke into Mariana's thoughts.

"He has gone to arrange for sheep," offered Lieutenant Marks.

"Sheep?" Miss Emily stopped slicing a lamb kidney. "What do we want with sheep?"

"We're having them for lunch tomorrow, Miss Emily." Marks nodded seriously.

Miss Emily's eyebrows lifted. "What sort of sheep are we expecting for lunch? I hope no one has invited the vulgar ones with orange splotches."

Marks gaped in confusion. At the table's end, Lord Auckland folded his napkin. "If I were you, Emily," he offered, a corner of his mouth turning up, "I should not wear wool at tomorrow's lunch."

Miss Fanny bent confidentially toward Mariana. "*Sheep* is one of my sister's favorite words."

"And now, dear Mariana," said Miss Emily, changing the subject, "you must hear the latest excitement from the Maharajah's court." She set down her porcelain coffee cup with a click. "We have just learned that while we were at the Golden Temple two evenings ago watching the fireworks display, someone performed an interesting feat of magic."

"Yes, indeed," Miss Fanny put in. "It is such a pity we missed seeing it happen. The story has all the romance of an Oriental Tale."

Miss Emily patted her mouth with her napkin. "You must have seen," she began, "the sickly-looking baby that the Maharajah keeps beside him all the time. The child is a political hostage, kept to ensure the loyalty of his father, a young man who assists the mysterious Faqeer Azizuddin, the Maharajah's Chief Minister."

Mariana caught her breath.

"The little hostage," Miss Emily went on, waving her knife over the butter dish as the standing crowd quieted to listen, "was present at the fireworks that evening. You may have noticed him, Mariana, when the Maharajah held him up to see the display."

Mariana nodded mutely.

"Apparently, the child disappeared immediately afterward, in spite of every precaution having been taken to ensure his security."

Miss Fanny leaned forward, her face alight. "According to the natives, the child *evaporated* from his servant's arms as he was being carried to the Maharajah's palanquin. Since that moment, no trace of the little one has been found. The Maharajah is said to be quite desolate at the loss of the child, who, he believes, brings him luck."

Mariana noticed Fitzgerald watching her speculatively from across the tent.

Miss Emily's eyes shone bright blue. "As if that were not enough, we are told that the child's grandfather is a well-known magician. The natives believe it was he who spirited the boy away, but this theory suffers from the fact that, at the time of the baby's disappearance, the grandfather was not at Amritsar with all of us but forty miles away in Lahore."

A burst of amusement came from the young officers. Behind Lord Auckland's chair, Colin Marks exchanged a whispered remark with another man, who threw back his head in suppressed laughter.

Miss Emily lowered her cup onto its saucer, her turned-up mouth making her look very like her brother. "Of course, that explanation is ridiculous, but I enjoy picturing the old man muttering spells in his room after supper, while miles away the Maharajah's hostage vanishes into the air."

Mariana tried to smile along with the others. Little Saboor's grandfather was a magician. What could that mean? She closed her eyes and saw the servant running toward her in the torchlight, his lips moving, Saboor bouncing in his arms.

Two seats away from her, Dr. Drummond cleared his throat. "Considering the carelessness of the natives," he intoned, "it is only surprising the child has not been lost before. He was probably stolen right in front of them while they were all looking the other way."

A wave of mirth circled the table. Mariana felt the color drain from her face.

"Are you all right, my dear?" Miss Emily frowned. "Take a piece of fruit."

"Oh, no, thank you very much." A lovely guava was within Mariana's reach, but she could not trust her shaking hands with the fruit knife.

"An enormous reward has been offered for the baby's return." Miss Fanny threaded her napkin into its silver ring and gave it a pat. "Is that not so, Mr. Macnaghten?"

The political secretary sat back in his chair and waved away a servant bearing a coffeepot. "Let us hope," he said, glancing toward the head of the table, "that the child is returned before anything happens to the Maharajah's health. Any illness he suffers now may be blamed on the child's absence. If it is serious, the illness might affect the treaty."

Lord Auckland had stopped smiling. "Do you think," he asked sharply, "that the disappearance of this child could harm our treaty negotiations, that the Maharajah might actually refuse to sign our agreement over the Afghan Campaign?"

"There are two possibilities, my lord," Macnaghten replied. "One is that the Maharajah may fall ill, delaying the signing of the treaty. The second is far graver."

The crowd around the table tensed. Mariana twisted her handkerchief in her lap.

"The natives are a treacherous lot, as we all know," Macnaghten continued, lifting his heavy brows. "There is a possibility that someone opposed to the treaty may have taken the child himself, and planted him in this camp."

"Planted him *here*?" Miss Emily stared, her cup poised halfway to her mouth.

Mr. Macnaghten nodded. "If that were the case and the child were to be discovered here, the Maharajah would certainly believe we had stolen him."

"*Stolen* him? Why should *we* do such a thing?" Miss Fanny's voice rose in astonishment.

At the end of the table, Lord Auckland twirled his butter knife. Mr. Macnaghten made a steeple of his fingers. "Because, Miss Fanny," he replied, "the Maharajah is quite convinced this particular hostage is responsible for all his present good fortune. In fact, it is said that next to the great Koh-i-noor diamond, the baby is Ranjit Singh's finest possession. He calls the child his Pearl of Pearls. He would naturally assume that we had abducted the child in order to procure his luck for ourselves. He might not, under such circumstances, sign our treaty. We might be forced to abandon the Afghan Campaign."

Abandon the campaign? Prickles of panic raced up Mariana's arms and legs.

Lord Auckland scowled. He made little stabbing motions with his knife at the tablecloth. "Are you certain of this, Macnaghten?"

Mr. Macnaghten did not look well. "My lord," he answered, "we must be mindful of the extraordinary power of native superstitions. The natives attach enormous importance to the oddest of things. Since the possibility exists that the child is here," he continued more briskly, "I should urge everyone in camp to look for him."

Mariana concentrated on breathing in and out, in and out. She dared not meet anyone's eyes.

Lord Auckland nodded. "You are quite right. We must ensure that this business of the baby does not interfere with our plans. As we all know, there is no time to be lost in signing the treaty."

He surveyed the crowded tent and raised his voice. "I recognize how unlikely this is, but if any of you should learn anything at all of this child's whereabouts, you are to report such information immediately to Mr. Macnaghten. Is that quite understood?"

Everyone nodded. The standing aides-de-camp, junior officers, and Harry Fitzgerald all murmured their agreement.

Mariana could bear it no longer. She pushed herself to her feet. "I beg your pardon, Lord Auckland, Miss Emily, Miss Fanny, but I have just remembered that my teacher is coming early today."

A male voice followed Mariana as she fled the dining tent. "Aren't these natives extraordinary," Lieutenant Marks was saying. "Imagine making such a fuss over a little black baby!"

MARIANA sat on the edge of her bed, her thoughts spinning. With everyone looking for Saboor, how long would it be before he was found and handed over like a lost parcel to the horrid old Maharajah—to die of grief and neglect while she stood helplessly by?

But she would *not* stand helplessly by. Within hours of the discovery, she would be on her way to Calcutta in utter disgrace. The Maharajah, claiming bad faith, would no doubt refuse to sign the treaty. Unable to establish supply lines or move troops across his territory, the British would then be forced to abandon their plan for Afghanistan. Unable to put their own puppet king on the Afghan throne, what chance would they then have of controlling Central Asia?

Everyone would blame her.

She dropped her face into her hands and let out a little howl of terror.

Who would betray them? Who knew of Saboor's presence in her tent? Did the sweeper know? Had he heard Saboor's voice while he was emptying her chamber pot? Had he overheard her talking to Dittoo? What of her palanquin bearers? They had already had the chance to see Saboor on three occasions. What of Dittoo's friends at his cooking fire? Had they guessed the identity of the child Dittoo slept with each night?

And what of the mysterious people who also knew, but had not revealed themselves?

She stood and began to pace the floor. There must be something she could do to keep Saboor's presence in the camp a secret. She must not allow herself to panic. Dittoo had certainly been correct to disguise him as a lost village child. That disguise could work. It *must* work.

Scuffling outside interrupted her whirling thoughts, and there was Saboor, rolled in his torn tartan gown and tucked under Dittoo's arm, chirping with delight as the blind dropped shut behind them, wriggling to get down, already reaching for her.

"What has happened, Memsahib?" Dittoo asked, his own face turning from warm brown to dusky gray.

"The English sahibs have guessed," she replied as Saboor wrapped his arms about her neck. "They have guessed that Saboor is here in camp—Lord Auckland says everyone is to search for him."

Dittoo put his tongue out in dismay, then smiled. "But then, Memsahib," he rejoined happily, "you have only to perform your magic and all will be well, is that not so?"

"No, Dittoo, it is *not* so," she snapped. "Don't be idiotic."

Hearing her tone, the child on her hip looked up, then laid a small sticky, calming hand on her cheek.

"AND so, Munshi Sahib," she said a little later, staring down at the ruined handkerchief between her fingers, "it seems that Saboor is in terrible danger of being discovered."

Her teacher stood where he had stopped as she began telling him her story. When she finished speaking, he turned and gazed out through the open doorway to the dusty compound with its drooping canvas wall.

"You and Saboor, God willing, will soon be safe, Bibi," he said, nodding seriously.

"Safe? Both of us?" Mariana gazed doubtfully at him, then at Saboor, who bounced, watching them, in Dittoo's lap. "But how, Munshi Sahib?"

"When Saboor came into your hands at Amritsar," the munshi answered, his eyes now on the child, "we were forty miles from Lahore. We have made two marches since that day. Lahore is now only twenty miles away. By tomorrow, having marched another ten miles, we will be close enough to the walled city for you to return Saboor to his grandfather's house there. You can do this at night, while everyone is sleeping."

"Return him?" Mariana jumped from her chair. "Of course! We will hide him until tomorrow night, and then I shall spirit him from camp after dinner, and hand him back to his family. No one will ever know." She clapped her hands. "What an adventure that will be! And by the next morning, the camp will have arrived in Lahore, and I shall simply slip back into my tent, and no one will be the wiser. Saboor will be quite safe again. Oh, Munshi Sahib, I am so relieved!"

"Exactly so, Bibi."

Her face fell. "But how am I to find the Shaikh's house?"

The munshi made a sweeping gesture, including in it himself, her, and Dittoo. "There is one other person besides the three of us who knows that Saboor is with you?"

"The groom, Yar Mohammad, knows." Mariana hesitated. "Also some mysterious people who have sent me messages, but I do not know who they are."

Her teacher gave a small, dismissive wave of his fingers. "Then," he said, "it is Yar Mohammad who will find the grandfather and arrange your journey."

AFTER two days in their care, Saboor had begun to play. While Mariana brooded over her interview with her teacher, he sat on the floor beside her, sorting her hairbrushes and thumping them experimentally on the striped rug.

After her meeting with Munshi, Mariana's relief had been replaced by an unexpected pain that had wrapped itself around her heart. Tomorrow night she was to give Saboor back to his own people, to grow into a man and live a native life. She would never see him again. When she was an old lady in a lace cap she would remember his luminous presence, his slow, beautiful smile, the happy little sigh he gave when she picked him up, the dear pressure of his arms about her neck.

His sweet company had consoled her since her loss of Fitzgerald. Now she must endure the months of travel back to Calcutta without Saboor, without Fitzgerald, with only the fading hope of a happily married future. She imagined the vicarage dining room in twenty years, and her father carving her a slice of mutton with elderly, shaking hands.

The baby pushed himself to his feet and clung, hiccuping, to her knee. She cupped his soft chin in her hand. "*Must* I return you to your family tomorrow?" she asked him.

He was getting better, and he loved her so. Surely Dittoo could hide him for one more day among the English tents. After all, they had hidden him successfully for three days already. Two days from now they would reach Lahore. Why not wait until then—at least until then? Surely they could keep him hidden if they were clever. . . .

Munshi Sahib would not approve of her keeping Saboor any longer, but Munshi Sahib did not understand how much she needed her tiny companion.

A little while after the sun had begun its decline, the muezzin of Sohani Kot arrived at his mosque. He climbed the narrow stair of its single minaret slowly, pausing several times on the way to catch his breath. Arriving at the parapet, he wiped his face before leaning out, his hands cupping his mouth, to chant the *azan* as he had chanted it five times a day for twenty years, reminding all those within the sound of his voice to offer their prayers.

His voice was still melodious and strong. It carried past the wall of the little town to the horse lines of the British camp where Yar Mohammad sat deep in thought, polishing a harness.

The groom raised his head, then set down his work, got to his feet, and strode toward the mosque.

Inside the courtyard, he rolled up his sleeves and plunged his arms into the cool water of the fountain. His lips moved in recitation as he washed for his prayers.

When he had finished, he felt a hand on his shoulder. He did not turn to see who was there, but waited, without speaking, while beside him, Shafi Sahib, too, made himself ready for his prayers.

Together, they studied the arriving men as they washed and formed rows facing toward Mecca. Yar Mohammad pointed toward a stocky man who stood nearby, his feet apart, his eyes closed, his hands clasped before him. Shafi Sahib shook his head.

Yar Mohammad subtly pointed out a second man. This time Shafi Sahib nodded.

Shaking their hands dry, Shafi Sahib and Yar Mohammad joined the worshipers as they stood, bent and bowed with the rhythm of their prayers.

By the time they left the mosque, they had chosen twenty-four men.

Chapter 22

We have no information yet." Faqeer Azizuddin motioned his assistant toward a pair of reed stools that waited in the shade. "If I knew your son's whereabouts, I would already have sent someone to bring him here." He tipped his head toward the Maharajah's silent yellow tent, twenty yards away, the saddled horse tethered beside it.

"You would have sent someone to bring him *here*?" Hassan sat down wearily. "Why, Faqeer Sahib? Saboor is ill. He must be allowed to come home to us."

The Faqeer drew his robe over his knees. "I know, my boy, I know your son should be with you. I have tried many times to persuade the Maharajah to send him home, but this is not the time to do it." He patted Hassan's arm. "Do not fear. We will find Saboor, we will look after him, and we will return him after the durbar. That I have promised you."

Hassan's eyes did not leave the Faqeer's face. "People say he was too weak to stand when he arrived at this camp."

The Faqeer nodded. "Saboor was weak when he came, yes," he agreed, "but he has recently become stronger. He has a reliable servant. The cooks have been ordered to make fresh food for him." He leaned forward. "Hassan, you know how I love you and your father. I am desperate at your pain and at Saboor's loneliness, but the Maharajah, too, deserves our affection. Who else has his energy, his curiosity, his courage? Who else could have forged the Punjab, beaten and impoverished after a hundred years of plunder and destruction, into this great kingdom?"

He opened his hands. "Like all men, he has failings. He drinks too much wine, he eats and sleeps too little. These failings are killing him. There are times when he cannot move his limbs, when he cannot speak. He will not take his medicine of ground pearls. All he wants is Saboor. I know it is desperation and not reason that leads him to believe in Saboor's power to heal him, but I cannot stand by and see my king die without trying to give him what he wants. If, at this moment, I could bring Saboor to him, I would do it."

"Will the Maharajah die because he is without my Saboor, or will Saboor die because he is with the Maharajah?" Hassan's tone was soft, but his face remained hard.

Faqeer Azizuddin did not reply. Both men looked up as a servant boy stepped from the parade ground and approached them. "Are you, sir, the Maharajah's Chief Minister?" the boy asked in a clear voice, after planting himself in front of the Faqeer.

"I am," answered the Faqeer.

"Then this letter is for you." The child held out a folded paper.

As the boy departed, Faqeer Azizuddin turned the letter over. "My old friend Shafiuddin," he said warmly. "How well I remember his hand! I was so sorry to have missed him when he was at your father's house." He smiled at Hassan. "Our friendship is as old as our childhood. Shafi was the best at kite flying. How daring he was then, leaning far out from the rooftops to swoop his kite with its colorful, glass-embedded string, cutting other kites from the air! Ah, those were wonderful days, running on the rooftops of Lahore with Shafi and Waliullah!"

He unfolded the paper, read it, then gave Hassan an appraising look. "Do you know," he asked, "the contents of this letter?"

"Sir, I do not."

"Then I will read it to you. '*Waliullah's grandson is at the British camp. You should know that we intend to return him to Qamar Haveli tomorrow evening. If you can arrange for the child to remain there undisturbed, we will be most grateful.*'"

The Faqeer folded the paper. He looked up. "Who are '*we*'?" he asked, his voice turning silken. "Who joins in Shafi's request besides you and my friend Waliullah?"

Hassan's face had relaxed. His eyes were shining. He did not reply.

The Faqeer stared into the distance. "So," he said at last, "I find myself alone with my king. My two oldest friends have taken the side of your son. Poor Saboor, poor Maharajah." He shook his head. "Take it," he said brusquely, holding out the letter.

Hassan slipped the folded paper into the pocket over his heart where it rustled against another, older letter.

Someone else had come. Near the yellow tent, a showily dressed eunuch attended by a trio of servants began to argue in a loud whisper with an armed guard. The guard signaled to the Faqeer with a raised arm.

Faqeer Azizuddin sighed. "What does that fool want? How I dislike these household eunuchs!"

The eunuch performed an elaborate salute as the two men approached. "My name is Gurbashan," he said grandly. "I have come to tell you that I know the whereabouts of the child Saboor."

He thrust his head back and beamed at the Faqeer, who blinked, but did not respond. Beside the Faqeer, Hassan stared at the man, his body tensing.

"I would know the boy anywhere," the eunuch added, waving an arm. "It was I who escorted him to—"

"Indeed," the Faqeer interrupted smoothly. "And how did you find him?"

The eunuch's smile broadened, displaying unfortunate teeth. "Faqeer Sahib, it is kind of you to ask, but, if you will forgive me, I have come to give this news only to the Maharajah himself."

The Maharajah's guards had heard. Two of them hurried into the tent, talking as they went. A high, cracked voice issued from inside.

"Come in," it commanded. "Come here at once, Aziz!"

A servant held the door hanging aside and gestured for them all to enter.

The air inside the little tent was cold. The Faqeer pulled his cloak about his shoulders as he lowered himself to the carpet beside the Maharajah's pillow. The eunuch edged up to stand beside the bed. Hassan watched from the shadows.

The wadded satin quilt had been thrown aside, leaving the Maharajah's fully clothed body to sweat on the thin mattress. Uncut since his birth, his hair stood twisted into a tight, iron gray knot on his crown. His beard lay unfurled and tangled on his chest. His seeing eye was open and bright with fever. A figured silver cup stood on a carved table behind his head.

"Yes, yes, of course I remember Gurbashan," he croaked impatiently, as the Faqeer began his introduction. He turned to the eunuch. "Speak, man, speak."

The eunuch gave another elaborate salute. "The baby is at the English camp, Maharaj," he announced in his dusky voice. "When I was visiting one of my friends there, I saw him myself."

"And how did you recognize him?" The Faqeer laced his fingers together.

"It was I, Faqeer Sahib, who personally escorted the child to this very camp from the Citadel. I would know him anywhere."

"Yes, yes, I know." The old Maharajah glared up from his pillow. "You are the one who made us wait all morning for Saboor before the procession. Go on, tell us which Englishman is keeping my Saboor." Color was already returning to his face. "Hah, Aziz," he added, "and you were telling me only this morning that there was no news!"

The eunuch paused dramatically. "The child," he declared, "is in the red compound where the British Governor and his ladies are quartered."

The Maharajah's sharp intake of breath induced such a fit of coughing that two servants were obliged to step forward, sit him up, and thump him on the back.

When the Maharajah was quiet again, the eunuch pulled a small silver knife from his cummerbund. Bending over beside the bed he drew a large rectangle in the pile of the carpet with the point of his blade.

"This," he said, pointing to its center, "is the compound where the Governor and the ladies keep their tents. It is surrounded by a high red wall and has three entrances."

The Maharajah propped himself on one elbow and breathed noisily, studying the marks on the carpet. "Hassan," he cried, looking up, "your son has been found! How did you discover him, Gurbashan?"

The eunuch showed his teeth again. "A man from the Citadel has recently been hired as one of the Governor-General's cooks."

The Faqeer shifted on the floor. "We know, Gurbashan," he said, a little wearily.

"The guarded main entrance is here, on the avenue." The eunuch stabbed the middle of one long side of his rectangle. "And the two service entrances are here, and here." He pointed to the ends of the other long side. "The tents of Lord Auckland and his ladies are arranged so, so, and so, and here is their dining tent." He drew three rectangles in the center of the space, then with a flourish, drew a fourth rectangle to form a square.

The Maharajah pointed eagerly to the carpet. "And my little Saboor is in one of these tents?"

"No, Maharaj." Bending, the eunuch put a finger on the left corner fronting the avenue. "The child is here, in the tent of a young woman who translates for the Governor-General's sisters."

Hassan drew an audible breath.

The eunuch stood straight, his silks rustling. "My friend said he has seen the same child being carried to and from that tent three times in the past two days."

"How could Saboor be in the Governor-General's compound?" the Maharajah demanded shrilly. "Has he been stolen by the British?"

The eunuch shrugged. "I do not know, Maharaj, but I can tell you this much." He drew a line of crosses along the back wall. "The child has been seen here, among the servants' cooking fires, and here, entering the translator's tent." He pointed, once more, to the corner.

"The girl? He was stolen by the *girl*? The girl they brought—" Wheezing, the Maharajah sank back into his pillow. "Aziz, tell me what this means!"

Hassan retreated to the shadows, a hand to the pocket over his heart.

Faqeer Azizuddin cleared his throat. "Whatever may be the truth of this matter," the minister said slowly, "we must think carefully before proceeding."

"Think carefully?" the Maharajah cried. "Why think carefully? I must have the boy in my arms by nightfall!"

"That can easily be done." The eunuch waved manicured fingers. "There are men in the city skilled in the stealing of children. We will pay one of them to do it," he added, as Faqeer Azizuddin stiffened. "I will go now and—"

"A child stealer!" Hassan lunged from the shadows and caught the eunuch by his shirt. He grasped a handful of satin at the man's neck. "Snake," he hissed, twisting the shiny fabric, his face distorted. "Son of shame!"

The eunuch squeaked with fright and clawed at his throat. His eye wide, the Maharajah wheezed on his bed. Without taking his eyes from the Maharajah, the Faqeer reached out, grasped the hem of Hassan's coat, and gave it a sharp tug.

"Maharaj," the Chief Minister said smoothly, letting go of the embroidered cloth as Hassan dropped his hands, "Gurbashan has been most clever to discover the whereabouts of young Saboor, but I must counsel *against* any plan to steal the child back."

"But why, Aziz, when stealing him is so simple?" The Maharajah attempted to raise himself again, but could not. He lay back on the pillow, his breathing strained. Pockmarks of past illness stood out against graying skin.

"It is my duty, Maharaj," the Faqeer said softly, "to remind you of the British, of their greed and their cleverness, and of our need to be most wary of them and their intentions. If they have, indeed, stolen the child, they have taken an unusual and uncharacteristic step. Consequently, we must expect a trap."

Hassan made a small sound.

The eunuch opened his mouth, but the Maharajah lifted a silencing hand. "Speak, Aziz," he said.

"It is possible," continued the Faqeer, "that by taking Saboor, the British hope to provoke us into doing what Gurbashan has suggested—sending thieves into their camp. If we do so, they will be waiting, and the thieves will be quickly discovered. The British will then have an excuse to break off the treaty negotiations, thus saving themselves from their mad attack on Afghanistan."

The Maharajah blinked.

The Faqeer tilted his head. "Without a treaty, their great army will not go to Afghanistan. It will instead remain on our border, aimed at us. After all, which is the greater prize—barren Afghanistan, with only dry fruit and camels, or this fertile plain with all its riches, including your priceless Koh-i-noor diamond?"

The eunuch fairly danced up and down in his place by the bed. "But Maharaj, I—"

The Faqeer raised his voice over the eunuch's. "As much as I dread the prospect, it is my duty to ride to the British camp with senior members of our court and request an open search of the red-walled compound."

"An open search?" The eunuch's voice cracked. "If the child has been stolen, he will never be found in a search! Tents have nooks and crannies. A baby as small as that one could survive for hours, drugged and hidden in a trunk, or carried in a sack!"

A rustling outside the tent told them the guards had heard their raised voices and moved closer to the door.

"Very well," replied the Faqeer equably, "in that case we can arrange a surprise visit to the compound, and an ordeal of some sort to identify the child thief: the rice test, perhaps."

"Give me my medicine, Aziz." The Maharajah took the figured cup from the Faqeer's hand, drained it noisily, then wiped his mouth and lay back against his pillow.

Gurbashan's face was dotted with perspiration. "But why should the rice test—"

Without looking in the eunuch's direction, the Maharajah pointed to the door. A servant rose and held open the hanging.

"The rice test," the Maharajah said thoughtfully, as the eunuch, his shoulders sagging, backed out of the tent. "How will you do it?"

"I will approach one of the senior British officers," replied the Faqeer promptly. "If they have indeed stolen Saboor, they will return him at once by some subterfuge, fearing the test. If they have not stolen him, they will protest but will submit to the test to prove their innocence. They will also work to find the child, in order to prove their good faith to us. In either case, we will win."

The Maharajah nodded. "Yes," he said, smiling at the yellow ceiling as Hassan and the Faqeer prepared to leave him, "the rice test. We will do it tonight."

"Tomorrow night, Maharaj, at midnight," the Faqeer said gently, from the doorway. "It is too late for me to speak to the British today. See," he added as the servant raised the door hanging again, revealing a rapidly darkening sky, "it is already evening. Sleep, Maharaj. We will have the test tomorrow night."

As Hassan and the Faqeer crossed the Maharajah's parade ground together, Hassan cleared his throat. "Faqeer Sahib," he began, "I am sorry that I was so—"

"Do not speak, Hassan." The Faqeer put a finger to his lips as they left the yellow tent behind them. "Walk me to my tent, but do not speak."

They walked in silence all the way to the main camp, the Faqeer striding purposefully along, his hands clasped behind his back, Hassan moving silently beside him, his eyes on the ground.

At his tent door, the Faqeer raised his arms to allow two of his servants to remove his coarse brown coat. "There is much for me to do," he said. "You will not see me for some time. Meanwhile," he cautioned, his eyes flicking to Hassan's breast pocket, "you would be wise to burn Shafi's letter."

Chapter 23

WEDNESDAY,
DECEMBER 18

"The rice test," Faqeer Azizuddin repeated the next morning from his basket chair at the British camp. He nodded gravely to his two companions, then glanced past them to the political secretary's spacious tent, whose doorway stood propped open with bamboo poles.

A bullock cart creaked by on the wide avenue, unnoticed. "The Maharajah does not require that I conduct the test myself," added the Faqeer. He returned his gaze to William Macnaghten's face and crinkled his eyes. "The Maharajah's other ministers and I will merely observe."

Beside Macnaghten, Major Byrne frowned with incomprehension. Macnaghten turned to him. "They think someone has brought that wretched little hostage here," he murmured. "They wish to perform some sort of test to identify the culprit."

Macnaghten breathed in, challenging the buttons of his frock coat, and shifted from English to Urdu. "And when, Faqeer Sahib, do you propose we perform this test?"

Faqeer Azizuddin smiled encouragingly. "At midnight tonight. The rice test is only successful if it comes as a surprise to those who are to be tested."

The sun had not yet reached its full height. It shone, colorless and painful to the eye, on the curving rise of the tent roof, and glanced upon the red wall whose left front corner, thirty feet away, abutted Macnaghten's allotted space.

"I knew they would try something like this," Macnaghten muttered to Byrne. "I was sure they would accuse us of taking the child."

Major Byrne gave a short honk, only partially disguised as a cough. "Do you suppose, William," he said behind his hand, "that the old man is doing this deliberately, to delay the treaty signing? He knows the passes will freeze soon. Is he trying to make us fail in our campaign?"

Macnaghten's foot, not quite hidden beneath his chair, began to twitch. "How, if I may ask, Faqeer Sahib," he inquired courteously, "have you come to believe the child was brought here?"

The Faqeer bent conspiratorially forward. "Ah," he replied, beaming, "this is just the place to have brought him! Whoever stole the child would have asked himself two questions. Question one is: which of the two camps is a safer hiding place for the little hostage? The answer is obvious. This is the safer camp, for here people would be less likely to recognize the child. Furthermore," he added, waving a hand toward the red wall, "what better hiding place could there be within this camp than the Governor-General's own compound?"

Macnaghten's fingers tightened on the arms of his chair.

"Question two," the Faqeer went on serenely, "is: what would happen if the child were discovered?" He lifted his shoulders, his palms raised. "Clearly, if the child were found in this camp, he, the *real* child thief, would not be blamed. No, indeed. If the baby were found in this camp, his disappearance would be blamed on the Supreme Government of India, the British Government!"

Putting back his head, he smiled, his eyes closed, signaling perfect happiness. "And so, we come at midnight to catch this child thief. After that, there will be nothing, no, nothing at all, to prevent our immediately signing the treaty."

His speech delivered, he opened his eyes and sat back in his chair as the political secretary, smiling at last, fumbled for the appropriate compliments.

After many politenesses, Faqeer Azizuddin departed down the avenue on his elephant, surrounded by his escort. Once out of sight of Macnaghten's tent, however, he called a halt and signaled to his mounted escort until one of them, an ox of a man from Mianwali, detached himself from the group and rode up.

The Faqeer leaned from his howdah. "You are to take a message, Mirza," he instructed, "to a man called Shafiuddin. I am told his tent is in that direction." He pointed to the end of the avenue and the British horse lines. The man nodded. "The message is this," the Faqeer continued, " 'There is to be a rice test in the red compound tonight, at midnight.' You must say this message comes from me. Do you understand, Mirza?"

The man nodded again, kicked his horse, and rode away.

THEY had found a thorn bush half a mile from camp and dismounted behind it. While Mariana watched, Fitzgerald took off his coat and spread it on the ground. "Mariana," he said as she sat down, impatient to hear why he had arranged this daring rendezvous. "There is something I must say to you."

She felt herself flushing. He was about to ask her to wait for him in Calcutta. "And I have something to tell you, too," she offered conspiratorially, imagining his response when she told him the Maharajah's baby hostage was at that very moment in her tent.

It was only after he sat beside her that she saw the expression on his face. "What is it?" she breathed, as an unpleasant feeling formed in her stomach.

The square, freckled hands that had once gripped her shoulders lay on his knees. He made no move to touch her. "I cannot see you again, Mariana."

"But Harry," she stammered, "we—"

He shook his head and finally offered her his clear green gaze. "I have thought about it ever since I walked you home from dinner. After we arrive at Lahore, Lord Auckland will sign the treaty. I will leave immediately afterward. If I am not killed fighting in Afghanistan, I will be sent to an army post somewhere in Bengal. I doubt we will meet again."

"But why?" She bent toward him, her heart aching, willing him to look at her, to fight for them both, to ask her to marry him. "I can wait for you in Calcutta. You can send for me after you return. *Why* should we not meet again?"

He shifted his body, moving away from her. "Please, Mariana, this is so difficult." He sighed. "I will never get permission to marry you, after the horrible things people have said. And if I did, I could never make you happy. You must find someone else."

"Harry, I can't bear this. You did nothing wrong. I would do anything—"

"And you will find someone, Mariana." Before she could touch him, he stood. "You will find yourself a nice husband before your year is over." He gave her his crooked smile. "It doesn't have to be Marks, you know."

SHADING her eyes from the setting sun, Mariana looked from face to face among the group seated in front of Miss Emily's tent.

Why must she be civil to Lieutenant Marks, when she wanted so desperately to be alone? How could she plan her campaign to win Fitzgerald back if she must attend to this simpering fool?

"I quite agree, Lieutenant Marks," Miss Emily was saying. "One must never forget the chasm that lies between our two races."

Miss Fanny reached for her wineglass. "But why should an Englishwoman *ever* spend more than a few moments with a native? The only ones we see, after all, are the servants."

"But Miss Fanny," Mariana offered, scarcely covering her impatience, "surely you have met the wives of Maharajahs. Did you not like them?" She kept her gaze on Miss Fanny, aware that Marks was trying to catch her eye.

Miss Emily opened her fan with a snap. "Fanny and I," she countered, "have seen a dozen Maharanis, and have found them hopelessly ignorant. Of course they are shut away all the time, poor creatures, with no one to talk to, but still, I cannot imagine spending more than a few moments together with such people."

"I agree entirely," purred Lieutenant Marks from his folding chair. A recent haircut made his ears stand out even more than usual. "In my opinion an Englishwoman should not show interest in *any* native, not even a native queen."

"But if we take no interest in them," Mariana asked tightly, "how will we learn *anything about India*?"

Miss Fanny made a small disapproving sound.

Marks's face creased into a lofty smile. "Ah, but Miss Givens, one cannot take an interest in the natives without becoming entangled in their affairs. It is uncanny," he added, nodding to Miss Emily. "Each time someone I know has shown the slightest concern for a native, the native in question has instantly overstepped the bounds of propriety and become unpleasantly familiar, even intimate." He fluttered a damp-looking hand. "One feels quite disgusted."

"And do you know of *many* such stories?"

Loathing had crept into Mariana's voice. Miss Emily glared across at her and closed her fan with another snap. "Of course, Lieutenant," she interposed, "no one in his right mind would—"

"Look!"

Stooped with apparent pain, Mr. Macnaghten approached from the direction of the dining tent, one hand pressed to his midriff. His face was ghastly.

"Lieutenant," breathed Miss Emily.

Marks sprang to his feet, took the secretary's arm, and guided him to a chair.

"My dear Mr. Macnaghten," said Miss Emily, leaning from her seat, a hand outstretched, "may I call Dr. Drummond?"

Macnaghten took a ragged breath. "No, thank you very much, Miss Emily. It is only dyspepsia. I shall be perfectly well by the evening. Meeting with Faqeer Azizuddin often has this effect on me."

Lieutenant Marks bowed to the Eden sisters, then to Macnaghten. "I beg your pardon for a hasty departure, but I must return to my men." He bowed to Mariana. "May I see you to your tent, Miss Givens?"

"No, thank you very much, Lieutenant," she replied stiffly. "I shall stay here for now."

AN hour later, not wishing to argue with her teacher, she spoke firmly. "I have asked you to see me at this unusual time, Munshi Sahib, because I have decided not to take Saboor to Lahore tonight."

Her teacher stood before her, the sunlight casting his shadow past the chair where she sat. In her lap, the baby flapped his arms as if trying to fly.

"I see no reason," Mariana continued, "why Saboor cannot remain with me until we reach Lahore. After all, we will be there tomorrow. Once the camp is settled, I can return him easily to his family, since they live in the walled city." She nodded decisively to indicate that the subject was closed. How could she give Saboor up today, of all days, when everything was going so wretchedly?

But her munshi did not let the subject drop. "Yesterday afternoon, Bibi," he said evenly, "you seemed delighted to learn that Yar Mohammad had arranged for you to take Saboor to his grandfather tonight. As I remember, you were very much afraid of his being discovered in your tent."

"I may have been frightened then," she countered firmly, while Saboor bounced up and down on her knees, "but I now see that I cannot travel all that distance alone at night without an escort."

Saboor clambered down from her lap, smartly dressed in a new regimental uniform of white pajamas and a tiny red coat with cross-belts. He tottered on his feet, smiling broadly at the munshi, then sat down on the floor with a thump.

"And how can I take instructions from Yar Mohammad?" Mariana added. "I am an Englishwoman. *He is a native groom.*"

"A native groom," her teacher reminded her gently, "who is willing to risk his life to escort you and Saboor to safety."

"Besides, Munshi Sahib," she said, a little too loudly, as Saboor got up and hurried unsteadily toward Dittoo, "no one will recognize Saboor now that Dittoo's friend has made him new clothes."

The munshi did not reply.

It *was* silly and dangerous to go all the way to Lahore with only Yar Mohammad to guard her. Hunching her shoulders stubbornly, she looked at the rug, wishing her teacher would say something.

At last, as the silence deepened, she told him the truth. "Munshi Sahib, I do not want to give him back."

Her teacher's face became grave. Ignoring the tears in her eyes, he offered her his reply. "It is one thing, Bibi, to rescue a little child from harm. It is something else to keep that child from his family, knowing that they love him and are longing to see him." It was the sternest statement she had heard him make.

"If you will permit me, Bibi, I will tell you a story." Without waiting for her consent, he clasped his hands behind his back, and began. "A man," he began in a singsong, his eyes fixed on the tent wall, "dreamed all his life of finding the Path to Paradise. Driven by his dream, he asked every person he met where the path lay.

"One day he met a wise man who pointed to an ordinary gate leading to an ordinary road. 'That,' the wise man told him, 'is the path you seek.' "

Mariana sniffed and wiped her eyes. How could she listen to fairy tales when all she wanted was to be left alone to feel her losses and her sadness?

"Following the path," the munshi went on, "the man came to a well. He pulled on its rope hoping for water to drink, but when the bucket came up, he saw to his astonishment that it held not water but jewels—diamonds and rubies, emeralds and pearls. Shaking his head, he lowered the bucket back into the well. 'What a foolish place to hide a treasure,' he said."

With a piercing shriek Saboor danced across the floor toward Mariana, who swept him up and kissed the top of his head. "Quiet, dearest," she murmured.

"As the man walked on," the munshi continued, "he saw a large, silken umbrella with a golden handle and golden fringes lying beside the path.

" 'This umbrella,' he said as he passed by, 'must belong to the same fool who has hidden his jewels in the well, for there could only be one man in this world foolish enough to leave his treasure in plain sight.'

"After a time, the path began to climb up the side of a mountain, winding its way to the top with many sharp turns—"

A fly banged obstinately into the tent pole. "Munshi Sahib," Mariana interrupted, forcing a smile, "you seem a little tired. Why do we not hear the rest of your lovely story another time?"

"No indeed, Bibi."

Her munshi had changed in the past few days. Why was he giving her orders: to pray, to return Saboor? Why was he suddenly so fond of the sound of his own voice?

"The path was steep, and slippery at the turns," he said, "but the man was determined to follow it. He climbed all afternoon until he arrived, exhausted, at a wide ledge. There, on a great rock, sat a giant. The giant wept, his head in his hands.

" 'What ails you?' asked the man.

" 'All my life,' wept the giant, 'I have searched for the Path to Paradise. Finding it gave me joy; but alas, as I traveled, I saw a well full of jewels. Giving in to temptation, I put a small ruby into my pocket.' "

A *small ruby*—her arms around Saboor, Mariana felt a stab of remorse.

The munshi rocked a little on his feet as he went on. " 'As I climbed this mountain,' the giant continued, 'the ruby began to grow heavy. It grew heavier and heavier until now, as strong as I am, I am too weary to continue, and I can never reach Paradise.'

"Leaving the giant behind," he continued, "the man climbed on until, after turning a steep corner, he was met by a powerful blast of wind. Terrified of falling, he clung to the side of the mountain until the wind died as suddenly as it had sprung up.

"When the wind died, the man noticed a small person sitting alone beside the path. Like the giant, he, too, was weeping."

Mariana eased Saboor to the floor, bracing herself for another illustration of her faults.

" 'As I traveled along this path,' said the small man, 'I saw a beautiful umbrella lying on the ground. I borrowed it, only to shade my head, and to make others believe I was a prince, since the umbrella symbolizes royalty. I meant no harm.' "

Make others believe I was a prince. If only she could take back those thoughtless words about Yar Mohammad. . . .

" 'But a wind came up and blew the umbrella away. In my struggle to save it, I exhausted myself. I am now too weak to go any farther, and I will never see Paradise.' Sobbing, the small person buried his face in his hands."

The munshi smiled. "Leaving the small person weeping behind him, the man climbed until he could climb no more. His eyes misted over with weariness, he could not see what lay ahead. Abandoning his quest, he crawled with his last strength to the edge of the path, and looked down. Spread below him was a green and glorious valley with sparkling brooks and gardens of fruit trees. Rising from the valley, a breeze carried with it the faintest hint of jasmine and roses. It was the Garden of Paradise."

His story was finished, but her teacher went on smiling, his eyes on Mariana.

Her father would agree. "Return the child," he would say firmly, after closing his study door. "It is the only honorable thing to do."

She sighed. "All right, Munshi Sahib," she said quietly, "I will take Saboor to Lahore tonight."

Chapter 24

"I told them I have sold Baba to Sirosh the tailor," Dittoo replied to Mariana's question, as he handed her the sleeping baby two hours after dinner.

"Sold him? To a *tailor*?" She still wore her rose dinner gown and shawls, although it was long past her bedtime. Her breath was visible in the tent.

Dittoo nodded his head decisively. "Yes, Memsahib. My friends think I have sold him to Sirosh for eight *annas*. They were only surprised I had not waited until Baba was fatter. They think I have made a bad bargain."

When Dittoo had departed, chuckling, she tucked Saboor into her quilts and sat down beside him, still wrapped in her shawls.

It would not be long before Yar Mohammad came to take them away.

The oil lamp threw shadows on the tent wall. She stroked Saboor's sleeping face. "I wish you and I were in Sussex, my love. It's nearly Christmas, you know. What a lovely time we would have—you in a coat with a little fur collar, with dozens of jam tarts all to yourself, and no one to sell you as if you were a Christmas turkey!"

But it was not to be. Nothing she desperately wanted was to be. Saboor was to leave her. Fitzgerald was already gone, Fitzgerald who had kissed her only twice, lovely, hasty, stolen kisses. Those kisses were all she would have when she returned, childless and husbandless, to England. But she had cried enough. She lay down beside Saboor, pulled up the quilts, and closed her eyes.

"MEMSAHIB, Memsahib, it is midnight." The resonant whisper roused her from heavy sleep. "We must be quick."

Shivering, she groped through the darkness to the doorway and pushed the hanging aside. A palanquin with woven-cane side panels stood before her in the starlight. Around it waited a dozen men, their breath coming in white clouds. Behind her, the baby sighed softly in his sleep.

Yar Mohammad appeared beside her. "These men," he said quietly, "will carry you through the back entrance and onto the road to Lahore. After three miles, you will change to another palki. The second one will be from the house of Shaikh Waliullah, the baba's grandfather. *Samjay* Memsahib, do you understand?"

She nodded, her heart quickening. *A groom who is willing to risk his life . . .* Was she, too, risking her life to take Saboor to safety? It was too late, now, to ask that question.

"I will not carry the palki, but I will be with you." Yar Mohammad's urgent whisper followed her as she reached for Saboor in the darkness. "Hurry, Memsahib, hurry!"

SOMEONE was talking loudly on the avenue as Mariana pulled her skirts up into the strange palki and held up her arms for Saboor. Distant torchlight flickered through the holes in the red canvas wall. The voice sounded like Major Byrne's, but why would the major be giving orders out there in the middle of the night? She tucked Saboor beside her, slid the palanquin's side panels closed, and laid her head on a thin pillow that smelled of hair oil. The activities of the camp no longer concerned her. What mattered was that she had been unable to find her bonnet in the dark. What would Shaikh Waliullah think of her, she wondered, arriving at his house without a bonnet?

The palanquin started off jerkily. Voices, pained and breathless, came from outside.

"I said the left foot first, Javed."

"Lift your pole higher, Saleem."

She opened her eyes. The men standing by the palki had not been wearing dhotis. The wrapped dhoti of the Hindu palanquin bearer exposed a man's bare legs as he moved. These men had not worn dhotis but *shalwars*, the gathered, full-length trousers of the Muslim. A hand on Saboor's sleeping body, she reached for a handhold as the palki lurched sideways. Whoever these men were, it was plain that none of them had carried a palanquin before. Four would carry, eight would trot alongside, awaiting their turns. How were they ever to travel three long miles like this?

They had stopped moving. Someone spoke nervously. "*Band hai. It's closed.*"

She sat up, slid aside the cane panels, and looked out.

To her right, the row of servants' campfires glowed, their flames spent. Near them, wrapped forms lay motionless. Somewhere among them was Dittoo. To her left rose the deserted kitchen tent. Holding on tightly, she craned her head cautiously out of the palki to look ahead. Before her, where the cooks' entrance should have been, there was only blank red canvas. Where was the yawning entrance, wide enough to admit a bullock cart of foodstuffs?

They knew. Someone had discovered Saboor's whereabouts and laid a trap. That had been the reason for Yar Mohammad's haste. That *had* been Major Byrne's voice on the avenue!

"Yar Mohammad," she whispered as loudly as she dared, and saw him instantly separate himself from the knot of bearers and approach the sleepy-looking coolies standing by the gate. She could not hear what was said; but over the murmuring of voices came the chink of coin on coin, then the palki moved forward again. As it moved she heard the scraping of canvas along its sides.

"Have no fear, Memsahib," came his quiet voice beside her after they had cleared the gate. "You and Saboor Baba will soon be far from here."

Her heart thudded. She *was* risking her life, as were Yar Mohammad and the other men. This must be like being in battle, except, of course, that she was unarmed. Curiously enough, she felt no fear.

She would tell her father the whole story of Saboor when she was out of the Punjab and it was safe to write without worrying that her letter would fall from the official mail pouch and into dangerous hands.

Papa would be proud of her.

•   •   •

"*UTO*. Get up." A soldier, his white cross-belts gleaming in the starlight, nudged his foot for a second time into Dittoo's ribs.

Dittoo opened his eyes. All around him and down the line of cold fires, men were sitting up, untangling themselves from shawls and sheets. Soldiers stood by, their weapons ready.

Beside him, Guggan grumbled. "All right, all right. I'm coming." Sita Ram cursed as he pushed his feet into his shoes.

Exchanging uneasy glances, the men stood. Prodded by the soldiers, they joined the servants straggling toward the front entrance of the compound, past the great tents of the English Governor-General and his sisters. Looking behind him, Dittoo saw guards arrive and stand at attention beside the closed kitchen entrance.

The groom Yar Mohammad had insisted that Memsahib and Baba leave tonight. He must have anticipated this exercise, whatever it was. Dittoo yawned. Well, it did not matter. Even with an army to help them find Baba, the British were too late. Yes, indeed. He knew because he had forced himself to stay awake long enough to see the kitchen entrance closed, then reopened just enough to allow a palki carried by amateur bearers to slide through. Following Guggan, he joined the file of servants.

"The rice test. It is the rice test." The word, carried back from the front of the line, caused Dittoo to stumble. He knew of the test, of its infallibility, of the panic of the guilty party, waiting to be discovered, trying desperately to bring saliva to his mouth.

Was the rice test to do with Saboor Baba? Were they looking for those who had stolen him? He shuddered. Perhaps not. Perhaps it was something else, some diamonds missing from the English ladies' jewel boxes. His body relaxed, then stiffened. No, it must be Baba. Memsahib had been certain his whereabouts would be discovered. She had been so frightened.

"They are looking for the Maharajah's hostage," said a voice behind him.

They would ask if he had seen the baba. His head jerking, he searched for a way to evade notice. There was none; they had seen to that. All along the column, red-coated Brahmin soldiers prodded the camp servants into line as if they were so many cattle.

There would be a terrible price to be paid for stealing the boy. The water carrier had told him that, merely for holding Saboor Baba at the moment when he disappeared, Baba's servant had paid with the loss of his nose. How much more had Dittoo done—hiding the child, feeding and clothing him, sleeping with him, rubbing him with mud to guard him from discovery?

He imagined with terror the heavy blow of the sword as it severed his nose from his face. He tried to walk forward normally, although his arms and legs felt as if they belonged to another man. He looked among the others in the line, hoping to distract himself with familiar faces. There was old Sirosh the tailor, bent double as always, helped along by his son-in-law. Ahead of them marched Jimmund, the servant of Miss Emily's little black dog, straight-backed, as tall as ever, as if even now he were walking a few paces behind Miss Emily, his canine charge under his arm. The fat dog boy, whose duties were less elegant, trailed miserably behind him.

"Keep moving," grunted a soldier.

Would he be put to death? Would they cut off his hands, his feet? Whip him in public?

"What is the matter with you?" whispered Mohan at his elbow. "You are walking like an Englishman."

The line of servants pushed its way through the folded front entrance and onto the avenue. There, by the light of dozens of torches, more soldiers waited, standing shoulder to shoulder, an impenetrable barrier to escape.

Dittoo kept his eyes down. If he were to look up and meet the eyes of the black-coated Englishmen who stood beside the wall, or those of the unfamiliar, turbaned courtiers beside him, there would be no need for the test.

They might torture him first, or question him first; or they might do both at once. What would he tell them about his memsahib? He had forgotten to wrap himself in his cotton sheet before joining the other servants, but there was no need. Sweat ran down his back and into the folds of his dhoti.

Why had she not protected him from this horror? Why had she run away, abandoned him, performed no magic to save him? Tears joined the sweat on his face and trickled into the stubble on his chin.

A soldier separated him from Guggan and Sita, motioning him to squat in the dust beside a boy who grinned happily as if they were playing a game. Alongside him, prodded and cursed by the soldiers, others folded themselves down, forming themselves into five parallel rows.

The fat, red-faced Major Byrne Sahib clapped his hands and coughed noisily. The murmuring along the rows instantly quieted. Beside him, his friend Macnaghten Sahib, the man with a mustache for eyebrows, also cleared his throat. The two Englishmen conferred for a moment.

"We are here," announced Macnaghten, "because we believe that, in the past few days, someone in this compound has committed a very serious crime." He stepped forward and paced, hands clasped behind his back, up and down between the first two rows. "This crime is so serious that it has been deemed necessary to perform the rice test in order to discover the identity of the criminal."

Behind him, the two elegant strangers, one wearing a coarse woolen robe, moved eagerly forward, scanning the faces of the squatting men.

The men near Dittoo began to talk among themselves. "Those men are from the Maharajah's household," declared one. "They have come to take the child thief away."

The soldiers shouted for silence.

"Each of you is to be given a small handful of rice." Macnaghten glared at the rows of men as if each one of them were guilty. "I will then ask all of you a question. The question is simple. It requires only a yes or no reply. When I have asked the question, I will come to each one of you to hear your answer. After giving your answer, you will put the rice into your mouth and chew it, then spit it into your hand and show it to me. Is that clear?"

He motioned to the soldiers, who began to move up and down the rows carrying trays on which rice lay in pale, ghostly piles.

Dittoo was too terrified to pray. He waited, frozen, as a soldier approached down the row, giving out handfuls of rice. Against the flaring torches, the man's tall shako and tight-fitting uniform gave him the look of a creature from a nightmare.

"Hold out your hand." The man's voice was nasal and superior. Dittoo held out both his hands, willing them not to tremble. With a flourish, the soldier scooped up a small amount of rice and poured it into Dittoo's open palms.

The giving out of the rice seemed to last all night. When at last it was done and the soldiers were shouting again for silence, Dittoo regretted his failure to enjoy the reprieve. Now it was too late for him. Macnaghten had begun to speak once more.

"Now, when I ask the question, you shall all listen carefully and be ready with your answer when I come to you." He raised a hand. "Many of you already know of this test. For those of you who do not, I can tell you this: It is a test of truthfulness. Whether you answer yes or no to my question, *if you are lying, I shall know it at once.* A man who tells the truth will have water in his mouth. His chewed rice will be wet. But," he added over the murmuring of the crowd, "a man who lies will have a dry mouth. His rice, when he spits, will be powder. Therefore, do not lie. I repeat, *do not lie.* Any man who lies will be most severely punished. Is that clear? And now to the question. *Silence,* do you hear? I require *absolute silence!*"

Soldiers moved among the men, threatening them with raised fists.

The two courtiers had come to stand beside Macnaghten and Major Byrne, peering into the faces of the servants nearest them. The crowd subsided.

"Do you, or do you not," thundered Macnaghten, "know the whereabouts of the child Saboor, the infant hostage of Maharajah Ranjit Singh? Once again, *do you know the whereabouts of the child Saboor?*"

How could this be happening? Paralyzed, Dittoo squatted, the rice unnoticed in his hands. Leaning forward from another row, Guggan looked at him, his eyes wide. When Dittoo tried to shrug, Guggan turned hastily away. Dittoo's eyes flooded. Even his friends must forsake him now. If they guessed at the real identity of his foundling, they, too, would suffer. How could he have been so reckless? How could he have trusted Memsahib?

Macnaghten, Major Byrne at his heels, stepped into the first row. He moved deliberately, listening to each man's answer, watching him chew, then spit. Soldiers held torches aloft, illuminating each servant as he was questioned.

They arrived at Dittoo's row and approached at a measured pace, the courtiers behind them, a soldier on either side, ready to seize the liar, the criminal, Dittoo himself. Dittoo tried to lick his lips, but his tongue had become as parched as old leather.

What was the question? Did he, Dittoo, know the whereabouts of the baby Saboor? Of course he knew Baba's whereabouts, for was the child not at this very moment on the road between this camp and Lahore City in the company of Mariana Memsahib?

If he were to answer yes, he would not be punished for lying, but he would certainly be punished for the part he had played in hiding the baba inside the red compound. And what of the oath he had made to himself? What would his loyalty, even his soul, be worth if he were to betray Memsahib and Saboor Baba? Perhaps it did not matter. Was Memsahib not, after all, a sorceress, capable of escaping any trap, of disappearing, if need be, into the air? Yes, indeed, and it was he, Dittoo, an ordinary man, who had been left to face this terrible decision. Snuffling, he wiped his eyes, then licked his fingers. All the water he needed inside his mouth was streaming down his cheeks.

Beside him the boy replied in the negative, chewed his rice, then, making a face, spat a slimy white blob into the dust.

It was Dittoo's turn.

He took a shallow breath. Yes, he knew the answer, but then again, perhaps he did not, for exactly where Memsahib and Saboor Baba were on the road to Lahore, he could not say. In fact, as he himself had never taken the road from Amritsar to Lahore, he did not have the smallest idea where they were.

"Well?" asked Macnaghten.

"Well?" echoed Major Byrne.

A perfumed breeze seemed to pass by, carrying away Dittoo's terror, drying his tears and the sweat on his face, allowing him to breathe deeply again as saliva rushed into his mouth and lay in a sweet pool under his tongue.

"No, Sahib," he replied firmly, "I do not know the whereabouts of the child Saboor."

The rice he chewed and spat out in a great glorious wet gob was filled with dust and other things, perhaps the bodies of dead insects, but never in all his life had Dittoo tasted anything as delicious as that little handful of rice.

Chapter 25

THURSDAY, DECEMBER 19

The palanquin's lurching progress along the dark road to Lahore seemed to go on forever. Inside, fighting nausea and unable to shut out the groans, cries, and occasional curses which punctuated each sway and jolt of the box, Mariana held Saboor against her and clung to what handholds she could find, grateful that the child, at least, managed to sleep through their ordeal.

Surely this nightmare journey would soon end. She could not guess how far her false bearers had carried her, but they must by now have covered most of the three miles to their meeting point with Saboor's family palanquin. Reaching cautiously past Saboor, she slid open a side panel.

From inside, it had seemed that they were racing along the road. Now she saw with distress that they were scarcely moving forward. The bearers seemed to be putting all their energy into moving the box sideways and bouncing it up and down.

It would do no good to scold them—they seemed miserable themselves—but she was exhausted and her head throbbed so much that she felt it would burst, and she was about to lose Saboor forever. She slid the door shut and, without caring whether the men outside heard or not, she wept with great, noisy, gulping sobs.

AT last, with a great chorus of groans, the men dropped her palanquin to the dust. Looking dizzily out, Mariana saw another palanquin standing beside the road. A group of efficient-looking men in real bearers' clothing waited beside it.

As she started toward the second palki she caught Yar Mohammad's eye and acknowledged his apologetic salute with a wave of her hand.

She pushed Saboor into the new palanquin, and crawled in after him. Within minutes, soothed by the rocking of Shaikh Waliullah's commodious old palki, she had fallen into exhausted sleep.

Sleeping, she missed hearing the lies the Shaikh's sirdar bearer told the guards at the Delhi Gate and the sound of the iron-studded door as it creaked reluctantly open, admitting the palanquin and its twelve-man team into the curving lanes of the walled city. She missed the groan of the Shaikh's own haveli doors as they swung wide to allow the palki inside, and the whispers of waiting servants as the palki was carried past two courtyards, past windows where lamplight gleamed and figures moved quietly behind latticed shutters.

She woke only when the palanquin stopped moving. Women's voices, hushed and excited, surrounded her as she pushed open a panel and looked out.

The palki had been set down beside a shrouded doorway. Behind curtains, lamplight moved and flickered. A slim hand reached for hers and helped her to stand.

The instant Mariana was on her feet, a dozen children darted past her skirts and flocked excitedly about the palanquin where Saboor still slept, thrusting their heads inside, all talking at once.

"Shireen-Jan is the eldest. She should carry him."

"But I am his reeeeeal cousin. I should do it."

"Be quiet, you'll wake him!"

What were children doing up at such an hour? There was no time to wonder, for she was being shown up a narrow flight of stone steps by two female servants with lamps. The girl who had helped her up now led her by the hand, while other women crowded the stairway, pointing and whispering as she climbed away from the excited little voices at the foot of the stairs.

The stair opened into a passageway. To the right, a heap of shoes lay beside a curtained doorway. The girl scuffed off a pair of embroidered slippers and glanced meaningfully at Mariana's feet. Remembering that Munshi Sahib never wore shoes indoors, Mariana removed her boots and found herself swept through the doorway and into a room crowded with women.

Oil lamps set into niches in the walls cast a golden light over the faces of a score of women who sat like nesting birds on a white-sheeted floor. Long shirts and fine, soft-looking shawls shrouded their bodies and hair. Toes peeped from beneath the hems of their loose trousers. Twenty pairs of eyes fastened on Mariana's gown with its tightly fitted bodice, billowing sleeves, and its six yards of wide, gathered skirts, so different from their own loose, vertical clothing.

The only native women Mariana had seen before had been dancing girls or peasants, their faces either painted and worldly or seamed with hardship. These were different. Shaikh Waliullah's family women were instantly recognizable as ladies of quality. While most had large features, a few of the faces turned to Mariana with open-eyed curiosity were delicate and fair.

Mariana's young woman guide let go of her hand and hastened away to sit among a group of girls her own age. All stared at Mariana before leaning together, their foreheads almost touching, to whisper among themselves.

Loosened veiling on some of the ladies' heads revealed hair parted smoothly in the center, hanging in a single plait.

Why were they all awake at such a late hour? A hand to her own hair, Mariana realized she had lost a great many pins. Curls swept across her face and brushed the back of her neck. Twenty pairs of brown eyes watched her over bent knees, past shoulders. What must she look like?

Across the room, a stout woman in white signaled to Mariana. "Peace," she said, in a baritone voice. She waved a hand, indicating the roomful of ladies. "We have been waiting for you. I am Safiya Sultana, the sister of Shaikh Waliullah." She pointed to an empty place on the floor beside her.

Mariana blushed as the woman studied her. Safiya Sultana's face could have belonged to a man. "So you are Mariam," the woman said.

Mariam?

"*Hai,* the poor thing," said a sympathetic voice, "traveling alone in the night."

Mariana arranged herself as best she could at Safiya's side, crossing her legs, feeling the bite of her stays against her ribs.

Safiya Sultana glanced toward the door at the sound of the children racing upstairs. "And you have brought my brother's grandchild, Saboor?"

There was no time for Mariana to reply, for at that moment the door curtain was jerked aside and a fat girl entered triumphantly, puffing with exertion, Saboor in her arms. His creased face lay on a plump shoulder, his legs dangled below her knees. He was still sleeping. The other children crowded about, touching him, arguing in whispers, while the roomful of ladies sighed and swayed in their places on the floor.

"Ah, my Saboor has come, he has come!" Burying her face in her shawl, one of the women began to weep loudly.

Her Saboor? Mariana stared at the woman.

"That is his grandmother," Safiya Sultana rumbled, nodding with approval. "She has waited a long time for his return."

The ladies' silent attention turned back to Mariana, who gazed at them avidly in return, memorizing each face, and each fold of their clothing. Few European women had visited a house like this, she knew. There was so much to see besides the ladies: the beamed ceiling of the room, the carpeted floor covered in white cotton sheeting. What did they keep in that painted cupboard in the corner?

By the window, someone gasped aloud. A birdlike woman pointed through filigreed shutters toward the courtyard below. "Someone has come, someone has come!"

Had they been followed from the English camp? Mariana barely breathed while the women around her fluttered.

Safiya Sultana raised a hand for calm. "We'll see what it is," she declared, pushing herself to her feet. "We'll see."

Too impatient to wait, Mariana followed her to the window. Other women crowded her, hemming her in, bracing their hands on her shoulders, trying to see what was happening in the courtyard.

At first Mariana shrank from the crowding bodies; but then, unable to avoid them, she relaxed experimentally. An old, gap-toothed lady in the crowd smiled and patted her arm.

A crowd had gathered in the courtyard below. Servants stood about, the flames from their torches illuminating the haveli's frescoed walls. At a shouted command, someone opened a low gate between the courtyards and armed men entered on foot, followed by a horse carrying two riders.

As soon as the horse was inside the little gate, the guards reached up and lowered one of the riders from the saddle. As they stretched him out in the dust, Mariana saw salmon-colored satin gleam in the torchlight. Elsewhere in the courtyard, men rushed to and fro. A man carrying a string bed darted out of a doorway and set the bed down opposite Mariana's window. In the shadow of a portico beside the string bed, an unoccupied platform waited.

From what Mariana could see, the haveli was not a single house but a three-storied building surrounding both this small busy courtyard and another, perhaps larger one, beyond the low gate. Several doors opened onto the small courtyard. Was all this part of the Shaikh's house? Were they really inside the walled city? She craned to see upward. Men had gathered on a roof opposite her window. They bent over the parapet, watching the scene in the courtyard from above.

"Ah," said Safiya Sultana, patting Mariana's arm, "it is only a case of snakebite. It has nothing to do with Saboor or with you, my dear." With a satisfied sound, she started away from the window.

"Snakebite?" Mariana had heard of the horrible effects of snakebite—the agony, the swelling, the bleeding mouth, the inevitable death. Could the man collapsed on the ground really have been bitten by a snake? She stared, unable to look away as two of the armed escorts lifted the satin-clad man by his arms. Bent under his weight, they carried him across the courtyard, his feet dragging behind like a condemned prisoner's, and laid him, kicking, onto the string bed.

Safiya Sultana motioned with her head toward another window. "If you want to see, come over here," she said, and led Mariana through the press of ladies.

This new window had a better view of the padded platform and the string bed with its twitching occupant. No longer empty, the platform now held a gaunt-faced individual wearing billowing white clothes and a high cylindrical headdress. Other white-clad men clustered nearby. The bejeweled second rider, now dismounted, stood wringing his hands over his stricken companion while the armed men milled about. Everyone except the man on the platform seemed to be talking at once.

"Is that Shaikh Waliullah?" Mariana whispered.

Safiya Sultana moved her head in assent.

So this was the great magician Miss Emily had talked about. He certainly looked like one, with his tall snowy headdress.

Mariana held her breath.

The torchlit scene, eerie already, was made more so by the sudden silence that fell as soon as the Shaikh raised a bony hand.

Although the *charpai* with its load of human misery could have been no more than a foot from his platform, the Shaikh made no move to touch his patient. Instead, he sat quite motionless, his back erect, his gaze fixed on the salmon-robed figure before him. For some minutes, the only movements in the courtyard were the convulsions of the man on the bed. Mariana narrowed her eyes, straining to see, wishing her window were closer to the platform. Was that a trick of the light or was sweat beginning to gleam on the Shaikh's face?

"Is he saying something?" she whispered into Safiya Sultana's ear. Even at this distance, it seemed wrong to make a sound.

"Yes," Safiya Sultana answered, then pressed her lips firmly into a straight line.

Mesmerized, Mariana watched.

A powerful connection seemed to have formed between the magician and his patient. It seemed almost as if another snake—a good, healing, invisible snake—had linked the two men together and was now at work undoing the virulent effects of the poison.

But there was not, and never had been, a cure for poisonous snakebite. From her first hour in India, Mariana had been warned never to walk outdoors, even on the streets of Calcutta, without laced boots. On her first day in camp, Major Byrne had instructed her to wear her boots all the time, even in her tent. Since then, she had heard stories of servants and even soldiers being killed by cobras, vipers, or other snakes.

Only recently, Dr. Drummond had recounted the story of a subaltern at the army camp who liked to walk about in a pair of bedroom slippers. "I warned him several times," the doctor had said, shaking his head, "but once he had been bitten, it was too late. What a terrible sight the man was—his leg was monstrous and livid. The poor fellow was in agony. 'Doctor,' he told me, before he lost consciousness, 'I should not be dying now if I had listened to your advice.' "

Murmuring rose from below. The body on the charpai had stopped twitching. Fascinated, Mariana watched it move, then sit up, no longer a terrible, suffering thing but a showily dressed man with a full curly beard who rubbed his face, then smiled.

With a grunt, Safiya Sultana took her arm and led her firmly from the window. "Well, that's done," she said briskly. "And now, Mariam, my brother has asked to see you, but first you must sit for another moment. It will be a little time before all those men have left."

The ladies had seated themselves once more as if they expected to sit in those same places forever. What hour was it?

"More men are coming, more men are coming. Look, look!" A girl of about fifteen, whose long reddish plait hung down to her knees, had pressed her face to the shutter.

Safiya Sultana sighed heavily as she lowered herself to the carpet beside Mariana. "Tell me what you see, Mehereen."

"Three men are riding into the courtyard—ooh, they are so beautifully dressed, Bhaji. They have swords and one has a big feather in his—"

Safiya Sultana waved a hand. "Only tell me what they are doing, Mehereen," she instructed.

"They have brought servants carrying covered trays. They are uncovering them and oh, there are shawls, so many shawls, although I cannot see how good they are, and they are leading in a horse, and one of the trays is heaped up with gold jewelry. Lala-Ji must have saved someone very important, someone very rich!" Her eyes alight, she turned from the window. "What does it mean, Bhaji? Are these gifts for us?"

"It means nothing, you will see." Safiya Sultana shook her head. "Nothing at all."

But the girl was peeping out again. "Wait! Why doesn't Lala-Ji look at the gifts? Why does he not show gratitude? The men look so disappointed, and now they are going away. They are taking their gifts and going away. Why, Bhaji?"

The sweet voice was suddenly so sad that Mariana felt a rush of desire to comfort the girl. Safiya Sultana patted the carpet on her other side. "My darling, we all know that Lala-Ji never accepts payment for this work. Come and sit beside me, Mehereen-Jani," she rumbled. She turned to Mariana. "The children call my brother Lala-Ji," she explained.

"But what if those gifts were from the Maharajah?" the girl persisted. "Will not his feelings be hurt? What if he becomes—"

"Mehereen, you must not ask questions. And now that those men have gone," Safiya Sultana continued, sharpening her tone, "it is time for Mariam to go down and meet my brother, and for all of us to go to bed."

"It is most unusual," she informed Mariana, "for him to meet a woman. Indeed, he has never met a foreigner, but it is his express wish to meet you before you return to your camp. His servant Allahyar is waiting now at the foot of the stairs to show you the way."

Pushing herself once more to her feet, Safiya Sultana braced herself on young Mehereen's shoulder. "And now, good night, and may God keep you, my child. In rescuing Saboor you have performed a great service for our family."

Leaning on Mehereen, she moved toward a curtained doorway at the end of the room and was gone.

Without Safiya Sultana, the room seemed somehow colder. Looking about, Mariana saw that there was no one left but a few yawning servants.

She rubbed her face, wondering what she and the Shaikh would speak about. Perhaps he would only greet her quickly, and then send her back to the British camp in his own palanquin. Hands braced on the wall, she descended the winding stair to where, at its foot, the promised servant waited.

His bush of hair was an arresting shade of red, but, as odd as the servant Allahyar appeared to her, she must have appeared odder still, for his eyes widened in astonishment as she approached. But what could they expect of someone who had been carried three miles in a palki by the clumsiest men in India, and then been awakened in the middle of the night to be scrutinized and stared at by a group of unknown women?

She lifted her arms to tuck her curls into a knot, but abandoned the effort, too tired suddenly to care what the Shaikh thought of her.

Except for a few torchbearers, the courtyard was deserted as the red-haired servant led her toward the painted portico where the old Shaikh still sat, upright on his platform. Of the patient and his bejeweled escort there was no sign, nor did there remain a single shawl or trinket from the trays of gifts that had been offered there only moments before.

The time had come to use the native manners that Shafi Sahib had taught her. Mariana inclined her head and saluted the old man, the fingers of her right hand touching her forehead. "*As-Salaam-o-alaikum,* Shaikh Sahib," she said.

When she looked up he smiled, seeming not to notice her rumpled dress and unruly hair. "And peace be upon you, daughter," he replied.

He patted his platform. "Sit down."

She smiled in return. Daughter. No one had ever called her that.

His voice was light and pleasing, which surprised her, since his elderly face was as dark and wrinkled as a prune. She approached the platform, which turned out to be covered in another white sheet, and sat down primly on its edge.

"The first part of your journey must have been uncomfortable," he said. His eyes held a force she had never seen before. "The men who carried you were not palki bearers. They were barbers and grooms. One was a soldier out of uniform. But all were good brave men."

She nodded, unable to take her eyes from his. *Willing to risk their lives . . .*

"And now," he went on, "I would like to express our gratitude for your rescue of my grandson. It is clear to us all that in this emergency you have acted with great courage and compassion, and with a kind of love that is very rare in this world."

Before she had time to flush with pleasure, he raised a brown finger. "And now, I would like to ask you three questions."

He did not wait for her to respond. "First," he began, "have you seen all that you wish to see of India?"

His eyes seemed to hold important secrets. What did he want her to say?

"No," she replied carefully, "not yet. But I still have the return journey to Calcutta before me. The journey is to take us four months, you see, after we stop at Simla for—"

"It is nearly dawn," he interrupted, his voice unchanged, "and you must be very tired. Perhaps you would like to answer my question truthfully."

She sat straighter. "—that is," she stammered, "yes—no, I have not seen all I wish to see of India."

Why had she tried to fool a magician? Under his powerful gaze, in spite of her deep exhaustion, she felt her imagination catch fire. "I have not yet seen the walled city, except for this house," she added, her voice betraying her excitement. "Until now I had never spoken to native ladies, or—"

"Thank you," he interrupted again, this time firmly. "You have answered my first question. And now the second." As he leaned toward her, his headdress seemed to reach up to the stars overhead. "Have you met my son Hassan, Saboor's father?"

This was not a trick question. "No," she replied.

"Very well, and now to my final question." He removed his headdress and stood it on the platform beside him. It was of starched white cotton, delicately embroidered. A tight, embroidered skullcap covered his head. Without his headdress, he looked entirely different.

"Have you ever loved before, as you now love my grandson Saboor?"

She looked across the dark courtyard, remembering the wave of passionate feeling that had rushed over her when she had first taken Saboor into her arms, and her agony when he had wept, caught in her shawl. The recognition and hope she had felt with Fitzgerald, sweet and compelling as it was, had been quite different. Her abiding, protective love for her father had been different. Even her love for Ambrose, great as it had been, did not compare to this. "No," she said.

"Very good," the Shaikh said briskly. "You have answered my three questions well."

He signaled toward the shadows. Allahyar, the red-haired servant, stepped out and stood waiting.

The Shaikh pointed through the low gate to where the second

courtyard lay blanketed in darkness. "One of our palanquins is waiting in the entryway," he told the servant. "Escort this young lady there, and tell the men that she is to be taken to a point seven miles from here, along the Amritsar road. At the seven-mile mark, she will be met by another palanquin. That is all."

Although she knew she had been dismissed, Mariana did not get up from the platform. Instead, a hand on the white sheet, she looked up into the Shaikh's wrinkled face.

"Shaikh Sahib, what you did earlier, the snakebite cure—"

Again he interrupted her in his clear, light voice. "What you have seen here, my child, is a spiritual trick, a matter of faith and practice. We, whom some people call Sufis, occasionally perform cures and do other things of that nature."

He raised a hand before she could respond. "But you should know that we are followers of the Path, not tricksters or magicians. Those of us who have permission to do so perform cures as a service to the people, but it is only a very small and unimportant part of our spiritual practice."

He studied her, as if he could read her very soul. "You must not speak of this, do you understand? Those who are told of these matters often do not believe what they hear. One must never, even by mistake, increase another person's disbelief."

Behind him, the sky had begun to lighten. He indicated by a slight movement that their interview had ended.

"Shaikh Sahib—" she said.

His expression had become distant. "You will meet Saboor again," he said, answering her unspoken question without meeting her eyes, "but not tonight."

As Mariana followed Allahyar through the low gate, a voice came from beyond the wall, its minor wail piercing the chill of the courtyard.

"*La Illaha Illa-Allah.*" There is no god save God. "*La Illaha Illa-Allah—*"

THE tall doors of Qamar Haveli thudded shut behind her. Mariana closed her eyes. In an hour, the British train would begin its daily march. Traveling toward her at its usual snail's pace, it would reach Lahore by midmorning. Shafi Sahib had been correct. Thank heaven for Dittoo, sender of palanquins and performer of many exacting tasks! Safe in her own palki, she would wait until the camp had arrived at its stopping place a few miles outside the city. Then she would easily rejoin it, unnoticed among other travelers busy with the raising of tents and the unloading of mountains of baggage.

She would be at breakfast in the dining tent with the Eden ladies, Lord Auckland, and all the others, by half past nine.

She yawned. What a strange night it had been. As she looked out at the brightening fields along the road, the torchlit scenes of the night before seemed more and more distant and unreal.

What was real, and tugged at her, spoiling all chance of pleasant rest, was the emptiness in the crook of her arm.

Chapter 26

**FRIDAY,
DECEMBER 20**

"Y"ou were sleeping in your *palanquin*? Sleeping in one of those musty instruments of torture? You *must* have been unwell." Miss Emily's eyebrows had risen until they were invisible inside her bonnet. Tilting her parasol, she studied Mariana carefully from the depths of her folding chair. "I cannot imagine myself sleeping so soundly in a palanquin that I failed to notice dozens of people searching for me. Lieutenant Marks has been quite beside himself."

Mariana tried to look innocent. "I am sorry, Miss Emily. My bearers did not wish to wake me, so they left me sleeping inside while the coolies were putting up my tent. I am sorry to have missed breakfast."

Of course, tired as she had been, she had not really slept. Dittoo had seen to that. As soon as she arrived he had rushed to her palanquin, and, ignoring her closed eyes, had recounted every detail of his own midnight adventure.

"Memsahib," he had informed her at least three times, his voice rising excitedly each time, "*aik dum,* all at once, the water rushed into my mouth, and I was saved!"

Now, at eleven o'clock in the morning, she could scarcely keep her eyes open.

"She is exhausted, Emily." Miss Fanny pursed her lips. "The child looks as if she has been wearing that dress for days. And look at her hair! Mariana, you really must go and lie down."

"In any case," Miss Emily persisted, unswayed by her sister's kindness, "I find it most tactless of you to have fallen ill, Mariana. I shall now be forced to watch the elephant fight all alone." She sniffed. "My sister's attachment to the animal kingdom must outweigh her attachment to me, for she has refused to attend the fight this afternoon. She does not, she says, watch animals kill each other for sport."

Miss Fanny raised her chin but said nothing.

"Be warned, Fanny," added Miss Emily, shaking her parasol in her sister's direction, "that the next time we are invited to some horrid occasion, I shall make a particular point of abandoning you. And speaking of horrid occasions, Mariana, please be recovered by Monday evening. We have been invited to dine with the Maharajah at his Citadel. I shall be expected to converse with him, and will need you to repeat to me every word he says."

Mariana winced. Maharajah Ranjit Singh who had hurt her Saboor—she would rather converse with a snake.

Miss Fanny sighed. "Have we really to dine with him? Oh, Emily, it is sure to be exactly like the dinners poor George has sat through— hours and hours of pointless conversation, dancing girls, red-hot food, awful wine—"

"I know, Fanny," Miss Emily agreed. "But what are we to do?"

"Ah, so Miss Givens has been found!" Lord Auckland ducked his head as he emerged, smiling, from the reception tent. Nodding in Mariana's direction, he pulled up his favorite basket chair. "What a relief for us all. I trust you are well?"

"She is not," replied Miss Fanny. "She is so exhausted that she fell asleep in her palanquin until just now. You must," she added, peering at Mariana, "have been *very* unwell last night."

Mariana looked at her hands. Would they please, *please* talk of something else?

"Perhaps, being ill, Miss Givens missed last night's excitement," Lord Auckland said, responding to her silent plea in the worst possible fashion.

She bent her head to express polite curiosity. "What happened, Lord Auckland?" she inquired.

"Exactly as Mr. Macnaghten had predicted," he answered with a satisfied little smile, "the Maharajah came to believe we had stolen that baby hostage of his and were concealing it in our own compound."

"After we had all gone to bed," Miss Fanny contributed, "at about midnight, a delegation of the Maharajah's courtiers arrived from the Citadel. Major Byrne rounded up *all* our servants and brought them onto the avenue, where he held something called a 'rice test.' All the servants were made to chew handfuls of rice, then spit them out onto the road, after being asked a question devised for the occasion by the mysterious Faqeer Azizuddin."

Lord Auckland winced. Miss Fanny put a hand on her brother's arm. "Only dear George, Major Byrne, and Mr. Macnaghten knew it was to be done," she said, her proud nod causing the rosettes on her bonnet to tremble. "It was all kept a dark secret beforehand, for fear the culprits might get away. What a shock it must have been for the poor servants to be rousted from their sleep by soldiers in the middle of the night!"

"Of course, nothing came of it." Lord Auckland brushed an ant from his sleeve. "There was never any question of the baby's being here. Anyone fool enough to bring that child inside this compound would have been found out at once."

"Do you know, George," Miss Emily said slowly, "Jimmund told me that, last evening as he was taking Chance for his late walk, a palanquin passed him. It caught his attention, he said, because it bounced and swayed as if none of the bearers had ever carried a palanquin before. And he insisted that there was something quite wrong with the way the bearers looked although I did not grasp what it was."

"How odd." Miss Fanny nodded politely as Major Byrne passed by. "A palanquin in the middle of the night. Did he tell you where he saw it?"

"He said it came from the direction of Mariana's tent and was on its way toward the back kitchen gate. He claims it passed him not five minutes before all the servants were rounded up for the test."

"What nonsense, my dears." Lord Auckland smiled affectionately at his sisters as Mariana hastily laced her trembling fingers together in her lap. He shook his head. "I cannot fathom why you let your servants talk to you at all, far less regale you with these absurd stories. Nothing of the sort happened, did it, Miss Givens?"

He folded his own hands over his middle. "Not that it matters," he added with satisfaction, "now that the treaty is at last to be signed."

"I saw no palanquin," Mariana said decisively. "If such a palanquin passed my tent, I knew nothing about it."

"I want to know," said Maharajah Ranjit Singh, peering down from his golden chair at his Chief Minister, "who caused the rice test to fail."

He tapped his fingers on the arm of his throne. "Who avoided my rice test and returned my Saboor to Qamar Haveli last night? Was it the same people who stole Saboor from the Golden Temple?"

He narrowed his eye. "And, Aziz, how do you *know* Saboor is at his grandfather's house?"

The carpet spread on the marble tiles of the marble pavilion kept the chill from Faqeer Azizuddin's bones, but it did nothing to slow the fresh breeze blowing through the fretted windows behind him. He drew his robe closer about his shoulders. The Maharajah had now recovered, but days and nights of tending him had given the Faqeer a fever.

"A goatherd saw Saboor in the Shaikh's courtyard this afternoon, Maharaj," he said for the second time. "That is how I know. A messenger came at all speed with the news. As to how his captors avoided the rice test, I do not know. Perhaps they had intended all along to leave for Lahore last evening, and only escaped the Governor-General's compound by chance."

The Maharajah made a snorting sound. He drew up a stockinged foot and rested it on the seat of his throne. "And you, Aziz," he inquired, studying his Chief Minister's face, "do not know who these captors are?"

An eloquent gesture, a tilt of the head, a rueful smile were all Faqeer Azizuddin would offer. "Do not worry, Maharaj," he said as he tucked his robe about his icy feet, "whoever stole the boy is certain to be found."

"I do not like it that they have evaded me twice." The Maharajah turned to the young man who crouched on his right side. "Who do you think they are, Heera?"

Heera Singh, court favorite, stopped stroking the old man's leg. His heavy emerald necklaces clicked as he raised his handsome head. "I think it was Saboor's family, Maharaj," he replied, peering nearsightedly at his king. "Real child thieves would never have returned Saboor to his own house. They would have kept him for themselves, for the reward. Had he disappeared entirely, I would have blamed criminals." He shrugged.

A corner of the Maharajah's simple turban had become unwrapped. It waved behind him as he bent toward the Faqeer again. "But why did the test fail? Saboor was living in the red compound. The servants there must have seen him. They all knew of the reward. Why did they not come forward for the money? Since they did not, how did the rice test fail to reveal their identities?"

Azizuddin stifled a sneeze. "The question was faulty, Maharaj," he replied. "The English officer in charge asked the servants only if they knew Saboor's whereabouts. Since the child had already been taken from the compound, the question was useless. None of them could have known exactly where he was. Had Major Byrne asked if anyone had *seen* the child, we would have had *real* results."

The Maharajah gave an unsatisfied grunt.

"We also know," the Faqeer added, "that Saboor was returned to Qamar Haveli last night *after* the city gates were closed. The only gate to be opened during the night was the Delhi Gate, which is of course the gate nearest to the Shaikh's house. It was opened twice, once to admit a palki said to be carrying a dying cousin of Shaikh Waliullah—"

"But it was no dying cousin, it was Saboor," the Maharajah interrupted crossly. Scowling, he rested his chin on his knee.

"—and once, a little time later, to admit Rajah Suchayt Singh, who had made the error of relieving himself onto a coiled snake after an evening's entertainment outside the city."

"Yes." The Maharajah's voice sharpened. "After hearing that your friend the Shaikh had cured Suchayt, I sent gifts at once, to show my respect. Although it was the middle of the night I sent shawls, gold, even a horse." He jabbed the air with a forefinger. "Your friend Waliullah returned them all."

His voice rose and cracked. "I do not like such treatment, Aziz. What does he mean by refusing my gifts? Does he think he deserves better gifts than those I choose to send? My men said he did not even look at them."

He turned a burning eye on his Chief Minister. "I tell you, Aziz, I do not like this business. I should not be treated with such disrespect. The man is too sure of himself. I am sure he is behind the stealing of my child. He must return my Saboor today. I want the boy. I need him." The old voice had turned plaintive.

The Faqeer shifted his aching limbs. "Maharaj," he said, altering his tone to a conciliatory whine, "why not leave Saboor with his family for a short while? After that, you need only ask and he will be returned to you. Remember, Maharaj, how you sat up, fully recovered, upon hearing from the eunuch that Saboor was found?"

When the Maharajah did not reply, the Faqeer pressed on. "The child was becoming sickly from so much traveling and excitement. To be constantly in your presence is too great an honor for a child so small. A few days in his own house will do him good."

It was not often that the Faqeer resorted to begging. When the Maharajah's expression subtly changed, the Faqeer seized the advantage and changed the subject. "And now, Maharaj," he added in a normal voice, smiling encouragingly, "what of the British? What of their plan?"

The Maharajah's face lit up. "Ah, Aziz, you know how to amuse me. These British are going to invade Afghanistan; they are going to put their own king on the throne there, thinking they will control all of Central Asia—how little they know, how little they understand!"

His shoulders shook with silent laughter. "What a gift they gave us when they arrived with their army, already too late to make the journey north, with no treaty allowing them to cross my Punjab! They have conquered half of India, and yet we have made fools of them, making them wait for my permission, making the Governor-General dance like a black bear on a chain! What a *tamasha*, what a show this has been!"

The Faqeer nodded. "Maharaj, you are indeed a master of delay."

The Maharajah was beaming. "Winter is tightening its grip on the passes, but why should we concern ourselves? Let the Governor-General's English soldiers and his Maharattas and his Bengalis suffer on the way to Kabul. Let their army grow weak." His expression hardened. "That weakness can only benefit us, who wait for the moment when the English will turn that same army against us. These English dream of conquering Central Asia, but one day they will see that my Punjab is the greater prize."

The Faqeer laid a tender hand on the royal knee. "Come, Maharaj," he crooned. "It is cold here. We will go to your room, where it is warmer, and talk more about the British."

The old man rose obediently, took his Chief Minister's arm, and began to shuffle, wheezing a little, in the direction of his private quarters. As he did so, the Faqeer bent and spoke into his ear. "The girl," he said softly. "Let us plan what we will do about the British girl."

The Maharajah straightened. "Yes, Aziz," he whispered back, clapping his hands, his face suddenly younger. "Ah, yes, there is much to be planned."

He gripped the Faqeer's arm. "What do you suppose the English will do when I make my announcement about the girl? I will let them think it is a condition for my signing the treaty. That will be a great show, yes, a very great show!"

As they rounded the corner into his private courtyard, the Maharajah nodded happily into his Chief Minister's face, the loose end of his turban fluttering behind him like a tiny battle flag.

SERVANTS scuttled to and fro across Shaikh Waliullah's courtyard, careful not to disturb the Shaikh on his platform. In a corner, a piebald cat sniffed at a bush. Distant clattering and the sound of children's voices echoed from other parts of the haveli.

The Shaikh smiled at Hassan. "I am glad, my dear son, that you were able to come so quickly last night. It must have been delicious to hold Saboor in your arms again, Allah be praised."

Sitting beside Hassan, Yusuf was listening to the slow groan of the water wheel on the roof. He always felt clumsy in the presence of the Shaikh. This peaceful courtyard was not his place. The men who sat silently here, moving only their eyes, were not his people. How much happier he would be galloping with Hassan across the ground outside the city, shouting aloud, celebrating Saboor's return!

Hassan was, of course, in no hurry to leave his home. Moving from man to man, he had greeted each of his father's companions with respectful grace. Why not? He was Shaikh Waliullah's son, the grandson of the renowned Shaikh 'Abd Dhul Jalali Wal'Ikram. Descended from great men, Hassan too would one day be great, for all his perfumes and expensive clothes. Yusuf was certain of that.

"Yusuf," the Shaikh said in his pleasant voice, as if reading Yusuf's mind, "wait a little. You will gallop your horse soon enough."

Yusuf lowered his eyes.

"I have called you here, Hassan, to tell you something of great importance," the Shaikh said, then paused.

Yusuf realized that he had never seen the Shaikh look so tired, or perhaps so sad. The old man's embroidered skullcap lay askew on his head. His back, usually as straight as a staff, curved forward as he studied his son.

"In my letter to you," he continued carefully, "I wrote that events pointed to Saboor's rescue by an unknown outsider."

The other men's eyes flickered. Although the Shaikh had not addressed him, Yusuf nodded. How could he forget that well-thumbed letter? *As Shafi Sahib is rarely wrong, I believe you may comfort yourself with this news.*

"The first event occurred soon after Mumtaz Bano was poisoned," the Shaikh said. "A man named Yar Mohammad came to us from the British camp. He described a vision he had seen, in which a female lion rescued a child from grave danger. We believed the child to be Saboor, but we were unable to identify his rescuer until Shafi Sahib received a message indicating that the lioness was an Englishwoman, a translator attached to the British Governor-General's camp. Even then, we could not tell when the rescue would take place."

Visions, messages—Yusuf's knee began to jog.

"Yusuf," said the Shaikh without looking at him, "you should listen. You have much to learn." He pushed his cap farther aside and scratched his head. "For many days, Hassan, we waited and prayed. We prayed when we heard the news that Saboor had disappeared from the Maharajah's camp. We prayed until last night when, as Yar Mohammad had foreseen and Shafi Sahib had predicted, the young English translator came, at much risk to herself, and delivered Saboor to us."

An Englishwoman—Yusuf twitched on his reed stool. After so many hopes and expectations, how was it that a woman, not he, had made this rescue?

"Now, my dear son," the Shaikh was saying, "we are faced with a serious problem for which there is only one solution."

No one moved. Perhaps it was the Shaikh's somber tone that brought silence to the courtyard. Except for the rattle and hum of the city outside the haveli walls, not a sound came from anywhere. Even the cat had vanished.

The Shaikh surveyed his audience. "Yar Mohammad's dream did not end after the lioness rescued the baby," he went on, speaking into the silence around his platform. "Having carried the child from danger, the lioness waited, standing over him, and when a second danger loomed, she lifted him in her jaws and moved away, out of Yar Mohammad's sight.

"According to Shafi Sahib and others," the Shaikh concluded gravely, "this signifies that the guardian is to remain with Saboor to protect him, perhaps for a long time, until he is grown."

The sky was white. Distant birds circled far above Yusuf's head. A *woman* to protect Saboor? Perhaps Shaikh Waliullah was so old and tired he had lost his reason. And why tell this long story? Why did he not come to the point, he who always told even the bitterest truth without hesitation? He glanced at Hassan, who was staring at the tiles between his feet.

"Hassan," the Shaikh said, finally, "I cannot know the depth of your grief over poor little Mumtaz Bano. But whatever your suffering, you must act to protect Saboor from further dangers. You must marry the foreign woman who has rescued him."

Chapter 21

Mariana sat outside her tent, her back to the sun, her hair spread in a damp cascade over the back of her chair. Where, she wondered, was Saboor now?

Perhaps, at this moment, he was playing with his cousins in the upstairs room where she had spent the hours before yesterday's dawn, his high, chirping laugh echoing down into his grandfather's courtyard.

Did he miss her? He must.

She fluffed out her curls. Newly washed, they would never remain in a smooth knot this evening at the Maharajah's dinner.

The whole story of Saboor was a tantalizing mystery. Why had he chosen *her* to rescue him? Why did she love him so? He was a native baby, after all, one of thousands and thousands of native babies, and yet when he curled his little toes, or peered at her over his thumb, she could barely keep herself from snatching him up and covering him with kisses from head to foot.

As she reached for her hairbrush, Dittoo approached. "Memsahib," he said, "a letter has been delivered to the main gate. It is for you." He held out a folded paper. "This letter," he declared, "is not from an English sahib."

He was right. The elegant script on the outside of the letter was not English.

She took it, frowning. "But who would write a letter to me in Urdu?"

The writing on the outside of the paper did not travel in neat lines across the page like an English letter, but in a curving diagonal that gave it a vaguely artistic appearance. She unfolded the page and bent over it, tucking her damp hair behind her ears.

"I pray that, God willing, your journey back to the British camp was safe and comfortable," it said. *"Saboor's return has brought joy to us all, especially to his father and his maternal grandmother, who have suffered very much. You have shown a warm heart and great courage in undertaking Saboor's rescue, and we are most grateful."*

How nice. It was a thank-you letter from Shaikh Waliullah.

In consideration of the fact that you are in India without your own family, it becomes difficult to arrange matters of importance concerning your future. However, the proposal we wish to make can most probably be brought to the senior sister of your Governor-General.

We have seen the love you hold for our Saboor, and we recognize that it is in his best interest to remain near you, but in order to ensure your continued, kind presence, we must observe the proper formalities.

Ladies of my family will therefore approach the elder of the Governor-General's sisters tomorrow, to propose your marriage to my son Hassan.

The letter floated from Mariana's fingers to the ground, its remaining lines unread.

Dittoo stared at the paper lying in the dust. "What is wrong, Memsahib? Have you had bad news? Is Saboor Baba ill?"

Unable to reply, she rose and swept past him into her tent, imagining the son, a younger version of the Shaikh, his ears jutting like his father's from under a tall headdress, while behind him a caricature of the Shaikh gave a suggestive wink.

Lieutenant Marks's words echoed in her head. *"The native in question has instantly overstepped the bounds of propriety and become unpleasantly familiar, even intimate—"*

This was so damaging. What would everyone think when a troop of native ladies arrived to ask for her hand in marriage? *What had she done?*

Someone had come. As she turned, her teacher stepped into the tent, the Shaikh's letter in his hand. "Bibi," he said, after greeting her, "I found this lying on the ground."

"I know, Munshi Sahib." Refusing to look at the letter, she raised her chin. "Please read it."

While she waited, her heart thumping, he opened the page unhurriedly and ran his eyes over the words on the paper, then put it on her table and stepped backward, waiting.

She searched his face. Where was his sympathy? "Munshi Sahib, what am I to do? Shaikh Waliullah wants me to marry his son! He wants to send his ladies to Miss Emily with the proposal!" She pressed her hands to her cheeks. "I must stop him, Munshi Sahib. Please help me write a letter that will make him stop!"

The munshi was silent for a moment. "If you wish, Bibi," he said finally, "I will help you to answer the Shaikh's letter. But I cannot do so today. You shall write your letter when I return tomorrow morning for our lesson."

Before she could say anything more, he excused himself and departed.

"I must say," Miss Fanny confided that evening, as their elephant turned, swaying, onto the road from Shalimar to the Citadel and the Maharajah's banquet, "that I am very glad our elephant has a *blue* face."

She gripped the railing of the silver howdah with gloved fingers. "Do you not agree, Emily, that blue is a becoming color for an elephant?"

"I do, indeed," replied Miss Emily from the corner where she sat, half-hidden under several shawls.

Ahead of them, preceded by the honor guard, the Governor-General, his own officials, and a native ambassador sent by the Maharajah, rode on other decorated elephants, surrounded by a swarm of liveried minions and servants and the inevitable crowd of local children braving clouds of dust to see the spectacle.

In her own corner of the howdah, Mariana prayed that the ladies would exempt her from their conversation. She needed to think about the past eight days, of all the things that had happened in that time.

Saboor had come to her and stolen her heart. Three days later, after reluctantly returning him to his grandfather's haveli in the walled city, she had seen a case of poisonous snakebite *completely cured*. She had met a great mystic Shaikh, and then, only that very morning, had received a proposal of marriage from that same Shaikh for his son. Even more extraordinary, *no English person knew about these events*.

At least she was over her panic about the Shaikh's proposal. Tomorrow, she and Munshi would write him a polite refusal, which would reach him by tomorrow afternoon. There would be no need to worry about native ladies calling upon Miss Emily.

She yawned. Yesterday she had tried to write to her father and also to Uncle Adrian and Aunt Claire in Calcutta, but, her head bursting with events she could not disclose, had been unable to think of anything to say. Dear Papa must wait, although her letters to him, when she *did* write them, would be sure to make up entirely for the gap in time.

"I am sorry that Mr. Macnaghten and Major Byrne have been made to ride that nasty sulfur yellow one," Miss Fanny observed, nodding toward the elephant ahead of them, "but since Major Byrne has told me that the treaty is to be signed at last, I doubt if they would mind riding a donkey."

"*I* think," Miss Emily frowned down at the dancing throng of village boys, "that Macnaghten and Byrne would mind a donkey very much indeed."

Mariana turned to gaze behind them toward their camp at the fabled gardens of Shalimar. At the sound of the call to prayer, whose last echoes still floated around them, the western sky had flooded the lacy buildings of the gardens with rosy light, turning cascades and pools of water into the stuff of dreams.

Dreams. Fitzgerald was *not* a dream. She would find a way to persuade him not to give up.

"Emily," Miss Fanny said suddenly, "I had forgotten the elephant fight. Was it dreadful?"

"It was unspeakable." Miss Emily shrank a little inside her wrappings; she tucked a maroon shawl with orange swirls more closely about her. "One of the mahouts was killed. He lay on the ground like a smashed doll, with his elephant standing over him, trumpeting. I believe the poor animal's heart was broken. I cannot bear talking about it."

While Miss Fanny made sympathetic noises, Mariana peered ahead, searching among the bodyguard for a familiar uniformed back. What an irony it was that her much anticipated proposal of marriage had come not from Fitzgerald but from a native. . . .

Miss Emily's voice broke into her thoughts. "Mariana, since the treaty is to be signed, I am certain your Lieutenant Marks will declare himself quite soon."

Mariana could think of no appropriate reply.

A brilliant mass of stars had appeared by the time the Governor-General's party arrived at the towering picture wall of the Citadel.

High on the wall, tile figures of animals, birds, and warriors seemed to dance in the torchlight, while below, accompanied by a cavalry detachment in chain mail and silks, a cluster of the Maharajah's dignitaries waited on elephant-back to receive them.

As Mr. Macnaghten moved forward to meet Faqeer Azizuddin, whose own elephant wore a pair of enormous orange tassels, Miss Emily turned to Mariana.

"As you can see, my dear," she said innocently, "it will be just as we described it, a simple dinner with our Sikh friends."

After the usual interval, during which elephants and horses milled about and Major Byrne and Mr. Macnaghten exchanged effusive greetings with a smiling Faqeer Azizuddin, the elephants fell into line and the gleaming procession with Lord Auckland at its head made its way through a high, guarded passageway leading to the narrow, protected gate of the Citadel.

"Good gracious! Look!" Miss Emily clutched her sister's arm.

To their left, a broad stone staircase led upward, turning as it climbed, toward bright light and the distant rhythms of Oriental music.

Instead of stopping, the elephants were making straight for the shallow stairway—Lord Auckland's animal first, followed by the ambassador's silver elephant, and then, its hindquarters swaying, the yellow elephant of Mr. Macnaghten and Major Byrne.

Miss Emily's bonnet bobbed with alarm. "You must assure me at once, Fanny," she implored, "that we are not about to climb a flight of stairs on a blue elephant."

But they were to do just that. As their mahout guided the great animal toward the stairs, the clear voice of a royal announcer began to call out their titles from a niche high in the wall.

"Oh, but this is so exciting," breathed Mariana, as they began their ascent, their silver howdah swaying and their elephant's state housings aglitter in the light of a hundred torches.

• • •

MAHARAJAH Ranjit Singh sat under a canopy of Kashmir shawls in the heart of a lamplit sandstone courtyard, his Chief Minister on the carpet at his feet, his nobles standing before him. On the Maharajah's seeing side, a stiffly smiling Lord Auckland perched on a golden chair near Mr. Macnaghten, who was to translate. The two men tactfully ignored the Maharajah's drawn-up feet and the pair of socks that lay discarded upon the rich carpet in front of his golden throne.

On the Maharajah's blind side, beyond the Misses Eden, Mariana smoothed her blue-and-white-striped skirt and listened to the murmuring of the crowd.

The Maharajah's chiefs were a wonderful sight. They looked even more romantic than the Honor Guard, who stood behind the British chairs, splendidly turned out in plumes and gold lace. Among them, a pale-looking Harry Fitzgerald, resplendent in gold braid and a black dragoon helmet with a red horsehair plume, kept his face turned away from Mariana.

How long had Major Byrne and Mr. Macnaghten been glaring at her like that? She let out her breath. Those two must *never* learn of the Shaikh's proposal.

Rising from some distant courtyard, fireworks burst noisily above them. Drums grew insistent and rows of dancing girls appeared. As the music quickened, Mariana felt her heart take up the rhythm of the drums.

She must enjoy this spectacle now, while it was still night. By daylight, the Citadel would surely prove to be a crumbling ruin, despoiled by the Sikhs after the glories of the Moghul Empire, full of filth, beggars, and starving dogs.

Perhaps everything in India was like Shaikh Waliullah—able to enchant only in the darkness.

Chapter 28

**MONDAY,
DECEMBER 23**

"While we are at dinner, Mariana," Miss Emily had cautioned on Saturday, "please remember that we British *never* notice gifts given to us by Oriental potentates."

The dancing girls had drifted away. A liveried servant appeared at the Maharajah's side carrying a tray heaped with jewels. Mariana tore her gaze away and stared for several seconds without thinking at a Sikh sirdar in a green-and-white shawl and emeralds, who smiled back delightedly.

While the English party studied the air, Ranjit Singh poked with brown fingers through the treasure on the tray. From the corner of her eye, Mariana saw him fish two diamond bracelets and a diamond ring from the pile, then reach for Miss Emily.

She glanced quickly across and was rewarded by the sight of Miss Emily staring into space, the bracelets already clasped onto one bony wrist, while, as if in some bizarre wedding ceremony, the Maharajah pushed the ring onto her finger.

He now returned to the tray and began again, his head tilted, to search diligently among the jewels.

At length, a rope of pearls in his hand, he rose and came to stand over Miss Fanny, apparently expecting to put the necklace over her head.

It was obvious that the midlength rope would not fit over Miss Fanny's large bonnet. Mariana risked another glance and caught the Maharajah's gleam of enjoyment as his small hands worked near Miss Fanny's impassive face, tangling the pearls more and more inextricably among silk peonies and velvet ribbons. His fumbling seemed to go on forever. Mariana stared sideways, fighting the desire to laugh aloud, grateful that she was to be exempt from this particular game.

As soon as this ceremony had ended, a fresh tray arrived, carried in by a beautiful young boy. As he set the tray in front of the Maharajah, a sigh passed like a gust of wind through the assembled British officers.

The Maharajah clapped his hands with pleasure. "*Wah, wah,* Governor Sahib, the wine has come," he declared happily.

"Do look at poor George," said Miss Emily in a stage whisper. "He looks as if he has been sentenced to transportation."

Moments later, someone pressed a wine cup into Mariana's hand.

Pursing her lips on the goblet's rim, she took an experimental sip. Bitter and blisteringly hot, the wine caused tears to rush into her eyes. Forced to swallow, she was certain she had scalded her insides.

"We had this wine at Simla," Miss Fanny was saying confidentially as she poured hers surreptitiously onto the carpet. "It tastes like bitter, fermented red peppers. Oh, dear, I see you've already tried it." She blinked into Mariana's burning face. "Are you all right? Poor George was in bed all morning after the last of these parties. Aren't we fortunate to be sitting on the Maharajah's blind side! The poor officer behind the major's chair has been on a *strict* diet of toast and water for days, and even he has not been able to avoid the wine."

For the next two hours, while the British officers stirred and yawned, the Maharajah drank steadily, his hand ever holding the golden bottle, ready to pour again.

Fitzgerald, who stood in the Maharajah's line of vision, was also being forced to drink. He now swayed puffy-faced in his place behind Lord Auckland's chair, his eyes drooping.

The toast-and-water officer had already been carried away.

"Are my brother and Mr. Macnaghten not brave?" whispered Miss Fanny, nodding toward the rigid-faced Mr. Macnaghten and Lord Auckland. "They know they must not offend the Maharajah, now that the signing is so very close."

• • •

AT last, several servants brought in a golden table and set it before the Maharajah.

Miss Fanny nudged Mariana and pointed to her timepiece as servants carried in dishes of food and set them out on the table. It was midnight.

Too tired now for hunger, Mariana picked at her plate while, before and behind her, the British and Sikh parties ate standing up. What was she eating, venison? Duck? What were those odd-shaped vegetables? The yellow rice tasted as if the cook had mixed into it all the spices for a Christmas pudding. Everything was like that, perfumed with a queer mixture of familiar and unfamiliar tastes.

Her nose ran from the red pepper. She put her handkerchief to her face and looked up to see the Maharajah bend down, his single eye fixed on her, and say something to the black-bearded Chief Minister at his feet.

Faqeer Azizuddin's glance became speculative. She looked down uneasily at her clothes. Had she spilled food on her gown? What were they staring at?

"Fanny, dear," Miss Emily said quietly, "I have eaten all I can bear to, and Ranjit will not stop feeding me. I have already deposited two quails, four balls of spiced meat, and a round of bread under my chair, and I fear I have used every bit of available space. Might I hire the carpet under your chair for the rest of the evening? I must find a home for two pears and a large sweetmeat decorated with gold foil."

"Of course you may, Emily," replied Miss Fanny in her stage whisper. "I do hope this evening does not go on much longer," she added mournfully. "The wine has soaked right through my best slippers."

THE Maharajah, still talking, was eating his dinner, including his rice, with one hand, sucking his fingers noisily. Having spoken for the better part of an hour with Lord Auckland and Mr. Macnaghten, he turned at last to Miss Emily.

This was Mariana's moment.

"Does the Governor Sahib not like women?" the king asked, his eye bright with amusement. "Is that why he has never married?"

Beaming, he reached into a serving dish, scooped up a handful of pomegranate seeds, and dropped them onto Miss Emily's plate. "Perhaps Lord Auckland would like to choose one of my dancing girls for himself? Or possibly my cup bearer?"

Mariana felt her face redden. How could she translate such an unsuitable question? Besides, he could not have meant *that* cup bearer, for he most definitely was a young man.

She looked to Mr. Macnaghten for help, but he was speaking, his head bent, to Lord Auckland.

"Ask her, Bibi," prodded the Maharajah, nodding to Mariana.

Miss Emily raised her eyebrows. "What is he saying, my dear?"

"He is asking whether Lord Auckland likes the dancing girls," Mariana said, firmly. "Please, do not say yes."

"The Governor-General likes, I should say," said Miss Emily carefully, "Lord Auckland likes the dancing girls well enough." She paused, pursing her lips. "But not as much as all that."

"Lady Sahib says that the Governor Sahib has enjoyed your entertainments," said Mariana stiffly, "but he is extremely busy and cannot take the time to see them again."

The Sikh sirdars greeted her answer with hoots of laughter.

The Maharajah also laughed, his head thrown back, his eye tightly closed, while at his feet the Faqeer gave a sphinx-like smile.

"Your sister is a very formal lady," said the Maharajah, turning back to Lord Auckland.

Hooting, the sirdars slapped one another.

"And," the king added, holding out his hands to be washed, "as to the matter of ladies, it fills me with happiness to know that I am at last to have an English wife."

An English wife? Mariana blinked. What game was the Maharajah playing now?

Beside the Maharajah, Mr. Macnaghten and Lord Auckland exchanged a look of puzzlement. On Mr. Macnaghten's far side, Major Byrne yawned into his handkerchief.

The Faqeer turned to Lord Auckland. "The Maharajah," the minister said, his tone velvety, "says he has entirely forgotten that three full years have passed since he wrote to your government requesting an English wife."

His smile broadened. "But now that the lady has arrived, he understands that this delay was due not to lack of desire by the Supreme Government but rather to a lengthy and careful search for the proper candidate."

Lady? Mariana swallowed. Why were all the sirdars staring at *her*?

"Women are necessary, are they not?" The Maharajah looked brightly from Lord Auckland to the Eden sisters. "Marriage between two families ensures love and friendship, does it not?" He shook drops of water from his fingers. "Our two families will now be joined forever, and the nightingales will never cease to sing in the gardens of our friendship!" Leaning back in his throne, he opened his hands expansively.

Mr. Macnaghten turned gray.

Beside Macnaghten, Lord Auckland blinked. "What is the matter, William?" he rasped. "What is the man saying?"

"Your duty," the Maharajah put in, waggling his fingers in Mariana's direction, "was to bring this young lady to Lahore, and mine is to offer the proposal."

Mr. Macnaghten closed his eyes.

Mariana's mouth dropped open. Not him, too! A second marriage proposal in two days, this one from an ancient, one-eyed Maharajah whose head came to her chin! Whatever was the matter with them all?

Miss Emily frowned. "What are they saying, Mariana?"

Behind Lord Auckland's chair, a glassy-eyed Harry Fitzgerald nodded on his feet. Was he even listening? Major Byrne's chin had dropped to his chest. Where was the odious Lieutenant Marks? Was anyone sober enough to stop this madness?

Mariana turned to Miss Emily. "The Maharajah has—"

"And there is good news," the Maharajah went on, his reedy voice gaining speed. "Auguries have determined that the correct day for the ceremonies is December twenty-fifth, only two days hence!"

What? The day after tomorrow? Christmas Day? Mariana twisted in her seat, searching the faces of the British officers. Why did no one stop him?

The Maharajah beckoned to someone standing in the shadows. "Therefore, Governor Sahib," he announced, "I will begin the formalities by showering coins over your head."

Miss Emily was leaning toward Mariana. "What are they saying? What is the matter with Mr. Macnaghten?"

Macnaghten's head swayed from side to side. Mariana glared hard at him, willing him to speak. *Respond,* she begged silently. *Pull yourself together and respond!*

This was Macnaghten's fault. Who had asked the political secretary to promise the Maharajah eternal love and friendship? Mariana's thoughts raced. Everyone knew that days ago Lord Auckland had given up hope of Ranjit Singh's joining in the British plan for Afghanistan. For all his expansive talk, it was clear that the old man would give little support to the campaign and would send no armies to fight beside the British. But what was the old king doing now? Would he refuse to commit himself even to a reduced treaty guaranteeing stability in the region and a safe passage for the British through the Punjab? Was he merely playing with them, calling their bluff, enjoying himself? Did he really want an English wife?

Would he refuse to sign the treaty unless she married him?

Sirdars murmured. Macnaghten blinked and raised his hands,

palms out. "Maharaj," he began shakily, "one moment please. Governor Sahib—"

"No, no," the Maharajah interrupted, waving an airy hand at Lord Auckland while a servant stepped forward with a silver tray, "there is no need to wait now, no need at all. You have made a good choice. She needs fattening, of course, but she has good teeth. I like nice white teeth."

"What is he saying?" Miss Emily tapped Mariana's knee with her fan. "What is going on?"

"Oh, Emily," Miss Fanny said anxiously, "I hope Mariana is—"

Dragging his gaze from the Maharajah, Mr. Macnaghten looked across at the three ladies. "He is speaking, Miss Eden," he said, his words a little slurred, "of Miss Givens's teeth." He closed his eyes again, clearly wishing he were somewhere else. "He likes them."

Miss Eden sat straight. "He likes Mariana's *teeth*? Her *teeth*? Really, these people are most extraordinary." She leaned across her sister. "Good gracious, Mariana, I thought you were on the Maharajah's blind side!"

Lord Auckland, his face the color of parchment, swayed in his chair as if already returning on his elephant to the British camp. He frowned as Mr. Macnaghten turned to him.

Mariana strained to catch his words. "—if we refuse," she heard him say, "—might claim bad faith—supply route across the Punjab . . ."

Sensing trouble, the officers behind Mariana began to shift nervously.

The old Maharajah reached for the tray of coins and began to fumble with its covering cloth.

What in heaven's name was the matter with Harry Fitzgerald? Why did he not intervene? Did he not love her? Why did he stand nodding on his feet while this preposterous scene unfolded, without making one single move to rescue her? Mariana wanted to stand up and shout his name. What sort of fool had she wanted to marry?

"Are you all right, my dear?" Miss Fanny reached across the space between their chairs.

Mariana's nose was still running from the pepper. With one hand she pressed her handkerchief to her nose, while with the other she gripped Miss Fanny's small, kind hand.

The Maharajah had lifted back a corner of the cloth.

The Sikh sirdars pressed closer, relishing the Maharajah's performance. A man in an emerald necklace laughed, his eyes on Mariana.

Why was Lord Auckland silent? Was he actually going to let the Maharajah have her in order to gain his treaty?

"Yes, yes," the Maharajah was saying, as if he were planning a picnic, while the bearded Faqeer at his feet nodded delightedly. "We shall have a grand wedding, the day after tomorrow, with more wine than ever, and many more entertainments."

Lord Auckland whispered something to Mr. Macnaghten, who looked desperately about him, then took a breath. "Most Excellent Maharajah," he began, "it is most—most—"

With a sigh and a heavy wave of his hand, he subsided into silence. Beside him, Major Byrne hunched over, his chin on his chest, snoring.

The old fingers were busy now among the golden coins on the tray. A picture formed in Mariana's mind's eye of her table with her letter from the Shaikh lying on its surface.

Had the Shaikh made his proposal to save her from this ordeal? Knowing of the Maharajah's plan, had he written to warn her, his letter worded so delicately that she had very nearly missed its true meaning?

"It becomes difficult," the note had said, *"to make arrangements concerning your future—"*

Coins dropped through the Maharajah's fingers as he leaned over and raised a fistful of gold over Lord Auckland's head.

Who could comprehend the native customs? If the old man dropped the coins, would that mean the engagement was sealed? Would it then be impossible to turn back? What would her family say to *this*?

Mariana could wait no longer. "Stop!" she cried, then rose clumsily, overturning her chair.

She crossed the carpet, her eyes on the Maharajah's raised arm, and stood before his throne.

The crowd that had moved back, murmuring, to let her pass, now pressed forward avidly. The Maharajah's hand stopped in midair as she offered him a full, breathless curtsy, her shaking knees locked together under her gown. Her ears rang. She had no idea what to say.

" 'How shall I tell thee of myself?' " Still in her deep curtsy, she began quoting from a legend Munshi was teaching her. " 'I cannot tell what has befallen me. I grieve day and night. Hunger and thirst have left me altogether. No joy by day; no sleep to my eyes. Heavy is my anxiety—' "

"What is she doing? What is she saying?" the Governor-General demanded loudly.

"*Shabash!* You have taught her Punjabi!" Still holding the coins, the Maharajah gave a high, wheezing laugh. He had fixed his eye on the decolletage of her low-cut gown.

Her cheeks blazing, she shot upright. The rest of the fable, and the point she was trying to make by reciting it, vanished from her mind, lost in a haze of fright and self-consciousness.

Searching her memory for something else, she found a Persian quatrain and began to speak again, ignoring the staring Governor-General and the suddenly attentive Harry Fitzgerald.

"Last night at the tavern I called for the cup.
'What lover,' I cried, 'leaves the last of the wine?'
As I lay on the threshold afire with joy,
Life came bearing gifts, saw my drunken state, and fled."

She looked up fearfully and saw the old king staring at her, his mouth ajar. Beside him, Miss Emily frowned furiously, pointing with little flapping gestures at Mariana's overturned chair.

Miss Fanny gazed from one face to another as if she were at the theater. Forced to translate Mariana's speech for Lord Auckland, Mr. Macnaghten seemed to be having difficulty with her Persian poem.

"Speak plainly, Bibi," ordered the Maharajah, impatiently, rattling the coins in his palm. "What do you want to say?"

Mariana glanced nervously behind her as the crowd of Sikhs began to edge forward. "How can I tell you that I am betrothed to another man?" she murmured.

There, now she had said it. Whatever else happened, surely the Maharajah must now abandon his pursuit of her.

Behind Lord Auckland's chair, directly in her line of vision, Harry Fitzgerald swayed from side to side, his eyes bulging.

The Maharajah's beard twitched. "What is this? To whom are you engaged? To whom is she engaged?" He turned to Lord Auckland and grasped him by the upper arm.

One of the officers behind Lord Auckland translated rapidly. Must she tell them?

"Speak!" commanded the Maharajah.

The crowd of courtiers rustled behind her in the waiting silence.

"I am engaged," she said clearly, "to Hassan, the son of Shaikh Waliullah of the city of Lahore."

Fitzgerald started so abruptly that he seemed to rise from the ground.

The lamps flickered, throwing an eerie light over the scene. In the crowd behind Mr. Macnaghten's chair, Mariana caught a glimpse of Lieutenant Marks's horrified face. She tried hard not to squeeze her eyes shut. Surely she would awaken soon to find this had been a bad dream.

She swallowed and glanced over her shoulder. The entire court seemed to be staring at someone standing at the back of the crowd.

In front of her, Lord Auckland had begun to swell visibly. Color, a dangerous red, was returning to his face.

"Emily, we *must* do something about George." Miss Fanny's whisper carried easily to where Mariana stood.

"Governor Sahib," the Maharajah said in a voice they had not heard before, "you brought the girl for me and now you have accepted another proposal for her? Is this a joke?"

Lord Auckland put a hand to his brow and closed his eyes. Perspiration had run onto his stiff collar.

The British delegation stirred and murmured as comprehension filtered through their ranks.

Fear made Mariana reckless. She plunged on, just as Mr. Macnaghten drew breath to speak. "Maharaj, it was *I* who accepted the proposal, on my own behalf. I did not consult Governor Sahib."

The Maharajah turned, openmouthed, to Lord Auckland.

Mercifully, Mr. Macnaghten had seen his opportunity. "If," he said, "the lady has given her word, it is not within the power of our government to force her to break it. However, Maharaj," he added, glaring at Mariana, "you may be sure the young woman will be suitably punished for this mistake."

Mistake. Mariana stiffened. The mistake of speaking up, of saving herself when no one else would do it, of taking the blame on herself for not marrying the old, blind Maharajah and saving all their faces?

She tried to catch Fitzgerald's eye, but he had turned away.

The Maharajah sat without speaking. At his feet, the bearded Faqeer fiddled with his cloak, his dark eyes darting this way and that.

Deprived of their translator, the Eden sisters gestured excitely for Mariana to come back and sit down. After a final trembling curtsy, she made her way past the Sikhs to her overturned seat.

"My dear girl, what do you mean by getting up and making a speech?" Miss Emily leaned past her sister, her eyes narrow. "What were you saying? What in the name of heaven is going on? It is quite clear that you have upset everyone, especially my brother."

Before Mariana could reply, the Maharajah broke the silence with a wheezing laugh that turned at once into a fit of coughing. Reaching to his right, he slapped the Governor-General on the leg, and held out his hand, palm up.

When Lord Auckland ignored his hand, the old king wiped his eye. "What a joke," he cried. "What a joke on us all! I tell you, Governor Sahib, there is no accounting for women. I have so many wives, and I tell you, the more wives you have, the more trouble you endure. You cannot imagine how my women fight with me."

Hiccuping, he thumped his black-bearded minister's shoulder.

"Perhaps you have been wise, Governor Sahib," he gasped, pointing mirthfully at Lord Auckland, "to have no wives at all!

"Now," he went on in a businesslike tone, interrupting Mr. Macnaghten who was attempting to speak, "since we are all brothers, we will have a great show at the wedding. You haven't seen one of our weddings, have you, Governor Sahib? We will have a fine show, a very fine show!"

A wedding?

"Wedding, Maharaj?" Mr. Macnaghten blinked.

"Of course," replied the Maharajah, spreading his bony arms expansively. "The girl and Hassan are already engaged. Why waste the wedding arrangements? We will celebrate the girl's marriage to Hassan here at the Citadel in two days. I know the boy," he added, his face suddenly unreadable. "We will have a fine show, a fine show."

With a groan, a government secretary standing behind fainted dead away.

Chapter 29

Mariana perched on the edge of her chair, her damp hands hidden in the folds of her skirts, as two officers carried the stricken man away. As they left, Mr. Macnaghten cleared his throat several times and then, slurring his words a little, recounted her speech in English for the benefit of the ladies. He spoke flatly, turning her poetry into odd-sounding English prose, translating her announcement to the Maharajah in the same tone he might have used to read a list of battle casualties.

Beside her Miss Fanny drew in a tremulous, audible breath. The Maharajah, his eye moving from face to face, watched from his golden seat.

No one looked at Mariana, not even the Maharajah, who appeared to have lost interest in her. Lord Auckland stared glassily ahead, his lips pressed into a thin line, his face as brick red as the pattern in the Maharajah's carpet. Mr. Macnaghten, who had sunk into his chair after his translation, avoided her glance. Major Byrne, finally awake, gave an echoing honk.

Coming from the political secretary's lips, her speech had sounded all wrong—intimate, suggestive of liberties offered and liberties taken. She must explain her behavior before they thought ill of her; but her head whirled and her thoughts would not order themselves.

"So," the Maharajah announced gaily, "there is much to do, much to enjoy! But we have business to perform. Tomorrow we will sign your treaty. The day after tomorrow, we will celebrate the wedding."

So, the treaty was to be signed *before* the wedding! Mariana's hopes lifted. Lord Auckland and Mr. Macnaghten exchanged glances. With the treaty out of the way, she could feign illness, even death, and avoid the wedding. In two days, the army would be on its way to victory in Kabul, and she would be having Christmas with the Governor-General's party as they traveled toward Calcutta, safe from further drunken evenings with the old king. She had done it! Having taken the blame on herself, she had prevented the Maharajah's using British faithlessness to back out of the treaty. She wanted to fan herself with relief, but refrained, fearful of drawing more attention.

"Excellent, Maharaj." Mr. Macnaghten's voice wavered, but his relief was plain. "We will sign the treaty, as you say, tomorrow." As he spoke, he seemed to savor every word.

She was a heroine, was she not?

Since her speech the Maharajah had not looked at Mariana, but she did not miss the speculative gaze of the bearded minister at his side. Why should she mind? There was no need to pay attention to these particular natives any longer.

She must write to the Shaikh thanking him for his proposal, explaining why she had spoken out at the dinner. What a good, kind man he was to have offered her such an elegant way to evade the Maharajah's wicked trap!

The evening was at last over. Permission for the Maharajah's guests to leave his presence had been asked and granted. The ladies got to their feet.

"I must tell you, Miss Fanny," Mariana murmured as they made their way forward to offer their good-byes, "what happened to me the other night at Amritsar as we were—"

Miss Fanny made a small but definite gesture for silence. "My dear," she said, holding up her hand, "do not speak of this. Whatever you say will only make your situation worse."

Worse? Beside her, Miss Emily moved forward, her sharp profile as still as if it were carved from ivory. There was no trace of color in her face. A chill crawled down Mariana's spine.

She gathered her skirts, preparing to climb the ladder into the howdah after Miss Fanny. Surely it would be all right. Surely, when they understood about Saboor and the Shaikh and the rice test—

"All I am able to do, Mariana," declared Miss Emily as she seated herself, "is to put your extraordinary behavior this evening down to the unfortunate effect of the Maharajah's wine."

She gestured for silence as Mariana tried to speak. "You have disgraced yourself and humiliated Lieutenant Marks. You have made us all look like fools."

Lieutenant Marks! "But Miss Emily," Mariana said, her voice sounding odd in her own ears, "I did it to save the treaty. Now that the treaty is to be signed, I can tell you what really happened at Amritsar after the fireworks display. One of the Maharajah's servants came running and handed me the baby, and I—"

"Baby?" Both ladies stared.

"Yes, the baby, the little hostage. I took him to my tent and kept him there until the night of the rice test."

She looked from one incredulous face to the other. "He is not yet two years old," she added, "and he was being ill-treated by the—"

"But my dear Mariana," exclaimed Miss Fanny, "this is madness! We were there all the time! How could we not have seen you carrying a great two-year-old child from the Golden Temple? You must give up this preposterous story. What can the Maharajah's hostage have to do with your being secretly engaged to a native while you were encouraging Lieutenant Marks?"

"Encouraging Marks? But, Miss Fanny, I—"

"Be quiet, Mariana! You have said quite enough." Miss Emily's voice held a chilling finality.

The remainder of the journey to the British camp took place in deep silence, with both Eden ladies staring fixedly into the distance, their chins held high.

Miss Emily spoke only when they had reached the entrance to the red compound. "Mariana," she said, after their blue elephant had dropped joltingly to his knees at the mounting stairs, "your behavior has put us all into a most distressing and awkward position. You are fortunate that my brother is a kind man. Whatever he may think of you, I am certain he will find a way to spare you the horror of actual 'marriage' to a native.

"I shall be very surprised if, by tomorrow afternoon, you are not already on your way back to Calcutta. But we shall say no more of this sad business now. Good night."

Without another word, she swept off in her best blond silk, leaving Mariana and Miss Fanny to climb down from the silver howdah in silence.

• • •

"WHAT is wrong, Memsahib?" Dittoo was wringing his hands. "What has happened?"

Mariana looked up from where she lay facedown on her bed. "Oh, Dittoo," she wailed, "it's horrible. They want to send me away to Calcutta, and all because of what I did to save their treaty!"

"Send you away, Memsahib?" Dittoo's chin began to wobble.

"No one will listen to me. I cannot get them to understand." She struck her pillow with a balled fist. "If they were so clever, why did they not speak out when that horrid Maharajah tried to betroth himself to me? Why did Fitzgerald do nothing?"

"The Maharajah betrothed himself to you?" Dittoo's eyes widened until white appeared all the way around their brown centers. "*Betrothed* himself?"

"No, but he very nearly did. *I* was the one who thought of a good excuse, so he would not be insulted and cancel the treaty. Now they all despise me." She sat up and wiped her face with her sleeve.

"I know one thing," she went on as Dittoo rummaged through the clothes in her trunk, searching for a fresh handkerchief, "the Shaikh is a great man. *He* understood the danger and sent his own proposal to be used as my excuse." She took a clean square of linen from Dittoo's fingers. "Of course," she added, blowing her nose, "he does not mean for me to marry his son."

"Marry his son?" Dittoo's expression was now a caricature of bewilderment. "The *Shaikh* wants you to marry his *son*?"

She glared at him. "Of course not. His daughter-in-law has just died. You told me so yourself. The Shaikh expects me to break the engagement on some pretext.

"The Shaikh is a marvelous, special native," she said as she rose to splash water onto her face from her washbasin. "I should never have doubted him."

Her towel in her hand, she moved to the open doorway. "Oh, Dittoo," she said, her eyes on the stars hanging in a bright web over the camp, "why am I not in Sussex, having Christmas with Papa and Mama?"

"SO, the young lady is to marry your assistant." The Maharajah held back his arms for a servant to take off his vest. He nodded rapidly, his beard shaking as he spoke.

"So it seems, Maharaj." Faqeer Azizuddin nodded solemnly.

The servant lifted the Maharajah's beard aside and began to remove the gold buttons from his silk tunic.

"Is this your doing, Aziz?" Ignoring the man working on his

clothes, the Maharajah peered up at the Faqeer. "If it is, I will give you many villages." His buttons removed, he flung his arms upward and the servant pulled his shirt over his head. "I never expected that foolish proposal to bear such sweet fruit!"

Naked to the waist, the old king sat down on the edge of his bed. "Ah, Aziz," he added, happily, "it is so easy to tease the British. Did you see Macnaghten's face tonight? What a tamasha, what a show! I had expected to confuse the British, but the lady's speech confused even me! But then I saw what she had done; saw the benefit to me from this engagement to Hassan."

The Faqeer's face had stilled. The Maharajah smiled broadly as he received a starched cotton tunic. "These English are children! Do you not see, Aziz, the gift the Englishwoman has offered me? After the wedding, I will send for my Saboor. Of course," he added, waving a careless hand, "when he comes, some relative of his must accompany him, to see to his needs. That relative will, of course, be the Englishwoman, his new stepmother."

He raised his chin, allowing the servant to lift his beard out of the starched tunic. "Your friend Waliullah may think he is getting the English girl for his women's quarters, but he is wrong. It is I who will have her for my Jasmine Tower!"

"We must remember, Maharaj," the Faqeer put in smoothly, "that the British will do all they can to extricate the lady from this marriage."

"After she herself has announced her betrothal before a hundred witnesses? Have no fear, Aziz," the Maharajah yawned as he stretched himself out on his bed. "The English may think themselves clever, but I, too, am clever."

"Indeed you are, Maharaj," Aziz agreed solemnly, as the servant carried in the Maharajah's satin quilt. "Indeed you are."

ILL and light-headed, Lord Auckland and the other male members of the British party sat huddled in the dining tent of the British camp. It was past two o'clock in the morning.

"There's no way out of it now." Major Byrne pulled up the collar of his frock coat. "She must marry the fellow, whoever he is. I am sorry for her, but she has done this to herself."

"Marry a native!" Lord Auckland's face gleamed in the candlelight. "Are you mad? Has everyone gone mad?" He brought his hand down heavily on the dining table.

Side by side, Major Byrne and William Macnaghten wiped their foreheads, but said nothing.

"There shall be no marriage." Lord Auckland's jowls shook. "I shall not be a party to such a disgusting scene."

He stared from face to face. "Miss Givens, however low her actions, is a Christian and an Englishwoman. While it is true that she has behaved abominably, it is our duty to protect what remains of her honor."

"She certainly did not look like the sort of girl who would throw herself at native men," Byrne said to Macnaghten under his breath, "but she must have been doing it all along. What an astounding thing, to announce to all of us and a hundred natives that she had secretly agreed to marry one of them!"

"To allow this 'marriage' to go forward would be indecency of the most virulent sort." Lord Auckland looked about him with reddened eyes. "And the worst of it is how helpless she has left us, after that brazen speech." He sighed bleakly. "And now that dirty, winking old Maharajah has invited us to the ceremony. Think how he is enjoying the prospect of our seeing her off to the consummation of her so-called 'marriage.' "

Byrne mopped his brow again. "But she has laid herself open to this," he pointed out.

Lord Auckland breathed deeply. "She has," he replied. "And now Ranjit Singh intends to celebrate her ruin, while we stand uselessly by. But he *must not*."

"Of course not, my lord." Gathering himself, Macnaghten spoke soothingly. "This whole display has already been in shocking taste. It must go no further."

Someone hiccuped. Macnaghten frowned. "The girl's behavior has been most unfortunate. Now we know her for what she is. She must, of course, pay for what she has done. But there is a way out. We will play for time. Tomorrow morning, I shall send word to Ranjit Singh that the girl has been taken ill in the night, and that the wedding must be put off until she has recovered. As soon as the treaty has been signed, we shall simply break the engagement and send her back to Calcutta. After all," he concluded, "the old man hasn't long to live. When he dies, all of this will be forgotten."

"And what," Lord Auckland inquired, glaring at the men around the table, "was that business about a letter? The Maharajah said he had sent us a letter *three years ago,* asking for a wife. No one told me anything about it. What happened to the letter?" His voice rose peevishly. "Why wasn't I told?"

Macnaghten shook his head. "I saw no such letter, my lord. Perhaps it never existed."

"Never existed? What do you mean, William? It is just the sort of thing that wretched old goat would do. Can't you see the opening we gave him? We might have lost everything over this business of an English wife. It is incompetence of this sort that causes the worst kind of trouble."

"If such a letter did come three years ago, whoever read it probably believed it was a joke," said a secretary thickly, "and threw it into the wastepaper basket."

In a corner of the tent, someone had doubled over.

"For God's sake, Fitzgerald," the Governor-General bellowed, turning in his seat, "get out of the dining tent if you're going to be sick. Think of breakfast, man."

"I can't think of breakfast, my lord," was all Harry Fitzgerald could manage before he stumbled away through the doorway.

Lord Auckland sighed. "It is time," he announced, "for us all to go to bed."

He rose from his seat and marched through the door, past the vomiting Fitzgerald, and with only a hint of unsteadiness, crossed the open space to his tent.

Chapter 30

**TUESDAY,
DECEMBER 24**

Clattering sounds told Mariana that Dittoo had arrived with her morning coffee. Restive and awake until late in the night, she had finally slept, only to dream of endings and the loss of precious things.

"Memsahib," Dittoo asked as he dropped the tray noisily onto her bedside table, "when will you marry Saboor's father? When is the wedding to be?"

Mariana opened her eyes. Her brain felt like lead. "Don't talk nonsense, Dittoo." She groped beside the tray for her timepiece. "I cannot possibly marry Saboor's father. He's a *native*."

Dittoo shrugged. "Memsahib, I have not wanted to say this before, but if Saboor's father wishes to marry you, then you should—"

"Dittoo, enough." It was six-fifteen. There was still time. She sat up and reached for her shawl. "Bring me my writing box," she said. "I have letters to write before breakfast. I shall write first to Miss Emily, explaining everything. Then I shall thank Shaikh Waliullah for his proposal, and tell him that I shall feign illness in order to avoid marrying his son—"

"But why avoid this good marriage, Memsahib? So many ladies would like to marry the son of Shaikh Waliullah." Dittoo shook his head as he put her inlaid writing box down on the table. "I am sorry to say this, but you are very old to be getting married. No Englishman has proposed for you yet, not even the tall one with fair hair who wears a blue coat."

Bent over to pull on her boots, Mariana winced. "I do not want your advice, Dittoo," she snapped.

When he had finally left, she sat at her table and took her pen and inkpot from the inlaid box. With a pang, she remembered the other officers avoiding Fitzgerald's eyes as the whispered translation of her speech flew from mouth to mouth around the Maharajah's canopied enclosure.

Fitzgerald, too, believed she had ruined herself with a native man.

She reached for a sheet of paper. After writing to the Shaikh, she would explain everything to Miss Emily. To write the whole story of Saboor and his grandfather before breakfast would be difficult, but it must be done. Without Miss Emily's forgiveness, she could never show her face in the dining tent again. After that, if there were time, she would send a note to Fitzgerald. He loved her. He would understand.

As she dipped her pen into her inkpot, Dittoo reappeared. "Memsahib," he cried breathlessly, "the sentry is here. He says some ladies have come for you on an elephant. They say they want to prepare you for your marriage."

"Ladies? Elephant? Dittoo, how can that be? The wedding is not until the day after tomorrow. Someone has made a mistake. Besides, the Shaikh expects me to claim fever or some other illness, and to cancel the wedding. Why would he send an elephant for me today?"

Dittoo flapped his hands toward the red wall. "I do not know, Memsahib, but an elephant is waiting on the avenue with ladies and an armed escort and many servants!"

As he went away to investigate, she shook her head, then bent again over her paper. *"Dear Miss Emily, I fear that the events of last evening have given a most unfortunate impression—"*

Dittoo returned almost instantly, more breathless than ever. "Memsahib," he puffed, "the sentry says the ladies are insisting you go with them at once. They say they have come a long distance and that already there is very little time to prepare you for the wedding. I have looked out through a tear in the wall, and what the sentry says is true. Are you sure you are not marrying Maharajah Ranjit Singh? The ladies' elephant is so—"

Mariana slammed down the lid of her writing box. "For heaven's sake, Dittoo," she shouted, "I am marrying no one!"

He looked so shocked that she changed her tone. "Please, Dittoo, go and find Mr. Macnaghten. Tell him that Shaikh Waliullah has sent an elephant for me. Say I must speak to him."

After Dittoo had shuffled hurriedly away, Mariana stepped outside. The compound was quiet, except for a few servants working near the kitchen tent. There was no sign of life at Lord Auckland's tent or at the tents of Miss Emily and Miss Fanny.

Mariana crossed quickly to the red wall. After dinner, both Mr. Macnaghten and Major Byrne had looked at her as if she were the lowest form of dancing girl. But, surely, Mr. Macnaghten would respond, now, when she asked for his help.

She put one eye to her special tear in the wall. There they were, waiting on the avenue just as Dittoo had described them—the lavishly decorated elephant with a curtained howdah, the liveried servants, the fierce-looking escort.

Up and down the avenue, the tents of the government secretaries lay silent, shrouded in the cold mist of morning. She felt a stab of panic. "Please be awake, Mr. Macnaghten," she whispered as Dittoo appeared on the avenue, hastening toward the political secretary's tent. *"Please."*

But Mr. Macnaghten was not awake, and the little servant who sat shivering beside his door was, Dittoo reported moments later, under the strictest orders never to awaken him unless the Governor-General wanted to see him.

"The ladies," Dittoo announced, rubbing his hands together, "are saying you must hurry, Memsahib."

"Perhaps the Shaikh wishes only to speak to me about the wedding," she said as Dittoo followed her back to her tent. She pushed aside the blind and stood uncertainly inside the doorway. "After all, it must be canceled as gracefully as possible."

The Shaikh. For all her uneasiness at leaving camp on a strange elephant, Mariana looked forward to meeting Shaikh Waliullah again. She had seen him only once, by torchlight, and yet she could still feel his powerful gaze upon her.

Someone else was at the Shaikh's house, someone she would give anything to see. *"You will meet Saboor again,"* the Shaikh had told her as the dawn light crept into his courtyard.

"Dittoo," she ordered, debating no longer. "hand me my blue-and-white gown. I am leaving with those ladies for the house of Shaikh Waliullah. I shall return by ten o'clock. If anyone asks for me, tell them I am ill, and am having breakfast in my tent."

Instead of writing a long letter to Miss Emily now, she would simply send a note asking to call on her in the afternoon while the men were away signing the treaty. That was a far more sensible plan. Her explanations would surely sound better when given in person.

THE elephant knelt down to receive her, the velvet curtain of its enclosed howdah jerking and swaying. Like someone in a dream, Mariana watched herself scramble up the ladder, over the railing, and through the parted curtains.

Three ladies sat upright inside, facing one another on red velvet cushions. One, an attractive woman of indeterminate age with oddly black hair and many rings on her fingers, greeted Mariana kindly in Urdu and pointed to the empty seat opposite hers. The woman's neighbor, a plain female with pockmarks and large features, stared at Mariana without blinking. A slender, sullen-faced girl with an enormous pearl and ruby tassel hanging from her nose ring gazed out at the sliver of avenue visible between the curtains, without acknowledging Mariana's arrival.

Where was Safiya Sultana, the Shaikh's deep-voiced sister?

Mariana sat down, arranged her skirts about her feet, and put a hand to her hastily pinned-up hair. The woman with black hair had painted her eyes, perhaps even her lips. Between her rings, her fingers were stained with an intricate pattern that resembled brown lace.

"When," asked Mariana as the elephant lurched to its feet, "will we reach Shaikh Waliullah's house?"

"Shaikh Waliullah's house?" The three women stared.

"No, no, daughter." The black-haired woman leaned across and patted Mariana's knee. "We cannot take you to the Shaikh's house. His is the house of the bridegroom. We are taking you to the Citadel to prepare you for your marriage."

"No." Mariana shook her head. "I am going to call on Shaikh Waliullah in the walled city."

"You are not." The pockmarked woman spoke with finality. "This is the Maharajah's elephant, and you are going to his Citadel."

The Citadel? Mariana's hand flew to her mouth. "No!"

"Yes, of course." The black-haired woman smiled and smoothed back her hair with a practiced gesture. "From now on, we are your family. It is we who will make you beautiful for your wedding."

Mariana jumped to her feet as the elephant started to move. "No," she cried, clutching a curtain for balance, "there has been a mistake. I cannot go to the Citadel. I want to get down! Please let me down—"

The three women leaned away from her, their arms raised in self-protection. "Sit down," ordered the black-haired one. "You will fall."

"But you do not understand. You must stop the elephant. I must get down. There is to be no marriage. It is all a mistake!"

Gripping a handful of blue-and-white silk, the heavy-faced woman tugged sharply downward, bringing Mariana back to her velvet cushion with a thump.

The sullen-faced girl turned from the gap in the curtains, her nose ornament swinging like a pendulum. Her pretty lip curled. "There is no mistake. No mistake at all. The Maharajah has given his *hukm*—his royal order—that you are to be prepared for your wedding tomorrow by his own ladies. What mistake can there be?" Her tone had an unpleasant edge.

"Quite right, Saat," nodded the black-haired woman.

"No!" Fright edging away conscious thought, Mariana shot to her feet again. "I *demand* to get down," she shouted in a high voice that sounded like someone else's. She reached for a handhold, missed, and staggered against an upright pole hidden among the curtains. Again she was tugged downward, but this time the black-haired woman swung her open hand at Mariana's face.

The woman's slap printed each of her beringed fingers on Mariana's cheek. "Sit down," she rasped, "before you injure one of us."

Mariana subsided in her seat, tears of shock wetting the burning place on her cheek. What a fool she was! How many times had she been warned of the dangers of her impulsive behavior? Even the soothsayers had told her to be careful. She should have known this was not Shaikh Waliullah's elephant. Only a queen would have such a heavily decorated animal, or such a large retinue of servants.

What a reckless fool she had been to get into the howdah!

But she must not panic now. Surely there would be a way for her to get out of the Citadel once they had arrived.

The Maharajah had given a royal order. What did that mean? Perhaps there was to be no wedding. Perhaps the old king knew the truth about Saboor's disappearance and intended to punish her in some even worse way for her involvement in it.

The howdah was stifling. Perspiration trickled down her neck. Were these the same queens who had murdered Saboor's poor mother? Had they been ordered to punish her? If so, what would they do? Would they beat her, starve her, torment her as they had tormented Saboor?

She had told Dittoo to lie about her leaving. *No one else knew where she was.*

Swaying on her cushion in rhythm with the queens, Mariana raised her chin and hid her trembling hands in the folds of her skirt while the elephant, accompanied by the Maharajah's servants and his armed horsemen, moved ceremoniously down the avenue. Whatever happened, she would do as Uncle Adrian had instructed her—she would remember who she was.

Through the gap in the moving curtains, she caught glimpses of the red compound wall, of Major Byrne's silent tent, more tents along the avenue, the horse lines, and then the flat, dusty landscape.

Chapter 31

I will *not* take off my gown." Mariana's voice seemed to come from somewhere else in the room. "I will not take off my gown, and I will *not* wear those," she declared, drawing herself up and pointing to the mustard-colored satin clothes the black-haired queen held out to her. "And I demand to see Faqeer Azizuddin."

The queens stared. "Are you mad?" The black-haired queen's painted eyebrows rose. "Who are *you* to be meeting the Chief Minister? Charan, Vijaya," she called, "she wants to meet Faqeer Azizuddin!"

Mariana stiffened as the heavy-faced woman from the elephant and a thin one with frizzy hair nudged each other.

"Where do you wish to meet him?" The frizzy one moved forward, derision in her eyes. "Will it be here at the Jasmine Tower, where no outsider comes? Or will you sit among his male visitors at his own house in the city?"

"She will do as she is told." The first queen turned to the heavy-faced woman. "*Hai*, Charan," she complained, "why must *I* be in charge of this foreigner? Why do these things always fall to me, while the others enjoy themselves, having their hair oiled and their legs massaged?"

Charan plucked a small green triangular packet from a tray. "I tell you, Moran, I never believed that story of the Maharajah wanting to marry her." She stuffed the packet into her mouth and chewed noisily on something that spilled red dye over her teeth. "He would never," she said with her mouth full, "marry one of these unclean women."

"Nonsense," snapped the black-haired queen. "Everyone knows he has been trying for years to get a European wife." She turned to Mariana. "Take that blue-and-white thing off."

"And if I refuse?" Mariana's cheek still burned where the queen called Moran had slapped her. Why did they want her to take off her clothes? Where exactly was she in this warren of tower rooms? Surely the low door by which she had entered was not the only way out of this sinister place?

The women looked at one another.

Moran gave a noisy sigh. "We will send for the eunuchs and have them undress you. We will enjoy that." Her smile showed a row of perfectly white teeth.

Mariana swallowed. "And if I do put these clothes on, what will you do then?"

"Then we will turn you into a beautiful bride."

"Who is she to marry? Who is the boy?" demanded a harsh-faced woman.

"The son of Shaikh Waliullah," Moran replied curtly.

"Oh, yes, of course," said the woman, "the one whose wife was poi—"

Mariana watched the woman redden and subside into silence under Moran's terrible stare. A part of her fear had subsided. If the queens knew she had stolen Saboor, they would have said so by now. So they had not brought her here to be tortured, only to be married.

The heavy-faced Charan turned humorless eyes on Mariana. "She will never make a beautiful bride," she declared. "She is too old. Her hair is a mess."

"She will be good enough." Moran turned to Mariana once more. "And now, will you take those things off, or shall I call the eunuchs?"

"WE should not do it now, Moran. It is too late."

Dressed in the long mustard trousers and shirt Moran had given her, Mariana sat on a bed while the black-haired queen and a stranger in red stood gazing down at her, their voices echoing in the little room. Her stays and chemise, her stockings and gown, her boots and her bonnet had all vanished, whisked off by a servant to some unknown place. She tried to read the women's faces.

An hour ago, compared to torture and death, marriage to a stranger had seemed a small price to pay for her impulsiveness. Now, as she watched the two women, unsure what they wanted of her, Mariana wondered whether the price was as small as she had thought.

"It will not heal in time. Her nose will be red and swollen tomorrow. It will look ugly." The woman in red was tall. Her eyebrows had been reduced to two thin, arched lines.

"Do not be foolish, Vijaya," replied Moran. "Where are we to put the *n'hut* if she is not pierced?" She snorted delicately. "How can she be a bride without a nose ring? There will be no swelling. I am putting a neem twig in the wound."

"Wound? Nose ring?" Mariana started up from the bed, but was immediately pushed down again. As she struggled, other women appeared, and more hands held her down. She fought an arm free and struck out blindly, catching someone's breast. She heard a grunt of pain above the tangle of restraining arms.

Moran gave a sharp order, and in an instant, two men appeared. "Do you want me to hold her head?" asked one in a high, smoky voice.

A pair of hands near Mariana's face worked on the end of a length of gold wire, filing it to a point. She shut her eyes against a sudden light. A powerful hand pressed down on her forehead. Someone had taken a threatening grip on her neck.

"Make her lie still, I want to put it in here," someone said. At once, Mariana felt a burning pain on one side of her nose. She gasped and struggled, feeling fingers poking into her ribs. The grip on her neck grew tighter. Gritting her teeth, she lay still.

"Give me the neem twig," ordered the same voice, and once again came the pain as something new and rough was thrust into the fresh wound.

The restraining hands were withdrawn. It was over. Mariana pulled up her legs and crouched, panting, on the bed, her back to a filigreed window, a hand protecting her injured nose. Furious at her tormentors, angry at her own helpless tears, she glared at the crowd of interested women that had collected in the doorway. The women did not speak. They looked at her, some holding their veils across their faces as if she were someone to fear. When they had stared long enough, they departed on silent, bare feet, glancing over their shoulders as they left her.

• • •

"DRINK this." A servant girl knelt beside her, a cup of red pomegranate juice in her hand. "You must not be afraid," the girl murmured. "You must be a beautiful bride. It is beautiful to wear the n'hut," she added wistfully.

"That's right, Reshma," agreed Moran from where she lay, stretched out on the white-sheeted floor. "We will make her beautiful, is that not so?" She yawned and got to her feet as gracefully as a cat. "Let her rest until I return."

Mariana probed her nose with her fingertips. It was terribly sore, and something hard stuck out of the wound. Her upper lip tasted of blood. She had told Dittoo she would return at ten o'clock. It must be past that now. Why had she not brought her timepiece? Surely she would be missed at camp. Surely, sooner or later, the British party would learn that she had been taken away to the Citadel. What would happen then? Would they order a search party? Would there be outrage at her kidnapping? Sympathy?

She raised the cup to her lips, then choked on the juice. How could she have forgotten? They were coming here! The treaty was to be signed here, at the Citadel! She had only to survive until her rescue this afternoon.

She looked about the room. Its doorway, the curtain pulled aside, led onto a stone passage. Outside, she could see a male hand and a white sleeve: a eunuch, posted there to prevent any attempt at escape. If her situation were different, she would want to know every detail of life in this tower, with its narrow, circular stair and its population of women and eunuchs.

There seemed to be plenty to do while she awaited her rescue. Moran rustled in and out, organizing women who carried pots of sweet-scented mud, bending to poke her fingers through a tray of seeds and pods that had been brought in for her inspection.

"Take these away," she snapped at the child who squatted silently beside the tray. "Do you think I cannot tell last year's *reetas* when I see them?"

A fat woman arrived to massage oil into Mariana's hair and scalp with padded fingers. As the woman worked, Mariana felt her eyes grow pleasantly heavy. When the servant had gone, she laid her cloth-wrapped head on the bolster and closed her eyes. Why not rest until Lord Auckland came and rescued her?

The thin mattress was quite comfortable, and a cool breeze entered through her window, shifting the air. She was nearly asleep when she heard a small sound at her bedside. The little servant girl they called Reshma sat doubled up on the floor, all face and knees, waiting.

The girl tugged her stained veil over her hair and glanced behind her. "Memsahib," she whispered, "have you seen the child Saboor?"

Mariana's breath stopped. *Saboor.* How did this servant know when she had said nothing to give herself away? Why was the girl crying?

"No, I have not seen any child called Saboor," she replied curtly, before turning her face to the window.

WITH the eyes of the Governor-General, the Misses Eden, and Major Byrne upon him, Mr. Macnaghten drew himself up in his folding chair. "Miss Givens left camp at dawn," he announced stiffly, "before I was awake. There was no time to send the Maharajah a message that she was ill."

He braced himself, waiting for Lord Auckland's response.

"Do you mean to say the girl vanished before anyone was awake?"

"She did," Miss Emily put in, "but not before she had written, asking to call on me after lunch. That is why I did not worry when she failed to appear at breakfast. Her servant reported at the time that she had a headache and would have breakfast in her tent."

"It is not surprising that she chose not to come to breakfast," Dr. Drummond contributed darkly from his basket chair.

Miss Emily's forehead creased. "It was only when she did not appear later that I sent to inquire, and discovered that she had gone off on an elephant at six o'clock this morning, promising to return straightaway, and that not a word had been heard of her since." Her hands tightened in her lap.

Lord Auckland tugged at his black brocade waistcoat. He looked unwell. "Where did she say she was going?"

Miss Emily pursed her lips. "Her servant said she intended to call upon the father of the man to whom she is 'engaged'—that magician, Shaikh Wallawallah."

"The Shaikh?" Lord Auckland snorted. "She wanted to call on a native Shaikh at six o'clock in the morning?"

"But the servant never believed it. He said that he tried to tell her the elephant had come not from the Shaikh but from the Maharajah, but she would not listen." Miss Emily sighed. "Apparently there were native women on the elephant who said they wanted to prepare her for her 'wedding'; but Mariana said that she was *not* to be married, and that she would be back before ten o'clock."

"Could she have been kidnapped by someone else?" Miss Fanny

looked up from her tatting needles. "The elephant could have belonged to anyone, could it not?"

"No, Miss Fanny," put in Major Byrne. "The elephant's escort was wearing chain mail. That eliminates everyone save the Maharajah. The girl was a fool to believe she was going to the Shaikh's house. She really might have—"

"Then that is where she is," interrupted Lord Auckland bluntly. He consulted his pocket watch. "We shall be leaving soon, and then we can discover for ourselves." He glared at Byrne and Macnaghten. "I cannot have female members of this party vanishing without warning."

"I fail to see," said the doctor, brushing a fly from his coat, "why the girl has done it. She is well-bred, and reasonably good-looking. We all expected her to marry young Marks. Why has she developed this sudden passion for native men?" He looked from face to face in the circle of chairs. "How did she do it, and when? How did the man manage to—"

A subaltern arrived and whispered to Major Byrne, who smiled broadly. "The elephants are ready," he told them. "The generals are on their way."

"The treaty!" Lord Auckland got to his feet. "The treaty at last!" He spread his arms. "Within a few weeks, we shall have control of Afghanistan, and of all Central Asia. What a proud time this is for England!"

TWO hours later, Lord Auckland sat perched on a golden chair in the Maharajah's fine little hall of mirrors. He cleared his throat. "Before we sign the documents," he said, a trifle too loudly, nodding to Macnaghten to translate, "I must ask the whereabouts of a certain member of our party."

Drops of perspiration ran down Lord Auckland's face, from his gold tricorn to his chin. Dark patches had appeared under the arms of his heavy brocade coat. His skin was turning gray. At a sign from the Maharajah, two fan bearers slipped through the crowd and waved peacock feather fans in Lord Auckland's direction.

Mr. Macnaghten's face, flushing as he translated the question, turned still pinker at the Faqeer's reply.

"May I inquire as to which member of your party is missing?" The Faqeer's voice was bland.

"How I hate the man," Macnaghten murmured to Lord Auckland. "No one is missing, as you suggest, Faqeer Sahib," he said, raising his voice. "Rather, we wish to confirm the arrival of Miss Mariana

Givens, our lady translator, who left our camp for the Citadel early this morning."

Perched on his golden throne, the Maharajah looked eagerly from face to face. Several of his sirdars smiled.

The Faqeer stroked his beard. "Then it would be well to discover for ourselves whether the young lady is gracing the Jasmine Tower with her presence." At a motion of his hand, a pear-shaped eunuch materialized before them. "Call one of the women servants," commanded the Faqeer.

"We shall soon be satisfied of Miss Givens's whereabouts," said Macnaghten, speaking in a normal tone to avoid giving the impression of secrecy, as the eunuch departed. "But my lord," he added, dropping his voice again as the Maharajah bent to speak to his Chief Minister, "as for our reclaiming the lady and forbidding this 'marriage' to go forward, I have grave doubts. I know nothing about native customs concerning women, but after listening to some of the Maharajah's more colorful remarks about them, I have drawn the conclusion that they are not the subject of polite conversation. Since ladies are not to be spoken of, I do not know how to broach the subject of canceling this wedding."

Lord Auckland's face had become the color of putty. "Well, Macnaghten," he replied bleakly, "you will have to think of *something*."

Macnaghten blew a long breath into the silence. "There is still, of course, a very slight danger that he may not sign the treaty if we upset him."

The eunuch reappeared. He was followed at a distance by a small, slovenly-looking servant girl. "This," he declared, stopping in front of the throne and waving a contemptuous hand, "is Reshma."

"Ah, Reshma." The Faqeer spoke smoothly from his place at the Maharajah's feet, motioning the girl to come forward. "Come closer, child. Tell us if there is an English lady visiting the ladies' quarters."

The girl hesitated, fiddling with her shabby veil. "Yes, Huzoor," she said tremulously, "there is an English lady in the *zenana*."

"Good. Send for her at once." Lord Auckland wiped his face as Macnaghten translated his command.

The girl, her eyes on her feet, did not respond.

"Speak, child," prompted the Faqeer. "You understand, do you not, that you are to call the English lady?"

"But I cannot bring her." The words rushed from Reshma's mouth. "She cannot be seen."

"What? What nonsense!" Frowning, Macnaghten spoke directly to the girl. "Tell her to come here at once!"

The girl's gaze remained fastened on the carpet in front of the Faqeer. "Huzoor," she whispered, "the lady is already wearing her yellow clothes. Her hair has been oiled. She cannot be seen. Soon they will put the *ubtan* on her skin."

"What does it matter about her hair or her clothes?" said Macnaghten sharply. "What has this 'ubtan' got to do with it?"

"What is she saying?" The Maharajah's single eye was bright with interest. He leaned forward. "Tell the girl to speak up."

The girl was near tears. "Ubtan," she whispered, "is the spiced and perfumed oil they put on the bride's skin to make it soft and beautiful for the—"

"That will do." His face reddening, Macnaghten coughed noisily.

Beside him, Lord Auckland wiped his perspiring face again. "What is she saying? When is the girl coming?" His voice had taken on a querulous note.

Macnaghten breathed carefully. "She is, that is, Miss Givens is apparently unable to come at present." He avoided the eyes of the Maharajah and his Faqeer. "She is indisposed."

"What? Well, we'll send for Miss Givens later. Let us get on with the treaty."

The Maharajah's golden table was carried out and set down with ceremony. The Sikh courtiers closed ranks, and the British generals and senior officers in their dress uniforms stood at attention.

Lord Auckland's speech, although filled with compliments, was brief. Throughout it, he looked as if he were about to faint, but he did not. He lasted through the reading and translation of the two documents, line by line, one in English, one in official Persian. He survived the Maharajah's speech, which was not a speech at all but a paean of elaborate praise aimed directly at him, to which he listened, smiling gravely, while the dark stains spread on his official dress clothes.

Macnaghten translated it all.

At last, taking a quill from the velvet cushion held out by a stiff-faced officer, Lord Auckland signed the treaty. The Maharajah followed suit, embraces were exchanged, and it was over.

"My lord," murmured Macnaghten after edging the Governor-General a little distance away from the crowd, "I have doubts as to our ability to retrieve Miss Givens from the Jasmine Tower this afternoon."

"Never mind the girl, Macnaghten," replied Lord Auckland, gripping his political secretary above the elbow with a trembling hand. "Take me away from here. I am going to be sick."

•   •   •

ROUSED by the smell of food, Mariana opened her eyes to find Reshma squatting beside her. On the floor beside the girl rested a tray of bread, orange-and-yellow rice, and something strong-smelling that looked like a chicken stew.

"You should eat now," the girl murmured, lifting the tray.

The light had altered. Below the window, trees cast long shadows across a wide, dry moat. Mariana sat up. "My people, the British! Are they here? Have they come? I must speak to them!" Loosened from its cotton bindings, her hair lay in oily ropes on her shoulders.

Reshma blinked. "The British sahibs with their many soldiers and their strange-looking clothes?"

"Yes. Are they here?" Why did no one in this country answer a question directly?

"No, Bibi, they have gone. They came, but they have gone."

"*Gone?* How can they be gone? They must be here. They must be asking for me."

Reshma looked away. "They asked for you, but we told them you could not be seen. After that, they went away."

Mariana was on her feet. "*What?*" she shouted into Reshma's face. "You told them I was not to be seen, and then they went away and *left me here?*"

The eunuch guard put his head around the door. The girl shrank away, an arm upraised. Mariana flushed. "Do not fear, Reshma," she said wearily. "I do not strike people."

"Bibi, look at yourself." The girl's chin trembled. "You are a bride. A bride must stay in bed in her yellow clothes until the day of her wedding. You cannot even have your food upstairs with the other ladies. How could you go there, to be seen by men?"

"Has she eaten?" Moran pushed, talking, through the door, followed by a slant-eyed servant woman. "We will do her eyebrows and other hair now. Come," she ordered, signaling the second servant to approach.

Before Mariana could act, Moran had pushed her onto the bed again. Her head immobilized by Moran's beringed fingers, her body pinned bruisingly down by other hands, Mariana struggled uselessly once more, tears of rage and pain leaking from her eyes as the slant-eyed woman pulled hair cruelly from her eyebrows with a cat's cradle of twisted string.

"Other brides do not behave like you," Moran snapped after Mariana had twisted out of her grip for the second time. "They know this work is for their beauty." She wiped her damp forehead as Mariana glared at her from the mattress. "*They* never complain."

Her heart thundering, Mariana gritted her teeth when the women examined the fine down on her arms. It was only when they untied the rope of her loose, gathered trousers and pulled them down that she screamed until her throat rasped and she could scream no longer. While Moran Bibi and several other women argued with her wails, telling her that it was necessary, that it was beautiful, the silent servant woman pressed a ball of something stiff and sticky against Mariana's tender skin, then tore it away. By evening, while a crowd of silent spectators watched from the doorway, the woman had pulled out every hair on Mariana's body, from her ankles to her chin.

Chapter 32

WEDNESDAY, DECEMBER 25

An angled shaft of sunlight shone through the window and lay hot against her eyelids. Still half-asleep, Mariana turned from the window and pulled the satin quilt over her face.

The ship of her dreams had returned again the previous night, carrying her swiftly through ever thicker fog, as steadily as if it were indeed piloted by Noah himself.

Why dream of calm when she was in this state? Why not dream of clinging, terrified, to the ship's foremast while waves broke over the deck and loose rigging whipped through the air, and lightning clove the fog, revealing a ghostly, tattered shore?

Tonight. Her wedding was to be tonight—Christmas Night.

She opened her eyes and touched the side of her nose with its protruding sliver of wood.

She winced at the memory of tiny drops of blood welling up on her softest places where the hair had been torn away.

She was not a bride. She was a lamb being prepared for the slaughter, a spectacle to be gaped at, prodded, and commented upon.

Yesterday after the servant raised Mariana's mustard-colored shirt, women and girls had crowded about the bed, staring.

"But," one woman had cried, as she stroked Mariana's midriff with painted fingers, "she needs no ubtan. Her skin is already white, and as soft as silk. No one in the Jasmine Tower has skin so white, so fine!"

"She has long legs, too," offered the woman with thin eyebrows.

Moran sniffed. "All very well," she had said, gesturing for Reshma to fetch another pot of paste, "but just look at the size of her feet."

Mariana flung off her covers and sat upright. She would go mad if she did not keep her wits about her. If she were to evade this awful marriage, she must have a plan.

"You showed quick thinking in a crisis," her father had said to her once, after she saved Jeremy's life. If only her brain would work quickly this time. . . .

Until now, resisting the queens had gained her nothing. She must save her strength and pretend to agree—allow them to pierce, pluck, oil, and dye her as much as they wished. Soon, perhaps this afternoon, there must be an end to this horrible preparation.

What then? How was she to get away before the wedding tonight? She could still see the eunuch squatting outside her door, but nonetheless, she must get away. She *would* get away. No power on earth could force her to marry the Shaikh's son. She would marry a laughing, familiar Englishman, not some dusky-skinned native.

What was he like, the Shaikh's son? Was he fat like the little girl who had carried Saboor up the stairs at the Shaikh's house? Was he raisin-faced, like his father? No, she would not think of it. It must never come to that. Her thoughts racing, she dropped her face into her perfumed hands.

"WIPE that *mehndi* from her face! You will give her brown patches!" Moran's irritated command reached Mariana from above as she lay on her back two hours later, her caked hair streaming over the end of her bed, her hands covered in a lacy design of drying mud.

She had not argued over the scented mud in her hair, or over the other things—the delicate tracings of the same mud now drying on her hands and feet, the bucket of slimy, boiled seeds with which they had washed the oil from her hair.

"Bibi," said a small voice, when Moran had gone. "Look, I have brought your food." It was Reshma. She set a tray on the floor and squatted beside it.

Mariana peered over the edge of her platform. A great, greasy round of bread leaked cubes of spicy-looking potatoes onto the tray. She shook her head, squeezing her eyes shut.

It was turkey she wanted, and her mother and father, and Baby Freddie, and Fitzgerald.

"Please eat," the girl whispered. "You will need food today."

Reluctantly, Mariana opened her eyes. There was something haunted about Reshma. From time to time, a sad, wounded look came over the girl. How frail, how underfed she looked, as if the very air of the Citadel were draining her life away.

"I cannot eat." Mariana shook her head and waved a dismissing hand at the food. "Have it for yourself," she added firmly. "Eat it."

The girl's eyes brightened. "You are good," she whispered, glancing first at the tray, then, carefully, at the doorway, "you are a good lady. That is why," she added, dropping her voice so low that Mariana had to lean from her platform to hear, "I am glad you are to marry the father of Saboor Baba."

Mariana jerked herself upright.

"You will be good to Saboor Baba, will you not, Bibi?" the girl murmured as she folded her potato bread. She raised her eyes, licking the grease from her fingers. "He is such a good boy."

Her little face, so eager at the prospect of her meal, filled suddenly with sorrow.

Footsteps echoed in the stone hallway outside the door. Female voices argued in a distant room. Where in his grandfather's house was little Saboor now? Was he upstairs with the ladies, or down in the courtyard with his magician grandfather?

Mariana glanced at the frail figure that crouched, eating hurriedly, in the corner. With her eyes, she measured the distance to the door. What was outside the guarded entrance to this tower? A courtyard, a garden, porticoes? Guards? After she had been taken down the elephant ladder, her arm gripped ruthlessly by the pockmarked queen, the palanquin she had been pushed into had threaded its way between many buildings. If she ran, could she find an open gate out of the Citadel before she was caught? If caught, how badly would she suffer?

She got up quietly, her mud-caked hair hanging heavily down her back, and crouched beside Reshma. "How far is it," she whispered, "to Shaikh Waliullah's house from here?"

"It is not far," said the girl promptly. "I think the Shaikh lives by Wazir Khan's Mosque."

"Reshma," Mariana murmured urgently, "take me there. Find a way for me to get out of the Citadel, and then take me to the Shaikh's house."

Reshma stopped eating. Mariana caught her gaze and held it. "You *must* do this, Reshma."

"I cannot, Bibi." The girl's greasy fingers trembled, as did her voice. "You must not ask me to do this."

"But why? Why not?"

"Bibi," came the answer, spoken so softly Mariana could scarcely make out the words, "if you disappear as Saboor disappeared, they will punish me as they punished Saboor's servant."

"What did they do to him?"

"They took a great, curved sword, and with one blow, they sliced his nose from his face."

ONE by one by one, the elephants heading the British procession slowed, then halted. The marching band fell silent. Lord Auckland leaned from his howdah, his fingers tapping impatiently on the railing. "Why must *every* journey to the Citadel be filled with interruptions?" He sighed. "How I wish this ghastly wedding business were already behind us," he told Macnaghten, who sat behind him. "I am already exhausted, and it's only six o'clock in the evening."

Staccato shouting erupted nearby. Lord Auckland straightened, abandoning his effort to see. Nothing was visible from his perch but the cavalry escort, an aimless crowd of liveried servants, and the usual swarm of excited boys from the nearest village perilously chasing one another under the elephants' moving feet.

He frowned. "I had hoped yesterday's treaty signing would be our last visit to the Citadel. What a wretched way to celebrate Christmas!"

A panting bearer loped past their elephant, a peacock feather fan in his outstretched hand. With another sigh, Lord Auckland settled himself in his seat.

"I was sorry to hear that the bridegroom's father has refused to speak to us until tomorrow," he said crossly. "That is most inconvenient, Macnaghten. The man behaves as if we have nothing else to do, as if the Afghan Campaign were nothing at all. Someone might have told us the old fellow was considered some sort of religious authority, that he held regular gatherings at his house. What fool told us he was a magician? But what does it matter now? All that matters is that our last effort at forestalling this miserable marriage has come to nothing."

The line of elephants started forward again, with the somberly clad Lord Auckland and Macnaghten together at its head. Behind them in the soft light of dusk, the Eden ladies bent their heads together, one black crepe bonnet nearly touching the other.

"I would much prefer to take the girl away with us tonight," Lord Auckland told Macnaghten, "but since we have had no contact with the Shaikh, we shall have to leave Miss Givens there until tomorrow morning."

He coughed, then fell silent. Beads of perspiration dotted Macnaghten's brow.

"I warned her." Lord Auckland shook his head. "When she first came to camp, I gave her my most stringent warning. 'Never,' I said, 'show interest in the natives.' "

The marching band had started up again. Macnaghten leaned forward to be heard. "Who could have guessed at her excitement over native men? It is terrible to imagine how she will suffer tonight."

Lord Auckland's only reply was silence.

Their progress slowed by a leaping, pushing crowd of native onlookers, they followed the city wall toward the Elephant Gate. Steadying himself, Lord Auckland searched the floor of the carved howdah for his silver-topped cane.

"Whatever Miss Givens's intentions may have been," he said as he sat up again, the cane in his hand, "her revelation saved the day. Accidentally, of course." His pale eyes brightened. "What a diversion the girl created after the Maharajah's marriage proposal! We could not have done it better ourselves."

"Quite so, sir," Macnaghten agreed, bobbing his head. "In fact, I have yet to think of a satisfactory response to that outrageous suggestion. Any refusal, no matter how well put, would have offended the old man, and might easily have had the effect of undoing our alliance. One cannot fathom the native mind. But what baffles me the most is how Miss Givens formed her own alliance with the Waliullah family. When could she have done it? She never left our sight."

Lord Auckland adjusted his top hat with precision. "I haven't the faintest idea, Macnaghten, but I do not wish to think of such matters now. Let us enjoy our relief at not having to participate in tonight's ceremony. I cannot say how pleased I was when you told me that this barbarian exercise is to be conducted by natives, according to their custom, and that we may leave it to the ladies to join Miss Givens as witnesses to her 'consent.' "

Macnaghten frowned. "I must say, I was most unpleasantly surprised at the behavior of the girl's munshi when he came to explain their marriage proceedings."

"Why?" Lord Auckland poked the end of his stick restlessly into the floor of the howdah.

"I found the man far too self-possessed for a servant, my lord. I did not like him."

Lord Auckland nodded. "Well, Macnaghten, this whole business is nearly over, thank God. I only hope my sisters keep their heads. They had some notion of getting Miss Givens to feign a swoon, then rushing her away on the pretext that she was too ill to give her consent." He smiled tightly. "It had not even occurred to them to wonder how they would manage this, with their only translator lying 'unconscious' between them."

He shook his head bleakly. "Why do we call this evening's spectacle a 'wedding'? Why do we not call it what it will be—an Oriental bacchanal? I can predict its course exactly, from deafening fireworks to screeching dancing girls, to poisonous wine, and finally to red-hot food."

"A proper wedding takes place in church," agreed Macnaghten. "How well I remember my own wedding day, how anxious I was, how lovely my wife looked."

He smiled to himself and crossed his legs.

"One thing is certain," pronounced Lord Auckland from the front seat, "Miss Givens is never to have a real wedding. We have tried everything to save her, and it is now too late. Tomorrow, she will return to us in utter disgrace. For all that she is to blame for her own misfortunes, I cannot help feeling sorry for the girl."

IT was quite dark before the fabled picture wall of the Citadel rose before them at last, its bright tile figures of battling elephants, horses, and warriors flickering in the torchlight.

"Welcome, welcome, most respected Governor-General Sahib! Welcome to the Governor-General and his party!" The Maharajah's ambassador, a smiling man in a striped turban, started forward to greet them, torchbearers running beside his velvet-draped elephant.

As Macnaghten gave his prepared reply, a flock of white doves erupted abruptly from a hundred small apertures in the wall. Their beating wings made the rushing sound of a sudden windstorm as, flying together in a spiraling white cloud, they flew in an arc, then in a circle, over the English party, before vanishing again into the wall.

"Kindest greetings and salutations from the Governor-General and his party," replied Macnaghten warily as the ambassador's elephant advanced.

Lord Auckland glanced upward at the wall. "If I were a native," he observed solemnly, "I might believe the appearance of those birds to be an omen of some sort. But I am not a native. I, praise God, am English."

Chapter 33

The thudding of artillery fire reached them through the filigreed window. Moran called sharply for silence.

"They have come," she announced to the crowded room, as braying trumpets and rattling drums followed the sound of the guns. "Send for the clothes."

"Who has come?" Mariana loathed the wobbly sound of her voice.

"Your husband, his family. They have come to take you away." Moran cocked her head and smiled. "Your husband has come for you, dressed in beautiful clothes, riding a white horse."

Mariana's throat closed. Uncle Adrian's instruction returned through the ringing in her ears. *Always remember who you are.*

Moran's eyes were fixed on Mariana's face. She frowned. "Bring a light, Reshma. I want to see how well her nose is healing."

The sour girl from the howdah sat against the wall. "This wedding is nothing," she said nastily, her nose ornament swinging like the tassel on a bell pull. "She has no relations of her own, no jewels, not even a copper pot for a dowry. How do we know the bridegroom is wearing beautiful clothes? *She* has sent him nothing to wear."

Murmurs of agreement filled the room.

Moran stopped peering at Mariana's nose, and pointed at the girl with beringed fingers.

"You, Saat, were you not a *dhoolie* bride, brought to the Maharajah's tent with no wedding dinner? Do not speak," she snapped, as the girl opened her mouth. "We have heard enough of your doings."

As the girl named Saat Kaur recoiled, a maidservant stepped into the room carrying a shiny cloth packet, followed by a eunuch holding a black velvet pillow on outstretched hands. An intricate emerald-and-pearl necklace, a pair of heavy gold earrings, and other jewelry lay on the pillow, stitched onto their places with black thread.

"These are your wedding clothes, and your jewels," said Moran, gesturing toward the bright packages. "Come, then," she ordered as she opened a mustard yellow veil the size of a bedsheet. "They will do the *nikah,* the marriage agreement, now. We are bringing you upstairs."

"Now? Like this?" Mariana wrapped her arms tightly around her middle. "But my clothes are all oily and—"

Moran tugged her to her feet. "You do not wear your wedding clothes yet. Lower the blinds upstairs," she barked over her shoulder to a eunuch as she draped the veil like a tent over Mariana's head and face, "and make sure the seating is ready. Come, be quick, and keep your head down." She put a hand on the back of Mariana's head and pushed it forward. "Do not walk proudly."

"No!" Mariana stood straight and snatched off the yellow veil. "I have already told you there has been a mistake. I have told you that the Shaikh does not wish this marriage to take place." She held the veil at arm's length, and dropped it onto the floor. "I cannot be married against my will," she announced, planting her feet on the tiles. "I will not participate in this wedding of yours." She folded her arms.

Everyone began talking at once.

"Wedding of *mine*? Against *your* will?" Moran thrust her face into Mariana's, her voice a loud, persuasive singsong. "Against your will, when you announced aloud to a hundred men at court that you were betrothed?"

She snatched up the veil and jerked it into place over Mariana's head. "As for the Shaikh," she sneered, "you are wrong. He has just now arrived with his son to take you away. You are only feeling shy." She raised her voice, as if speaking to a deaf person. *"Brides always feel shy."* There was a murmur of assent and giggles from the crowd.

"Tell the eunuchs to wait," Moran added over her shoulder. "We may need them to take her upstairs."

Bodies crowded against Mariana. Hands pushed her head down. Bent over, she tottered helplessly toward the tower stairs.

Chattering women propelled her up the stone steps. There was no need to guess where she was; as soon as she reached the head of the stairway, she was assaulted by a blast of noise. Lights flickered through her veil as she was pushed outside and across a carpet, then nudged onto a platform like the one she'd just left, this one covered with scratchy, metallic cloth.

Her breath dampening her face, she listened through her veil.

Her attendant ladies were leaving. As their whispers faded, a rustling sound signaled the arrival of two other women who sat down, one on each side of her.

After a moment's silence, a familiar voice spoke into her ear. "Mariana," it said, in English, "is that you?"

Mariana tore her imprisoning veil from her face. There, like two tardy rescuing angels, sat the Misses Eden. Both were wearing black, as if they were in mourning.

At the sight of Mariana's face, Miss Emily started, her eyes wide.

"Oh, Miss Emily, Miss Fanny," Mariana choked out, "I am so glad to see you. Please help me. They did so many things—"

Should she describe her ordeal to two spinster ladies?

Miss Emily produced a handkerchief and pressed it mutely into Mariana's hand.

"But, Mariana," Miss Fanny whispered, staring, "what have they done to your nose, to your hands? Why have they wrapped you up like a parcel? I must say that yellow does *not* suit you. Why is your face all shiny?"

Miss Emily found her voice. "Perhaps there are things," she intoned, "that are better left unmentioned."

Mariana looked about her. She and the Eden sisters now sat in a darkened enclosure connected by a covered passageway to the ladies' tower door. The sides and back of the enclosure were of thick canvas, while the side facing the courtyard had been made up of thin cane screens lined with fine muslin. Through the screens, she could clearly see a brightly lit gathering of men, no more than ten yards away.

Was that Lord Auckland in a silver chair?

"Can they see us?" she breathed.

"No, my dear, it is the oddest thing," replied Miss Fanny. "As we approached, we could see nothing at all. We had no idea what was inside this enclosure, and yet from here we can see the courtyard perfectly."

"I am so glad you have come, Miss Emily," Mariana said eagerly.

"I had feared no one would come to save me. But why are you wearing black? Has someone died?"

Miss Emily tightened her black-gloved hands in her lap, then spoke briskly, allowing no further interruption. "No one has died, my dear, but I am sorry to say that we have not come to save you, although my brother and Mr. Macnaghten have certainly tried their best to prevent this disaster."

What had Miss Emily said? Mariana's mind whirled.

"This 'wedding' business of yours," Miss Emily went on stiffly, "has gone too far to be stopped. You must marry the man to whom you say you are betrothed." Black ribbons quivered under her chin. "I cannot imagine how I shall explain this to your aunt and uncle after they trusted me to guard your safety and your reputation. . . ."

"But Miss Emily, I cannot marry the Shaikh's son. It was never, Shaikh Waliullah never—"

"Mr. Macnaghten is to call upon the Shaikh tomorrow afternoon," Miss Emily broke in firmly. "He did his best to arrange a meeting for today, but the Shaikh was too busy to see him."

Too busy to see Mr. Macnaghten and cancel the wedding? Impossible! Mariana shook her head vehemently. "Miss Emily, I cannot possibly marry—"

Miss Emily ignored the interruption. "As much as it pains me to say so," she went on, "you are the sole author of this dreadful situation. We *all* warned you to keep away from the natives. I shudder to think what you could have done to invite a proposal of marriage from one of them."

Thundering in Mariana's brain joined the pounding of her heart. She could scarcely breathe. "Miss Emily," she shouted, "I invited *neither* this proposal *nor* the Maharajah's!"

Desperate, she turned to her other side. "Miss Fanny, I—"

Miss Emily raised a finger. "Do not appeal to my sister. Fanny quite agrees with me. You, my dear, did not stop at merely soliciting a marriage proposal. You announced your engagement before the Maharajah's entire court, and then went away on his elephant. Had you not done those things, there might have been some way out." She smoothed her black skirts. "As it is, nothing can be done until tomorrow morning when Mr. Macnaghten will come to the Shaikh's house to collect you and return you, sadder but wiser, I am sure, to our camp at Shalimar."

Her teeth clamped shut to prevent herself from shrieking with rage, Mariana gazed out over the crowd of glittering Sikhs and black-clad Europeans.

"What is that scent you are wearing, Mariana?" Miss Fanny inquired. She had covered her nose with her handkerchief. She shifted on the platform beside Mariana, her taffetas creaking. "It has quite given me a headache."

"The second thing we have come to say," Miss Emily interposed in a repressive tone, "is that no word of these events is to escape the British camp. My brother has issued instructions to all those who were present at the Maharajah's dinner and to all who are present this evening that no mention of this 'marriage' is ever to be made in either personal letters or official dispatches. As far as we are concerned, these events will *never* have happened." She coughed delicately. "As far as he is able to do so, my brother has determined to preserve your reputation. It is not, of course, within his power to preserve your honor."

Mariana could not take her eyes from the throng outside her enclosure. Of course they would gossip. They would all talk about her. How she despised Miss Emily, Miss Fanny, Mr. Macnaghten, every one of them. If he were here, she would hate Fitzgerald, too.

A loud gasp came from the passageway.

It was the torturing Moran, now glittering with jewelry, layers of maroon silk rippling about her. Without pausing to acknowledge the English guests, she rushed forward and cast the yellow veil for a third time over Mariana's face.

"Shameless girl," she hissed. "The court solicitor is coming to hear your consent! How foolish you are to uncover yourself!"

She sat down on the platform, her jewelry clashing. Beside the now-enshrouded Mariana, Miss Emily rustled and sniffed.

"I do *not* wish to know what that rude woman was saying," Miss Emily declared, "and I shall be very glad when this absurd ceremony is finished."

Mariana raised a corner of her veil and looked out. An elderly, bearded man in a knitted skullcap shuffled toward the ladies' enclosure, aided by a stocky person in plain-looking clothes.

Miss Fanny nudged Mariana. "Is that square young man to be the bridegroom?" she whispered.

Mariana repressed a whimper. *Bridegroom.*

Another man followed the first two. He wore a tall headdress. Shaikh Waliullah. Mariana stiffened, despair welling inside her. Why had the Shaikh spoken of her courage, and of the love she felt for Saboor, then cheated her of her honor and her life?

The trio of men waited uncertainly before the wall of screens until two eunuchs appeared, carrying chairs.

"Ah," declared Moran, sighing gustily, as the three men seated themselves before the screen, "it is time."

Shaikh Waliullah raised his head. For a moment, although she knew he could not see her, Mariana felt his powerful gaze reach through the screen, and pierce her heart.

"This," murmured Miss Emily, "seems more a fancy-dress party than a wedding. I must say that if I had ears like open carriage doors, I should not have chosen a costume involving a foot-high tubular headdress."

Mariana dropped her veil into her lap and stopped her ears with her fingers.

Bodies shifted beside her. Something was being said. She pushed her fingers harder against her ears.

She took them away when an elbow dug into her side. "Answer him," hissed Moran.

"Is she present?" an old man's voice asked.

"Yes," Moran answered. "I, Moran Bibi, declare that she is present."

"And does Mariam Bibi," rasped the ancient voice, "give her free consent to marry Hassan Ali Khan Karakoyia?"

Free consent?

"What are they asking?" inquired Miss Fanny in her stage whisper.

"Speak," ordered Moran.

Mariana breathed in. "No," she said grimly and distinctly through her veil. "I do *not* give my free consent."

"What does *'nay'* mean?" Miss Emily demanded. "Are you saying, Mariana, that you refuse to marry the man?"

Miss Fanny drew in a sharp breath. "I think she is very brave, after all the things these people have—"

"You will say yes." Menacing fingers pinched Mariana's arm.

Mariana blinked. On second thought, to refuse would be a mistake. Moran would only return her to the rooms downstairs and inflict more punishments upon her. But if she consented, she would leave for the Shaikh's house within hours. Had it not been her plan to escape the Citadel at any cost?

"I consent," she croaked.

"What did you say, Mariana?" asked Miss Emily and Miss Fanny in unison.

Mariana did not reply.

Bent over in her greasy clothes, she half listened as instructions were given and prayers recited in drawn-out Arabic. When clashing music started up in the courtyard, Moran tugged at Mariana's veil. "Tell your ladies to join the other English people," she commanded, "while we dress you in your wedding clothes."

Sick at heart, Mariana stumbled down the stairs again. What had the old man said? What was her husband's name?

BATHED at last, her hair dried, her eyes painted, and her skin massaged with almond oil, she stood drooping with fatigue. Moran, her own eyes ringed with dark circles of fatigue, tied the drawstring of Mariana's crimson wedding pajamas and tugged a matching brocade shirt over her head.

"There." Moran stood back. "Now we are nearly ready."

The watching women nodded.

"No, her hair is not right." The heavy-faced Charan chewed as she spoke. "Look. It is like a rat's nest."

A rat's nest! Would she ever recover from the insults of the past two days?

Moran lowered a crimson dress of fine embroidered tissue over Mariana's brocade shirt. "Why is everyone criticizing?" she muttered, as she broke the basting threads that had restrained a heavy, fringed veil into a neat square. "Pah! Do they all think I have never before dressed a bride?"

With a snap of thread, she freed the pearl-and-emerald choker from the velvet pillow. "Be still," she ordered, putting the necklace over Mariana's head and jerking the fastening cords tight.

After rummaging in a wooden jewelry casket, she pulled out a dozen straight ropes of pearls, each with a hook on one end and a large, lustrous pearl on the other.

"Here. These will help," she said as she tugged at Mariana's hair. "They will be our wedding present to you."

She stood back and narrowed her eyes. "You look all right." She nodded. "You make a nice bride. The clothes they sent are good enough. They are not very elaborate, but after all, they have had a death in the family."

What did Moran mean by "not very elaborate"? Mariana had never worn such fine clothes in all her life.

One piece of jewelry remained stitched to the pillow. Moran pulled it loose and approached, her eyes on Mariana's nose.

Backing away, her hands before her face, Mariana shook her head. "No," she cried. "No!"

Moran let out a noisy sigh. "Can you not hear the sounds from upstairs?" She gestured impatiently toward the window, her many rings flashing. "We must take you there now. There is no more time to waste." Gripping Mariana's chin, she tweaked out the neem twig and forced the gold nose ring through Mariana's nose with one decisive gesture. Her work accomplished, she stood back, her head cocked.

"Now we are done," she said.

Mariana gazed at the brown tracery decorating her hands, as elaborate as the marble filigree of the window of the room in which she stood. She studied her four rings, two of rubies and pearls, two of emeralds and pearls, the enamel-work bangles on one wrist, the heavy gold circlets on the other, the seed pearls and gold thread decorating her sleeves. Other jewelry lay on her forehead. Her nose, having burned fiercely when the ring was first put in, now merely ached.

"Remember one thing, bleed heavily tonight," Moran advised carelessly as she unfolded the heavy fringed veil and draped it over Mariana's face. "Bleed as much as you can, all over the sheets. It makes the family happy."

ON her platform in the ladies' enclosure once more, Mariana drooped with exhaustion. She made no more attempts to see through her new red veil. Outside, musicians nearly drowned the noise of male conversation.

Miss Fanny spoke from close by. "A stout woman is coming this way. Who is she?"

"I don't know," Mariana replied crossly, wishing they would all go away.

Bodies moved on the platform, making room for the new arrival, who promptly wedged herself into the too-small space beside Mariana.

It was not a queen. "Peace, daughter," intoned a baritone voice. Thick fingers grasped the fringed crimson veil and raised it. Mariana glanced upward—into the satisfied face of Safiya Sultana.

"You are pretty, as I knew you would be," said the Shaikh's sister, dropping the veil.

Pretty she might be, married she might be, at least according to them, but Mariana had made up her mind that as soon as she was safely out of the Citadel, this Oriental charade must end. Her mother had never mentioned blood when she gave her terse, ugly description of the origin of babies. Mariana had no intention of performing any wifely duty with the Shaikh's son, far less whatever grisly ritual they had in mind for her. She would make that clear to Safiya Sultana this very instant.

As she opened her mouth to speak, Moran spoke beside her. "We should let the foreigners see the bride."

Moran was there! Mariana closed her mouth again, unwilling to risk the scorn her announcement was certain to provoke from the queen. Her announcement to the Shaikh's sister would have to wait.

Someone lifted her veil again. Their black-bonneted heads together,

Miss Emily and Miss Fanny stared at her through a tunnel of crimson and gold tissue, their mouths forming perfect O's of mute surprise.

Mariana gazed steadily back. She would never speak to them again, never.

Safiya Sultana's stout body shifted against hers. When Mariana had brought Saboor to the haveli, the Shaikh's sister had not hurt or humiliated her but had only thanked her for the service she had performed. Safiya Sultana, at least, appeared to be kind and sensible, although Mariana could not guess what cruelties *she* might offer a family bride.

"We will complete the formalities and take you home as soon as possible, daughter," Safiya Sultana said, wheezing a little. "It is not our intention to spend time here. These men can have their drinking party without us."

"The bridegroom is coming," someone announced.

Everyone seemed to have gone away, save the Eden ladies and Safiya Sultana. In the middle of a tired yawn, Mariana sensed an abrupt change in the atmosphere around her.

"Most extraordinary," Miss Emily's voice declared. "How can he see through that great tangle of beads and pearls?"

As someone sat down beside Mariana, Safiya Sultana began to recite something in a quiet singsong. "Now the bride and groom must see each another," the Shaikh's sister said, when she had finished.

Miss Fanny gave a muffled sound as Mariana's veil was lifted again, this time all the way back, freeing her face.

Someone thrust a looking glass with an intricately carved silver border before her. Leaning forward, she saw herself and gaped, astonished at her reflection.

Rimmed with black *surma,* the eyes that stared back at her were shapely and strange. Between unfamiliar arched eyebrows, a gold pendant set with jewels rested on her forehead, its pearl rope hidden in her hair. Her hair, no longer brown but a rich auburn, curled softly on her shoulders, interlaced with strings of pearls. A wide ring of fine gold wire circled through her nose, its pearl and ruby beads touching her lips.

Was this creature really her? She made an experimental face and put out her tongue, just as the mirror was tilted to one side, and she saw not herself but a pair of shocked brown eyes. Holding his own ropes of gold and pearl aside, the man in the headdress looked briefly into her face before someone dropped her veil.

"May Allah Most Gracious bless you both and give you long life," intoned Safiya Sultana.

• • •

A N hour later, stiff with apprehension, Mariana sat upstairs at Qamar Haveli, surrounded by the Shaikh's family women. The Waliullah ladies, so benign when she last had seen them, now seemed like a crowd of vultures, staring, waiting.

"That is not the same girl who brought Saboor," pronounced an old woman, dropping Mariana's now damp veil over her face again. "The queens have sent someone else."

"Of course it is the same girl," said two other women at the same time. "Look at her nose, her skin."

The veil was pulled away again. "So it is," agreed the old lady, peering closely at Mariana. "For all their malice, they know how to prepare a bride. I would never have believed she could look so lovely. That girl was as plain as a cooking pot."

Half an hour ago at the Citadel, Miss Emily's voice had cut through the noise of the crowd as she and Miss Fanny were led away to their palanquins at the end of the evening.

"What an extraordinary transformation, Fanny," she had said, her voice floating back over the marble courtyard. "I find it astonishing that an ordinary-looking English girl could be made to look so exactly like a native. A white native, I mean, of course. What a pity the bridegroom was invisible under all those—"

"Yes, and I thought she made a very pretty native."

"*Really,* Fanny."

Mariana shifted. What were these women waiting for? Whatever it was, it must be even more horrible and disgusting than what Mama had described.

Her body felt clammy. She clutched her knees to her chest. Here in this upstairs room there were no eunuch guards, no armed men at the door. She imagined herself running through darkened streets in her bride's clothes, looking for the way to the British camp at Shalimar. . . .

Safiya Sultana sat in her accustomed place against the wall. Determined to finally tell Safiya of her refusal to continue this charade of a marriage, Mariana crawled to her side, dragging heavy embroidery and fringes behind her.

"I must speak to you," she began as the other women murmured in surprise. "I must tell you that—"

Safiya frowned. "Not now, daughter. It is time for you to leave."

"No, please, I must tell you now—"

Before Mariana could finish speaking, Safiya Sultana nodded to a group of young girls, who got to their feet and came toward them, holding their hands out to Mariana. How innocent they all seemed, these Waliullah females, the girls blushing, Safiya Sultana nodding contentedly to herself against the wall.

The only choice left was to fight, but Mariana had no more strength to protest or to struggle against restraining brown hands. Defeated at last, she got to her feet meekly and let the girls lead her to a corner room at the end of a veranda.

Inside were two string beds, both turned down, their sheets sprinkled liberally with red rose petals. An oil lamp glowed on a carved table. By its light, Mariana watched the girls run away, looking back over their shoulders, giggling through their fingers.

She sat down. The oil lamp looked like a reasonably dangerous weapon, but of course, it was lit and would start a fire if she tried to use it. Who would enter the room and advance upon her? What would they do to her?

There was a sound at the door. Ostrichlike, Mariana tugged her veil hastily down and peered through its fringe to see the curtain move aside and a figure in white pause before entering the room.

The bed creaked as the figure sat beside her. She did not turn her head. She could scarcely breathe. Attar of sandalwood scented the air. Where had she smelled that before?

"You didn't look foreign when I saw you, but then I couldn't see much in the mirror."

His voice was pleasant, like the Shaikh's, but without inflection, as if he were simply stating a fact. Beside her, a hand moved on his knee. It was a beautiful hand, perfectly shaped, with curved fingers. The hand lifted, pointing to a corner of the room.

"You should take off those heavy things and your jewelry," he said. "Put them on the trunk over there."

No longer burdened by her elaborate clothes, she might be able to put up some real resistance. In the corner, her back to him, she removed her nose ring and tugged, grimacing, at the pearl strands in her hair. Were they to be alone? How long could she avoid looking at him?

"I am glad to lie down," he said. "I have ridden forty miles today, from Kasur."

She dropped her veil and her pearl-embroidered dress onto the trunk. Still wearing her scarlet tunic and trousers, she steeled herself and turned. The Shaikh's son lay full length on one of the beds, his eyes closed, his hands behind his head, his lips parted under a full mustache. His beard was thick and neatly trimmed.

It was the tall man in the embroidered coat whom she had followed from the durbar tent a month ago, the same man who had later appeared, weeping, beside her near the howitzers, who had even then worn attar of sandalwood.

He did not look like the Shaikh at all.

His eyes remained closed. Barely breathing, Mariana crept to the other bed. She lay down silently, arranged the quilt over herself, then leaned over to turn out the lamp.

The bed beside her shifted and groaned. She froze, her arm still extended, praying he was only turning in his sleep.

He was not asleep. His eyes met hers as he pushed himself up and sat on the edge of his bed.

Without speaking, he got to his feet. As he padded toward her, she twisted away from him and rolled her carefully prepared and perfumed body into a ball on the far side of the bed, her eyes screwed shut, her fist in her mouth. Her ragged breathing seemed to fill the room.

There was no sound from outside.

His weight came down beside her. "Show me your face," he said.

When she did not move, he took her by her shoulder and turned her to him.

She could only look up, her body clenched against invasion, too terrified even to blink.

He studied her, his fingers still on her shoulder, his eyelids drooping just as Saboor's did when he was sleepy. "They were correct," he said. "You do not look foreign."

His eyes were ringed with dark smudges as they had been when she had first seen him. Now, his expression altered. His breathing gathered speed. His eyes on her mouth, he leaned over her, then pulled back when she flinched away, her eyes wide.

"So," he told her softly, "you are afraid of me."

He took his hand from her shoulder and turned away. "There is no need for fear," he said in a muffled voice, his back to her. "You rescued my son. I am in your debt."

He stood. "Sleep, Bibi," he said softly, as he returned to his own bed. "Go to sleep."

Chapter 34

**THURSDAY,
DECEMBER 26**

Mariana swam to consciousness through a thick mist. As the events of the previous night returned, she lay still, holding her breath, and listened. Was he still there, in the other bed?

Silence.

She opened her eyes and put a hand to her neck. Forgotten when she took off her other jewelry, her choker now hung loose, its scratchy cord wrapped about her throat, its pearl-and-emerald beads entangled in her hair.

Daylight filtered into the room through closed shutters. On the trunk in the corner, her fringed veil and the rest of her jewels lay where she had dropped them. Her tissue dress had fallen from the trunk and lay on the floor, its pearl embroidery gleaming in the striped light from the window.

She turned her head cautiously. The bed next to hers stood unoccupied, its sheets wrinkled, its quilt thrown aside.

She drew up her knees, enjoying the cool air on her face, and the warmth beneath her covers. Last night, when Hassan had left her to sleep, she had been too exhausted to feel the relief that now bathed her from head to foot. What luck! She was safe and unharmed. Mr. Macnaghten was coming today. She was nearly free.

Someone pushed the door curtain aside. A small girl stepped shyly into the room, a neatly folded set of clothes in her hands.

Rose petals, crushed to a deep purple, marked the floor tiles, Mariana's pillow, the sheets of both beds. The girl looked at them, and then at Mariana, a question in her eyes.

Unable to think of anything to say, Mariana smiled.

"Come, *Bhabi,*" the child piped, beaming in return. "I will show you where to bathe." She held out the russet-colored package and a soft-looking shawl of the same color. "You will wear these to meet the ladies. They are waiting for you in the big room." Her face sobered. "Of course, you must understand that our house is still in mourning for poor Mumtaz Bha—" She pressed her lips together. "I should not be speaking to you, a bride, of these things," she added.

Mariana began to untangle her choker. "I would rather wear my own clothes. Please ask someone to bring my own things from the Citadel. They are my best clothes, you see."

Yes, her chemise, her stays, her stockings, her blue-and-white silk gown. Wearing them again, she would feel entirely herself. She must look like an Englishwoman again when she met Mr. Macnaghten.

The child was a birdlike creature whose thick, glossy braid fell below her waist. "Bhabi, your own things have not come from the Citadel."

Mariana waved a hand. What did it matter? Her clothes were the least of her worries. In the past three days she had lost more than a borrowed gown and her good set of stays.

"Safiya Bhaji had these clothes made for you," volunteered the child. "It will make her happy to see you wearing them." She held out a silk drawstring pouch. "And see, she has sent you a beautiful gold necklace."

Safiya Sultana. Mariana turned the intricate necklace over in her hands. Did the Shaikh's sister know what had happened—or not happened—the previous night?

MARIANA shivered as she poured steaming water over her shoulders with a vessel that looked like a teapot. Last night, when he leaned over her, Hassan's skin had smelled hot beneath the attar of sandalwood he wore, as if it had been scorched.

She put down the teapot. He would surely have felt it within his rights to do whatever he wished with her last night, but he had not. He had given her one considering glance, and then left her alone. She would always remember that kindness, and the sweet, burnt scent of his skin.

A short while later, she balanced nervously in the doorway of the big room, removing her new embroidered slippers with their upward-curling toes. She blushed as she added them to a pile beside the door.

How odd to feel self-conscious over something that had *not* happened.

Safiya Sultana beckoned, pointing to an unoccupied place beside her on the cloth-covered floor.

The women whispered as Mariana made her way through them and crouched down beside the Shaikh's sister. A familiar-looking gap-toothed aunt patted her knee. On Safiya Sultana's other side, a very old lady smiled into the air.

Mariana's new clothes felt alien and voluptuous. Without stays and petticoats, her body felt unfettered and exposed. She reached up to touch the unfamiliar smoothness of her hair, now hanging down her back in a silken plait, so unlike her own flyaway hair that it could have belonged to another girl entirely. Her oiled and hairless skin had a smooth, indecent texture.

There were children in the room. She looked for Saboor, and saw him near a doorway with a group of other children, too far away to notice her. His bubbling laughter reached her as a girl of six or seven, eyes alight, dragged him across the floor, her hands under his arms.

"An-nah!" He had seen her. He bounced, shouting in the little girl's arms, reaching out for Mariana. "An-nah!"

The room stilled.

How sweet it felt to hold Saboor again! She kissed the top of his head and breathed his baby scent greedily as he reached up to play with the gold buttons on her long silk shirt.

A collective sigh gusted about her.

Safiya Sultana sniffed. Was she weeping? Still rocking Saboor, Mariana glanced up to see Safiya wipe her eyes with her white cotton veil.

Her sigh filled the room. "These are painful times," the Shaikh's sister pronounced in her baritone voice. "Painful times. We all remember that when our dear Mumtaz Bano died, her child was left alone among strangers at the Citadel, his life in danger."

She looked at Mariana. "We also remember that, after this brave young foreigner saved Saboor, my brother, seeing her courage and her love for our child, determined it is the will of Allah that she remain beside Saboor, to protect him from harm, and to help us raise him to his manhood." She paused, clearing her throat. "It is for this reason that we have joined her in marriage to Hassan."

We have joined her in marriage.

The Shaikh's proposal had been genuine! Mariana loosened her hands on Saboor's body and turned away to face the wall as nausea rose from her belly to her throat. Moran Bibi had been right. Miss Emily had been right. The proposal *had* been genuine, and she had accepted it in front of a hundred people, including Harry Fitzgerald, her blue-coated Fitzgerald who had kissed her and made her happy.

She had done all of this to herself.

A worried voice spoke beside her. "Is the bride ill?"

The bride. Fighting back tears, Mariana watched Saboor scramble away. How would she ever face Mr. Macnaghten and the British camp? How would she ever convince them that she had honestly believed her marriage was a sham? And what of her family? What of poor Mama and Papa who still waited at home for news of her engagement to an Englishman? . . .

"Allah alone," Safiya Sultana was saying, "knows the pain and confusion it has caused us to have our dear Mumtaz Bano's death followed so quickly by Hassan's marriage to this foreigner. We all suffer for Mumtaz's mother."

A little distance away, a small woman in white clothes rocked silently.

Mariana swallowed hard. *These* people did not want her. How could they? Of all of them, the only one who really wanted her was Saboor.

He was now in the arms of his fat cousin, who held him away from a dozen small, reaching arms. His eyes on Mariana, Saboor wriggled to get down, then hurried over to her and sat, with a sweet little thump, on her lap.

She wrapped her arms gratefully around his body and pressed her cheek against his head. If only she could take him away from here, they would be so happy alone together. . . .

Safiya Sultana sighed again. "But we must remember how greatly Hassan's new wife loves our Saboor. Her affection for him is plain to see. We have noticed her face soften as he approaches her; we have seen it fill with light. It gives us comfort to see her love for our motherless child. We all know of women who feign love for a widower's children in order to gain entry into his family. We pity the motherless child who must endure the hatred of his father's second wife."

Mariana sniffed, wishing she had a handkerchief. She had certainly never wanted to "gain entry" into this native family.

"Perhaps," said one lady softly, nodding at the woman who sat trembling with age at Safiya Sultana's stout side, "this foreigner will love Saboor as Bhaji Tehmina loved Safiya and Waliullah when they were orphaned as babies. Such love is rare indeed."

Lured by beckoning children, Saboor slipped away again. Mariana wrapped her arms about her legs and stared through the window at a cloudy sky, imagining herself back at the British camp. She pictured the camp preparing for the return journey to Calcutta, its bustling activity so different from the stillness of this room in the Shaikh's house.

Mr. Macnaghten would arrive soon to call upon the Shaikh. There was no need to fear that she would miss him—he would be clearly visible, sitting beside the Shaikh's platform in the courtyard, and the ladies would rush to the windows to see the foreign gentleman. She would go down to meet him, and once there, would insist that he take her back to the British camp. By the evening, disgraced or not, she would be in her own tent, standing over her trunks before she dressed for dinner, telling Dittoo which of her gowns to pack.

The ladies had fallen into contemplative silence. Outside, rain had begun to fall, splashing onto the windowsills, drumming on the flat, tiled roof over their heads.

The honor guard would have left already to join the march to Kabul. Fitzgerald must hate her now.

Mariana smoothed her silk shirt over one knee. What if something happened to Mr. Macnaghten and he never came? She shivered. What if he did come, but she was somehow prevented from leaving with him? Would the British then simply leave her behind? No, surely not. They would not abandon her here forever, never again to eat her own food, or hear the familiar cadence of her own language.

But they had left her at the Citadel and gone away.

If only she knew her future!

But someone here in the haveli knew her future. How could she have forgotten? Whatever her feelings about his marriage proposal, Mariana was convinced the old Shaikh possessed profound knowledge. When his eyes had met hers through the reed screen last evening, they had seemed to hold some promise she did not understand.

She leaned toward Safiya Sultana. "May I please," she said as sweetly as she could, "offer my salaams to Shaikh Waliullah?"

"What?" Safiya Sultana looked startled. "Why, daughter, you cannot see him today. He is not at home until the afternoon, and then he will have visitors."

"*Nani, Nani!*" All the ladies looked up as a tall boy with the callow beginnings of a mustache rushed into the room and stood, breathing hard in the doorway, his eyes drifting to Mariana and Saboor.

"Armed men have come from the Citadel!" he reported anxiously, jumbling his words. "They are waiting in the courtyard. They say they have come to take Saboor and the European lady away with them. You are to have their clothes packed. They say Saboor and the lady are to live at the Citadel forever, as guests of the Maharajah!"

Mariana felt the blood leave her face.

A question hung in the air. The boy answered it before it could be asked. "There are no men in the house, save Uncle Bilal, Allahyar, and me."

A woman shook her head. "Only Safiya's grandchild, a servant, and Bilal, the impractical one, the dreamer, the teller of tales. This is not good, not good at all."

The children playing on the floor gaped at the tall boy, their chattering abruptly stilled. The little girl who had been reciting nonsense rhymes to Saboor stopped speaking and looked up.

A woman spoke from the corner of the room. "It is wrong," she protested loudly, "for them to take the child away. How can he go to the Citadel? He is not the Maharajah's slave!"

Safiya Sultana turned a silencing glare upon the woman. "Yahya, my darling," she told the boy over the patter of the rain, "go downstairs. Tell the Maharajah's men that it will take a little time to make Saboor and the lady ready. Tell them also that Saboor has a fever. Tell them we have had a case of smallpox among the stable hands."

The boy hesitated. "But Nani—"

Anxious voices whispered around Mariana. "Why can we not hide them?" "There are so many hiding places in this house." "My children know them all. Surely we can—"

Safiya Sultana nodded sharply. "Go, Yahya."

All eyes were upon the boy. He flushed, then turned stiffly away. Without looking back, he crossed the rain-spattered veranda and clattered down the stairs.

Safiya Sultana surveyed the room calmly, her eyes resting on the only woman in the room who was dressed like a servant. "Bina," she ordered, her expression daring anyone to speak, "bring us fruit."

After the old maidservant had pushed her feet into her shoes and shuffled away, Safiya Sultana cleared her throat. "Spies," she said harshly. "There are spies in this house." She raised a hand, subduing the shocked cries that followed.

Mariana looked from face to face. *Spies?*

"We do not know how many of our servants have been turned against us," Safiya went on, "but we must not blame them too much. They may have been tempted with gold, or they may fear for themselves or their families. But we do know that, among our staff, there will always be some who can be trusted, even with our lives.

"Now," she said, "we have only a few precious moments to save Saboor. Under no circumstances can we allow him to fall again into the hands of the court. The Maharajah, as we have all heard, may die at any moment. Should he die, Saboor's life will be worth less than a cowrie shell."

Blood thudded in Mariana's temples. She looked for Saboor, and saw him in the arms of a spindly girl who watched Safiya Sultana, her mouth open.

Safiya searched the faces around her. "When Mumtaz Bano died," she continued, "we ourselves could not help Saboor. We could only wait here, praying with all our strength for his safe return. We did not know from which quarter help might come. Now, when he is once more in terrible danger, our circumstances are different. This time, with help from Allah Most Gracious, we ourselves will save him."

A dubious sigh blew through the room.

"This time we have among us," Safiya went on, drawing her audience with her, "our bride, the young *Angrezi* woman who, disregarding the peril to herself, took Saboor from his servant's arms at the Golden Temple, and with her own hands brought him safely home to us."

Heads swung in agreement. A shy-looking girl nearby met Mariana's eyes for the first time.

Safiya's pudgy finger poked the air. "She alone among all of us is able to leave this house in the necessary manner. Our bride has experience of the world outside, while we have only knowledge. She will do the needful—will you not, daughter?"

This last was not really a question; it was a deep-voiced command. Still, Safiya had left the way open for Mariana to refuse. Her thoughts galloped. *Leave the house in the necessary manner.* What did Safiya mean? Having never seen the street outside, she could not know how many men passed hourly before the haveli's great carved doors. If a passerby had seen the Maharajah's men enter, an interested crowd, three or four deep, must already have collected there.

Mariana wiped damp palms on her knees. She and Saboor would never leave the haveli unnoticed.

What would happen to them if they were caught? She did not need to ask. She knew enough of the Jasmine Tower. No one would protect Saboor from the wrath of the jealous queens. No one would save her from the wrath of the Maharajah.

Rain entered a corner of a nearby window and trickled down the wall. Safiya Sultana waited, her eyes on Mariana's face.

Saboor watched her from across the room with the same round, expectant gaze that had melted her heart outside the Golden Temple. Had it only been eleven days before? That gaze had made her feel capable of anything.

"Yes," she replied, for the second time since yesterday. "I will." She breathed in. "I will do whatever you need."

Chapter 35

Safiya Sultana turned to the young girl who had come to Mariana's room. "Zareen, go and bring me the oldest *burqa* you can find. Ah, here is Bina with the fruit," she added in a warning tone, as the elderly maidservant shuffled through the door bearing a tray of oranges and guavas.

All murmuring stopped. "Spies," hissed someone, under her breath.

Taking a guava and a sharp knife from the tray, Safiya Sultana cut out a wedge of rosy flesh with practiced hands, dipped it into a little heap of salt on the tray, and handed it elaborately to the elderly lady beside her. "Eat this, Ammi-jan," she shouted into the old woman's ear.

The old lady took the fruit with a palsied hand, put it obediently into her mouth.

Safiya Sultana's face betrayed no anxiety. Mariana edged toward her on the floor, hoping to absorb some of her calm.

"Leave the tray with us, Bina," Safiya told the maidservant, "and call Allahyar. Tell him to come up here at once. He is to stand outside the door for my instructions. Go, and close the door curtain on your way out."

She leaned over to Mariana. "Look at these women before you," she said quietly in her man's voice. "They are my family. Some are wise, some unwise, but all are good-hearted in their own way." She put a hand on Mariana's knee. "Together, we are about to undertake a journey as far from our own experience as the ocean voyage that brought you here. Some of our ladies will not believe that you can succeed in the escape I have in mind. Others will see the sense in it and will have confidence. In any event, our prayers and our hearts will be with you."

Mariana swallowed, trying not to think of the danger.

"I most certainly hope," Safiya Sultana added more loudly, frowning around the crowded room, "that none of you breathes a word of what we are about to do. Children, stand up."

Mariana watched a dozen children straighten reluctantly and stand in a solemn brown-skinned row.

Safiya Sultana regarded them sternly. "You must all leave the room now," she said. "Secrets can be difficult to keep. If you are not here, none of you can, by chance, betray your little brother."

Betray. Mariana shivered. Beside her, Safiya Sultana gave off a stout calm.

The whispering children rustled out, the larger ones carrying the smaller, leaving only Saboor. The ladies waited, moving only their eyes until a deep cough heard through the curtain revealed the presence of a man.

Safiya Sultana signaled for attention. The ladies leaned forward to listen over the patter of the rain.

"Who is there?" Safiya called out.

"It is I, Allahyar, Begum Sahib," replied a male voice.

"He is Lala-Ji's personal servant," one girl Mariana's age whispered to her.

"Allahyar," ordered Safiya Sultana, "you are to go to your uncle the storeroom keeper and get from him a small ball of opium."

Mariana blinked. Opium?

A slurred response came from behind the curtain.

"There is no use," Safiya Sultana said firmly over the drumming of the rain, "in trying to tell me that your uncle does not take opium. He has done so for thirty years."

The ladies smiled.

"Ji, Begum Sahib," said the male voice, after a pause.

"You will bring the opium here," Safiya Sultana went on, "and you will also bring a basket from the storeroom, the largest basket we

have. You will then wait outside until a lady comes from this room
and joins you. You will tell no one of these instructions. Do you
understand me?"

"Ji, Sahib."

"Go, then."

Safiya Sultana studied Mariana as if she were seeking something.
"My daughter," she said, her deep voice softening, "here is what you
will do."

Mariana nodded. Unlike the malicious queens at the Citadel, Safiya
had treated her like a daughter. Overcome with gratitude, Mariana
felt a sudden urge to bury her head in Safiya Sultana's well-padded
shoulder.

"I have sent for an old burqa," the Shaikh's sister added a little
gruffly, "the long veil that our Punjabi women wear out of doors. We
shall put it over you, to conceal your face and hair, and your clothes.

"Wearing the burqa, you will go downstairs. After passing through
the kitchens, you will leave this house by the rear door. Allahyar, my
brother's personal servant, will accompany you. He will walk a few
paces in front of you. You will," she paused, her eyes moving from
face to face, daring anyone to object, "be posing as Allahyar's wife."

"But what of Saboor?" Mariana heard herself ask.

"The Maharajah's men may be watching the rear door," Safiya
Sultana warned. "Saboor, therefore, will not be with you as you pass
out of the house. He will instead be lowered from that window."

She pointed across a tiled veranda to a window that gave onto the
street below. "In a basket."

The women all tried to speak at once. Safiya Sultana held up a
commanding palm.

"Do we not," she asked the room in general, "lower a basket to
Vikram Anand, the sweetmeat seller below, when we wish to entertain ourselves with his *jalebees,* his *luddoos,* and his *gulab jamons*?
And has not that same sweetmeat shop stood below our window for
the past three generations?"

A thin lady near Mariana smiled as the room subsided. "Of course,
Vikram's best customer is Safiya herself," she whispered.

"I have confidence that Vikram will help us," Safiya told Mariana.
"He is known in the city for his charity and his level head."

Mariana stared at the rain outside the window where Safiya had
pointed. How did Safiya Sultana know what people in the city said
about a sweetmeat seller?

Safiya nodded. "Allahyar will take Saboor from the basket. You
will follow him as he carries the child toward the Delhi Gate. You will

then follow him through the gate and onto the road. There, you will be overtaken by one of our own palanquins."

The gap-toothed aunt lifted her hands. "Where is she to go?"

Safiya Sultana frowned.

"She should go to Kasur, to Hassan, of course," contributed another woman. "He is her husband. Where else should she go?"

A wave of assent spread through the crowd.

"But Shalimar is right here." Her heart thumping, Mariana shook her head. "Kasur is miles and miles away. Surely I *must* take Saboor to the British camp."

Instead of answering, Safiya Sultana signaled to the shy girl. "Aalia, bring me a pen and ink, and some paper."

Turning to Mariana, she smiled grimly. "The world is a strange place, Mariam, and the will of Allah Most Gracious is not for us to know. Wherever else you may wish to travel, this time you will journey, God willing, to Hassan's camp at Kasur."

Mariam. The solicitor at the Citadel had called her Mariam. Mariana started to give the correct pronunciation of her name, but saw that Safiya Sultana was now busy writing letters.

The burqa arrived. Zareen gathered up the yards of cotton cloth that made up the burqa, and fitted its embroidered cap carefully over Mariana's head.

The dusty folds fell to her feet, causing her such a fit of sneezing that she did not hear what was being said through the curtain. Sniffing, she looked through the grill of cotton cutwork before her face, and saw that it offered a narrow, impaired field of vision. So this was what the women were able to see when they were out of doors. Could they see enough to avoid accidents? There was no side vision whatever. She moved her head experimentally to and fro, and saw the ladies nod their approval.

"Now," someone said, "no one will know she is foreign."

Inside her cotton tent, Mariana sneezed again. No one would even know she was *female,* she thought.

She looked for Saboor. He now slept in the lap of one of his aunts, his body limp, a rim of something brown and sticky around his mouth.

Safiya Sultana pushed herself to her feet, the sheaf of letters in her hand, and took a book covered in heavy silk wrappings from the carved corner cupboard. She stood before Mariana, swaying slightly, her eyes half-closed, murmuring something. Finished, she took a deep breath and blew three times in Mariana's direction.

"Take these," she said. Reaching under the burqa, she pushed papers into Mariana's hand. "These are letters to our relations who live between here and Kasur. They will keep you and Saboor, and they will furnish you with fresh bearers. Come, then."

Seizing Mariana's arm through the folds of cotton, she led her to the door, and held out the book, still in its wrappings. "Kiss the Qur'an Sharif," she commanded.

Mariana did not at all wish to kiss someone else's holy book, but Safiya Sultana pressed it against her lips through the cotton veil, then held it up, allowing her to pass under it on her way out of the room. Mariana would have preferred Safiya to embrace her, but there was no time for that. There was no time to be afraid, or even to bid the ladies good-bye.

"May Allah Most Gracious guide you." Safiya Sultana's deep voice followed Mariana along the tiled veranda.

Through her peephole Mariana made out the slight figure of a man with orange hair, the same servant who had guided her to the Shaikh the first time she had come. He nodded and started for the narrow stairway that led down to the great kitchens below. The stairway was dark. She felt her way carefully down, holding the dusty burqa away from her feet.

THE kitchens were hot and smelled of heating fat and half-cooked spices. Women squatted on the floor, away from the fiery heat of the wood stoves, slicing onions and crushing a yellow ball of paste between two stones. Through an open door, Mariana could see rain splashing onto a small brick courtyard. This was the way out that Safiya had described.

Allahyar signaled. Mariana stepped into the courtyard after him, and within moments was drenched to the skin.

Across the courtyard, a low door led into a narrow cobbled alley with an overflowing gutter running along one of its sides. Had she been able to extricate her hands from the sodden burqa Mariana could have touched the houses on both sides of the alley at once.

Icy water ran down inside her fitted cap and dripped from her cut-work peephole. As she watched, Allahyar strode past an armed man loitering halfway down the alley. Was he one of the Maharajah's men? As she hurried to catch up with Allahyar, Mariana failed to see a loose cobblestone. Falling, she reached forward to save herself, and instantly doubled into a ball as her trapped hands forced the heavy burqa to drag her head downward.

The gutter beside her stank. One side of the burqa had fallen into the running water and was now drenched in filth. As she scrabbled for the papers she had dropped, a pair of hands grasped Mariana's arm through the soaked cloth. Allahyar's disgusted face passed close to hers as he hauled her to her feet, then disappeared as he moved off.

The bustling, familiar British camp had never seemed so distant, but Mariana no longer cared. If Safiya Sultana had carried out the other part of her plan, Saboor waited, drugged and helpless, in a sweetmeat shop below Safiya's veranda window, while other armed men patrolled the city lanes, ready to pounce on him and carry him away to the Citadel.

She must hurry. Ignoring the wet and the cold and the stench of sewage, she toiled along the alley and past the armed man, hugging the wall opposite the gutter, her whole being intent on escape. Reaching the alley's end at last, she shuffled out onto a wider cobbled lane, and found herself beside a small shop that had been built into a corner of the Waliullah haveli's wall.

"I would not mind having you beside me in battle," Papa had said once. What would he think of her now?

VIKRAM Anand, maker and seller of sweetmeats, was accustomed to seeing a basket lowered from the upper windows of Qamar Haveli. The ladies upstairs enjoyed his cooking, none more than Safiya Sultana herself, who sent for his wares by this simple method at least once a week. He had it on authority that this important lady had described his jalebees as the best in the city. He was, therefore, unsurprised when a basket appeared from above and dangled near his elbow.

He pushed aside a bowl of flour and wiped his hands on his clothes.

"Oh, Vikram," called a deep, familiar voice from above. "Do not sit idle when there is work to do. Take our basket and do the necessary."

Vikram leaned from his sheltering overhang and pulled the soaking basket toward him. It was heavy. He pulled the sides apart and peered inside. There, with rain lying like tears on his face, lay Saboor Baba, the child sought by all of Lahore.

There was no mistaking the child's identity. Vikram knew of every betrothal, wedding, and birth in the city. Hadn't he himself made the luddoos, each covered in a gossamer sheet of silver, that had gone to all the great houses, announcing the birth of this very child?

Had anyone seen? Glancing anxiously about, he reached into his shop for a banana leaf, and quickly covered the laden basket, hiding its dangerous contents from view. Working as rapidly as he could with the wet rope, he untied the basket and put it hastily behind him, out of sight. That done, he arranged himself once more in his usual place, and breathed deeply.

It was said in the city that Shaikh Waliullah's grandson brought the Maharajah luck. Perhaps that explained the curious desperation the child's disappearance had brought out in the old man. How many times since Saboor Baba's vanishing had the Maharajah sent high officials into the streets to investigate his disappearance, to ask the same questions each time they came?

Vikram stirred his vat of boiling milk. Even after everyone knew that the child had somehow found his way home to the haveli, these visits had not stopped. Only this morning, a showily dressed eunuch had come, asking for the child.

Vikram had been unwilling to answer then. Now he knew the truth. A daring escape was to be made. He nodded to himself. One glance had told him the baby in the basket was drugged. For that, he was grateful. There was no knowing how long they would have to wait. He frowned with pride as he stirred his milk, feeling the weight of the Waliullah family's trust upon his thin shoulders.

A man who sits all day frying sweetmeats on one fire and boiling down milk on the other has patience, but Vikram Anand needed to wait only a short time before an orange-haired man appeared, standing beneath the dripping canopy in front of his stall. Allahyar was well known to Vikram. He came several times a month to collect sweets for the men's side of the household. Often he stopped to pass the time of day, enjoying a moment to watch the life of the city pass by the little shop.

"Have you," asked Allahyar cautiously, without preamble, "a package for me?"

Vikram noticed for the first time the female in a filthy burqa who stood behind Allahyar. Confused, he looked silently at his hands. *Do the necessary,* Safiya Sultana's voice had said.

Allahyar's eyes darted to a pushing crowd by the main entrance to the haveli, not thirty feet away. "Perhaps the lady Safiya Sultana has sent something for me?" he asked.

Vikram Anand made up his mind. "Ah, yes, the lady Safiya Sultana *has* sent something. Shall I give it to you in the basket?"

The tense face before him relaxed slightly. "No, I do not want the basket."

Vikram reached behind him and lifted the banana leaf from Saboor's sleeping form. Allahyar's face creased into a smile.

"I am to tell you," he told the sweetmeat seller, as he hoisted the sleeping baby out of the basket and onto his shoulder, "that in consideration of your trouble, there is something for you in the basket."

After Allahyar strode off, the woman shuffling after him, Vikram Anand felt in the bottom of the basket. His fingers found a coin. It was a gold Mohur.

Nodding gravely, he tucked the treasure into his clothes. The Waliullah family had a sense of occasion that separated them from the other families of Lahore. A few copper coins would have been enough, considering the small work he had done. But that would have devalued the child. To put the coin on Saboor's body where it could be seen would have devalued Vikram. By hiding the gold coin under the child, Safiya Sultana had, in one gesture, complimented Vikram and demonstrated her family's love for their baby.

"Oh, Vikram, are you expecting to keep my basket?" called a deep voice two stories above him.

He should have known someone was watching.

Chapter 36

By the time the Maharajah's armed men forced their way into Qamar Haveli, Yar Mohammad the groom had been waiting in a doorway opposite Vikram's sweet shop for nearly three hours.

"Move out, move out!" An unsatisfactory meal of dry bread forgotten in his hand, Yar Mohammad had watched the soaking horses clatter past, their riders' shouts interrupting his thoughts. He had watched their leader pound on the haveli door, demanding admittance for his men and for a carved palanquin carried by bearers wearing scarlet loincloths and turbans.

These armed men, he knew, could be on no errand of mercy. He remembered the previous afternoon at the British camp, when he had hurried from the horse lines to Shafi Sahib's neat tent.

"I have seen something," he'd said as he entered, his eyes roving to a new feature of Shafi Sahib's tent, a string bed in one corner where a man lay, breathing heavily, his face covered in a poultice of boiled leaves.

"Speak," Shafi Sahib had replied from where he sat on his own bed near the door. His prayer beads dangling from his fingers, he had gestured toward the figure on the bed. "You may speak in front of him. That is Ahmad, Saboor's servant."

Yar Mohammad willed himself not to stare at the injured man who, if he lived, would forever wear the mark of shame on his face. He imagined himself in the man's place, with rough hands holding him down on his stomach, and other hands jerking his head back by the hair while the swordsman prepared to bring down his heavy sword. Who could not have respect for such a man who would sacrifice so much?

"I have seen a great dust cloud enter the city and surround Shaikh Waliullah's haveli," Yar Mohammad began.

Shafi Sahib's beads ceased their clicking. "Go on."

"After that, the vision became unclear. Something seemed to come from the haveli and pass out through the cloud. I am almost sure there was a snake somewhere nearby, but all I can say for certain is that I saw the dust cloud."

Shafi Sahib frowned at the wall of his tent, his eyes moving as if he were looking at something Yar Mohammad could not see. Yar Mohammad allowed himself a glance toward the man in the corner. Faced with such a punishment, would he, like Saboor's servant, have refused to speak?

"As you know," Shafi Sahib said, "a cloud of dust signifies an emergency." He closed his eyes and rubbed his forehead. "As it happens, Shaikh Waliullah is to be absent from his house all tomorrow morning. I suggest you go into the city at dawn, and keep watch outside the haveli door until Shaikh Sahib returns."

Yar Mohammad stiffened. "Will there be danger?"

"Of that I am not certain," Shafi Sahib had replied. "But, Yar Mohammad," he added, smiling, "it is you, not I, who received the little vial. If it is His will, Allah Most Gracious will keep you safe."

A crowd began to collect in the rain as the horsemen pounded upon the carved door of Qamar Haveli.

Tightness in Yar Mohammad's chest told him that this was indeed the emergency of his dream. These men had certainly come in search of the child Saboor, intending to take him as a hostage to the Citadel. They also must intend to take Memsahib, as she was now the child's stepmother. Why else would an elegant palanquin with a team of bearers have followed the horsemen inside?

The horsemen had carried swords and matchlocks. Armed with only his curved kukri knife, he would be useless.

The crowd at the door grew larger. Raised voices argued over the family's response to this new crisis. Would the Shaikh perform magic again? Would the Maharajah punish him? As he listened, coils of terror wrapped themselves about Yar Mohammad's heart. What unknown, dangerous work had been entrusted to him? What if, unsure of his mission, he made a mistake so terrible that he endangered them all?

Coolies passed his doorway, bent beneath heavy loads of charcoal and rags. Horses trotted by, their riders wrapped in dripping shawls. A picture rose in Yar Mohammad's clouded mind of Shaikh Waliullah and Shafi Sahib seated side by side in the upstairs room at Qamar Haveli. *"You and no one else,"* the Shaikh had told him, while Shafi Sahib nodded his agreement, *"will know when the time has come to act."*

Yar Mohammad stepped onto the wet stones and started toward the Delhi Gate. He would go back to Shalimar, to Shafi Sahib. Some day, perhaps, he would be braver, would know how and when to act, but this time he needed advice.

He had not taken three steps before a familiar-looking red-haired man hurried past him, followed by a stumbling figure in a stained burqa. The red-haired man's eyes shifted from side to side as he walked, as if he were afraid of being observed. On his wet shoulder lay a sleeping baby.

The man was Allahyar, the servant who had conducted Yar Mohammad to meet the Shaikh and Shafi Sahib, a day that still rang in Yar Mohammad's memory. The sleeping baby was, without question, Saboor Baba. And, if he were not mistaken about her manner of walking, the struggling figure in the filthy burqa was the English memsahib.

As she hastened past him toward the great stone gateway, the woman lifted the edge of her burqa away from a pair of ruined slippers. Oh, yes, it was Memsahib. No woman of the city would reveal her ankles thus. He must warn her not to give herself away! Uncertain no more, he fixed his eyes on her back and lengthened his stride.

Men and animals crowded the street near the old public bath, blocking his way. Afraid he might lose sight of the odd trio, he elbowed other men aside, bruising his shin on a fruit seller's stall, jostling a blind man's hand from his guide's shoulder. Then, he was through the gate and past the heaving crowd at the entrance to the caravanserai, the rest house of travelers. The crowd thinned, and there they were again, the redheaded man, the lady, and the dozing child.

As he drew breath to call out to Allahyar, Yar Mohammad found himself flung abruptly aside by an outstretched arm as a wide old palanquin drove past, its bearers shouting warnings as they ran. Recovering his balance, he looked ahead in time to see it halt and Memsahib's burqa-clad figure climb inside. As he began, panting, to close the distance between them, he saw Allahyar thrust the baby inside and slide the door shut.

Still running, he watched helplessly as the bearers lifted the poles to their shoulders and started off again in the direction of the Delhi road. Desperate, he searched the crowd for a sign of Allahyar, but the redheaded man had vanished. As the chill rain soaked through his thin clothes, Yar Mohammad began to trudge resolutely along the road behind the speeding palanquin, his shoulders hunched against the cold.

S O intent had Yar Mohammad been on following the three figures before him that he failed to notice two men who stood in the crowded shelter of the Delhi Gate, staring after Allahyar and his companions. He missed seeing a smartly dressed eunuch turn to a lanky, sallow-faced young man, and gesture with long arms toward the sleeping bundle on the man's shoulder.

"I know that child," Gurbashan said excitedly, ignoring the water dripping from the end of his nose. "I would know him anywhere."

He put his mouth next to the young man's ear. "It does not matter how he has come to be on the road in the company of servants," he whispered. "That is the child Saboor. I am telling you, it is he. How could I fail to know him after I spent four days taking him to the Maharajah's camp? I recognized him once before, whatever they may say, and I have now recognized him again."

"Shall we follow them?" asked the young man dubiously, staring after the stumbling woman.

"No," replied the eunuch. "I know where they are going. Why give only information, when we can present Saboor himself to the Maharajah and get the full reward? I know exactly how to get the brat. Come with me."

I T was late afternoon before the eunuch Gurbashan and the sallow young man had made inquiries at a certain narrow alley in the city. They now stood in a damp mist, by a low door, jostled by noisy strangers, waiting for the man they sought, while music floated from the adjoining houses and the pungent smell of perfumes mixed with the wet filth of the street.

"I do not like this," the young man said, his feet dancing nervously on the stones. "I do not like this at all."

"If you do not like it," snapped Gurbashan, looking hastily behind him, "then be gone. I will keep all the reward for myself."

A narrow-faced man stood before them, studying them with lifeless eyes. Although he was not old, he had no front teeth. Behind him stood a boy whose face was round and ruddy beneath a layer of dirt. Both were dressed in rags. The narrow-faced man and the boy waited, saying nothing, gazing hungrily at the eunuch's clothes.

"I understand," said Gurbashan, drawing himself up, "that you are well versed in the stealing of children."

The man offered no reply. The boy behind him stared.

"I want to know how good you are." The eunuch lowered his eyes and poked the ground in front of him with a sandaled foot. "We desire the services of someone who can do what we need."

The man drew his lips back, revealing more toothless gums. His hair was matted and dusty. The ruddy-faced boy smirked.

"I have stolen more than thirty children," the man replied. His lisping voice was as flat as his eyes. "I sell them for labor, or I sell them, especially the girls, to these places."

He tilted his head toward a row of open-windowed houses, the only ones in the city where women were not hidden but displayed.

"Some," he added, "I sell to the beggars."

Perspiration gleamed on the sallow forehead of the eunuch's companion.

The dead-eyed man shrugged, palm up. "Why is your friend so afraid? He is too old for my services. Besides, it is not I who deforms the children." He pointed with his thumb at an impossibly twisted man lying in a doorway. "It is others who break their bones to arouse the sympathy of the pious. They know how to—"

The eunuch hastily raised his hands. "How do you work?"

"The work takes skill," the man answered. "I know how to enter a house silently, in the darkness. I can drug a child without killing it." His half smile disappeared. "The children I steal do not cry out."

Gurbashan's companion gulped noisily. The eunuch scratched his head, his eyes on the cobblestones. After a time, he nodded. "All right," he agreed, "but remember, if the baby is not delivered in perfect condition, you will get no money."

"You told me you would frighten the child thieves with threats," protested the sallow-faced youth as Gurbashan propelled him away, a long arm about his shoulders. "You said you would warn them that they would be tortured to death by the Maharajah's soldiers if Saboor Baba died."

"When did I say that? I never said such a thing," snapped the eunuch, turning to look quickly behind him as they reached the alley's
end and rounded the corner into a wide lane.

"*WHAT?*" Lord Auckland's face, reflected in the silver table orna-
ments, had turned crimson. "You say the girl was not there when you
called at the Shaikh's house? You say she had gone off without a word
on some native errand, when she knew perfectly well that you were
coming to fetch her?"

His jowls quivering, he glared at Macnaghten. "They must have
hidden her somewhere in the house. Why did you not protest, demand that they produce her? If she were not there, why did you not
insist on having someone take you to her?"

Macnaghten speared a piece of fish with his fork before replying.
"Your lordship may have forgotten," he said evenly, "that natives of
the Shaikh's class seclude their women. It was, therefore, impossible
for me to go to Miss Givens. It also seemed to me—although here I
must rely on my experience with natives—that the Shaikh was telling
the truth."

It was true. As surprised as he had been at the girl's absence, he had
not questioned the Shaikh's promise that Miss Givens would, God
willing, present herself at the British camp four days from today. The
man was clearly someone of importance among the natives. He had
spoken with unmistakable authority.

"Shaikh Waliullah has given me his word that Miss Givens will call
on you and your lady sisters four days from today when this camp
reaches the city of Kasur." Macnaghten watched Lord Auckland push
potatoes angrily onto his fork. "I therefore take full responsibility for
her safe arrival, barring, of course, some unforeseen accident upon
the road." He raised his hands. "I assume that she will then remain
with the camp for the return journey to Calcutta."

Aides murmured at the far end of the table. "Four days from now,"
observed Lord Auckland darkly, "you will not be at this camp. *You*
will be partway to Kabul with the army."

Macnaghten's appetite left him. It was no use talking to Lord
Auckland; the man was an ass. He put down his knife and fork and
refused the rest of the dishes. His toes wriggling inside his shoes, he
waited for dinner to end.

SHAFI Sahib let out a gentle sigh. "Yar Mohammad," he repeated,
"you must take the road to Kasur." The string bed creaked under

him. "I am certain that Memsahib has taken Saboor Baba to his father. She must have done so—there is no sign of her at this camp."

Yar Mohammad said nothing. At a loss, unable to keep up with Memsahib's palanquin, the groom had followed the road as far as Shalimar, then stopped at the British camp, hoping to find her there. He had waited for hours, posting himself near the guarded entrance in the red wall. As night fell, he had gone to the back of the red compound and entered by the kitchen gate, to discover Dittoo sleeping by a cooking fire.

"No," Dittoo had said, shaking his head, "Memsahib has not returned."

Yar Mohammad was weary. His head ached from trying to decide what to do.

"Go, brother," Shafi Sahib told him. "Go now. You must travel all night. With luck, you will find a bullock cart that will carry you. But you must go. Otherwise, you will not find them on the road tomorrow morning."

Chapter 31

In a corner room at the Citadel, the Maharajah leaned from his low bed and spat into a carved silver bowl.

He spoke with effort. "What am I to believe, Aziz? Is Saboor at his house in the city, ill with smallpox as his family claims, or is he at the British camp, as the eunuch insists?"

"Only Allah knows," replied the Chief Minister tenderly.

The Maharajah coughed weakly, his eye closed. Azizuddin drew closer to the bed.

"I hope he is not at his house," the Maharajah said. "If he is anywhere on the road or even at the British camp, Gurbashan's child stealers will be sure to find him."

"Child stealers?" The Chief Minister's neck went rigid. "You have allowed the eunuch to hire child stealers?"

"I am old, Aziz. I am weary of everything." The Maharajah shivered. "Today, I have not the heart even to tease the British. I need my Saboor."

"Ah, Maharaj," Aziz said softly, a hand on the bedcovers, "you are tired only because you are unwell. Why, only two days ago we were—"

"Leave it, Aziz," his king interrupted, turning his head away. "Without my Saboor, I will not live another three months."

After some time, the old man's labored breathing became regular. Aziz signaled for a servant to take his place beside the bed, then he stole quietly away.

"STOP, stop!" Mariana thumped with her fist on the roof over her head. She could wait no longer to relieve herself. "Get off, Saboor," she snapped, pushing the little boy from her lap. "You are making Mariana feel worse.

"Oh, dear," she murmured as he crawled away, his face puckered into a baby glare. Feeling a pang of guilt at her impatience, she slid open the panel and looked out. They were passing a place where thorn bushes grew thickly along the road. This was exactly what she needed. "Stop, I say," she repeated, pounding again. "Stop!"

She pushed a tangle of curls from her face. Yesterday, after their escape from Qamar Haveli, she had balled up her filthy burqa and hurled it from the moving palanquin. Since then, dressed in the rust-colored silks Safiya Sultana had given her, she had entertained Saboor in a creaking box with no view of the passing landscape and no idea where they would finally stop. This was not at all like the long journey from Calcutta to Simla with Uncle Adrian and Aunt Claire. She missed Uncle Adrian's arrangements—tea and coffee, and regular opportunities for the ladies to retire discreetly into stands of bushes along the way.

Dear Uncle Adrian. So much had happened since she had last written him. How would her aunt and uncle respond when they learned the truth? She imagined Aunt Claire being carried insensible to her room, leaving Uncle Adrian to sit alone, shaking his head, Mariana's explanatory letter in his hand.

But for all its fright and discomfort, what a time this had been! Surely Uncle Adrian would understand the adventure of it. No Englishwoman could ever have been prepared for marriage by Indian queens, or seen a case of fatal snakebite being cured by a Shaikh. No one Mariana knew had stayed with natives while traveling in India, but she had. Last night, Safiya's female relatives had crowded around her in the large village house where she had been taken. Some had asked indecent, prying questions about her clothes and habits, and some had stared, veils drawn over their mouths and noses, as if she were some evil fairy. One narrow-eyed woman had even shooed her own children away, looking fearfully over her shoulder, as if Mariana's presence alone were enough to poison everyone in the house. How could Safiya Sultana be related to people like that?

The palanquin had stopped at last. She peered out again. Her bearers had understood her needs, and chosen well. It was a pity she had nothing to give the nameless sirdar bearer, for he had stopped in a neat clearing where upturned stones had been arranged near a heap of cold ashes. Surrounding the clearing, thorn trees and bushes offered her their protection.

"Go to the bearers, there's an angel," she said, patting Saboor on his back as he clambered after her out of the palki. "Take him to do soo-soo," she ordered, as she started for the bushes.

Like all the bearers along the route, the men had turned their backs the instant she emerged, but they welcomed Saboor when he danced over to where they had squatted down to rest. She stepped carefully, skirting the largest of the bushes, looking for a good hiding place.

The bearers' voices filtering through the bushes grew faint.

She crouched down gratefully. This evening, if all went well, she would arrive at Kasur. Once there she would ask the palanquin bearers to wait, she would kiss Saboor good-bye, and then hand him over to his father.

She shifted her feet among the leaves. There would be no need for conversation with Hassan, or any long farewells. She would simply climb back into the palanquin and return to the British camp. Once there, she would somehow live without Saboor or Harry Fitzgerald.

The camp should not be difficult to find. After leaving Shalimar, it would, like her, have followed the road to Kasur. Moving over much-traveled terrain with no rain since the downpour on the day of her escape with Saboor, it would most likely arrive there when she did, in three days' time. Only heaven knew what the British party would say to her when she reappeared, out of nowhere, four days late, having missed Mr. Macnaghten at the Shaikh's house.

A squirrel leaped from branch to branch above her head. It was too late to worry about what would be said to her when she rejoined the camp. Of course, the Shaikh's family expected her merely to call upon the Eden ladies in order to assure everyone of her good health, and then return to the haveli without Saboor. But once she was safely at camp, she had no intention of leaving again. Sixteen days of adventure were more than enough.

Not even Safiya Sultana could persuade Mariana to spend the rest of her days in a walled city house with a group of native ladies.

She smiled. Her departure from the haveli had not been graceful, but it had been effective. Yes, the queens, Shaikh Waliullah, Safiya Sultana, and the aunts were entirely behind her now.

Soon, even her lovely little Saboor would be only a memory. She sighed.

Ants marched past her, toward the carcass of a beetle. What would a future palanquin ride be like without Saboor's edgy little self, all elbows and feet, scrambling over her, trying to open the panel, insisting that she bounce him on her lap?

As she half stood, fumbling with the rope of her Turkish trousers, shouting erupted from the clearing. Through the thicket, raised staccato voices reached her.

Something was wrong. She swiftly retraced her steps, her heartbeat quickening. Near the edge of the bushes, she stopped.

A man's voice spoke with gritty authority. "We want her gold. That is all."

Thieves! Where was Saboor? She leaned forward, desperately afraid to make a sound.

Another man spoke, closer by. He punctuated his words with hollow thumps, as if he were slapping the top of the palanquin with an open palm.

"We wish you no harm," he said, his voice a tenor whine. "We only want your money and your jewelry. If you throw them out of the palki, we will leave you in peace. Give us your gold. That is all we want, nothing more."

"You fool," barked the first voice, "she is not in the palki. You are talking to yourself, Suraj."

Mariana held her breath.

"Oh, Begum Sahib," the first man rasped, raising his voice, "come out of the bushes."

From his tone, it seemed he could see her, that he knew where she was. She strained her eyes through the undergrowth, but could see nothing. She stood still, all of her being focused on quieting her breathing.

"Come out. We will not harm you."

Sounds of scuffling and grunting were followed by a sharp male cry. "If you come out now," the first man added, the roughness in his voice turning to poison, "we will not harm the child."

Saboor's wail started on a low note and rose swiftly to a high pitch, where it remained, drawn out, wavering like an infant version of the call to prayer.

Allah-hu-Akbar, God is Great. A thorny branch lay at Mariana's feet. It was too long. She jerked it from its place, braced her slippered foot against it, and with one sharp motion, snapped it in two. It was not much of a weapon, but it would have to do.

The branch over her head, she rushed, screaming, from her hiding place and into the open, as an agonized shriek from one of the thieves drowned out the sound of Saboor's wail.

The bearers huddled in a terrified circle on the ground, their arms protecting their heads. Beside the palanquin, his weapons clanking, a small man in dirty clothing had turned toward the sound of the cry, Saboor in his arms.

Two more thieves, one of them bloody and sobbing, backed away toward the road, flailing their arms as if warding off an invisible demon. The injured one began to run jerkily, bent double, clutching at his leg. Shreds of red-stained cloth hung from his shoulder. Blood ran into the dust from behind his knee.

"Put the child down," shouted a voice Mariana knew well. "Put down the child and be gone! Sons of shame. Pigs! Dogs!"

The thieves did as they were told. The small man beside the palanquin dropped Saboor to the dirt and ran, his clothes fluttering, across the clearing and onto the road without stopping to help his friends. The third man turned and followed him, dragging away their gabbling companion.

Mariana threw down her stick, knelt in the dust, and gathered Saboor, still howling, into her arms. When she looked up, the thieves had vanished. The bearers now gaped at someone sitting on one of the upturned stones, his head buried in his hands.

It was Yar Mohammad, of all people, the tall groom from the British camp. Beside him on the ground lay a heavy, wicked-looking knife, the blood on its downward-curving blade filmed with dust. He was weeping.

YAR Mohammad did not look up at the sound of approaching feet, but he saw before him the mud-stained slippers of the memsahib, guardian of Saboor, whom he had last seen clothed in a filthy burqa at the Delhi Gate days earlier, and who had just now run, wild faced and screaming, from the bushes, her veil fallen to her shoulders, a thorny branch in her hands. The slippers were pointed toward him. They waited.

He would not weep before a woman. Heavy with shame, his eyes on the ground, he got politely to his feet. Perhaps she would go away soon and leave him to his grief. He needed to forget the sickening feeling of the knife as it cut down through the flesh of the brigand's shoulder, separating muscle from bone. The act had felt like an execution. Worse, in his horror, while sweeping his knife sideways and out of the way, he had cut again, this time slicing the tendons at the back of the man's leg.

The memsahib seated herself on a stone in front of him. Glancing at her, he saw that her face, still gray from fright, was now filling with curiosity. From her lap, Saboor Baba regarded him intently.

"You have done a brave thing, Yar Mohammad," she said in Urdu, frowning up at him, "but how have you come to be here? Why are you not at camp, at the horse lines?"

"I have followed you since yesterday," he said, then hesitated. "I thought I had lost you until I saw the palki, then the baba."

She looked puzzled. "Why have you followed us? How do you know Shaikh Waliullah's palanquin?"

How should he answer? He had walked most of the night and part of the morning, looking on the road for that very palki.

She pointed to the ground. "Sit," she said. "Speak."

He lowered himself to the ground and extended his arms over his knees.

He watched his fingers pick indecisively at one another. She was the Guardian. After what she had just done to save Saboor, he could have no doubt of that truth. Perhaps it was his duty to tell her of his dreams, of his wondrous meeting with the Shaikh.

He sighed. The story would take some time to tell, and he was not a teller of stories. "There is so much . . ." he began.

"There is time," she said kindly. "Begin at the beginning."

He would not begin at the very beginning, for Shaikh Waliullah had forbidden him to speak of the vision in which he received into his hand the small ceramic vial.

"One morning at the British camp," he began, watching a beetle hurrying over a dried leaf, "I had a dream of smoke, and of a lioness. . . ."

When he had finished, the Englishwoman stared off into the distance for a long time without speaking.

"A lioness," she said at last, her voice sounding far away. "Shafi Sahib, interpreter of dreams. That is why I felt I was being watched. . . ." Her voice trailed off.

"Tell me one more thing," she said, sitting straighter. "Why were you weeping?"

Yar Mohammad bit his lip. "I did not mean to hurt the thief so badly." He glanced to where his kukri knife lay in the dust. "He will never walk again. If he had been a horse with that wound, I would have been forced to cut his throat."

•   •   •

THE British camp had done its traveling for the day. Hours ago, teams of coolies had erected the durbar tent and the red compound wall. Since then, the dead-eyed man and the dirty-faced boy had waited, squatting beside the avenue in the shade of the durbar tent, watching the folded entrance to the red compound.

The boy spat into the dust. "We should have made that eunuch come with us, Jagoo. He would easily recognize the child. How do we know we have not missed him?"

"Be quiet." Jagoo turned his flat gaze on the boy. "We haven't missed him. The eunuch swore that he is here. Stop giving advice and watch for that bent-over manservant the eunuch described. He will lead us to the brat."

Since yesterday, they had traveled with the camp, walking anonymously toward Kasur, lost among a crowd of laborers and baggage animals. As soon as the camp had been erected, they had posted themselves at the back of the compound and watched the kitchen entrance. They had seen not even a glimpse of the child.

"Perhaps he is ill," Jagoo had said. "Whoever has him is being careful, keeping him out of sight."

They had stolen their food by day and slept in the open at night, making their own small fire with pilfered charcoal. Now, as they waited by the durbar tent, interesting people passed by them on the avenue. Some were children, ripe for stealing, but none answered the description of the child Saboor for whom the eunuch was willing to pay such a rich price.

"We have missed him," insisted the boy.

"You know nothing." Jagoo's voice was less certain than before.

The boy scratched himself. "I know something," he said as they watched a passing bullock cart. "I know that Hassan Ali Khan, the father of Saboor, has been sent out of Lahore on the Maharajah's work. And I know where he is."

Jagoo stopped chewing his wad of betel and tobacco. "What is this? What have you not told me?"

"The child's father is at Kasur. Before we left the city, while you were asleep, people were talking outside our door. They said Hassan Sahib, the son of Shaikh Waliullah, has gone to Kasur to get tax money for the Maharajah. He is not more than ten miles from here."

Jagoo's blow caught the boy cruelly on his temple, knocking him sideways against the canvas of the durbar tent.

"The eunuch is a fool," he rasped, as the boy crawled to his knees, a hand to his head, "and so are you!"

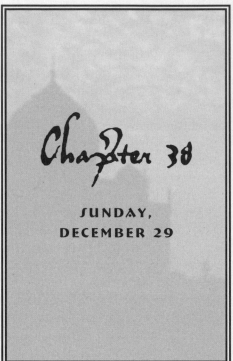

Chapter 38

It was dark by the time Mariana's palanquin stopped outside the little walled city of Kasur. She half listened, yawning, while her bearers asked a passerby the direction of Hassan's tents.

"An-nah!" Saboor murmured in her ear as he tugged at one of the enameled bangles on her wrist.

Soon she would be back at the British camp, back in familiar clothes, although nothing there would ever be the same as before.

How exciting, how filled with promise, even the dullest camp day had seemed only a short time ago! Now, after the scandal, even the White Rabbit would find it hard to take her part. Lord Auckland, she knew, was lost to her forever. She was not speaking to the Eden sisters. If she were lucky, Major Byrne and the doctor would ignore her. If she were unlucky, they would make unkind remarks. Mr. Macnaghten, thank goodness, had already left for Afghanistan. But there was no sense worrying about it. For all the unpleasantness it promised her, she could not deny that the British camp was where she belonged.

Now, at least, they would stop telling her to avoid the natives.

She could always count on Dittoo, Yar Mohammad, and Munshi Sahib. And there was another ray of hope. According to Yar Mohammad, the great Shafi Sahib was staying at the camp. It was maddening that the interpreter of dreams had been so nearby all along, attached somehow to the army or the government in the curious way of natives, and she had not known. Perhaps, if she asked him, he would interpret her dream of the guided ship. Perhaps he would give her hope for the bleak days to come.

"Come here, Saboor," she said, beckoning the child who had crawled to the foot of the palanquin. "See?"

When he crept back, she dropped her thin silk veil over his face, and then pulled it off in a quick gesture, watching his smile broaden, waiting for his bubbling laugh.

It was Shafi Sahib, of course, who had sent the message, delivered by Yar Mohammad, on the night she had first taken Saboor. "*You have done well. Wait for your instructions. Tell no one what you have done.*" She tried to imagine his face. Did he, like Shaikh Waliullah, radiate a mysterious power?

According to Yar Mohammad, Shafi Sahib was a Punjabi, and the old Shaikh's childhood friend. It could be that he had already left the British camp, to spend time in Lahore with the Shaikh. How disappointing that would be!

The palanquin began to move. Tired of her game, Saboor had climbed onto her lap in order to pull on her gold chain. Cooing to him, she unwound his fingers, remembering Shaikh Waliullah's house, and the view from the ladies' upper window. Perhaps, at this moment, the Shaikh and Shafi Sahib, both wearing tall headdresses, conversed in his courtyard by the painted portico, while the Shaikh's female relations sat together on the sheet-covered floor of the upstairs room.

She sighed. The Shaikh's sister had been so strong, so motherly. Mariana would have liked, just once, to have wrapped her arms about Safiya Sultana's bulky form.

As for the Shaikh, she now understood that she was more to blame than he was for her reckless marriage to Hassan. But even that did not matter now.

Perhaps it was a good thing that it would take months and months for the now army-less camp to return to Calcutta. She needed time to decide on her future. Tied to a native stranger, unable to marry, should she return to England and live quietly with her family? Or should she remain in Calcutta and brave the gossip, hoping to see Fitzgerald again, a man she could never wed?

The palanquin thumped to the ground.

With a little sigh, Mariana swung her feet out through the open panel, and stood, waiting while Saboor, who liked to do it himself, clambered out on his own.

The night was cold, the air sharp. Stars made a dazzling tapestry overhead. A large tent with a curving roof loomed before them. Outside, by a flickering fire, two men leaned on bolsters, a smoking hookah between them. Seeing her, one of them stopped speaking in midsentence.

Servants of various sizes stood around her palanquin. As Mariana hoisted Saboor to her hip, all gaped in momentary astonishment, then spun about, turning their backs to her as men everywhere had done since she left Lahore.

"Saboor Baba," she heard one of them murmur. "The memsahib has brought Saboor Baba."

Ordering her bearers to wait, she paused by the entrance, then, coughing to announce her presence, pushed aside the door hanging and entered.

The tent was vacant and icy cold. Sandalwood hung in the air, igniting her memory. She hesitated. Someone had followed her inside, a lamp glowing in his hand. She turned.

His eyes on the child in her arms, Hassan Ali Khan put the lamp down and approached her, his hands extended to take Saboor, his face a mask of tenderness.

Saboor immediately wrapped his arms around his father's neck. Hassan kissed him several times, then frowned at Mariana, one hand stroking his son's small back. "Why have you brought him here? What has happened?"

His gaze was as intense as it had been the night of their wedding. He was lighter skinned than she remembered. She saw that his nose was crooked, as if it had once been broken. She saw that his naked feet were long. They were not as beautiful as his hands.

"Four days ago, after you left the haveli," she answered, shivering from the cold, "armed men came from the Citadel to take Saboor away. To save him, your aunt Safiya had him lowered in a basket from an upper window."

A string bed stood in one corner of the tent. Hassan sat Saboor on the bed, then bent over a trunk at its foot. He straightened, an embroidered woolen shawl in his hands. He held it out. "From a window? Then?"

On her shoulders, the shawl smelled of tobacco leaves. "The basket was lowered from a window to a sweetmeat shop, where your father's servant Allahyar picked him up. Pretending to be Allahyar's wife, I followed them through the Delhi Gate. Then your family's palanquin came and I got into it with Saboor."

He picked Saboor up again, and pointed to the bed. "Why don't you sit down?"

"No." She backed away. Let this moment be over quickly. Later there would be time to grieve for Saboor, to remember. "I must leave."

Hassan, too, wore a shawl. Thrown over his long coat, it fell in elegant, finely embroidered folds over his shoulders and down his back. He jogged Saboor gently up and down, his cheek against his son's. "You should rest," he said, as if he had not heard her. "And I must ask you, what has happened to your burqa? Why was your veil not on your head, just now, when you got out of the palki?"

"My veil? My burqa?" She stared. What did her clothes matter?

His tone developed an unpleasant edge. "You were not properly concealed. My servants saw you. My friend saw you."

She had worn no burqa on the journey. That explained why the women had stared so, why the men had turned away from her. Palki bearers and servants had seen her without it. Safiya Sultana's friends, her relatives, her *male* relatives had all seen her uncovered.

It was too late to argue over customs. Besides, none of those people would see her again. "I fell down on my way out of the city," she said tersely. She reached under her borrowed shawl and pulled out her loosening braid. "The burqa was soaking wet and filthy. I threw it out of the palanquin."

Elongated by the lamplight, his shadow loomed over her. "You cannot walk about uncovered." He fixed his eyes on her as if he were teaching her something important. "You are my wife. If you behave like a foreigner, you bring shame on me, on my father, on my family."

"*Shame?* But I *am* a—"

"Foreigners allow their women to wear indecent clothes, like that thing you wore at the Maharajah's dinner when you made that shocking announcement before the court. People are still laughing. . . ." His voice trailed off.

Mariana's cheeks warmed as she remembered the deep curtsy she had made to the Maharajah in her low-cut gown. "I do not care what people think of me," she snapped, putting out her chin. "I care only for Saboor."

All she wanted now was to be left alone. She stepped toward Hassan, and touched Saboor's cheek. "Good-bye, my little lambkin," she murmured.

She had said the same words to her little brother when she kissed him for the last time. Like Saboor, Ambrose had been asleep, but his face had been dry and hot, not healthy and glowing like Saboor's. Forcing grief aside, she faced Hassan.

Her tongue felt thick. She sniffed, wanting to wipe her nose on her veil, aware that her face was smudged with dust from the road. "I am leaving now," she said stiffly. "You will not see me again."

As she started away, he took a step toward her and caught her arm. "It's night," he said brusquely, pulling her from the doorway with one hand. "You cannot travel now." He watched her over Saboor's head, as if uncertain of what she might do next. "Call on your people tomorrow on your way back to Lahore."

"Lahore? No!" Mariana tugged her arm away. Her braid had unraveled. She raked her hair back with her fingers. "I am not going back to Lahore," she said loudly, glaring at him. "I am going to the British camp right now!"

"Do not attempt to leave this tent." His voice had become level, his eyes as unreadable as closed doors. "I am dismissing your bearers and setting a guard outside. You will go nowhere until tomorrow morning." He sighed, then lifted the door hanging. "A servant will bring you food and hot water."

"You cannot make me stay behind while my people return to Calcutta! You—"

The hanging closed behind him with a dusty thump.

The little lamp bathed the tent in a dim light. Mariana's very bones ached from four days of palanquin travel. Wrapped in Hassan's shawl, she sat down on the bed.

How dare he criticize her and tell her what to do!

She had hoped to leave before there was time to feel the loss of Saboor, but now hurt overwhelmed her, reminding her of the agony she had suffered after little Ambrose's death. Why, knowing the risk, had she given her heart to a child who was not, and could never be, hers?

Voices murmured outside the tent. Hassan must have taken Saboor outside to his friend. She would never let him hear her weep. She pushed a fist into her mouth and bit down on her knuckle, her face crumpling as Saboor's had done that first evening in her tent.

It was green in Sussex. She would find things to do there. She would help Papa with his sermons, and visit Charlotte and Spencer and Baby Freddie. She would sketch or study singing, or the pianoforte. She would not even mind changing the flowers or counting the silver. Half-married to someone she would never know, she would learn to live without a nice English husband or fair-haired babies of her own.

"Memsahib, Memsahib!" The hoarse summons of a servant came from outside, accompanied by the sound of a tray being put down. "Your food has come!"

YUSUF Bhatti did not look up when Hassan returned to the fire, his baby in his arms, nor did he mention the raised female voice that had come from Hassan's tent. Poor fellow, married by his father's command to that odd foreigner who had already behaved so badly in front of the court. Everyone knew about the woman, about her speech to the Maharajah. How could she have done it?

Now she had shouted at Hassan loudly enough to be heard by Yusuf, the guard, and all the servants.

When she had entered Hassan's tent, her face uncovered, her veil falling, her body moving suggestively under her thin silks, Yusuf had looked away, mortified for his friend. Even now, he could not meet Hassan's eyes.

But there was one thing he should say. As a friend, he must tell Hassan what he had learned.

"Did you see the hill man waiting outside?" He gestured with his chin toward a long man who crouched silently by the doorway.

Hassan, who had been murmuring to his son, raised his head.

"His name is Yar Mohammad. He is a groom at the British camp. He is acquainted with Shafi Sahib and with your father."

"He is?" Hassan turned to look.

Yusuf pulled a bolster toward himself and leaned against it. "After Saboor and the foreign lady left your house four days ago, someone sent Yar Mohammad to protect them on the road. He says he followed the palanquin carrying Saboor and the—ah—lady all the way from Lahore to Kasur."

His face averted, Hassan leaned over the child in his lap and drew one finger along a pattern in the carpet.

Yusuf sucked in his breath. Hassan must be thinking of the trail of shock and embarrassment his foreign wife would have left behind on that journey. Why had he not thought to leave the woman out of the story until the end?

"On the road, Yar Mohammad heard shouts coming from a clearing," he continued. "He went to investigate, and found three armed brigands robbing your family's palanquin. One of them had laid hold of Saboor and was threatening to hurt him if the lady did not turn over her jewelry, but the lady was not in the palki, as he believed."

Hassan's finger froze on the carpet.

Yusuf grunted in sympathy. "The other two thieves were standing with their backs to the road. Yar Mohammad ran up behind them and pulled a knife. As he was dealing with them, the lady charged, screaming, from the bushes, waving a thorny branch over her head. Without hesitating, she ran straight for the man who held Saboor."

Hassan tightly wrapped both his arms around his son. He shook his head. "I am not surprised," he murmured.

When the food came, they ate without speaking while the child drowsed beside his father. Later, with the child asleep and Hassan's eyes heavy, Yusuf signaled a servant to cover them with a quilt where they lay.

Yusuf stared into the flames. It was now clear that the English-woman's bold action in taking Saboor from the Golden Temple had not been accidental. She might be shockingly behaved, but she had courage. Like a wild animal, this woman would kill to protect those she loved.

He called for another quilt. Still, he thought as he stretched out, his head on the bolster, it seemed impossible that the honor of guarding the child Saboor had fallen not to him, Hassan's soldier friend, but to this uncivilized female.

"Foreigners," he said softly, shaking his head. "Foreigners."

"GET up!"

Something bumped against the string bed, tugging Mariana from sleep. "You must get up." The voice above her was urgent. "Something has happened."

Except for the starlight that shone in through the open doorway, the tent was pitch-dark. "Go away," she muttered, squeezing her eyes shut. "Leave me."

Hassan sat down on the edge of the bed, pinning her beneath the quilt. "Listen," he said, his words almost too rapid to understand. "Two strangers from Lahore have been asking for my camp. A villager overheard them talk of stealing a child. He says they are dangerous-looking men. He has come to ask for our protection for his own children, but it is not a village child they want. It is Saboor."

Awake now, Mariana stiffened under her quilt. "How can that be? No one knows he is here. Everyone thinks he's at Qamar Haveli, ill with smallpox."

"Not everyone," Hassan said harshly. "Why else would child thieves be looking for this place?"

She pulled her arms from the covers, then crossed them hastily over her chest to avoid touching him. "But why worry when your camp is full of armed men?"

She felt his eyes on her in the dark. "Child stealers hide during the day and work at night. They are silent and dangerous. You must take Saboor tonight. To the British camp," he added after a pause.

"The British camp?" She felt a rush of hope. "To stay? For how long?"

He turned away from her, toward the starlit doorway. "I don't know. If these child thieves fail, more will come. As long as the Maharajah lives, they will come."

She remembered him weeping silently beside her near the howitzers on the first day of the durbar.

Hassan leaned across her body. "My son," he said softly, "is more precious to me than my own life."

His face was near her breast. His tense weight and the burnt scent of his skin were making her dizzy. "Do not fear," she heard herself say, as she put a hand carefully on his embroidered sleeve. "I will take Saboor to the British camp."

He sat up and gripped her shoulders, his beautiful fingers tight on her bones. "Go now, before the child thieves come. Take Saboor across the Sutlej, to British territory. Hide him even there, especially when the camp is moving. Do you understand?"

His face was now very close to hers. She took a ragged breath, then nodded.

He stood, and started for the door. Mariana found her slippers and followed him in her tarnished silks, his tobacco-scented shawl over her shoulders. Outside, the ground was lit by a bright moon. Holding her back with an outstretched arm, Hassan gave an order, then moved off to fetch Saboor.

Soldiers and servants stood at attention, their backs to her. Even the bearers squatting beside the Shaikh's palanquin had turned away. She recognized the silent, shadowy figure by the doorway as Yar Mohammad.

"I will try to visit you," Hassan told her when he reappeared a moment later. "And," he added, as he put Saboor into her arms, "this time, you will have a proper escort, so there will be no need for you to be attacking highwaymen with sticks and branches."

He made a sound that could have been a laugh. She could not read his face. "Go," he said to the bearers.

THE fire outside Hassan's tent had long been cold by the time Jagoo and the ruddy-faced boy arrived. It was nearly dawn. Motionless, the boy strained his eyes in the darkness, waiting for Jagoo to return from his work.

He winced as an icy hand clamped his neck. Jagoo pointed silently toward the clearing where they had set their own small fire.

Jagoo's hands shook from cold as he lit the fire. A rancid smell came from him. His clothes bore fresh grease stains. He raised his lifeless eyes to the boy's. "The child is not there. Nor is the woman."

For the boy, any failure was painful, no matter who was to blame. He tensed his shoulders against a blow.

But Jagoo moved closer to the flames, instead. "When I did not find him with his father," he said, rubbing his arms, "I searched the tent." He drew back his lips and pointed through the scrub trees. "Go now, and see if the child sleeps with the servants."

Reluctantly, the boy stood, pulling his ragged shawl over his shoulders. "And if the child is not in the camp?"

The fire sputtered. "We will find him." Jagoo spoke without looking up. "Not tomorrow, but soon. We know where the father is. That is all we need to know."

"All we need to know? Why?"

Jagoo spat into the flames. "You ask too many questions. Go. If the child is not here, I will leave in the morning. While I am gone, you will watch for anyone leaving this camp."

Without another word, he stretched out on the ground and closed his eyes.

Chapter 39

**TUESDAY,
DECEMBER 30**

"What will you tell your friends now?" Mariana asked, an hour before dawn, as Dittoo, smiles wreathing his face, reached into the palanquin for Saboor. "You did say, after all, that you had sold him to Sirosh, the tailor."

"I will tell them, Begum Sahib, that Baba cried all the time and annoyed Sirosh's wife." Dittoo's grin broadened as Saboor reached up to pat his face. "I will say Sirosh forced me to take Baba back and return his money. My friends will not question me—they will only call me a fool."

"Be careful," Mariana cautioned as Dittoo set off toward the line of servants' cooking fires, Saboor under his arm.

She sat up and swung her feet out to the ground. Dittoo had called her Begum Sahib, a salutation reserved for married women. She had never seen him so happy. Was he happy for Saboor, or for her?

AT one o'clock that afternoon, she stood in the middle of her tent, fumbling her way into one of her gowns.

Having arrived well after midnight, she had then marched with the camp at 6:00 A.M., which had given her reason enough to sleep through breakfast. But now, as much as she dreaded it, she must go to lunch. She could no longer put off meeting the camp.

She bent stiffly, her stays biting into her, to tie her boots. Last night, with Saboor beside her in the palanquin, she had dreamed that she had stolen him from the Maharajah only moments before. In her dream she had regarded her future with a fearless calm. If she could only bottle that feeling of calm, she would take a spoonful of it every morning.

Her skirts smoothed, her bonnet tied, she stepped from her doorway and started resolutely toward the dining tent. It would be all right. Whatever they might say in private, the Eden ladies would never be unpleasant to her in public. She, on her part, would be civil, even though she had vowed never to speak to them again, after they refused to rescue her from her wedding.

"Miss Givens, how delightful to see you!" The White Rabbit did not look as delighted as he tried to sound. He swallowed, his Adam's apple bobbing, as he straightened from his bow. "May I escort you to the dining tent?" He offered her his arm.

Government officers murmured and elbowed one another as Mariana approached the dining table. When the Rabbit pulled out her chair, Major Byrne stood abruptly and stalked out, his exit punctuated by a quiet but distinct honk.

Seated near one end of the table, Mariana surveyed the company with growing unease. Dr. Drummond was there, and Lord Auckland; but of Miss Emily and Miss Fanny there was no sign.

A few empty seats from her, Dr. Drummond glanced in her direction without meeting her eyes. "It is a pity," he declared, "that the Eden ladies are both so unwell with coughs and fevers."

Unwell! So she, the pariah, was to be the only woman at table. Who knew how all these men would behave without the Eden sisters? Mariana searched the faces around her. Eyes moved rapidly away from hers.

A servant offered her a platter. Thankful for something to do, she helped herself to a mutton chop. What a pack of cowards these people were!

At the head of the table, Lord Auckland cleared his throat noisily. "Would you mind, Miss Givens," he said, addressing her at last, speaking through his nose, "wearing a pair of gloves the next time you come to a meal? I am finding it difficult to enjoy my lunch in the presence of such dirty hands."

Mariana looked down at her hands. The delicate tracery from

her wedding was still there, now faded to an unpleasant yellow, incongruous against the lace edging on her sleeves. She had forgotten all about it.

Someone sniggered.

Her chop turned to poison, Mariana dabbed her mouth with a faded napkin. "Certainly, Lord Auckland," she said clearly, before pushing back her chair.

Fury made her strong. In one motion, she rose to her feet and swept from the tent, her chin high.

YUSUF stretched his legs on the carpet, careful to avoid knocking over the dishes from their afternoon meal. He raised a greasy hand. "Hassan, your cook has been resourceful, as always. I have eaten too much." A compliment often solicited the truth.

His curiosity about the lady wanted satisfying. He took an orange. "At least Saboor is safe," he continued. "It seems," he added carefully, spitting orange seeds into his hand, "that some of these foreigners have good hearts."

Beside him, Hassan stared southward, toward the Sutlej River. "Yes," he replied absently, "some of them have good hearts." He sat upright. "Yusuf, I must visit my son."

Hassan had seen his son only last night. Yusuf swallowed a mouthful of orange. "Well, then," he answered, "go today. By tomorrow the English and their camp will have crossed the Sutlej. Twenty miles is already a long return when your negotiations with the Kasuris succeed. After all, you have those people in a tight noose."

Hands outstretched over a water basin, Hassan nodded to his servant. "What do I care for the Kasuris and their treasure?" He shook water from his fingers. "Saboor may spend months in the British camp. He has already suffered at the hands of strangers. I must see for myself that he is comfortable and safe."

Yusuf nodded. He might be a soldier, but he was not stupid. Hassan clearly wished to see his new wife again, although he would never say so. Safe the child would certainly be, with that wild woman for company. As far as his comfort, a child could grow accustomed to anything. He, Yusuf, certainly had, raised in the cold of Kashmir by two uncles and a grandfather, with his mother dead and his father away, serving in the Maharajah's army.

"I am leaving now," Hassan was saying. "If Allah wills, I will enter the British camp by nightfall. If I find my baby comfortable and safe, I will bid him Godspeed and return here."

Yusuf rubbed his face and repressed a sigh. "Be careful, my friend.

Stay off the roads. If someone follows, you will lead him straight to your son."

"No one will follow me," Hassan replied, glancing sideways at Yusuf, "if I'm wearing your clothes and riding your horse."

Yusuf gave a snorting laugh. "And if you wear my clothes and ride my horse, then whose clothes am I to wear, and which horse am I to ride when I accompany you?"

Smiling at last, Hassan reached out and gripped Yusuf's outstretched hand.

AN hour later, the sun had dropped behind the branches of a dusty tree. Under the tree, Jagoo, the ruddy-faced boy, and a gaunt stranger with matted hair bent over a jumble of hoof- and footprints in the cracked soil.

The stranger straightened and squinted into the distance. "And these are the tracks you want me to follow?"

Jagoo turned his dead gaze on the boy, who nodded. "Yes," the boy told the stranger. "This is where the two men mounted before they rode away." He pointed south, in the direction of the river.

"Well?" Jagoo turned to the stranger. "Can you track them?"

"Of course," replied the stranger. "I can track a stolen cow through the walled city of Lahore. I told you that. There is no one in this area who can follow tracks as I can."

While Jagoo watched, the tracker squatted over the prints again. "I can tell you this," he said, looking up. "There are two riders. Both are gentlemen. Their shoes are not patched, and their footprints are regular. They are no low-caste people accustomed to carrying heavy loads. The first one has a slim foot. He is thinner than his friend, who is heavy. The heavy man's right foot turns in. As to the horses, one has a small cleft in its right rear hoof, and the other has a variation in its gait, tending to advance sideways from time to time."

Trailed by the ruddy-faced boy, Jagoo and the tracker walked rapidly away toward the southeast, their eyes on the ground, their unclean cotton garments flowing smoothly around them.

Chapter 40

Just before sunset, Hassan and Yusuf reined in their horses. Hassan stared ahead, a hand shading his eyes, then nudged his mare close to Yusuf's. "There," he said, pointing to a horizontal cloud of smoke and dust that lay over the flat line of the horizon.

Both men were armed. Hassan's pistol was serviceable, but his sword was better for show than for fighting. Yusuf had his own pistol, his triangular-bladed dagger with the hunting hawk carved into its blade, and a heavy curved sword hanging at his side. If it came to a fight, he preferred hand to hand.

Hassan breathed deeply as they kicked their horses and moved off again.

"First we will find Shafi Sahib," he said, "and then I will see my son."

"AND so," Hassan said politely, after they had found Shafi Sahib's tent and been invited inside, "I have come to assure myself of Saboor's safety."

Hassan, who had begun speaking as soon as he entered the tent, was still standing before the string bed with its elderly occupant. Behind him, Yusuf kept his eyes from the empty bed against one canvas wall.

Shafi Sahib read his thoughts. "Ahmad, Saboor's servant, has gone out," he said. "He is recovering very well from his wound."

For all his toughness, Yusuf could not help wincing at the thought of what the man had suffered.

When his servant boy entered, dragging a canvas chair, Shafi Sahib got up from his bed and sat in the chair. "It will be difficult," he told Hassan gently, "for you to enter the compound openly. Unfortunately, you are not welcome there."

He crossed his legs and reached for his beads as his two visitors lowered themselves to the string bed.

Hassan stiffened. "Why, Shafi Sahib?"

"I fear," answered the old man, "that the English people have been gravely displeased by your marriage." He pressed his lips together. "They do not look upon us as their equals.

"Your wife," he went on, ignoring Yusuf's snort, "may be suffering as a result, although her suffering will not affect Saboor. The English are unaware of his presence here." He raised his chin, warning Yusuf not to speak. "In any case, it is not anyone's feelings that would keep you from entering the Governor-General's compound by ordinary means. It is the two well-armed sentries who are forbidden to allow strangers past the gate."

"What then?" Hassan's voice had flattened. "Must we kill both sentries before I may see my child again?"

"Oh, no, my boy, that will not be necessary." Shafi Sahib leaned back in his chair. His beads clicked softly. He turned to Yusuf. "If you will give us permission?" he said politely, his eyes straying to the door.

It took Yusuf a moment to understand that Shafi Sahib wanted to speak to Hassan alone. Then, wondering whether Hassan was about to learn one of the Shaikh's spiritual tricks, Yusuf pushed himself hurriedly to his feet and with apologies left the tent.

THE tracker stood, bent double, over the dust of the avenue. "It's too dark," he reported, straightening. "I cannot see the hoofprints any longer. As soon as it is light we will return and continue from here." He pointed to where smoke rose from a ramshackle bazaar, just visible beyond the avenue's end. "I am going to get food."

The ruddy-faced boy shrugged. "The child isn't in this camp. We have been here already. We—"

"Quiet!" barked Jagoo. "And what if the horses are there now?" He jerked his chin toward the horse lines. "Among so many other mounts, how will you find their tracks tomorrow?"

The tracker smiled, cracked teeth large in his gaunt face. "You do not know my skill." His tone held confidence, but his eyes had become wary.

The three men were crossing the avenue when two riders came into view, passing among pack animals and groups of coolies, a tall groom on foot beside them.

The tracker started, then snatched at Jagoo's shirt. "Look!" he hissed.

One of the horsemen turned in his saddle to glance at them, a hand on his sword. "One man is slim, the other heavy," the tracker murmured to his companions as the two riders continued down the avenue. "Both are gentlemen. One horse likes to move sideways from time to time. They are now with a groom, but that is the only difference."

Signaling the others to follow, he crossed the avenue.

The avenue was broad and crowded. The air held the scent of charcoal fires and cooking. A bullock cart heaped with firewood passed, led by a boy singing at the top of his voice. Laughing groups of young men pushed one another. Englishmen strode past carrying carved wooden walking sticks, lips pursed, their black clothes smudged with dust.

The two horsemen and the groom continued along the avenue until they reached the same high, red canvas wall where Jagoo and his companion had waited fruitlessly only four days previously.

His eyes on the riders, the tracker strode along the margin of the avenue, followed by Jagoo and the boy. When the horsemen stopped at the guarded entrance, the three men faded into the blackness beside the wall.

The uniformed sentries stood at attention by the gate, ignoring the lively activity in front of them. Jagoo pushed past his companions and edged up to the red wall, near the two horsemen, who had stopped a little distance from the sentries. Once there, he bent and feigned a fit of coughing. The two riders had begun speaking to each other. Jagoo stopped coughing and listened.

"He said to turn left as you enter," Yusuf Bhatti was saying. "Her tent stands alone in the corner, there." He pointed to his left, where the red wall turned away from the road, thirty yards away.

Nodding, Hassan dismounted.

"May the Most Gracious guide you," Yusuf offered, reaching for Hassan's hand. "I'll stay here in case, Allah forbid, something goes wrong."

Hassan waved, then started toward the entrance, his lips moving as he walked.

As Hassan moved away, Yusuf leaned from his saddle. "You are allowed through the gate, are you not, Yar Mohammad?" he asked the groom.

"Ji, Sahib."

"Then go inside and guard Memsahib's tent."

Jagoo had crept near to hear the two men's words. When he turned back to look at the road, he stopped short, eyes wide. Beside Yusuf Bhatti's horse, Yar Mohammad, too, froze where he stood. Yusuf jerked upright in his saddle, blinked, then blinked again.

In the time it had taken for the onlookers to glance away, Hassan should have covered ten or twelve feet of the distance from his horse to the red wall. But he was not there. Yusuf, Yar Mohammad, the tracker, Jagoo, and the ruddy-faced boy all searched the avenue with their eyes. Hassan was nowhere to be seen.

Yusuf smiled to himself. Now, he was sure of it. Shafi Sahib had told Hassan one of the secrets of the Karakoyia Brotherhood. He also knew for certain that he would never learn what that secret was.

"LIGHT the lamp, Dittoo, it is too dark to read."

Inside her tent, Mariana sat up, propped on several pillows, an open letter in one hand, Saboor's arm in the other.

"Saboor darling, sit down," she pleaded as he tugged away from her. "See, you can play with my ribbons. They are there, on the bed."

"An-*nah*." He pronounced the last part of her name carefully, his eyes fixed on hers, then dropped down and, digging his hands and knees into her lap, crawled toward the little bedside table. She pulled him back, holding her letter safely out of the way, as he reached for the tinderbox.

His little body felt so soft under his clothes. She retrieved him, kissing a little hand that smelled of babyhood and dust. He pulled it away and wrapped his fingers around her gold necklace.

"And take Saboor away," she told Dittoo, unclasping the small fingers. "He is everywhere at once."

Dittoo shambled out from the corridor, wheedling as he came. "A-*jao*, Baba, come, I will find you something very nice for you, yes, very nice."

"An-*nah*, I want An-*nah*!" Saboor complained as Dittoo carried him, kicking, to a corner of the tent.

His health had certainly improved. Mariana made a kissing sound. "Shhhhh, Baba. There, there, my love, it is only for a little while."

She held her letter to the light while Dittoo's singsong nonsense floated across the floor. Three months old, yet new to Mariana, Mama's firmly written words carried with them the very air of home.

> We all missed you dreadfully at Freddie's birthday party. Several neighbors came and Freddie rushed about with their children until he became overexcited and had to be put to bed.
>
> He spends more and more time with Papa. I pray that he will, in time, take Ambrose's place in your father's heart.
>
> As for you, my darling, remember that you are not bound to marry in India. If no young man there makes you happy, you are to come home. Do not rush into a misalliance in order to please us.
>
> If you should return unmarried, our shoulders are broad enough to bear whatever society has to say.

Those reassuring words did little to take away the jolting pain Mariana had felt when she read a second letter that had come together with her mother's. *It saddens me immeasurably,* Fitzgerald had written from the army camp, *to know what scandal, what utter disgrace you have brought upon yourself. I excuse myself immediately after dinner each night to escape hearing the shameful things our officers are saying about you. How could you have associated so recklessly, so indecently, with a native man? Who will dare to be your friend now?*

It was no use hoping. Fitzgerald was gone forever. Who *would* be her friend? Mariana's call on Miss Emily had been even more unpleasant than she had expected.

"You have not only ruined yourself, Mariana," Miss Emily had declared flatly from her pillows, "you have also grievously wronged Lieutenant Marks. We shall not easily forgive you. We shall not mention it again," she had continued, as she adjusted the ribbons on her bed jacket, "but I will say this. You must accept your just deserts. Wear gloves to meals and do not attempt to join the conversation. Only pray that, one day, you will be forgiven."

Her duty done, Mariana would not call on hateful Miss Emily again. Miss Fanny was no use either. "It would have been better if you had not come to India, Mariana," she had said mournfully. "You are much too adventurous for this country."

No, she would never seek their approval again.

Although the Eden sisters and Lord Auckland, even all the other officers combined, could not frighten Mariana, one thought did bring her an ambushing panic. Once the scandal reached England, it would break her family's heart. She could bear being an outcast here in

India, but the thought of her family at home suffering for her mistakes was too miserable to endure.

Of course, Lord Auckland had given orders that her story not be repeated; but there had been a hundred witnesses to her declaration before the court, to her wedding—

Such a tale was too dark, too exciting not to be told. Within days of the camp's arrival at Calcutta, it would certainly escape Lord Auckland's censorship and swiftly reach every drawing room in the city, to be embellished with false, damning details of her bold enticement of native men. From there, it would spread, carried by every fresh ship bound for England.

Her letter lay on the bed beside her. Mama and Papa loved her. They would go on loving her, no matter what she did, no matter what society thought. She longed to sit down to Sunday lunch with them all, even the always critical Aunt Rachel. . . .

Why not leave now? Why not arrange to travel by palanquin ahead of the camp? Lord Auckland and his sisters expected to stop at Simla for several months on the way back to Calcutta. Even after they resumed traveling, they would stop many times along the way, to allow local Rajahs to entertain Lord Auckland. It might be a year before the camp arrived in Calcutta. If Mariana left within a few days and traveled without stopping, she would reach there many months ahead of her story. If she were fortunate, a passenger ship would be waiting on the Hooghly River. She might well be on the high seas long before the scandal broke in Calcutta.

Uncle Adrian would arrange everything, of course he would! She would write to him as soon as the camp crossed the Sutlej River into British territory.

In England, she would have time to explain, to prepare her family and their friends. It was, perhaps, too late to worry about society, but she could protect her family from hearing malicious lies from other lips.

In the corner, a pacified Saboor squealed with pleasure. Mariana pushed away sadness. She had always known she must leave him. He would be happy without her. As long as he had someone to guard and to love him, he would be quite safe. Hassan's fear must surely be exaggerated.

Someone scratched at the door blind. Dittoo stopped singing and stood before it, Saboor in his arms.

"An-nah." Distracted, Saboor fixed his eyes on the doorway as Dittoo turned and rushed toward the bed, his feet thumping on the striped rug, and thrust the child at Mariana.

"I have come to see Saboor Baba," said a male voice from outside.

Who was that? Who knew Saboor was here? Mariana held her breath and pushed Saboor down beside her on the bed, and covered him with her shawl. "Quiet," she cautioned softly, a finger to her lips. "*Chup*. Do not speak." She nodded to Dittoo.

"Who is it?" he asked, his voice cracking with nerves.

"It is Hassan Ali Khan," said the voice with some annoyance. "Open the blind."

Mariana sucked in her breath. Beside her, Saboor struggled to sit up.

Dittoo flung aside the blind. Hassan stepped in from the darkness outside.

"Abba! Abba!" As Dittoo stooped his way backward out of the doorway, Saboor scrambled off the bed and danced to his father. His face tilted upward, he braced himself against a Turkish-trousered knee.

Something about Hassan reminded Mariana of Saboor. It was the candor in his expression, perhaps, or a softness in his eyes. He looked strained. His coat smelled of horses. Rings gleamed on his hands. Behind her back, Mama's open letter beckoned from the bedspread.

She hardened herself against him. "Yes, Saboor is safe here. But there is something I must tell you."

Hassan did not look at her. Instead, he surveyed her tent. "How can you live like this?" He poked a long finger at her sparse furniture. "Where do you sit?"

She pointed to her upright chair, wobbly now from hard travel. "There, but that is not—"

"Where are your furnishings? Your carpets? I can't have my son living under these conditions. For all we know, he may be in this camp for months."

"I—"

"You need better arrangements," he interrupted, frowning as he lifted Saboor into his arms. "I must make them tonight."

Saboor wrapped his arms about Hassan's neck. Father and son regarded Mariana with identical gazes.

"A letter has come for me," she said firmly, changing the subject. "I must return to Calcutta at once."

Hassan waved a dismissing hand. "It is late, Mariam," he said curtly. He put down his son. "I must hurry."

"But that is not how you—"

Before she finished speaking the door blind closed behind him.

Chapter 41

Saboor stared past Mariana's worried face, refusing to meet her eyes or acknowledge her kisses. "How has he become like this?" she wailed, as she handed him to Dittoo. "He could not have gone deaf in one minute. What is the matter with him?"

"I do not know, Begum Sahib." Dittoo bounced the passive, unsmiling child, then shook his head. "I have never seen such a thing before."

Saboor's abrupt change of mood had begun the moment his father left them. As the door blind shut behind Hassan, Saboor had gone still. It seemed as if his whole being had turned suddenly inward, out of Mariana's reach.

For an hour she had rocked him, crooning, searching her memory for a cause. She had examined him with nervous fingers, looking for signs of the spider or scorpion sting that might have paralyzed him somehow. Finding nothing, she had crooned his name and tried to force him to look at her, but he would only stare past her, his energetic, affectionate little self replaced by a stiff, unloving stranger. She was baffled. What could they have done or said to change him so? Surely he had not divined her plan to leave him and return home? But if he had not, why had he retreated into silence, as if his heart were crushed?

"Please, Dittoo," she implored, "do something."

A bath did not help, nor did Dittoo's arguing or Mariana's embraces.

Later that evening, Mariana sat up waiting, still dressed, with Saboor asleep beside her. Hassan would return soon. When he did, she would find words to explain her leaving. For now, all she could do was to sit while the timepiece at her bedside ticked away the passing time.

Mariam. He had called her Mariam.

ON the moonlit avenue, Jagoo nodded to the boy and moved along the red wall near to where the riders had pointed. Here the canvas sagged and billowed. He sat down again and stretched his body out, as if readying himself for sleep.

But he did not sleep. Instead, he began gently, unobtrusively, to smooth away stones, twigs, and small obstructions from the ground under the wall.

It was nearly midnight. The traffic had died on the avenue. Bats swooped overhead. Hollow coughing came from nearby servants' quarters. In the distance, men laughed. Someone was singing.

The tracker yawned. "I want to eat," the boy whispered beside him. "I can smell cooking over there." He jerked his chin toward the horse lines.

They watched Jagoo take things out of a cloth bag. First came something that looked like a greasy leather pouch. Next came a ten-inch knife.

Jagoo motioned to the boy, a silent, significant gesture. Then, the pouch concealed again in his clothes, the knife between his teeth, he slid in one smooth, soundless motion under the red wall, and was gone.

Horses approached on the avenue. The tracker stiffened instantly, his breath hissing as the two riders came into view again, this time followed by a laden donkey cart.

The tall rider dismounted and started toward the guarded entrance. From where the tracker sat, he could make out that the man's lips were moving. The tracker turned his head and glanced at the boy, who had gripped his arm, his eyes wide and worried. When the tracker turned again to look at the place where the tall rider should have been walking, the avenue was empty.

The tracker shook the boy's fingers from his arm and stood. Keeping his body flat against the wall, he crept away, leaving the guarded entrance, the laden donkey cart, and the second horseman behind him. Breathing hard with fright, he hurried to the corner where the red canvas wall turned away from the avenue. Once around the corner, he ran through the dark, his clothes billowing and flapping around him, his sandals slapping on the hard clay ground.

ATTENDING to a personal need, Dittoo crouched behind the thicket of guy ropes that supported Memsahib's tent, his face turned to the red wall. He looked over his shoulder, his dhoti draped discreetly about his legs, considering for the hundredth time the extraordinary fact of his memsahib's marriage to this man Hassan.

How would his life change after this event? Time would tell.

One thing was certain. No wife of Hassan Ali Khan Sahib would be allowed a male servant. But, without maidservants for Memsahib, how could Dittoo escape going into her tent? Without him, how was she to have her morning coffee, or her bed made, her lamp lit or her side table dusted?

The canvas beside him trembled. He looked along the wall in time to see an arm, then a leg, then a whole man appear silently from under the wall near Memsahib's tent.

Dittoo hastily adjusted his clothes and crept closer. When he was near enough to see the man clearly, he stopped and held his breath.

The man had not seen Dittoo. He stood, a shadow in the moonlight, and reached with a swift movement under his long shirt. His loose cotton trousers dropped to the ground.

He stepped out of them and then, naked under his shirt, began to smear something from a greasy pouch onto his legs and buttocks. That done, he pulled off the shirt.

Yar Mohammad had come, hours ago, to guard Memsahib's tent. Ghostlike in his gray shawl, he now sat gazing into space beside her doorway, unaware of the naked intruder who had now finished smearing his chest and back. As Dittoo watched from the shadows, the man bent over, his skin gleaming faintly, and withdrew something from his discarded clothes.

It was a long, cruel-looking knife. Dittoo went cold.

Too terrified to move, Dittoo crouched by the canvas wall, as silently, slowly, his eyes fixed on Yar Mohammad, the intruder crept forward, the knife ready in his hand.

Dittoo found his voice. At his yell of warning, Yar Mohammad jerked his head up. Seeing the man, he reached, scrabbling, for his own weapon.

At that instant, a third man appeared. Before Dittoo could make another sound, the man began to run toward them. Dittoo held his breath. Whoever this was, he must have seen the scene beside the tent door. Was he a guard or another assailant?

He was neither. It was Hassan Ali Khan Sahib himself, breathing hard, running full tilt at the intruder.

His hands gripping his face, Dittoo watched Hassan Sahib throw himself forward past Yar Mohammad. Ignoring the raised knife, he drove the intruder into the doorway of Memsahib's tent, bringing the door blind thumping, unrolling to the ground.

Gasping and spitting, the two men grappled in the stony dust. Fighting to gain a purchase on the greased body, Hassan Sahib cried out as the naked man slid from his grip and darted toward the red wall.

The intruder flung himself down, caught the canvas wall with one hand and began, lizardlike, to slither under it, still holding his knife; but Yar Mohammad was too quick for him. Throwing himself at the man, he caught one greased ankle, then another, then, grunting with effort, dragged the intruder by his feet from beneath the wall and across the ground to the tent.

Naked, bleeding, and covered with dust, the man wept aloud as Hassan Sahib grasped him by the hair.

"Piece of filth," Hassan Sahib rasped as he beat the man's head on the ground. "My wife, my son!"

"Oh, Sahib, have pity!" the man wailed. "I am only a small thief in search of trinkets. Had I known it was your family—"

"Pig! Son of shame! I know who you are, what you want. Yar Mohammad, get his knife!"

Dittoo shivered as he watched Yar Mohammad turn the man roughly onto his stomach and force a knee into his back. What a pity he himself was too old to help!

Shouting came from the entrance. Someone was arguing with the sentries, trying to get in. A moment later, a guard appeared, followed by a burly man who strode behind him, dragging a frightened-looking boy.

"I know nothing, Huzoors, nothing at all." Arms over his head, the boy cowered before the sentry, babbling with fright.

"Be quiet. See, guard, I told you there were others," said the burly man. "I only wish I had caught the one that ran away."

As the sentry poked at the greased man with his bayonet, Dittoo suddenly remembered Memsahib and Saboor Baba. He stepped over the fallen blind and into the tent.

"Memsahib, Memsahib," he whispered, uncomfortably aware that Hassan Sahib would likely shout at him for entering, "are you all right?"

He fumbled across the floor in the darkness, found his way around the bed to the little table in the corner, and lit the lamp.

AWAKENED by Dittoo's frightened shout, Mariana had reached for her boots. Then, her heart pounding, she had seized the lamp and dropped to her knees beside her bed. "If someone has come to harm you," she had whispered to the sleeping Saboor as she wrapped him in one of her shawls, "they must kill me first. Oh, Saboor, if only I had a sword . . ."

Now as she sat upright on the edge of her bed, her dressing gown skirts spread widely about her, she could see Hassan by her open doorway, his back to her, his shoulders heaving.

An authoritative male voice spoke. "You take charge of them. Say you caught them yourself. Yes, yes, of course, that is what a sentry is supposed to do. Now be gone, and good night."

Here was Dittoo, holding the lamp aloft, and now, suddenly, there was Hassan, smelling foul, his face and clothes streaked with grease and dirt. He looked at her without speaking, his whole soul asking for Saboor.

Behind him Yar Mohammad craned to see inside.

Mariana pushed her skirts aside and got down on her knees. While Dittoo held up the lamp she lifted the edge of the bedspread. There under the bed lay Saboor where she had hidden him, wrapped in a nest of her shawls, his head turning toward them, his eyes open.

"An-nah."

"There, darling, it's all right now."

As she took hold of the shawls and pulled him toward her, she felt someone strike her violently from behind. Her back arching involuntarily, she let go of the shawls and clutched at her spine.

"Why, why?" she stammered, her face crumpling in pain, searching the four surprised faces above her.

Panting with shock, she tried to crawl away as Yar Mohammad's urgent voice pierced the ringing in her ears. "A snake must have bitten her. This is what happens when a viper strikes. They think someone has struck them from behind—look at her hands!"

A snake! She struggled to speak, to tell them she had looked under the bed, that she had even brought the lamp, but her voice had abandoned her.

Still on all fours, she watched Hassan, his hands outstretched, snatch his son from the terrible nest of shawls. As her sight dimmed, she saw her four-poster bed upturned and Yar Mohammad pounce, a heavy blade flashing in his hand.

Someone gripped her wrists. "There. Two puncture wounds."

Her bitten arm was on fire. She felt herself being dragged across the floor. "Lift her from the other side," someone said. "We must get her to Shafi Sahib."

"No," another voice said, "she'll be unconscious soon. Yar Mohammad will fetch Shafi Sahib. Go, Yar Mohammad, take my horse."

Shafi Sahib. Friend of the magical Shaikh, interpreter of dreams. Why would the great Shafi Sahib come to her? Who was sucking at her wrist, spitting and cursing? Who prayed aloud, while a baby wailed, hopelessly?

An alien creature had invaded her body, and was scorching her from the inside. Too weak to cry out, she could not tell them of her agony, or beg them not to touch her. She thrashed, gurgling, and there was rustling and silence and a voice began to recite in an undertone.

She sank into blackness.

THE ship rocked. She could not see rigging above her, but she could feel the rolling of the deck. She strained to see ahead, and there, through the fog, glimmered a brilliant light. The waves beneath her murmured something she could not understand. Longing to reach the light, she tried to stretch out her hands. The ship was taking her there, taking her there.

SHE could breathe. The burning, although fierce, had abated, and she could breathe, shallow breaths at first, then deeper, sweeter ones. As she drank in the air, the voice went on, soothing and healing her. There was no sound of a baby crying. The light shone through her eyelids.

When she opened her eyes, she saw a blur of faces. Then the light went out and the singsong murmuring ceased. "Get another light," said someone. "I must be able to see her."

Did she know that voice?

"Who must see me?" she murmured into the darkness. What was this dark place? What language were they all speaking?

Several voices spoke at once. "Are you all right?" "Have you recovered?" "Can you breathe?"

"Yes." Her voice sounded curiously distant. Something unpleasant had dribbled from the corner of her mouth. Her hair was drenched. The pain in her arm was nearly gone.

"Can you sit up?"

"Yes, but I do not wish to," she said weakly.

Someone sighed. She heard the rustling sound of someone standing up. "Since she is now all right," said the familiar voice, "I shall go back. Yar Mohammad will see me to my tent."

WHEN she opened her eyes again, the lamp had been relit. The interior of the tent looked quite odd from where she lay on the floor near her desk. Her dressing gown had bunched itself uncomfortably around her legs. Her chair stood a few feet away. Her bed now lay on its side, spilling bed linens over the striped floor. Dittoo, holding Saboor, sat motionless in the corner. Hassan crouched beside her, a hand to his head. Near the door, his eyes fixed on the sky outside, sat a heavyset stranger.

"I think," she said, "I would like to go to bed."

As Dittoo scrambled to his feet and began to scoop up the bedclothes, Saboor trotted toward her. He sat down with a little bump by her side, then reached out, round-eyed, and patted her arm. She tried to smile.

At a rustling outside the tent, she raised herself onto one elbow. In the doorway, their feet upon the fallen blind, stood the Misses Eden, their two faces fixed in horror as if they had come suddenly upon some fearful accident or scene of torture.

For a moment, there was silence. But for the quivering of Miss Emily's skirts, Mariana would have believed the figures in the doorway to be a delirium-induced tableau.

"I hope I have not caused a disturbance," Mariana said carefully.

Hassan pointed meaningfully at his mouth, then at hers. Mariana scrubbed her chin with a corner of her dressing gown, and found it had been smeared with something pink and slimy. She closed her eyes and subsided to the floor, doomed, but too ill to care.

Miss Emily found her voice. "We have been called here, Mariana," she said, ignoring everyone else, "by the servants, who heard some very unexpected sounds coming from your tent. Get up at once. You are coming with us."

Hands raised Mariana. Illuminated by torches carried by Miss Emily's servants, she was half-carried past Hassan, past Dittoo and Yar Mohammad.

"Fanny," she heard Miss Emily say, "tell one of the servants to call the sentries."

"WE shall not ask you to explain now," said Miss Emily crisply, as she tucked Mariana into her bed, now hastily reassembled in her own large drawing room. "There will be time for that when you are sufficiently recovered. You shall sleep here until we march tomorrow."

Through half-closed lids, Mariana could make out Miss Emily's little sofa, her bookstand, and several tables, each with an oil lamp. Someone had put a cold compress on her forehead. Miss Fanny stood beside her sister, her lips tight.

"My sister and I," Miss Emily declared, turning to Miss Fanny who nodded without speaking, "are determined to mention this to no one, at least for now. We request that you do the same, until something has been decided. In the meanwhile, you should rest.

"Whatever you have been up to," she added darkly, "is certain to have been most exhausting."

Mariana floated into sleep.

Chapter 42

"Do not be foolish, Yar Mohammad," Shafi Sahib said from his seat on a borrowed mule, shortly after dawn. "How can you not see the importance of your work?"

The groom strode silently at the animal's head, Shafi Sahib's reins in his hand. Around them on the march, the brass ankle bells of the camels chinked and sang.

Perhaps he should have kept quiet and not bothered Shafi Sahib with his troubles, but his sense of failure had been too great. What had he done to earn the little ceramic vial that had been put into his hand? What had he found to offer those about him in this strange and powerful time?

"Of course your work is important," the old man continued, letting go of the saddle with one hand to search for something among his garments. "What would have happened if you had not been there to stay Yusuf Bhatti from slaying the madman on the road to Lahore when these events first began? Without your intervention, the man would have died, I would not have received his message, and we would not have guessed at the identity of the Guardian."

Encouraged, Yar Mohammad looked up.

"It was you," Shafi Sahib added, gripping the saddle one-handed, his beads held daringly in his free hand, "who delivered our messages to the young guardian memsahib, you who provided the child's first morsels of food after his rescue. You fought for them on the road to Kasur and sat guard over Saboor's place of refuge when the child thief came to steal him. It was you who recognized the viper's bite, and summoned me to save the Guardian's life."

The old man smiled down from his swaying perch. "You, Yar Mohammad," he said, his voice lifting, "have been given the duty of protecting the Guardian. Your little vial was full when you showed it in your dream to Shaikh Waliullah. I believe it is full even now."

Shafi Sahib was tired. The old man's head drooped. Yar Mohammad walked on, breathing deeply of the morning air.

"I understand we had some excitement last night," remarked an aide-de-camp as he helped himself to omelette aux herbes Indiennes in the dining tent. "It seems that two men tried to rob this compound."

Lord Auckland looked up, scowling. Mariana stared down at her plate. The Eden sisters made a point of looking neither at each other nor at Mariana.

"Yes," said another aide. "One of them tried the old trick"—he coughed delicately—"of covering himself with grease."

The first aide smiled broadly over his buttered toast. "I heard one of them actually got past the guard and tried to get into the tents, and—"

"Absolute nonsense!" Major Byrne's face had reddened. He cleared his throat noisily. "Nothing of the sort, nothing of the sort." Avoiding the Governor-General's eye, he inclined his head gallantly toward the Misses Eden. "Your compound is impregnable, ladies. You must have no fear on that account. Both men were caught by the sentries well before they attempted to get in."

He glared at the aides. "Do not let these young men frighten you. They have no idea what they're talking about. And now, ladies, Lord Auckland," he concluded with a decisive little nod, "if you will excuse me."

Miss Emily regarded him silently over the rim of her coffee cup as he strode away.

Lord Auckland nodded vaguely in Byrne's direction, then pushed back his chair. "Emily, my dear, it seems that we are to be relatively safe from the natives this morning. I thought we might take a drive before lunch. There may be some interesting ruins on the way to Kasur." He smiled hopefully at his sister from beneath dusty eyebrows.

"I am so sorry, George," said Miss Emily, glancing reproachfully at Mariana, "but Miss Givens was quite ill last night. I cannot go out until Dr. Drummond has seen her."

Mariana pushed smoked fish onto her fork. *Miss Emily,* she ordered silently, *take the drive, take the drive!*

"I had hoped," Miss Emily said, as they waited in her drawing room for Dr. Drummond, "that we had heard the last of your extraordinary behavior."

Mariana touched the healing puncture marks on her wrist. She would not explain or apologize, whatever they said to her.

"But not at all." Miss Emily rose from her seat and crossed the tent to her little bookshelf. "Since then," she went on, turning back to Mariana and folding her arms across her bosom, "you have not ceased to astonish us. Is there any point in my asking why we found you last night lying on your floor in your nightclothes in the company of not one but two strange native men?"

Mariana's bed, now tightly made, stood on one side of the tent. No one looked at it.

"If you are going mad," Miss Emily pronounced as she lowered herself to the sofa beside her sister, "your behavior can be explained, although, of course, it can never be excused."

She opened her hands. "Why, Mariana? Why the foul-smelling native men? Why the unexplained baby? Why the overturned bed, the general disarray?"

"There was a viper," Mariana said as coolly as civility allowed, "under my bed."

Why did she bother to tell them anything?

A servant bowed in the doorway. "Doctor Sahib has come," he said in polite, accented English.

Dr. Drummond stood over her in his old-fashioned clothes, smelling of tobacco. "Now, Miss Givens," he said, bending to look cautiously at her over the tops of his spectacles, "how are we feeling today?"

He pursed his lips. "I understand," he continued, nodding toward the sofa and the upright Misses Eden, "that the timely arrival of these ladies at your tent last night prevented your meeting a most unpleasant fate.

"What none of us can grasp is how these things keep happening to you. Do *you* know, Miss Givens? Hmmmn?"

They already believed her a lunatic. Nothing she told them would change their minds. She turned over her wrist. "A snake bit me last night." She pointed to the marks. "I was very ill then, but I am much better now."

"Now, Miss Givens," the doctor said reprovingly, looking not at her but at Miss Emily, "we all know there is no cure for poisonous snakebite."

"Yes, Dr. Drummond, but—"

"No cure at all," he repeated in a firm tone, smiling falsely. "You had a narrow escape last night, to be sure, but we all know that it was *not* from poisonous snakebite. Nonetheless, if it will make you feel better, I will have a look at those marks.

"She could, of course," he said to the Eden ladies, taking Mariana's wrist in his hand, "have been injured by one of the men. Miss Givens, do you mind coming to the light?"

Injured by one of the men indeed! If Miss Fanny had not been watching, Mariana would have made a face behind the doctor's back.

He turned her wrist this way and that, looking down his nose at the two small marks. After a moment, he nodded. "You may sit down now, Miss Givens.

"These are clearly puncture wounds," he pronounced, drawing out his words, pointing a stubby finger at Mariana's wrist. "They *do* resemble marks left by the fangs of a snake, but if they *are* bite marks, the snake would have been of a rare, nonpoisonous variety. In any case," he went on, "as they are nearly healed, the marks have nothing whatever to do with the events of last night." He shook his head. "I really do not know what to make of all this."

"May I please," Mariana asked, struggling to keep her tone level, "tell you the *real* story of what happened last night?"

Greeted with silent surprise, she took a deep breath and plunged on. "The thieves we discussed at breakfast this morning," she began, "were child stealers. They did indeed get into the compound. In fact, they nearly got into my tent."

Miss Fanny's mouth opened. "*Nearly* got in? But Emily and I saw them clearly!"

"No, Miss Fanny," Mariana disagreed patiently. "*That* was the bridegroom from the wedding, and another man I had not seen before."

Miss Emily's face turned pink. "Are you trying to tell us," she cried, "that the filthy creature beside you was your *husband*?"

Mariana glared at her. "No, Miss Emily. I said I would *not* marry him. I am certain you heard me say so. In any case, he was dirty because he had fought with a child thief who had gotten into the compound, and was trying to steal his baby from my tent."

"Baby?" Dr. Drummond's jaw hung open.

Miss Emily was now scarlet. "You will not speak to me like that, Mariana," she snapped.

"*Whose* baby?" The doctor was looking avidly from face to face.

"I think, Dr. Drummond," said Miss Emily, her eyes narrowing, her tone a potent combination of charm and force, "that we have no further need to take up your valuable time."

"But, Miss Eden, we have not yet discovered—"

Miss Emily smiled thinly. "Thank you so *very much,* Dr. Drummond. Fanny, please see the doctor out."

Mariana caught the doctor's disappointed glance over his shoulder as Miss Fanny, mute and very pale, ushered him from the tent.

Miss Emily's gaze was inescapable. "The baby, Mariana, is the key to this entire disgraceful story, is he not? Your 'father-in-law' is Shaikh Wallahwallah, the magician grandfather who was said to have spirited the Maharajah's baby hostage from the Golden Temple."

Mariana nodded.

"The missing baby, therefore, is now your stepson."

Mariana nodded again.

Miss Emily's voice would have been triumphant if it had not been so deadly. "In that case, the child in your tent was Maharajah Ranjit Singh's hostage, the child whose disappearance caused the Maharajah to fall ill, thus delaying our treaty negotiations. Delaying, in fact, the very Afghan Campaign for which we have all come so far and worked so hard."

Her eyes bored into Mariana's. "It was not *magic* that caused the child's disappearance, was it, Mariana? It was a *conspiracy* in which you played a part. Are you, or are you not, the thief who stole the child from the Golden Temple?"

Miss Fanny gasped.

It was pointless to deny the truth. "It was I who stole Saboor, Miss Emily, but there was no conspiracy." Mariana raised her chin. "I tried to tell you so, after the Maharajah's dinner party, after I got up and spoke—"

"Later, you lied to us repeatedly on the subject. When questions were asked, you deceived and betrayed us."

It was true. She had lied to them.

"I should have guessed before now." Miss Emily shook her head. "It was all in front of me. Your disappearances and your sudden headaches all began after that baby vanished. You fell asleep in your palanquin the morning after the rice test. When I consider that awful scene last night . . ."

She closed her eyes. "Call one of the servants, Mariana," she said, shaking her head. "I shall not say another word until I have had tea."

"*I* think," remarked Miss Fanny timidly as she stirred sugar into her cup, "that we should allow Mariana to tell the *entire* story."

Miss Emily raised a hand. "Absolutely not, Fanny. I cannot bear any fresh horrors."

"There may be details we have not understood," Miss Fanny persisted. "But even if there are not, I should like to hear Mariana's side. It is, after all, a most *interesting* story."

Miss Emily sniffed, but did not argue.

"The baby's name is Saboor," Mariana began, responding to Miss Fanny's nod. "His mother was poisoned by the Maharajah's queens. He had been ill-treated by the queens *and* by the Maharajah. He was forced on me suddenly by his own servant, who feared he would die. I returned him secretly to his family on the night of the rice test."

The ladies stared at one another. Mariana took a sip of her tea to steady herself. "The Shaikh then proposed that I marry his son. I was horrified, of course, but when the Maharajah announced that he wanted to marry me himself, I used the Shaikh's proposal as a means to refuse him. I honestly believed the Shaikh's proposal was not serious, that it was meant only to save me from the Maharajah. I was tricked into going to the Citadel."

Miss Emily sat immobile, her teacup partway to her lips. Mariana plunged onward. "On the morning after the ceremony, the Maharajah sent armed men to the Shaikh's house to fetch the baby and *me*. I was forced to take the baby away in the rain, in disguise." She shivered at the memory. "Then child thieves came to steal him. The one who nearly got in was covered in grease. He had a knife."

"Grease? Was he—?" Miss Fanny's eyes danced naughtily over the hand at her mouth.

"*Fanny!*" Miss Emily put her cup down sharply.

"Saboor's father caught him just in time, but the struggle was messy because of the grease. That is why he smelled so awful." Mariana sighed. "He *had* been wearing nice clothes."

Miss Emily drummed her fingers on the arm of the sofa. "Who, then, was the square man with no neck?"

"I do not know. A friend of Hassan's, I think. He was not supposed to look at me, as I am married. He and a groom and someone else came in to help after I was bitten by the snake."

"Ah, the snake." Miss Emily sighed pointedly.

"I *was* bitten, *after* the fight." Mariana touched her wrist. "I thought I should die from the pain. I fell down, something horrible poured from my mouth, and then I fainted. They sent for someone who cures snakebite by reciting verses—"

"I see." Miss Emily raised her hands. "All *politesse* was flung away as soon as you were to be seen rolling on the floor and foaming at the mouth. More native men were summoned, mumbo jumbo was recited, and you recovered." Her hands dropped to her lap.

Mariana refused to look away. "I know it sounds fantastic. . . ."

Miss Fanny let out her breath. "And we all believed camp life was dull!"

"I blame myself." Miss Emily shook her head. "I should have had your tent put closer to mine. I should never have allowed you to be pushed off alone into a corner of the compound with only a native manservant and no woman to confide in. That is precisely how young girls get into trouble. And you, Mariana, you have a genius for trouble." She folded her hands in her lap. "This wild behavior must stop at once."

"But Emily," Miss Fanny protested, "she only—"

Miss Emily ignored her sister. "First," she announced, "that baby is to be returned immediately to the Maharajah. The child's welfare is no concern of ours. I will *not* spirit the Maharajah's hostage out of the Punjab like a thief in the night. And as for you, Mariana, our only choice is to send you to Calcutta at once. You are a danger to yourself and all of us. I shall speak to my brother this afternoon."

The air around Mariana seemed to go cold. Her training and manners forgotten, she jumped up. "No, Saboor cannot go back! If you send him to the Maharajah, he'll die of grief, and it will be *all your fault*!" She turned on her heel, then started for the doorway without looking back.

There was no time. Before Miss Emily went to Lord Auckland, she and Saboor must escape once more. With only Yar Mohammad and Dittoo for company and nowhere safe to take refuge, she and Saboor must become gypsies, traveling at night, hiding from people who did not care for them, who thought only of rewards or politics.

To her shame, the previous evening she, too, had chosen England over India. In her haste to forestall her own ruin, she had put her troubles above Saboor's. In the hours before the child thief came and the snake coiled itself beneath her bed, she had chosen Mama and Papa over the Shaikh and Safiya Sultana, Freddie over Saboor, eau de cologne over attar of sandalwood.

How could she have failed to see that, willingly or not, at every fork in the road she had taken the path leading to India? How could she have failed to notice that each choice had been made as if she had, indeed, been on a ship piloted by someone else? Now, when she was about to lose him, she knew for certain that she was Saboor's true guardian, as Yar Mohammad's dreams had foretold.

How could she ever have thought of leaving India?

"Mariana, sit down. Emily, *I am shocked.*"

Mariana had never heard Miss Fanny use that tone.

"Whatever we may think of her, Mariana *is* the child's stepmother. It is for her to decide what is to be done with him."

Before a startled Miss Emily could reply to her sister's declaration or Mariana return to her seat, a bumbling sound came from outside.

"He gave me no peace." Unshaven and untidy as ever, Dittoo nodded apologetically as he pushed his way inside, rumpled and out of place in Miss Emily's grand tent, a freshly bathed Saboor wriggling in his arms.

"No one saw us," he added as he lowered Saboor to the carpet. He tipped his head carelessly at the two ladies. "They had already seen him, had they not, last evening?"

"An-nah, An-nah." Saboor danced, chirping, to her. Gripping her skirts, he tried, panting with effort, to climb onto her lap. She felt herself flush with pleasure as she reached for him.

His clothes were starched, his cheeks ruddy. He sat straight on her lap, his thumb in his mouth, gazing at the two English faces before him.

"These are Angrezi ladies," Mariana said instructively, kissing the top of his head.

"*Rezi,*" he echoed seriously, then slipped down and marched, not to Miss Fanny who was already holding out her arms, but straight to Miss Emily, who sat quite still, her hands clasped tightly in her lap.

He leaned against her skirts and peered into her face, his head tilted backward, his little red coat bunched up, a small, familiar fist resting on her knee.

"Well," she said at last, looking down, her thin lips beginning to turn up, "well, well, well."

"He must," declared Miss Fanny, as Miss Emily took Saboor under his arms and lifted him, still sucking his thumb, to her lap, "come to my tent and stroke the spotted deer."

MARIANA lay in her own tent at midnight, enjoying her solitude, relieved that her bed had been returned to her own tent, that she was safe at last from the scrutiny of the Eden ladies, their ladies' maids, and assistant ladies' maids.

Her head felt heavy, but her body felt as light as air. The sisters had not sympathized, but they had been fair.

"We shall not, for the moment," Miss Emily had said later, "—and I emphasize *for the moment*—mention to anyone the whereabouts of Saboor or the events of last night."

"Do not tell her I said so," she had murmured to Miss Fanny as Mariana listened behind them on the way in to lunch, "but I fear we may have done the girl a disservice. She is young, after all, and the baby *is* very sweet."

Mariana looked across her tent. The furnishings Hassan had ordered to be brought inside after the fight looked quite comfortable arranged along one wall—the thick carpet from which Dittoo had beaten pounds of dust, the pair of bolsters, the low carved table.

She slipped out of bed, and, after making sure there were no snakes about, lowered herself uncertainly to the carpet, loosened her hair, and leaned back on a purple bolster. Hassan had also provided a satin quilt. She pulled it to her chin.

What a comfortable little arrangement! It was a pity she had never had her own native furniture before.

She yawned. She had wanted to call on Shafi Sahib today, but there had been no time to find his tent. Munshi Sahib had given her a wonderful lesson. The poem he had brought her had been beautiful, but difficult to translate.

> *I gave my heart to three qualities I found in you.*
> *To be taken from these has caused my torn heart pain.*
> *But if you suffer, it is worse for me.*
>
> *I do not fear for you,*
> *Alone on the field of battle.*

"Dittoo," she called, "raise the door blind."

This moment was perfect enough to make one wish to travel forever. The sky through the open doorway was awash with stars. A plaintive melody drifted in from the distance. Saboor slumbered peacefully on the bed.

She had seen Hassan through the same doorway after the snake bit her, his back to her, his shoulders heaving, his beautiful coat stained and torn. She had not said good-bye to him, or thanked him for saving her life. Glancing behind her as she was taken away, she had caught a single glimpse of his exhausted face. He had met her eyes, then looked away.

She pushed a tangle of curls from her face. By this time, he must be on his way north to Kasur. The British camp, now moving south, would cross the Sutlej tomorrow morning. Every day the space between them would grow.

Dittoo greeted someone, then backed hurriedly away.

Hassan stepped quietly in through the doorway. He stood there, his gaze traveling to the bed where Saboor lay sleeping, then to her. He had a cut on his cheekbone. His ruined coat had been replaced by a shawl.

He sat beside her on the carpet. "Let me see your wound," he said without preamble, pushing the quilt out of the way and reaching for her hand. An uncut emerald set in gold gleamed on his finger as he raised her wrist to the light.

"I must thank you for what you did last night," she said a little weakly, distracted by the pressure of his fingers. "I might have died. Was it you who sucked the poison?"

He did not answer. Instead he released her wrist and sat back against the bolster, his face turned from hers. The shawl across his chest moved up and down.

"I have received an urgent message from Kasur," he said. "I must start back tonight. I had hoped to cross the Sutlej with your camp, but I cannot."

"It *was* you," she whispered, her fingers on the healed wounds, remembering the agony in her wrist and the voice praying by her side.

He said nothing, nor did he look at her, but a wave of feeling seemed to come from him, as if he were speaking to her without words. It crossed the space between them, gaining power, mixing with the scent of sandalwood, reaching every part of Mariana's body. Her breathing deepened.

A small sound came from the sleeping Saboor. Hassan glanced toward the bed. "When people ask us where you are," he said softly, turning to Mariana, "we will tell them you have gone to stay with your relatives."

"With my relatives," Mariana repeated, as his eyes searched her face. That would imply that she had run away from his family, from him. But it was suddenly far more complicated than that. "No," she stammered. She ran her hands over the satin quilt, searching for the right words. "No."

He rose to his feet. She knew by the way he held his body that he was about to leave her.

"The Maharajah will most likely die soon," he said. "After that, the succession, Allah willing, will be smooth." He moved to the bed and lifted Saboor. "If it is not, there is a chance you may not see us again. If you do not, have courage, and remember me and my family." His eyes closing, he embraced his son.

Starlight streamed in through the doorway and lay at their feet. "Shafi Sahib will remain with you and my son." Hassan stepped closer to her and handed her the child. "Even while he is small, Saboor should be instructed in the ways of the Brotherhood. One day, God willing, he will be a great man."

She could not speak.

"Yar Mohammad, also, will stay with you. He is now in my family's pay. I am sure he will think of a way to hide Saboor during your journey." He paused. "If I can, when it is safe, I will come for you." His voice had thickened.

"You will come for *me*?" she repeated.

"Yes." With a sharp intake of breath, he bent and caught her mouth with his.

She did not try to escape him. She stood, trembling, the sleeping boy in her arms. His mouth was firmer than Fitzgerald's had been. His eyes were open.

Approaching footsteps broke the silence around them. Hassan released her and looked out through the doorway. "Shafi Sahib is coming," he said, in another voice. "He must have come to say good-bye to me, and to talk to you of your journey." He smiled apologetically. "I must go out and meet him."

He stepped through the doorway, then turned and looked hard at her. *"Khuda Hafiz,"* he said. "And may God protect you." He raised his hand, just as his father had done when she left Qamar Haveli after returning Saboor.

Mariana stood still, holding the child tightly against her.

A moment later, Hassan's respectful greeting drifted into the tent. She looked about her. Shafi Sahib, the mysterious interpreter of dreams, was nearly at her door. She must do something. She laid Saboor on the bed and wiped her palms on her skirts. What would she say when they met? She could not touch his knees or his feet as the natives did, but she must make some gesture, however subtle, to show her respect. She could never treat Shaikh Waliullah's friend as if he were an ordinary person. Until she saw them again, Shafi Sahib would be her link to Hassan and his family.

Someone was removing his shoes outside the door. Brown fingers grasped the reed screen and held it aside. Her munshi stood before her, blinking a little in the half darkness.

"Peace, Bibi," he said mildly. "I trust you are well?"

• • •

THAT night, she woke as a light wind sighed around the tent. The fog of her recurring dream had lifted at last. Over water that sparkled and shone, her ship now sailed parallel to a rocky shore, while behind her, tied to the ship's stern, an energetic little dinghy bounced on the waves.

They were not alone. Ahead of them, a plain and powerful Arab *dhow* sliced purposefully through the water, its lateen-rigged sail creaking in the wind. Beside the dhow and a little behind it, a narrow, gondolalike boat moved smoothly through the waves, propelled by oarsmen, its prow carved to resemble a bird. Between Mariana's barque and the dangerous-looking shore plied a long, serviceable barge, piled high with leather and straw.

She searched the distance. There, above the horizon's edge, rose the graceful masts of an Indian river yacht.

IT was, after all, not Yar Mohammad but Dittoo who found a way to hide Saboor as they traveled. "No one will look for him at so great a height," he declared, nodding fiercely to emphasize the cleverness of his solution. "We will need only to take care that Saboor is not seen when we bring him across the avenue."

The next day he had tramped away, a bribe of a newly hemmed cotton shawl in his hand, to make Saboor's travel arrangements.

Later, as she rode beside Miss Emily in one of the carriages, Mariana caught sight of Motu the elephant behind them in the distance, a massive swaying shape among a dusty sea of carts and baggage animals, the tiny figure of Hira Lal seated on his neck, carrying the Governor-General's great durbar tent and the grandson of Shaikh Waliullah of the Karakoyia Brotherhood to Calcutta.

GLOSSARY OF URDU WORDS NOT DEFINED IN THE TEXT

A

abba	*diminutive of father*
Allah	*God*
ammi	*diminutive of mother*
Angrez	*English*
anna	*a coin: one sixteenth of a rupee*
attar	*scented oil*
azan	*Muslim call to prayer: given five times a day*

B

baba	*diminutive for a male child*
Begum Sahib	*polite form of address for a married lady*
bhabi	*polite term for a young female relative*
bhaji	*polite term for an elder female relative*
Bibi	*polite form of address for a young woman*
burqa	*woman's head-to-toe covering made of many yards of cotton*

C

caravanserai	*overnight stopping place for travelers and their animals*
chapatti	*flat disc of unleavened wheat bread: the bread of the people*

D
dal — *lentils*
dhoolie — *litter for carrying a woman*
dhoti — *Hindu loincloth*
durbar — *meeting between heads of state*

G
Gurkha knife — *heavy knife with downward-curving blade used by Gurkha soldiers*
Granth Sahib — *sacred text of Sikh religion*
gulab jamon — *sticky brown sweetmeat*

H
haveli — *large walled-city house, built around a courtyard*
howdah — *litter or seat with railings, for riding on an elephant*
Huzoor — *polite form of address, equivalent to "my lord"*

J
jalebi — *orange, pretzel-shaped sweetmeat*
jan or jani — *darling*
ji — *yes; also used after someone's name to denote respect*

K
kameez — *long shirt, usually of cotton, worn over loose trousers (pajamas or a shalwar)*
khabardar — *be careful!*

M
mahout — *an elephant driver*
mehndi — *henna paste, used for dyeing the skin and the hair a russet brown color*
Memsahib — *polite form of address for a European woman*
Moghuls — *emperors of India in the sixteenth and seventeenth centuries, responsible for much of India's finest architecture and design*
muezzin — *man who gives the Muslim call to prayer*
munshi — *teacher, especially of languages*
murshid — *a spiritual guide or teacher*

N

namaste   *traditional Hindu greeting*

neem   *tree with astringent bark, used to clean teeth
                     and heal wounds*

P

palki or **palanquin**   *litter carried by bearers, often used for long-
                     distance travel*

Q

qamar   *moon*

qul   *third day of mourning, when the entire Qur'an
                     is read for the benefit of the departed soul*

Qur'an   *sacred text of Islam*

R

reetas   *seed pods that are boiled, then used for washing
                     the hair*

S

salaam   *traditional Muslim greeting meaning "peace"*

shaikh   *leader of a Muslim spiritual brotherhood*

shalwar   *wide, gathered cotton trousers worn under a
                     knee-length shirt*

sirdar   *noble (as in Sikh sirdar) or leader (as in sirdar
                     bearer)*

sufi   *Muslim who is also a follower of a spiritual path*

surma   *black powder, used as eyeliner*

T

tasbih   *string of beads, used to count prayers or the
                     names of God*

tulwar   *curved sword*

Z

zikr   *Sufi practice of repeating God's name with spe-
                     cial head movements, for the purpose of spiri-
                     tual gain*

ABOUT THE AUTHOR

Thalassa Ali was born in Boston. She married a Pakistani, and lived in Karachi for a number of years. Although she has since returned to the United States, her deep connection to Pakistan remains unbroken.